PRODIGIES

A NOVEL

PRODIGIES

A NOVEL

BOB ARMSTRONG

An Imprint of Roan & Weatherford Publishing Associates, LLC
Bentonville, Arkansas • Heber City, Utah
www.roanweatherford.com

Library of Congress Cataloging-in-Publication Data
Names: Armstrong, Bob author
Title: Prodigies/Bob Armstrong | Prodigies #1
Description: Second Edition. | Bentonville: Mad Cat, 2025.
Identifiers: LCCN: 2021934994 | ISBN: 979-8-89299-118-6 (trade paperback) |
ISBN: 979-8-89299-119-3 (eBook)
Subjects: | BISAC: YOUNG ADULT FICTION/Westerns |
YOUNG ADULT FICTION/Steampunk | YOUNG ADULT FICTION/Superheroes
LC record available at: https://lccn.loc.gov/2021934994

Hat Creek trade paperback edition November, 2025

Cover Design by Casey W. Cowan
Interior Design by Casey W. Cowan
Editing by Lisa Lindsey

To Rosemary and Sam

1

---◆・◆・◆---

FILCHING APPLES FROM the market vendors was easy, but Daniel McCormack was careful not to get greedy. His rules were simple—take only one at a time and never hit the same vendor twice in a day. The king of the vendors was a big, mustachioed Sicilian whose voice echoed off the tenements of the Five Points. "Freshest apples! Fresh from the orchard!" He carried a walking stick, but Daniel could tell by the way he moved that he had no trouble with his legs. The stick was for rapping filchers on the side of the head, something Daniel had seen a time or two. Daniel took particular pleasure stealing from the Sicilian.

Daniel waited for the crowd to thicken with housewives and domestics stocking up for the evening meal. When he was satisfied he had cover, he slipped between hips and elbows until he reached a position just behind a pair of women in kerchiefs, who inspected the goods and muttered in what Daniel took to be Polish. Beside them, a colored woman in a black dress and white apron held an apple aloft for inspection.

"This one's no good," she said, pointing to a dark bruise.

"Best apples in New York!" the Sicilian insisted.

The Polish women let out a stream of syllables. It sounded as if they doubted the Sicilian too.

The Sicilian flashed his teeth in anger as Daniel looked up through the space between the arm and breast of one of the Polish women.

"You no like, take the boat to Brooklyn!"

One of the Polish women pointed at a pile of fuzzy yellow peaches and asked in English, "Sweet?"

As the Sicilian extolled the virtues of his peaches, a narrow gap developed between one of the Poles and the colored woman, now giving a golden apple the once-over. Daniel flung an arm through the gap and withdrew an apple from the table so rapidly that the movement did not register on either of the women. He slipped the apple under his shirt, pivoted, and sidestepped between women and men until he had placed half a block between himself and the vendor.

As long as the vendors thronged the streets, Daniel could find something to eat. Fruit and vegetable sellers were the easiest pickings, but sometimes a body needed something hot. Daniel had worked out techniques for palming a hot pretzel or two or even filling his pockets with roasted chestnuts, which on a fall day had the advantage of warming his outside before they warmed his insides. Hot corn girls were also easy to rob, but after the first time he cleaned a brazier of sweet, buttery corn, he couldn't bring himself to do it again. The hot corn girls looked even hungrier than Daniel.

Stealing food was something he'd learned to do after his ma had been taken away to the bughouse. Before then, she'd worked hard to bring food home, even if it was just bread and potatoes. And on a good day, she'd come back from the house where she worked with the butt end of a ham or a soup bone and maybe a penny candy in her pocket, and she would sing songs from what she called the Old Country and even pick Daniel up and dance a jig with him. But on the bad days, she'd come home and drop into her bed and sleep with her eyes open and an empty smile on her face. Sometimes, she'd not come home at all, staggering in the next morning, crying and promising it would never happen again. Then, there had been the really bad nights, when his ma had gone to her bed after telling Daniel not to let her leave their room, nights she'd spent crying and making sick in a basin, her face gleaming with sweat, the room fouler than the cesspit in the cellar of the old tenement. Things would be better for a time after those nights, but sooner or later she'd get back to working late, as she'd call it.

He knew now that working late meant smoking opium in a den down on Mott Street. And he knew as well where his ma was now. After the leatherheads raided his ma's usual den, a few swells who were slumming with a bowl of Hap Wong's finest had been escorted quietly to their homes uptown, but the ragged smokers from the Five Points had been hauled off in a paddy wagon. Opium had ruined their minds, so they'd been taken to the bughouse. Daniel had been told so by the lady from the mission, who'd turned up accompanied by a thick-necked young leatherhead in order to take him to the orphanage. Daniel had had no desire to see the inside of the old brewery that was now the home of last resort for the children of the streets. He'd taken the church lady's hand and begun walking with her until they were out the door and descending the back stairs of the tenement house. Then he'd pulled away suddenly, ducked under the outstretched arms of the leatherhead, and jumped over the railing and onto the staircase of the next building, leaving the copper red-faced, breathless, and furious.

Since then, he'd been feeding himself on the streets and sleeping wherever he could find a hidden dry place for the night. But with winter coming on, he would have to find some place warm. That would mean some place crowded, maybe with people he wouldn't want around him while he slept. Money, he decided, was the difference between safety and danger.

For months, walking the streets of the Five Points, the Bowery, and up Fifth Avenue to Satan's Circus, Daniel had been watching men and women removing coins and sometimes paper bills from wallets and handbags. He had been learning how and where people stored their money and what kinds of defenses they had against probing fingers. Daniel felt confident he could dip a hand into a swell's coat pocket, especially one staggering out of a saloon after a night of carousing, and come away with enough money to buy a safe place to sleep for the night.

Still, he knew that lifting a wallet would make him a thief. And his mother had always told him she was not raising a thief. Stealing food was different. It hardly counted as crime at all. But if he stole money only to buy food or a safe place to stay, was that really any worse than stealing food? With his adolescent brain spinning over rights and wrongs, he nearly walked into the backs of the crowd that had gathered on a street corner. From the other side of this flesh wall, he heard a singsong voice. "Three shells, one pea. Four-to-one if you see."

Daniel slipped between two of the onlookers and saw a man standing behind an upturned box and holding out three walnut shells in his hands. The man wore a tall hat over a side-combed slab of glistening black hair and a brocade vest over a white silk shirt, the sleeves of which had been rolled up to expose his supple wrists and long, delicate fingers.

"I invite you to inspect these shells. You will see no secret compartments, no springs, no doors. They are shells as nature made them. And please inspect this dried pea, if you will. I will now place the pea on the playing surface and place the three shells flat-side down on the surface. All is on the level, no tricks, no illusions. Now I cover one pea and begin to move."

The man slowly began to move the walnut shells, moving the left shell to the middle, the middle shell to the left, exchanging the left and the right shells.

"And which shell contains the pea?" he asked.

"That one there," a shoeshine boy said, gesturing to the shell on the right, which the man lifted to reveal the pea.

"You're a natural, kid," the man said as he began moving the shells more quickly. He repeated the procedure at a slightly faster pace, shuffling the shells until he challenged the onlookers to tell him where the pea had ended up. And again the onlookers were right.

"Now we do it at full speed," he said and began moving the shells so fast they were almost a blur. "Now, can anybody tell me where it is?"

"The middle one," said a large and menacing man with a thick set of salt-and-pepper whiskers.

The man behind the box lifted the middle shell, but it was empty.

"No, no. It was the one on the right again," a thin old man with the look of a sailor called out.

A lift of the shell revealed that the old sailor was right.

"And so you see, this is a game that rewards those with a fast eye. But even without a fast eye, the rewards can be great. Why? Because I will pay you four-to-one odds if you can tell me which shell contains the pea. And as I have only three shells here, even if you guess randomly, the inexorable and inevitable laws of probability dictate that over time you will win more than you lose. Who would like to take a chance at ten cents a guess?"

The crowd pulled closer to the box now that money was in the air. Those who had ten cents to spare considered the possibility of turning them into fifty cents. Those who had ten cents to spare and a few years of schooling considered the possibility of turning fifty cents into two dollars fifty, and two fifty into seven fifty. Those who had experience of street-corner games of skill and observation put their hands in their pockets and waited in anticipation of a fight breaking out.

After a few moments of anxious self-appraisal, in which it seemed the crowd, with one mind, looked for a volunteer to test the shell man's offer, a man in a bowler hat and a black suit, shiny from wear, stepped forward. Carrying the satchel of a traveling salesman and wearing the ragged shoes of a tramp, the man looked as if he once carried dollars to spare and now could scarcely spare a dime. He put his dime on the box, and the shells began to move again.

The shells moved no more rapidly than they did moments before, but Daniel saw that this time the shell man occasionally bumped them against one another as he shuffled them about. At the end of his movements, he invited the old drummer to make his guess. The drummer pointed to the middle shell. It was empty.

"Not that one," said the old sailor. "He bumped the shells together and transferred the pea. It's in the shell on the left!"

The man behind the box smiled, lifted the shell, and showed that, sure enough, the pea was there. "Too bad you didn't put a dime down, Captain. You'd be forty cents richer."

Daniel saw the big, bearded man whisper something in the sailor's ear and turn to the man behind the box.

"I'll front him a dime, and I'll take a guess myself," he said, placing two dimes on the surface.

The shells again began to move and again began bumping. When they stopped, the sailor pointed to the shell on the right. The man behind the box lifted the right shell to reveal no pea. Then he lifted the middle shell and showed that the pea was there. The big man gave the old sailor a disgusted look.

"Try again? I'll improve your odds. Payout's five-to-one this time."

As the big man bent to investigate the walnut shells, the breeze picked up the aroma of hot corn. Daniel turned to see a hot corn girl approaching with a basket filled with cobs fresh from the brazier. After eating only apples so far that day, he figured a hot cob of corn would fill an empty place. Setting aside his caution about speaking to adults, Daniel wormed between onlookers to the big man's side.

"I know where he puts it, Mister."

"Oh, you do, do you?"

"I been watching close."

"Watching so you can grab the dimes and run, more like it."

The shell man laughed at the bearded man's joke. It seemed to Daniel to be a forced laugh, too loud and too long to be real. The kind of laugh the leatherheads had when they were hauling a kid into a wagon. The kind of laugh that meant trouble. Daniel felt that either of these men might haul off and slug him if he stuck around, but at the same time he smelled the hot corn, and he heard his stomach rumbling. His best chance at a meal was to help somebody win money from the shell man.

While he was trying to decide what to do, the big man lost another pair of dimes, one for himself and one for the sailor. After shaking a fist at the old sailor, the big man grunted, turned his back, and pushed his way out of the crowd.

"I'll make it a six-to-one payout this time," the shell man called. "The laws of probability guarantee your profit!"

Daniel squeezed between bodies and followed the big man, tapping him on the back and stepping aside to be ready to run, just in case.

"I'll tell you what I seen, and if you win, you'll give me a dime? Okay?"

"And if I lose?"

Daniel didn't want to think what the man would want if he lost.

"You won't lose."

"Whisper it. I don't want these stiffs to hear."

Even with the big man bending at the waist, Daniel had to stand on tiptoes to speak into his ear, a deformed and twisted piece of cartilage that told of years of bare-knuckle fighting. When Daniel had finished, the man stood and placed a heavy hand on the boy's shoulder.

"If this is a trick to make me lose another dime, you and that greasy-faced gyppo will regret it."

"No trick. Just don't forget my dime."

The man put a hand in his pocket and came out grasping a silver dollar. Daniel looked at the dollar and then at the crowd, which was beginning to thin. Then he saw the big man nod and smile and elbow his way back to the table.

"Seven-to-one! Seven dimes to one dime bet. That's a seven hundred percent profit, gentlemen!"

"I'll put a dollar down and tell you where the pea is. That's if you have seven dollars on you."

The air seemed to thicken in Daniel's lungs, and he had to force air in and out. Seven dollars. It used to take his ma a week to make that much money.

The shell man removed his hat and straightened his hair. He seemed to look into his hat as if it were his purse and he were counting his money.

Voices in the crowd began to call out.

"Take his bet, ya four-flusher!"

"What's the matter, afraid Big Jim has your number?"

The big man himself, Big Jim, placed his dollar on the table and then held his ham-sized fists in front of his chest and began cracking his knuckles, creating a series of cracks and pops audible above the din from the spectators. The shell man, after looking to the left and right and seeing his exits blocked, removed a coin purse from an inside pocket and counted out a pile of seven dollars, which he first held out to Big Jim for his inspection.

With a wave of the hand from Big Jim, the crowd went silent. The shell man took the pea in his thumb and forefinger, held it out for all to see, and then placed it below a shell. Then, in a flurry, he began to move the shells, faster than ever before. Daniel noticed sweat forming on the shell man's brow. He was concentrating so hard. So hard on fooling the crowd.

Suddenly, Big Jim reached out and seized the shell man's arms.

"Hey! What gives?"

"I know where the pea is."

"I'm not done yet."

"I know you're not done yet. You haven't cheated me out of my money."

At that, Big Jim lifted the man's arms and revealed that all three shells were empty. There was no pea under any of them.

"You're not done yet because the pea is still stuck in that little fold of skin under the top joint of your left ring finger."

As Big Jim said this, he lifted the shell man's hand and turned it, giving the man's shoulder a painful twist, to reveal the pea, stuck exactly where Daniel had told him it would be. With the crowd as his witness, he pocketed the stack of silver dollars the man had placed on the table, then reached into the man's coat for the change purse.

"Hey, that's robbery!"

"You owe me four dimes."

Big Jim counted out the four coins and gave the shell man back his purse. The man stuffed the purse back in his coat, picked up his table, and sidestepped away from the crowd, which was egging Big Jim on to teach him a more permanent lesson.

"Knock his block off, Jim."

"Kick his teeth in!"

"Flatten the louse!"

Big Jim glared at the crowd and silenced them and turned and handed Daniel a pair of dimes.

"I was fronting the sailor with these, so you can have 'em both."

"Thanks, Mister." Daniel spun and looked for the hot corn girl. There she was, just up the block. Then he felt that heavy hand on his shoulder.

"How'd you know?"

"What?"

"The trick? How'd you know his trick?"

"I don't know. I just saw it."

The big man lifted his hand to let Daniel go.

"You be careful," he called out to Daniel's retreating back. "You can get in trouble just seeing things."

Feeling newly wealthy with two dimes in his pocket, Daniel caught up with the hot corn girl and asked her to take two fat cobs off the coals. He handed her a dime and took his eight cents change and hauled himself up on a barrel outside a brewery to eat. He placed one cob under his jacket, feeling the warmth spread from his belly out to his fingers and toes. Then he peeled the other, juggling the cob from right to left hand to keep from being scalded by the steam, all the while savoring the aroma. Once it was cool enough, he bit into the corn, too hungry to bother picking out the strands of silk.

With the first cob finished, he pondered what to do with the eighteen cents he had left. Fifteen would buy a bed for the night, though he wondered if a fifteen-cent bed was really any better than a hidden corner in an alley. A gust of wind flicked a fat drop of cold autumn rain his way to make the decision for him. This would be no night to sleep in an alley. He considered saving the second cob for later but realizing he was still hungry, removed it from his jacket, peeled it, and chewed it down to the cob before the rain could build up to full force. The street was emptying out. The workingmen who'd stopped to watch the shell man after work had made their way home or to a saloon, probably the latter. The wives who'd been to market to buy a loaf or a basket of potatoes had finished their errands. A lamplighter was firing up one of the few lamps on the street that still functioned. It was time to find a bed.

A fifteen-cent bed meant Mother Flanagan's, a rookery located in a back house down Butchers' Alley. Daniel hoped to reach Butchers' Alley while some light remained, so he ran the two blocks to the entrance, where he paused and caught his breath, peering into the shadows cast by the tenement back houses and the laundry flapping and turning brown in the foul air.

"It's just an alleyway," he told himself.

Daniel stepped into Butchers' Alley and felt a hand reach out of the darkness of a doorway and grab him by the throat.

"You owe Mister O'Donnell eight dollars and forty cents."

The hand that held him belonged to a big man, bigger than Big Jim, but thicker and not so tall. His words came from a fleshy cave of a mouth protected by an irregular array of yellow stalactites, and he glared with yellowy eyes from above a flattened nose and below a single eyebrow that sprawled across the upper part of his face like a monstrous caterpillar. Daniel recoiled and tried to wriggle out of the man's grasp, but the hand that held him was a heavy slab of meat, and the powerful fingers were wrapped most of the way around his throat.

"Who's Mister O'Donnell?"

"I am," said the shell man as he walked down the alley. "And you ruined my game. And now that I come to think of it, you don't just owe me eight-forty. You owe me for every dime I might have made off that collection of rubes and for every dime I might have made off their friends and families. Why, today's losses might be only the tenth part of what you owe me."

Daniel scanned the darkness of the alley for aid. None was forthcoming. Few would dare linger in Butchers' Alley, and those who would were unlikely to be Good Samaritans.

"I can think of two ways a boy like you could pay off a debt like that," Mr. O'Donnell said. "Bull, bring him to me for a better look."

The thickset man wrapped another hand around Daniel's arm and marched him toward the entrance to the alley, where Mr. O'Donnell awaited. The shell man reached out a hand to smooth his hair and drew a finger along Daniel's thin, straight nose and thinner lips.

"You're not an irredeemably ugly boy, are you? Bull, let go of his neck. I want to see his face when it's not all bunched up and red."

Mr. O'Donnell put a hand on each of Daniel's shoulders and stood him up straight, while bending close to look at him from in front and in profile. "Skin's smooth, no obvious scars, and we saw today that he likes helping strange men." Mr. O'Donnell straightened and gave a self-satisfied smile, removing his hands from Daniel's shoulders as he did so.

Daniel saw an opportunity in the moment before Bull's hand again wrapped around his arm. He spun and ducked in one movement, and Bull grabbed only a phantom. Daniel feinted to his right and saw Mr. O'Donnell shift his balance in that direction to block him, opening up a gap between the two men. Daniel dove through it, hit the jumbled paving stones with his shoulder, and rolled back onto his feet. As he began running for the mouth of the alley, he saw the silhouette of a man appear and block his escape. Behind him, he heard the first steps of Bull and Mr. O'Donnell. Ahead of him, he saw a pile of broken bricks, left behind by workmen who had been shoring up the sagging foundation of one of the tenement buildings. In two steps, he reached down for two palm-sized chunks, pivoted, and threw them at his pursuers.

The first caught Bull in the face, causing the monster to stop and reel back in agony, his hands covering what was left of one eye. The second struck Mr. O'Donnell square in the mouth, shattering teeth and driving the splinters into his throat. The shell man put one hand to his throat and with the other struck his chest as he tried to expel the fragments. The men were still feeling the shock of their injuries as Daniel's second projectiles struck them, one flattening O'Donnell's nose and the other hitting Bull square on the Adam's apple. The brick fragments had only just found their targets when Daniel spun and advanced on the man at the entrance to the alley, carrying a piece of brick in each hand.

"You'd best move, Mister, or I'll do the same to you."

In the flare of a match, Daniel saw Big Jim. He watched as Big Jim drew back his jacket to reveal the butt end of a revolver.

"Gentlemen, I think you'd best go tend to your wounds before you get some that can't be tended."

Bull and Mr. O'Donnell staggered out of the alley, the former half blind and both breathing laboriously.

"Now, boy, tell me how you learned to throw like that."

2

THE PALL OF smoke drifting over the sycamores told Lincoln Henry that there would be no school on the September morning when he set out, in his best clean shirt, to start the fifth grade. It was black, oily smoke, too thick and dark to be emerging from the Johnsons' smokehouse.

Lincoln broke into a run, even as he heard his mama call to him from behind.

"Lincoln, you stop now!"

There was fear in her voice, just as there had been the night before when she'd told Lincoln's papa, "Them riders been coming closer every night this summer."

Lincoln hadn't followed his parents' words that night. He'd been lost in his lines again. Mama had set him to cleaning the sleeping loft in the cabin, and he'd found a spiderweb up in a corner under the roof beams. Lincoln had picked up the old twig broom to sweep out the web—his mama couldn't abide spiders in the house, always said her powerful mislike of creepy crawlies of all kind come from growing up in the Delta, slapping and scratching at chiggers and gnats—but the shine of the silken lines in the lamplight had caught his eye. He'd followed the patterns of the silk as they traced a glowing circle in the air. The cabin, his parents, and the world outside faded away as he stood as high as he could to figure out the come-togethers and see how the spider had built its home.

Sometimes, the whole world just seemed to Lincoln to be nothing but lines and come-togethers. He saw them in the curve of a snail's shell when he went for a swim down at the creek and in the patterns of the honeycombs Papa brought in from the hives. His mama would sew him a new pair of britches for church, and all through the service, while the preacher was talking about Moses and the Promised Land, Lincoln's eyes would fix on his own legs as he figured out the come-togethers in the homespun cotton. Soon, his mind would wander far beyond the church, to the lines in the skeletal wing of a dead sparrow or a towering chestnut tree. He'd start to see how you could understand how things would move and whether or not something would break by comparing the length of the lines or the shape made by the come-togethers. He called this "figuring the big-littles."

Miss Cadbury had smiled the first time he'd told her about figuring out come-togethers and big-littles.

"You mean angles and ratios, Lincoln."

She'd given him a book she said was written by an old man named Euclid who had his picture on the title page. He wore a long white beard and a kind of baggy, white dress. The book had Miss Cadbury's name in it and the name of the woman's college she'd attended up north before coming south to—as she told her students—help bind up the nation's wounds. It was plain to see from this Euclid's book that he had a powerful interest in drawing lines and making shapes, starting out with three corners and squares and slowly getting more curvy and fancy. According to Miss Cadbury, Euclid and another old man in a dress, Pythagoras, had written down the rules for come-togethers and big-littles and all kinds of shapes a long, long time ago.

As he'd stared at the spiderweb the night before, Lincoln had been looking forward to telling Miss Cadbury about it. He wanted to work out the rules the spider followed to make a web that could curve so pretty and so strong, and he had an idea that those same rules could be used to build a house that would hold up in a twister.

Of course, this year he was supposed to go with the older children and sit in Mr. Delacroix's class. He was a little scared of Mr. Delacroix, who didn't put up with any backtalk or monkeyshines and punished students for every "ain't" and "I done" they let through their lips.

"You will learn to read and write and speak the King's English," Mr. Delacroix always said when he caught a child speaking in slang, even after school, even at the swimming hole.

Lincoln's friend, Leon, had earned himself a smack on the backside once when he said to Mr. Delacroix, "Didn't white folks fight a war to send that old King back to England?"

Like all the children, Lincoln was afraid of Mr. Delacroix's passion for the rules of grammar and proper deportment. But what scared him even more was the conversation he'd had when school had let out in June. Mr. Delacroix, tall and broad-shouldered and with every one of his close-cropped hairs held in place with Macassar oil, dressed in a dark suit with a high, stiff collar even in the heat of a Tennessee June, had called on Lincoln to come back into the school just as he'd been about to run off with Leon and the other boys. The teacher had led Lincoln into his empty classroom and gestured with his long piano player's fingers for him to sit. Then, he had given Lincoln a rare smile, showing off his neatly arrayed white teeth and causing the long scar on his right cheek to scrunch up.

"Lincoln, Miss Cadbury says you are a very talented boy," he'd said in that funny accent of his. Some people said Mr. Delacroix talked funny because he was from New Orleans, and people there speak French. Other people said he talked funny because he had spent time up north in a city called Boston, where everybody had red hair and came from a place called Ireland. Still others said he talked strange because, even though he was a colored man, he wanted to be an Englishman like Mr. Shakespeare, a writer whose stories he was always reciting.

"She says you have a special talent with geometry and with mathematics."

Lincoln had looked down at the floor, trying to find some come-to-gethers and big-littles he could figure out, anything rather than meet Mr. Delacroix's gaze.

"It's a good thing to have a special talent, Lincoln. Our people need boys and girls who have talents. We need them to build those talents. Do you understand?"

"Yes, sir."

"People who are good with geometry and mathematics can become scientists. Do you know what a scientist is, Lincoln?"

"Yes, sir."

"A scientist might help people like your father, and a lot of the other men in this community, who are trying to feed a family on forty acres of scrubland. A scientist might do experiments with different kinds of plants, find out how to make them grow faster and put out more seed. Or if you don't want to be a scientist, somebody who is good with mathematics might become a kind of merchant who lends money to people so they can buy a strong plow horse, or buys a man's corn crop and sells it somewhere else for a higher price. Our people need merchants like that because at the moment they're selling their corn to men who don't want to buy it at any price. Do you understand that?"

Lincoln did not, in truth, understand about becoming a merchant or making seeds grow faster. And he did not know why Miss Cadbury, who had always been so nice and friendly to him, would talk to scary Mr. Delacroix about him.

"I like looking at lines, sir, and figuring out the come-togethers. I mean, the angles."

"You like angles."

"And big-littles. Ratios, I mean. My papa showed me how he uses ratios when he has to dig out a stump. A longer piece of lumber gives him a better ratio, makes him stronger, so he can pry that stump."

"You want to spend your life pulling stumps, Lincoln?"

"I like tools."

"Tools?"

"I think I could make a better house or a bigger school."

"Tools are useful, Lincoln. But there are enough colored men using tools. We need more colored men owning tools. For you to own tools, tools that could help our people, you need to learn a few other things. You must learn how to communicate, how to express yourself, how to enunciate words and comport yourself like a man of science and culture. And that, Lincoln, is what we will set for our task next year. We will develop your understanding of the rules of grammar and punctuation. We will read and recite the works of Shakespeare. And we will work on your posture, so that when a teacher is talking to you, you will not look down at the floorboards. It is my responsibility, Lincoln, to prepare you for a world in which a young colored boy can look forward to opportunities to develop his special talents for the betterment of his people and the world. And that, young man, is what I intend to do when we meet again in September."

Now September had arrived, and there would be no teaching. Black clouds blocked the sun as Lincoln entered the schoolyard. Scattered papers, splintered chairs, and shattered glass littered the ground. One sheet of paper, blown by the wind generated by the flames, tumbled toward Lincoln and came to a stop at his feet. It bore one of the simple drawings of Mr. Euclid. Three lines with three equal come-togethers. An equilateral triangle, he knew now, with the name coming from the same word as "equality," which President Lincoln proclaimed when Lincoln was just a baby.

A crying woman emerged from the trees and ran toward Lincoln. He didn't recognize her with her red face and her hair hacked away from her bloodied scalp. The strange woman shouted Lincoln's name in a voice that sounded like Miss Cadbury's. She knelt and seized Lincoln in a desperate embrace, but he pulled away, drawn by the hypnotizing presence of the flames.

Miss Cadbury cried out, "No, Lincoln, no!"

She grasped Lincoln's head and forced him to turn away from the school and toward the sycamores.

"Go to your mother, Lincoln. Go to your mother. Don't look."

A shriek came from the trail at the point where it bent around the sycamores. Lincoln's mother came into view, and even from this distance he could see her eyes widen in shock and terror. "Oh my Lord, no!"

Lincoln's mama collapsed to her knees as if struck with a length of lumber. Lincoln freed himself from Miss Cadbury's control and ran to her.

"Mama, Mama, we be fine. I'm going to figure all the come-togethers so's I can build us a new school. It's gonna be a better school with a roof that don't leak. You'll see."

But his mama continued to cry. Lincoln looked back to the school and saw now what she saw. She wasn't looking at the burning school. She was focused on a high, dead branch of the old cottonwood that provided shade on the hot days when Miss Cadbury took the young ones outside for their lessons. A rope tied to the cottonwood swayed slowly in the kind of stretched-out circle known as an ellipse. At the bottom, marking time like a pendulum, was a shirtless black man, his body turned away from Lincoln and his mother. On his back were lines, deep and dark as furrows but all jumbled up like twigs piled together.

Lincoln saw, below the hanged man, a pile of clothing that he knew contained a shirt with a stiff, high collar. He looked at the lines on the man's back, saw where they met, figured the come-togethers, and saw in his head where each man had stood with a whip in his hand, how hard he'd flicked it, how much strength it had taken to break skin. It was just a matter of big-littles—the ratio of the length of the whip and the speed of the man's arm—to see how easily the man's skin had been torn into such a mess. Life was a matter of big-littles—the strength of the riders versus the weakness of Mr. Delacroix, the fear in his mother's face against the hope she had for her son. Someday, maybe, Lincoln would figure a way of using the big-littles to his advantage.

3

UNCLE STANISLAS WAS going to be cross. Lily had been practicing for weeks, but she still could not remember all the steps of her Highland sword dance. The problem was the music sounded so much like a clogging song that she had to force herself to remember not to land on her heels. She would forget to point her knees up, or she would drop her arms to her sides, and by the time she stood up straight like a daughter of the Highlands, she'd end up losing the count. It was harder than her flamenco. When she lost track of where she was in the flamenco, all she had to do was stomp her heels a little harder and clap her hands faster, and it seemed like part of the show.

When she'd started dancing during what Uncle Stanislas called the entr'acte, she'd discovered that it was possible to cover for any mistake by switching to a jig and singing "Dixie." But that had been in Tennessee. Now they were in Illinois. That wouldn't do here.

Lily Mandeville had not always performed in the circus, nor lived as part of the traveling community of what the townspeople referred to as oddballs and foreigners. She'd lived in mill towns and cities, where her mother had struggled to earn a living by tending steam-powered looms and taking in washing and mending. Her mother had put Lily to sleep at night with stories of her father—a dashing cavalry officer who fought with

General Custer's Fifth Michiganders and was personally credited with saving the general's life when Custer's horse was shot from under him.

Lily had lived in overcrowded tenements and drafty cabins, the living quarters becoming colder, dirtier, and smaller as her mother's coughing grew more frequent. She had no memory of better times on the small farm where she'd been born, mere months after her father had ridden off to the war from which he never returned. Nor of the day the bank took back the farm when her father's cavalry pay ceased coming through.

Lily was eleven when her mother brought her to the circus, where her father had once been a featured trick rider. She had been introduced to a man she was to call Uncle Stanislas, who'd smiled and noted her resemblance to her blue-eyed, blond father and had been disappointed to hear she had not been taught to ride. After that first meeting, her mother's illness had worsened quickly, and Lily soon returned to the circus to stay.

Since then, she had earned her keep giving out handbills, selling candies, doing laundry, and acting as an all-purpose servant for the performers. She ran errands for the midget tumblers, whose backs and legs often hurt on account of the impact of their performance on their twisted little bodies. She helped Madame Mystere, the fat lady fortune teller, get into her shiny silk costume before the show. After the show, she helped Madame wash herself, reaching under folds of flesh with a soapy cloth.

But now, at thirteen, she was old enough to start earning her keep. In a circus, Uncle Stanislas had explained, everyone is part of the act. He had attempted to apprentice her to the wire walkers, but though her balance was good, she was deathly afraid of heights. She had shown promise on a practice wire a foot above the ground, but when she climbed the tower the first time, she had swooned and been caught by Tommaso Largo, who declared her unfit for any performance above the height of a table.

Uncle Stanislas had tried to train her to be a magician's assistant, but though she was learning the skills of confusing the eye and secreting objects in the palm of her hand, her breaking point came when she was placed in the sword box. Lily had broken out in a sweat as soon as the box was closed around her neck. She knew the swords would not pierce her flesh, but a small part of her mind whispered to her that she would forever be locked in the box. It was worse when she was placed in the disappearing closet and was swallowed up in the blackness. Her screams had brought the entire circus running, even Madame Mystere, though running was not perhaps the most accurate word.

The dancing entr'acte was Uncle Stanislas's idea. Lily would dance between each circus act in a different national style, making the entire evening into what he called "A Salute to America, Land of Many Peoples." She needed at least three dances. The flamenco was one. Uncle Stanislas said a Bavarian dance, performed in knee-length leather pants with thick needlepoint braces and a felt hat, would be popular with the squareheads in Wisconsin and Minnesota, though Lily never remembered the steps and mostly slapped her knees and ankles at random.

Uncle Stanislas had recently asked Madame Mystere, who doubled as the circus's seamstress, to sew a harem girl costume, though both agreed it would be at least a year before she would fill it out. Lily had been doing an Indian princess dance, which consisted mostly of hopping in circles while emitting savage war cries, but the last few times she performed the dance, it had yielded raspberries from customers who had seen real Indian dancers at Wild West shows.

Lily found a quiet place in an alley behind the lodging house, where she shared a room with Madame Mystere. Maybe if she worked through the steps slowly by herself, she'd feel more confident when she stood in the parlor and practiced with Mr. Szabo, the circus's accordion-playing clown. Lily closed her eyes and began humming "Loch Lomond" but was nearly knocked to the ground by a furry projectile.

She opened her eyes to see a pair of mongrel dogs. The dog that had struck her was some mix of terrier and bulldog, low to the ground but powerful in the chest and legs and equipped with a wide jaw and thick neck. From its mouth, a live rat dangled. Rounding the corner of the alley and coming at the terrier was some kind of sheepdog— long-legged, built for speed but strong enough to fend off predators. The pursuer caught up with its shorter quarry and pounced, and the two animals hit the paving stones in an explosion of fur. A hideous chorus of snarls erupted from the two animals, the terrier uttering its muted noises through clenched jaws that held tightly to the chittering rodent. With the terrier unable to fight back without losing its prey, the sheepdog went on the attack, sinking its teeth into the muscled back of the shorter animal.

Lily recoiled in horror and moral outrage. The sheepdog was being an utter brute.

"You stop that this instant!" she shouted.

She stepped forward, waving an admonishing finger at the taller animal. The sheepdog released its grip. The terrier growled up at it.

"Now, which of you caught the rat?"

Both dogs looked her way.

"You couldn't both have caught the rat."

They continued looking her way.

"Well, all right then." She looked at the sheepdog. "You flushed it from hiding." She addressed the terrier. "And you caught it. So, you both had a share in catching it, and you can both share in eating it."

The dogs looked up at Lily and whimpered.

"No. There's no point complaining. It's only fair."

The rat, noticing the lull in activity from the dogs, renewed its wriggling attempts to escape. It backed out from the terrier's slackened grip and launched itself along the broken cobblestones, but with a word of warning from Lily, the faster sheepdog pounced, holding the rat firmly by its long, leathery tail.

Lily, who detested rats after one night too many in lodging houses infested with the creatures, called the sheepdog to her.

"You'd better finish off that rat if you don't want it getting away. Smash its head against the paving stones."

She mimed the action to the animal, as if she were holding the rat's tail with her own teeth and swinging the rodent onto the ground. The dog seemed to nod and began to do the same, once, twice, three times, until the rat's skull shattered. After a few more words from Lily on dividing the spoils, the two dogs took turns taking bites from the bleeding carcass, then began to walk off, side by side.

"No more fighting for you two," Lily said. "There are plenty of rats to go around."

As the dogs trotted away, all signs of aggression gone, Lily heard the sound of playing cards. She turned to see Uncle Stanislas practicing fancy card shuffles. He didn't look as cross as Lily expected.

"I was practicing, Uncle Stanislas. I got interrupted."

"Practicing what?"

"My dance."

"My Lillian is no dancer."

"No, Uncle, I can learn to be a dancer."

"No. Lillian is—" Uncle Stanislas pursed his lips and furrowed his brow. Then, he smiled again. "Lillian is Dog Girl. No, she is Canine Child. Is no matter. We find you name. But first, we find you dogs."

4

LINCOLN HENRY WAS so tired, he dropped straight into sleep without spending his usual hour figuring come-togethers. Normally, his baby sister, Annabelle, kept him awake with her babbling or her crying out for feeding, and if it wasn't her, then it was his brothers, George and Thomas, tossing and kicking on the same straw mattress. But this night, sleep came almost as soon as Lincoln lay down.

With no school to go to, he had spent the day picking rocks from the back pasture on the land his papa had bought with wages he'd earned during the war. While Lincoln worked, his papa again told him the story of how this came to be the Henrys' land. Papa hadn't waited around to be given any forty acres and a mule. He'd set off to cut timber for the Bluecoat armies, while Lincoln's mama had taken in washing and fixed meals for officers billeted in the old plantation. When the war ended and the old plantation owners had been forced to sell property to pay their debts, Lincoln's papa had bought his forty acres through a white northern land agent. When the transaction was completed and Lincoln's papa went to look at his new land, he was surprised to find that it wasn't the rich bottomland he thought he had purchased. Instead, the land meandered up a holler into the hills and was more suited to rooting hogs than to growing cash crops. So now, Lincoln's papa dug out rocks, hacked at roots, and hauled manure up from the pile beside the barn in a ceaseless effort to improve another pinch of the back pastures every year.

At first that day, Lincoln had tried to make a game out of picking rocks. He'd taken the iron pry bar, longer than he was tall, and set it up with logs as balance points—what Miss Cadbury had called fulcrums—in order to lift rocks out of the ground.

He'd enjoyed figuring out the best place to put the pry bar and how much force it would take him to lift a rock. Then he'd had the idea that the bigger rocks would be easier to move if he could figure out how to break them, so he'd taken to inspecting the rocks mighty carefully and noticed that what seemed like a single solid piece like as not wasn't. Some were all different kinds of rock stuck together like old stew left too long in a pot. If you could figure out the come-togethers of the rock, you could find the weaknesses, like where the glue of hardened gravy might hold tight to a rough-textured potato but let go from the smooth skin of an onion.

Lincoln had tried taking his papa's pickaxe and striking rocks just at the right spot to break them. Lincoln enjoyed the look of astonishment on his papa's face when he saw that his son had shifted more big rocks than he had. But still, that pickaxe was mighty heavy, and after a few hours of it, no matter how clever he was at working out the come-togethers, Lincoln's muscles were powerful sore.

And so, Lincoln was sleeping so soundly he didn't hear the clip-clop of the horses' hooves, nor the jingle of bridles, nor the whickering of the animals. He didn't wake until the gunshots began and his mama screamed in terror and then shouted at Papa to stay in the house and not get himself killed. Lincoln looked down from the sleeping loft and saw Mama holding onto Papa, giving him a great big bear hug.

"You stay here, John!"

"They gonna burn us!"

"No they not. They just want to put a scare in us."

Papa shook free and pulled up a floorboard. From underneath he pulled out an old Enfield muzzleloader. "I'll go put a scare in them."

Mama moved to block the front door. "No you won't. They gonna put a bullet in you, you try that."

There were more gunshots, but Lincoln could tell they weren't coming toward the house. There was something in the sound, a kind of sliding, bending noise that reminded him of the sound a bird makes flying away from you. The guns were pointed in a different direction, he was certain. Sound must work with come-togethers too.

"They're shooting in the air," he said. "They riding over to the cornfield now."

Mama turned and looked up at him. "Lincoln, you go back to bed."

"You can hear it in the sound. They not so close now."

Mama and Papa stopped for a moment and listened. The riders were going away.

"These the same men that killed Mister Delacroix, Papa?"

"The same men or the same kind of men. Makes no difference."

Papa shooed Mama back from the window and peered out a corner of the window.

"What do they want, Papa?"

"They want us to sell our land and go away. But it'll take more than—" Papa stopped, his eyes fixed on some new terror. "Fire!"

Papa stepped past Mama and opened the door. Lincoln climbed down and joined Mama at the window and beheld a constellation of lights through the doorway—a scattering of small fires burning in the cornfield. It had been hot and dry for weeks, and the corn was just about ready for picking, and now the stalks flared up like a field full of torches. There was no more shooting, just the sound of the riders fading away. Papa ran out to the shed and grabbed a shovel and a bucket. He called to Lincoln and placed the bucket by the well, then ran off to the first of the fires. He swung the shovel like an axe and brought it down on the stalks, then beat on them with the flat of the blade and covered the embers with red clay soil.

"Lincoln. Pour water on this one, then bring me another bucket."

Papa moved over to the next closest fire, which had already grown to twice the size of the first one. He hacked and raked the burning stalks into a pile. This time, instead of putting out the burning stalks, he began to dig a dirt moat around the flames to stop them from spreading. Lincoln came to him with a bucket of water.

"Here, along this side!"

Lincoln tossed the water onto the advancing edge of the flames and heard the flames hiss as he turned to fill the bucket again.

Ahead, he saw Mama, now directing the two younger boys to gather up straw and sticks and anything else that could burn from in front of the house. In her arms she carried baby Annabelle, who howled into the night like a wildcat.

"Lincoln," she said, "put some water on the roof."

"Papa wants water for the corn."

"Ain't gonna be any corn in the morning. I want us to have a roof."

Lincoln filled a bucket and climbed the ladder and doused the roof, noticing as he did so that sparks were indeed drifting on the wind. Mama was right. Their corn crop was good as gone already. Lincoln climbed back down and filled the bucket again and doused the roof. Looking back toward the field, he saw that his papa was nearly surrounded by fire as he cut down swathes of corn. Lincoln ran to his side and threw down another bucket of water, but the flames seemed to jump back up.

"Mama says we gotta protect the house."

Papa looked around at the burning cornfield, then placed a hand on Lincoln's shoulder. "Mama's right. Let's go."

For the rest of the night, Papa dug a firebreak around the house and the barn, while Lincoln tossed one bucket of water after another on the ground, turning the red soil into a muddy wallow. The younger boys took their turns as well, throwing pitchers of water on any spark that flew over the firebreak. Mama placed Annabelle back in her bed and let her cry and then picked up the pitchfork and joined in with Papa, turning up clods of soil to form a barrier that they hoped the flames would not jump.

By morning, the fire in the field had burned itself out, and the house and barn were still standing.

Lincoln walked with Papa through the cornfield.

"Everything," Papa said. "Every ear of corn. Every turnip. Every head of cabbage. Burned it all before we could sell it for cash money or put it up in storage for the winter."

"But they didn't burn the barn or the house."

"They didn't want to burn the barn or the house. That's worth something to them."

"What are we gonna do now, Papa?"

Lincoln's papa held out the shovel that he still carried in his hands, the shovel he'd been using to pat down isolated smoldering coals. "You're gonna stay here with Mama. I'm gonna go to work with this."

5

DANIEL MCCORMACK WOKE to the aroma of chicken broth boiling. He could almost taste the rich, fatty soup and the doughy dumplings that Mrs. Kleinschmidt had taught him to call matzo balls. His nose detected bread dough rising as well. There'd be fresh bread for shabbos—the day of prayer and rest that started at sundown on Fridays. Maybe Sophie, the Polish girl who helped Mrs. Kleinschmidt around the house, would make a few of those little potato dumplings Daniel loved so much. All that activity in the kitchen warmed the rooms in the apartment above Mrs. Kleinschmidt's store. Daniel knew it was late, but he wanted to enjoy the warmth a little longer.

For a moment, Daniel congratulated himself on the great luck that had brought him to Mrs. Kleinschmidt, but then he remembered his ma, locked up in the bughouse. A warm bed and a full belly were nice, but this place was only a stepping-stone to getting Ma back.

"Daniel, my little prince, time for sleeping is over."

"Coming, Missus Kleinschmidt."

He jumped out of bed and hauled up his new trousers and shrugged into his new shirt and jacket, admiring yet again the smooth sensation of the fabric, which he had been told came from all the way across the ocean. He descended to the kitchen and discovered, to his pleasure, a steaming bowl of the chicken soup laid out for him, along with a thick slice of the sweet, yellow egg bread called challah.

Mrs. Kleinschmidt pinched his cheek and pointed to the table. "A big, hot breakfast I made for you today. Mister McGuire says you'll need it."

Daniel lapped up the soup, just cool enough not to blister his tongue.

Mrs. Kleinschmidt set a basket on the table beside him and placed in it another loaf of the egg bread, wrapped in a cloth, and several hard-boiled eggs. "A long day, I'm thinking. Maybe you won't be back in time for shabbos. Maybe I'll have to have Sophie come in tomorrow to be my shabbos goy and light my lamps and kitchen fire."

Mrs. Kleinschmidt had always called Daniel her shabbos goy, a term Daniel now knew meant a non-Jew who could do work that was otherwise forbidden on the Jewish holy days. But as Big Jim found more and more work for him to do—often on Friday nights—this title had passed increasingly to Sophie. Daniel looked at the stove, and Mrs. Kleinschmidt must have caught his expression.

"Not to worry," she said. "I cook a nice, fatty brisket when you return. I should let you starve because you have to use your magic eyes for Mister McGuire?"

Mrs. Kleinschmidt smiled, then placed a hand on Daniel's forehead, frowning slightly. She turned to the door and removed a woolen scarf from a hook. "Keep this around your neck and your hat around your ears. God forbid you catch a fever from those cold winds by the river."

So, it was another day and from the sound of it another night of watching the docks. Ever since he'd met Big Jim McGuire at the crooked shell game, Daniel had been spending days and nights watching buildings and boats, leatherheads and sailors. He'd watched big houses uptown, where smoke billowed from half a dozen chimneys, and gates opened and closed to let gleaming black carriages in and out. He'd watched offices down by the Battery, where message boys carried urgent dispatches between buildings, and occasionally a wagon guarded by armed men would deliver a case so heavy it would take a pair of men bigger than Big Jim to carry it. And he'd watched the docks, making note of how many crates and barrels went back and forth, how many men came off each ship, where they went, whether or not they had the gait of men out for a good time with a pocket full of their wages.

Daniel knew that the observations he made helped Big Jim and his friends plan robberies. And he knew that Mrs. Kleinschmidt worked with Big Jim, helping him to sell the goods his men stole from the houses and ships and offices. Daniel had figured that out after he wandered through the stockroom behind Mrs. Kleinschmidt's dry goods store and came upon a case of silverware stamped with the same crest he had observed on the door of a carriage he had seen at one of the houses he'd watched. This was doubly odd, since Mrs. Kleinschmidt didn't sell such fancy goods in her store. He then realized that the stockroom contained a number of other items—fur coats, silk shawls, paintings—that were different from the simple tools and kitchen goods and bedclothes on sale in the dry goods store.

By the time Daniel realized he was serving as the eyes of a criminal gang, he'd begun to grow accustomed to the warmth, comfort, and steady meals at Mrs. Kleinschmidt's. He sometimes noticed familiar faces among the orphans and urchins in the street when his work with Big Jim brought him to the Five Points, and he knew from their ragged clothes and gaunt faces that life would be much harder if he hadn't met up with Big Jim.

On his travels around the city, he also kept an eye out for the shell man and his giant helper, fearing what would happen if they found him and suspecting that the protection of Big Jim might be his only hope. And though he knew that Mrs. Kleinschmidt made money off the crimes that he made possible, Daniel also felt the childless woman's concern for his health and safety and even something like love. Still, she could not replace his ma, and he knew his ma would disapprove if she found out he was working for a gang of robbers. The thought of his ma conjured up again for Daniel a picture of the two of them at some time in the future. He liked to think that, come the spring, Ma would be better. She wouldn't be sad and sick, and she wouldn't need Hap's opium anymore. She could get a good job, maybe in a dry goods store like Mrs. Kleinschmidt's, and Daniel could use what he'd learned around Mrs. Kleinschmidt's store to help out. They wouldn't be rich, but they'd have food and a warm place to sleep.

Big Jim's heavy steps on Mrs. Kleinschmidt's back staircase brought Daniel back to the present.

"Finish your soup," Mrs. Kleinschmidt said. "You don't want to keep Mister McGuire waiting."

Big Jim stepped into the kitchen, his usual bowler hat pulled down low on his head, his shoulders and chest straining the brass buttons on his waistcoat.

"Time to earn your keep, boy."

Daniel raised the bowl to his lips and downed the last mouthful, then stuffed the last morsel of bread in his mouth and followed on the heels of his employer. Reaching the street, Daniel ran to keep up with Big Jim's long strides. They had at least a mile's walk to reach the docks, and Daniel knew from experience that the pace of their journey was not likely to slacken. Still, that gave him enough time to ask a question that had been burning in his heart and his head for months. Already panting, he struggled to control his breathing.

"Jim? Can I ask you a question?"

"You can ask. Doesn't mean I'll answer."

"How does somebody get out of the bughouse?"

"You're asking about your ma?"

"They told me her brains were scrambled, but that ain't true. She was just awful sad. But if I could get her out of the bughouse, I could make her happy."

Big Jim stopped suddenly and pulled Daniel into an alleyway. He bent at the waist and placed his face up against Daniel's, a meaty hand on the boy's shoulder.

"From what I've heard about your ma, it's going to take more than that to make her happy. Her sadness is a kind of sickness."

"You never saw her. Some days she sang old songs, and we danced."

"And some days she couldn't get out of bed and couldn't stop crying? Some days she smiled in her sleep, and a gun going off in her ear wouldn't wake her? I've known men brought low by the same sickness as your ma."

"She's not sick. We were poor, and she had to work so hard to buy food. But if you paid me money so I could watch things, she wouldn't have to work so hard. So she wouldn't be sad."

Big Jim's eyes turned hard at the mention of money, then he relaxed his scowl and smiled. "You want money? It's not enough that Missus Kleinschmidt gives you a warm bed and all the food you need? You're not happy with a nice, new suit of clothes keeping out the draft?"

Big Jim stood and tugged on Daniel's shoulder and led him back into the street at a faster pace. As Daniel ran to keep up, he compared the comforts he now enjoyed to his mother's life, chained up in a cellar like others in the bughouse, if the whispered descriptions he had heard of hospitals for the insane were accurate. He had to do something about that, regardless of the cost in money or in danger.

Daniel stepped directly in front of Big Jim and halted. "I know what you do, Jim. You get Missus Kleinschmidt to sell the stuff you steal. You've got money to pay me."

Big Jim didn't reply, instead pointing to an alley and the back door of a dockside tenement. He looked up and down the alley first, then opened the door and ushered Daniel into a dim back entrance leading to a series of uneven stairs. They ascended to an attic piled with rotting garbage, water drops from the ceiling catching them as they negotiated a route to the dusty window that gave out on the waterfront. Big Jim sat Daniel down and handed him two lamps and a box of lucifers and gave him his orders. He would watch for patrolling leatherheads or guards on the dock and keep an eye on the window of a nearby saloon, where a lamp would be lit when the crew was ready to go to work. If the going was clear, Daniel would reply by lighting one lamp. If not, he'd light two.

"You're our Paul Revere, boy," Big Jim said with a rare smile.

Daniel didn't feel like Paul Revere. Wasn't he a hero, watching out for British soldiers? Daniel didn't know a lot about heroes but figured one thing they didn't do was skulk around filthy cabbage-smelling tenements, acting as the eyes of robbers.

Big Jim went through the plan as Daniel eyed the scene forty feet below. Men lounged on the nearest dock, smoking, looking out to the gray waters of the bay, apparently waiting for the changing tide to bring in a ship.

On Water Street, a team of broad-chested draft horses hauled a cart, piled high with barrels, past a toothless old man who held out one hand to a group of passing stevedores while feeling his way along the street with a white cane. Daniel noticed from four floors up and a half a block away that the blind man quickly cast his eyes down to a cigar butt at his feet and, when the stevedores passed, reached down to pocket the cigar.

Big Jim repeated that Daniel needed to keep an eye out for leatherheads and ships' watchmen and also for watchers for other gangs.

"Like the blind man?" Daniel asked.

"What about him?"

"He ain't blind. I saw him pocket a cigar butt."

Daniel's eyes could indeed spot things quickly, like the shell man palming the pea, and it took all of his visual gifts to detect the hint of a smile that raced beneath Big Jim's beard.

"You told me you know what I do. Well, I know what you do. You're a watcher for a gang of thieves. You help us steal something good, and we can help you get your ma out of the bughouse."

Big Jim took his leave, and Daniel was alone with the creaking of the old floorboards, the skittering of rats in the walls, and the whistling of wind around the window frames.

The sounds made Daniel shiver even though he was still warm from the rapid pace of his walk, and the worrying feeling was made worse by having his back to the door. He remained standing with his face in one corner of the window, so he could keep his eyes on the street and the docks, and so he'd be as hard as possible for others to detect. He noticed, as he had on previous watching missions, that standing still for more than ten minutes at a time was a lot harder than it looked. After two hours, Daniel's feet and hands grew numb with cold. No heat reached the empty attic, but the damp sea air had no trouble pushing through the walls. As he looked out at the water, Daniel noticed a change—the dark blue-black of the ocean worked its way toward the city, pushing the gray-green of the East River back upstream. A dead dog slowly floated toward the dock, seagulls squabbling over the right to peck at its sodden fur, its eyes long since removed from their sockets.

The tide had turned. A ship inched closer, its sails furled, a thin cloud rising from one funnel. Daniel made out the striped red, white, and blue flag that he had been told meant it came from France. He didn't know much about France, except that it was a country that produced many fine things—silk dresses, ladies' hats, the kind of booze they didn't have in cellars in the Five Points. He watched as the harbor pilot brought the ship in snug to its berth and the mooring lines were cinched up.

As he watched the stevedores unload the ship, Daniel noticed a peculiar pattern to the movements of the men. One stevedore in particular caught his attention. He was younger than the others, not slow and stiff in his movements. He had his own way of lifting boxes. Where the others would slowly raise the box and slide it onto a wheelbarrow, then push it just fast enough to avoid the harsh words of the foreman, this man worked up a sweat loading his wheelbarrow and racing it to the cart, where he unloaded it with equal dispatch. It was as if the others knew they had years of lifting ahead of them, while this man just wanted to get this work over with today.

And there was something else. When this man would approach the stack of boxes, he would not simply go to the nearest one. He would look ever so quickly at the foreman and point to one or another with his forehead, and the foreman would nod or shake his head. After the foreman gave a nod, the man would place a box in a cart pulled by a swaybacked chestnut mare. When the foreman shook his head, the man would place a box in one of the other carts. Daniel noticed that no other stevedore placed cargo in the cart pulled by the chestnut.

Daniel had overheard some of the language of his employers since coming into Mrs. Kleinschmidt's care, and he understood that this was what they called an inside job. The young stevedore and the foreman were the gang's inside men.

Every fifteen minutes, a pair of leatherheads walked past. The coppers knew they needed to keep their eyes on the docks to keep cargo from vanishing into the underworld, but they also knew better than to send men down to the waterfront alone. Daniel didn't know if fifteen minutes would be enough time for Big Jim and the gang to take off with the cart. That old chestnut didn't look much like a racehorse. The blind man, whichever rival gang he worked for, also kept his supposedly sightless eyes on the scene. Daniel had a feeling the man would get a cosh on the back of the head when the robbery began.

A wintry pall of coal smoke and pregnant clouds brought an early twilight to the city as the special wagon filled up. Once it was almost dark, a lamp came to life in the saloon window. Daniel checked for the leatherheads. They had passed a few minutes before. The coast was clear if Big Jim could act fast. Daniel struck one of the lucifers and lit a single lantern, placing it in the window to signal safety. After he did so, he noticed something in the fading light. The foreman turned from the dock, removed a watch from his pocket, and pointed at it while giving the blind beggar a questioning look. The beggar responded with a shrug.

The foreman knew that the beggar wasn't blind. The foreman must have been working with the beggar. Daniel's mind raced through the implications. Was the foreman double-crossing Big Jim and working with a different gang? Or was this whole thing a setup, a trap set by coppers to lure Big Jim and his gang into action? Maybe one of their inside men was actually a copper in disguise. Daniel grabbed for the box of lucifers and struck one so he could light the second lantern and cancel the all-clear. The lucifer sparked and sputtered. He struck another. No spark at all. He felt in the box. Wet. After lighting the first lamp, he'd placed the box under a leak in the roof. He struck each remaining lucifer with mounting panic.

Down the street, he could see men approaching, men he'd seen before with Big Jim. The robbery was beginning. He had no time to warn them. For the first time, he noticed something unusual about a pair of large boxes that had been sitting all day by themselves near the horses. Holes. Air holes. It was a trap.

He opened the window so he could shout a warning, and as he did so noticed a ragpicker's handcart in the street, not far from the first of the mysterious boxes with the air holes. Without further thought, he threw the burning lantern onto the cart, where it shattered and doused the rags with burning kerosene. Then he tossed the unlit lantern onto the fire, causing a second, larger burst of flames.

Big Jim needs a warning light? That ought to warn him.

A cry arose from the ragpicker and from the stevedores and the inhabitants of the lower floors of the nearby tenements. A call went up immediately for buckets and water. Big Jim's men stopped and watched. Suddenly, the top burst off the first of the air-hole boxes, and two men jumped out, moving stiffly but in a hurry to get away from the flaming cart. Big Jim's men turned and ran. The foreman tackled the stevedore, who had been depositing the designated boxes in the cart and, as he wrestled the younger man, called out for the men to emerge from the other boxes. Legs stiff and cramping from a day in a tight space, they gave chase to Big Jim's men. The blind beggar pointed up at Daniel's attic and called to the armed ambushers.

"Up there! It came from up there."

Two of the armed men detached themselves from the chase and ran to the tenement. As Daniel heard the men rush up the stairs, it occurred to him, too late, that he could simply have lit the second lamp from the flame of the first.

6

UNCLE STANISLAS HAD warned them that these Swedes and Germans were a tough audience. "Lutherans," he'd said. "Grim Protestant squareheads. They pay a quarter to come to the circus just so they can complain about the show."

Uncle Stanislas was right. As the ringmaster welcomed the audience, Mr. Szabo sneaked in behind him to start his usual clown antics, a choreographed routine in which Mr. Szabo would imitate Uncle Stanislas's gestures and facial expressions in exaggerated mockery, then adopt ever-more-unlikely casual poses whenever Uncle Stanislas turned to catch him in the act. It had never failed to loosen up a crowd. Well, never before Wisconsin.

Then Madame Mystere came on to start her mind-reading act. "I ask for one volunteer to come forward so that I may demonstrate how I peer into men's souls."

A thickly German-accented voice called out, "Only God can see into men's souls."

Madame Mystere had dealt with revivalists and believers of all stripes before, so she hastened to clarify. "You are correct, of course. I was speaking in the language of poetry and metaphor. I cannot see into your souls, and I cannot tell fortunes. But I can see how your character and experience have marked you and how they have laid out a path for your future."

"She's a fortune teller!" the German cried, leading others from his congregation to join in.

"A witch!"

"An abomination!"

Mr. Szabo, still in his clown makeup, came on to distract the audience with a rendition of "Amazing Grace" on the accordion, giving Madame Mystere a chance to bow and leave the ring.

As Madame Mystere retreated behind the curtain, Uncle Stanislas directed all eyes to the high wire where, at the sound of a cymbal crash and behind a puff of smoke from a handful of flash powder, Tommaso Largo stepped forward into a chasm as calmly as if he were crossing the street. It was an entrance that typically elicited gasps and sometimes even brought forth prayers for Tommaso, particularly from young women whose eyes were drawn to his tight knit pants and singlet.

Here, the audience seemed divided between those who felt cheated because the wire wasn't high enough and those who felt he was setting a poor example for children who would be inclined to climb onto the barn roof. Tommaso walked across, returned to the halfway point, and began to juggle twenty feet above the ground. As usual, while juggling three eggs, he let one fall, to demonstrate what might happen to his own brain were he to lose balance.

The audience did not interpret the action that way.

"The man can't even juggle."

"We paid good money for this."

When he finished his act, the overriding sentiment from the audience was one of disappointment that they'd paid a quarter to see the circus, and the most dangerous act of the show had just ended without injury.

Uncle Stanislas sent Mr. Szabo out again with his accordion and the instruction to "play something German."

As the familiar sounds of "O Tannenbaum" drifted backstage, Uncle Stanislas approached Lily, who had just finished helping Madame Mystere out of her costume and was now laying out props for the midget tumblers, who usually opened the final act and led up to Uncle Stanislas's climactic magic show.

"I think tonight we give them a different act."

"You mean—"

"Lillian the Lycanthrope."

"What's a lycan-whatever?"

"Is big word for werewolf."

"But I've only just started training my dogs."

"You finish training when the clown finishes playing Christmas song."

Lily and her dogs had been nearly inseparable ever since Uncle Stanislas had seen her communicate with them in an alley in Springfield. After she called them back to meet him, he had been amused when she insisted on asking their opinions on the question of traveling with the circus. Did they have masters already? Would they like to travel with the circus?

"The dogs say yes," she had told him.

In the months that followed, as the circus moved on to Peoria and Rockford, keeping to smaller cities where audiences would be more starved for entertainment, Lily came to understand her bond with the animals. She realized her communication with the dogs wasn't really a conversation. They did not, in truth, have a full understanding of English. Nor did they have a complex vocabulary in their growls, yelps, and barks that corresponded to words. Rather, she felt that when she opened her mind in a certain way, it bonded with those of the dogs, allowing her to sense the world as they did and allowing her to direct her thoughts into their minds. She still spoke out loud when communicating with them, in part because, as a human, putting thoughts into words came naturally, and in part because speaking out loud would be better for her act.

Now, after a few weeks of training, she knew she could communicate with the dogs, and she could ask them, maybe even order them, to do things, but she didn't know how to make that into a circus act. Uncle Stanislas had suggested making them jump through flaming hoops, but she had scotched that idea.

"Galahad is afraid of fire."

Galahad, she informed him, was the name of the long-haired sheepdog.
"What about other dog? Terrier?"

"It wouldn't be fair to ask Lancelot to do something Galahad won't do."

"How about they walk on hind feet? Is funny, like little furry people."

"No, they would both find that beneath their dignity."

Once she had bathed the dogs and brushed their fur and given them regular meals, their solemn dignity had indeed become evident. This was fine, up to a point. After all, Tommaso Largo was a dignified man, and he was usually the most popular performer at the circus. But a circus also needed performers who didn't worry about their dignity, who enjoyed casting it off and trampling it underfoot, like Mr. Szabo during the part of his clown show when his pants fall down to reveal a lady's undergarment underneath.

Shortly before their arrival in the little Wisconsin town, Lily found the balance she needed for her act when Uncle Stanislas presented her with a third dog, a little hairless thing with a ridiculous Mexican name and an even more ridiculous bark. She had named the dog Sparky.

Mr. Szabo's fingers teased out the final notes of "O Tannenbaum" with additional arpeggios and sustained quavering notes, giving Lily the chance to round up the three dogs and fit Sparky into his costume, which Madame Mystere had just finished sewing that morning.

"Ladies and gentlemen, for the first time anywhere, the one, the only, Lillian the Lycanthrope!"

Tommaso pulled back the curtain for Lily, who paused before walking into the ring with Lancelot and Galahad. Sparky remained hidden in the back. She issued a silent prayer that the three dogs wouldn't have stage fright. She issued another for herself. She had danced for larger audiences than this, but she had never spoken to this many people, and she had never imagined how to inhabit a character as mysterious and magical as Lillian the Lycanthrope.

Tommaso cleared his throat and reminded Lily to step through.

"Hello. I'm Lillian. I'm not really a lycanthrope. That's a werewolf, which is like a kind of magical wolf that can take human form or a person who can take wolf form. I can't do that. But I can talk to dogs. You might think that's not so special. You probably talk to dogs. But with me, they talk back, and we have a conversation."

She heard some laughter. It wasn't the kind of happy, friendly laughter that Mr. Szabo normally would get. It was a mean laughter. A laughter that told her the audience thought she was a stupid girl, or maybe a crazy one.

"These are my friends, Lancelot and Galahad. I call them Lancelot and Galahad because they are brave and loyal."

At this point, she produced a short length of rope from her pocket, looped it around her wrists, and, using her teeth and the fingers of one hand, tied her hands together.

"We're going to pretend that somebody has taken me prisoner and tied me up. Lancelot and Galahad are so brave and loyal, they will free me."

She walked the length of the front row, giving audience members the chance to inspect the rope and see that it had been tied in a proper knot. Then she called to the terrier.

"Lancelot, Lancelot. Come here. Now, do you see the rope? See how it's tied? I want you to take the rope in your teeth and pull it loose, just like we practiced. No, not that part. You have to pull that little piece to make the knot loose. Yes. That's right."

Lancelot pulled the central part of the knot enough to loosen it, then, under her direction, pulled the other strand free.

The man with the German accent, who had started the heckling that forced Madame Mystere from the ring, called out, "That's easy. You made it so loose you could shake it off."

Lily turned to the sheepdog.

"Galahad. Here, Galahad, please take this rope up to the gentleman in the back row, the one who just spoke. Give the rope to him and invite him to come down and tie me up."

Lily had been practicing this rope trick with knots tied by Tommaso, but Tommaso was too kindhearted to pull the rope tight against the girl's skin. This bully would know no such restraint.

"Is he shy, Galahad? He isn't afraid of dogs, is he? Maybe you need to prove to him that you're well mannered. Do you see that seat behind the gentleman? Please go to that seat and sit politely."

Galahad turned back down the row he was in, climbed to the next level of seating, and walked carefully until he came to the vacant space, then calmly pulled himself onto the bench, turned around, and watched Lily, awaiting further instructions.

"You see, sir? Nothing to be afraid of."

For the first time, members of the audience laughed in a way that didn't sound and look as if they were mocking the circus, though there was some mockery directed at the man. Looking around him in dismay at being the butt of a joke, the man stood as if to get things over with and strode to the stage.

"Thank you so much, sir. Now, Lancelot, we are going to pretend that this gentleman is a villain. Do you remember what a villain needs? Could you bring me something to make this gentleman a villain?"

The terrier ran to a bag of props and pulled out a black mask. Additional ripples of laughter ran around the stands as the audience pictured the man in a mask.

"I'm not wearing that!"

The ripples became a crashing wave.

"That's fine. We'll just pretend you're a villain. Now, I'd like you to tie me to this tent pole. However you'd like. Pretend I'm your prisoner."

The man took the rope from Lily's hands and examined it, a look of skepticism mixed with anxiety on his face. He reached his arms awkwardly around Lily's body, making an effort not to touch her, and wrapped the rope tightly around her waist and arms, twice. He pulled the hemp taut against the bare skin of Lily's forearms. He pulled more forcefully than Tommaso ever had. Lily felt the rope burn and knew her flesh would be red for some time. She shouldn't have goaded the man so much. He was getting back at her.

The man panted his beery breath all over Lily, his face red and shiny with sausage-smelling sweat, his teeth yellow in the circus lamplight, as he inspected his handiwork.

"Thank you. Does anybody wish to inspect this gentleman's knots? Make sure he did a good job? Ma'am, with the yellow dress in the front row. Would you like to take a look?"

The woman shook her head. Evidently, the people knew the angry man well enough to trust that he wouldn't spare a young girl any discomfort when tying her to a tent pole.

"Very well. Now, since we have a villain tying up his captive, I think we need a hero to free the captive, don't you? Ladies and gentlemen I would like to introduce the fourth and final member of this act, my new friend, Sparky. Sparky, please come out."

Lily strained her neck to see Sparky emerge from the opening in the curtains, walking on his hind legs, wearing a suit of clothes with a sheriff's star, a tiny brown holster from which the butt of a derringer emerged, and a miniature ten-gallon hat. A roar of laughter swept through the tent. Galahad and Lancelot both looked mortified on behalf of their new, small colleague.

"The sheriff is here. But he needs his horse. Lancelot, could you be the horse?"

Lancelot cocked his head and looked at Lily. She was sure she saw him raise an eyebrow. But just when she feared he might balk at this request, Lancelot galloped toward Sparky, who took a running leap and landed on the sheepdog's back.

To a resounding round of applause, Lancelot galloped around the ring with the Chihuahua on his back. So far, so good. But could the little dog loosen those tight knots?

Lancelot walked behind Lily to place Sparky within biting distance of the knots. She felt the tiny teeth against her skin as Sparky attempted to grasp the rope where it cut into her wrist. She felt him tug at the rope and slide it back and forth over the newly burnt skin. She felt new chafing as the dog pulled from different angles or worked on different parts of the rope.

In front of her, the man began to smile.

"You're doing fine, Sparky. Just keep trying different parts of the rope until one starts to loosen."

She felt a barely perceptible movement against her skin—one part of the rope shifting ever so slightly.

"I think that was it. Keep working at it."

Sparky pulled again, and the knot felt momentarily tighter. But then he pulled from a different angle, and Lily felt some slack. It continued like that for another minute. Tighter. Looser. Tighter. Looser still. As Sparky loosened one section of the knot, Galahad moved him into position so he could reach another section. In another minute, the rope came free, and Sparky shook his head in triumph, waving the rope end for the audience to see.

The applause was deafening.

Uncle Stanislas strode back on stage and called out in triumph, "Ladies and gentlemen, I give you Lancelot, Galahad, Sparky, and Lillian the Lycanthrope."

Lily had saved the show.

7

LINCOLN HENRY HAD never seen so many people at the railway camp. Folks on foot and riding all manner of horse and mule streamed toward the mountain's big rock face, while farm wagons and fancy carriages, carrying families all trucked out with hampers and blankets as if they were going to a picnic, kicked up dust along the dirt road. Otis the stable keeper's boys called out to passing riders and drivers, offering oats and clean water in the shade of the pine trees. Lincoln's mother, who cooked six days a week for the workers on the Richmond and Nashville Railway, labored with other camp women over batches of cornbread and fritters, seizing on this opportunity to turn butter and cornmeal into hard cash. Around him, Lincoln, now fourteen, saw boys his age rushing up to the mountain laden with platters piled with gleaming, golden goodness.

Unbidden, numbers began rushing into his head. How many pounds of butter and cornmeal would it take to satisfy the men, women, and children? How many gallons of water would their horses drink waiting for the trip back down the valley? Then more numbers and then ratios and angles. How far did the tunnellers have to dig to punch through to the other side of the mountain? How much higher would the tracks have to climb? What angle would the railbed make with the horizon?

And then beyond that, the numbers that governed his papa's work on the railway—the length and weight of his sledgehammer, the force those numbers created when the hammer struck the rock drill. And the numbers all bundled up inside of the big steam drill he'd seen the day before as the crew from the New Haven Steam Drill Company moved it into place in front of the cliff. How, he wondered, could his papa's numbers come out on top against the numbers in that steam drill?

"Lincoln! Where your head at, boy?"

His mama's voice woke him from the dream of numbers and angles and ratios. She was coming his way with a hamper filled with cornbread, his brothers, George and Thomas, trailing along in her wake.

She had a hard look in her eye, though truth to tell that wasn't saying anything much new these last few months, ever since she'd pulled herself up from her sickbed after the fever had taken young Annabelle in the winter. Fever had run through the railway camp, with workers living elbow-to-elbow behind thin canvas walls that did little to keep out the blasts of winter.

Lincoln's family had begun following the moving camp the summer before, after the riders returned and destroyed another crop. With no corn to sell or to feed to their milk cow and their pigs, Lincoln's parents had been forced to sell their forty acres for a fraction of their value. They'd sold the sow but taken that year's weanlings as well as the cow with them to the camp. With the money from the sale of the sow, they'd bought enough feed to keep the weanlings growing until they could be butchered, cooked, and sold to hungry railway men.

Some of that money was set aside to keep the cow fed and producing milk through the winter. The rest went into a locked box that Mama carried everywhere she went, not trusting the rootless wanderers who followed the rail. Through the fall and for the first part of the winter, Lincoln had seen a look of hope on her face every time she put a week's worth of milk money in the box. That money and Papa's wages would buy them another farm somewhere far from Tennessee. She explained all of that to him one day, while he watched her counting the coins in the lockbox.

"We gonna have our own land again, Lincoln. This time in a free state."

"Teacher said they're all free states now."

Miss Cadbury was still the only teacher Lincoln had ever known, except for that one afternoon two years before with Mr. Delacroix. There was no school in the railway camp, except perhaps for Lincoln, who drew shapes and figures for his younger brothers and Otis's daughter and attempted to explain the concepts that were so clear in his mind that he could no more break them down into simple steps than a hawk could provide point-by-point lessons on flying.

"Well, 'course she say that," Mama said. "They's all free states for Miss Cadbury."

Mama had looked angry when she said that but not hard. She still had some fondness for Miss Cadbury that could not be completely over-whelmed by the horror of the day the riders reduced the school to ashes and Mr. Delacroix to carrion, nor by the despair when their farm was stolen from them by men who used torches and guns to bring down the price. Despite all she'd seen, she'd still had hope that day.

Now, in addition to her new hard look, she had a cloud of fear over her face as she handed Lincoln the hamper of cornbread and arranged a cloth to trap the warmth.

"There's a mess of hungry folk up by that rock. Warm cornbread sells better than cold, so I don't want to see no lingering. I'll be up there presently with another batch."

"Yes, Mama."

"George and Thomas, you listen to your brother, and you help him sell that cornbread."

The younger boys nodded. Lincoln, growing rapidly since his thirteenth birthday, shrugged off the efforts of his brothers to help with the hamper. He began to trot as best he could, with his arms held out wide to carry the hamper.

"And you stay away from that infernal machine, Lincoln."

Mama knew well how that machine had captured his imagination, ever since his papa had come home talking about the steam drill that could power through a rock face faster than a whole team of the strongest men. Papa had explained that it worked with the same power as the steam engines of the trains, heating water to make the steam push wheels and gears to drive a drill into the rock. Lincoln understood that steam power could do some wondrous things, but he surely desired to see a steam engine that was strong enough to drill through rock.

When he reached the clearing in front of the cliff, he saw the biggest crowd of people in one place that he had ever seen, with more still coming up behind him and his brothers on the road. Knowing Mama would be angry if he let his cornbread get cold and stale, he willed himself not to look at the gleaming metal shape that squatted in front of the cliff, cordoned off by ropes and guarded by two stern-looking men.

He set George and Thomas to walking through the crowd, calling out "fresh cornbread," and made his way slowly after them, noting whenever one of them pointed out a hungry customer. At a penny a piece, he slowly felt the weight of the coins accumulate in the knotted kerchief Mama gave him to use as a change purse. It was a big hamper, though, and Lincoln feared he would miss the excitement if he didn't sell out soon. He felt a powerful dread that he would be bent over his change purse making a sale when the machine exploded into action.

His heart jumped when a man in soot-covered dungarees with goggles propped up on his forehead approached and asked for a piece of cornbread. With tools dangling from his belt and an enticing aroma of lubricating oil floating up from his clothing, the man had to be the mechanic himself. Lincoln wondered for a moment if he could trade a piece of cornbread for a closer look at the machine. Truth to tell, he'd gladly trade one of Mama's pies for a gander.

As Lincoln handed the mechanic the largest piece left in the hamper, a man in a stovepipe hat, his cravat loosened, his jacket off and sweat stains spreading out from under his arms, confronted the man.

"What's keeping you? Is there some problem with the drill?"

"No, sir," the mechanic said. "But they sent the wrong drill bit. This one's likely to overheat if we go at it too long. I've asked them to send up a different bit."

"Damn it, McTaggart! I've got a hundred potential customers waiting for a demonstration. Every minute they're forced to wait is another opportunity for their doubts to grow."

"If we go ahead with the wrong bit, the metal might overheat, sir. Hot metal becomes soft. I canna drill rock with a stick of taffy, sir."

The face of the man in the stovepipe hat reddened. "Damnation! I'll open up another keg of beer and try to keep them entertained. I'll give you two hours, and then we'll have to go ahead regardless. You just keep that drill working."

Two hours! Lincoln would have plenty of time to sell his cornbread before the machine started. He might even have a chance to get a closer look. He felt a surge of hope that the drill bit would arrive in time. He surely wanted to see the machine working at full speed. No sooner had that thought crossed his mind than he tried to take back his hope. The machine and the mechanic and this man in the stovepipe hat were all out to beat Lincoln's father, the steel-driving man who had won the right to race against it by driving his hand drill in the rock faster than anyone else.

Lincoln reminded himself what was on the line—one hundred dollars to the steel driver who could beat the steam drill. One hundred dollars which, combined with the savings from Mama's cooking, would buy the Henrys a piece of homestead land somewhere out west. The owner of the machine must have been powerful certain to offer that much money. But if the machine could beat a man as strong as Papa, these other men in the silk ties and fancy hats, smoking those fat cigars and drinking mugs of the owner's beer, would surely want to buy machines to dig tunnels for their railways.

It didn't take long for Lincoln's hamper to be emptied down to crumbs. Around that time, he saw Mama come up the road with a second hamper, and he and George and Thomas ran to help her sell its contents.

By the time they were down to the last few pieces, it was looking like everybody who wanted cornbread had already bought some, so Mama gave the boys the remaining pieces and took them to see Papa, resting in the shade of a tarpaulin stretched out near the rock face, right up beside the rope that kept the crowds away from the big steam drill.

"I thought you had better things to do than watch this foolishness," Papa said as Mama approached.

Mama produced a chicken leg wrapped in cheesecloth from the bottom of her empty hamper and passed it to Papa. "Thought I did, too, but since the entire camp is up here, ain't nothing to do back in our tent. Might as well make some spare change off of these fools, got nothing better to do than watch a man work himself to death."

"Now, Bessie, ain't nobody working himself to death here. This dang fool machine like as not won't even start."

Lincoln spoke up. "They're waiting for a different drill bit. The one they have might overheat and warp the drive shaft."

Papa smiled. "Bet you a busted drive shaft cost these men more than it cost them to pay me my hundred dollars. Could be an expensive day for them."

"Could be an expensive day for this family," Mama said, "if you work yourself into an early grave."

Papa's smile faded as he looked at his three boys. "Bessie. Maybe we best talk about this later. Lincoln, why don't you take your brothers over to that man selling candy? Here's a penny for each of you."

Lincoln led his brothers to the candy man, looking back over his shoulder at the tense exchange between Mama and Papa. He knew his mama was worried. Now he thought about it, so was he. Papa had been unsteady on his feet the evening he beat all the other workers to win the chance to race against the machine. How much harder would this race be?

Now Lincoln wanted to know more about the machine, not because it was new and shiny and worked with the magic of numbers and ratios, but because he wanted to know if his father had a chance against it. He wanted to know if fighting the machine would kill his papa.

When George and Thomas ran ahead with their pennies, Lincoln turned to make sure neither Mama nor Papa was looking his way. He also looked back to where the machine's owner was laughing and pouring beer for the crowd of customers. Nobody was watching him. He turned quickly and ran up to the rope on the far side of the machine, where the mechanic stood with a wrench in one hand, an oilcan in the other, and a look of concentration on his face.

"Excuse me, Mister Mechanic."

The man turned, saw Lincoln, and raised an eyebrow.

"You bought some of my mama's cornbread."

"So I did. Your mama is an excellent cook."

"Thank you, sir. I'll be sure to tell her."

The man gave Lincoln a puzzled look. "Was there anything else?"

"Yes, sir. If it's not a bother."

"I don't know if it is or if it isn't. Not until I hear what it is."

"That's right, sir. The thing is, it's my papa you're racing against and—"

"You want inside information."

"No, sir. Well, not really. I'm just a little scared. And my mama's mighty scared. How fast does my papa have to drill that rock to win this race?"

"Faster than any man can, son."

"But if he tries real hard, do you think he could hurt himself trying to beat your machine?"

The man sighed, looked over the machine at Lincoln's father, and shrugged. He was not an unkind-looking man, with his wisps of red hair falling below a crushed flat cap, a scattering of freckles across his nose and cheeks, and a smudge of oil on his forehead. He looked, though, like a man who might be more comfortable talking to machines and coaxing another bit of power from them than talking to a worried fourteen-year-old boy.

"Your daddy looks a brawny man. I'd say if any man can beat this machine, he can. And I think if he can't, he looks like a man who has the good sense to put down his hammer and rest before he does himself harm."

Lincoln felt a little reassured by the signs of kindness on the man's face, enough at any rate that his curiosity reemerged. He was closer now than he'd ever been to a machine, and he began to scan it from one end to another, taking in every shaft and gear he could see.

His mind began to fill up with numbers. The size of the gears. The length of the shafts. He knew a magic thing to do with numbers to tell him how long it was around a circle if you knew how far it was across.

And he then could figure how far a drive shaft would move forward, given the size of the gear it was attached to.

Soon, he began to calculate ratios of big gears and little gears and think of how much drilling power one turn of a big gear could generate if it caused a little gear to spin around a dozen times. Somewhere in his mind, some other thoughts pushed their way in. How much would all that spinning heat up that metal?

He knew that you could start a fire by spinning wood fast enough against a wooden block—that was called friction. And he knew that a lucifer rubbed across a block of wood wouldn't catch fire, but one rubbed across rock would. So, rock must create much more friction. He knew as well that when metal was hot enough, you could bend it. He'd watched blacksmiths at work and seen how something as strong as an iron bar could bend like a willow after time in the hot coals. There had to be a way of putting numbers together that would show how fast the machine could drill rock before it overheated.

"Son!" The mechanic was holding him by the shoulder and calling into his ear.

"Yes, sir?"

"You having a spell there?"

"No, sir."

"Thought you were about to start rolling around on the ground or something."

"No, sir. Just thinking."

"Some powerful thinking, I'll bet. What was taking hold of your young mind?"

"Your machine. And numbers, and ratios, and power."

"Well, I'll be. You're a born mechanic, boy."

With a grin and a look back to make sure that his boss was occupied with customers, the mechanic lifted up the rope that separated the machine from the crowd and invited Lincoln to take a closer look. The mechanic expressed his delight at finding somebody who appreciated his machine as much as he did. To be sure, he explained, the owner, Mr. Vandenberg, appreciated it for the money it might make him if this demonstration went well and enabled him to return to Connecticut with a satchel filled with sales orders and bank drafts.

But Lincoln appreciated it as a mechanical wonder that took the laws of mathematics and geometry and made them into power. Lincoln appreciated it as a work of art in which dozens of parts came together with perfect timing to create something greater than any of those parts. The mechanic invited Lincoln to look closely at the couplings, where the drill bit connected to the drive wheel, where the drive wheel connected to the drive shaft, and the drive shaft to the piston. He pointed out to Lincoln the details that would interest only a born mechanic. He showed the boy the inertia wheel, a heavy not-quite-circular wheel that would be driven into its rotation by the force of the piston's movement, and which would then continue moving forward because of its lopsided weighting, keeping the engine moving while pressure built in the cylinder to drive the piston forward again.

He explained how to read the pressure gauges and how to relieve excess air pressure. He pointed out the fire box and explained that for this demonstration the machine would use the purest and hardest anthracite coal because it burned hotter and would keep the engine turning faster. He invited Lincoln to look closely at the steel of the drill bit and see how it had been discolored by heat and to feel a slightly misshapen portion of the cylinder where it had warped for the same reason. He pointed out the cans of petroleum oil he used to lubricate the couplings and where oil was injected into the cylinder to keep friction from causing additional warping inside, which might make the entire machine grind to a halt, leading to a dangerous buildup of pressure and quite possibly an explosion.

"The devil doesn't know what to do with mechanics," the man said with a laugh. "Because Hell seems so much like home to them."

Lincoln interrupted the man's laughter. "How fast does this go?"

"Sixty revolutions per second."

As he continued examining the machine, one ear tuned to the mechanic's explanations, Lincoln let the numbers wash over him. Sixty movements of the big piston, sixty turnings of the big flywheel—that would add up to how many turns of the drill? And how much force was pressing that drill bit against the rock? He looked toward his father, still talking to Mama, and his father's numbers came to him—the length of his arms, the length of his hammer, the weight of the hammer, the force with which that hammer would drive his papa's drill into the rock. It took him little time to see that Papa could not possibly match the steel-driving power of this machine at sixty revolutions per second.

Unless. Unless it had to move at less than normal speed.

"What happens if you don't have the right drill bit, sir? And how about that bump inside the cylinder?"

"Cylinder's down about ten percent already because of the bump. And I'm going to have to disengage that bit from time to time to keep it from binding in the hole. Let's say if that good bit doesn't get here, we're not good for much more than half speed."

Half speed. Lincoln thought on that for a moment and saw that just maybe Papa could beat this machine. He glanced at the owner in the top hat and saw the man looking impatiently at his pocket watch. He pictured the owner pushing the mechanic to speed up past half speed, well past half speed. He pictured the drill bit binding in the hole and snapping off, or pressure building up inside the cylinder and the entire machine bursting like an overstuffed pie in a hot oven. He saw the impatient man snap his watch closed and begin making his way to the machine.

Lincoln quickly thanked the mechanic and excused himself before he could find himself in a heap of trouble. As he sneaked around the other side of the machine, he heard Mr. Vandenberg say to the mechanic, "I can't make them wait any longer. You'll do it with the drill bit you've got."

Lincoln ran up behind his father and tugged on his sleeve.

"Papa. You can beat the machine."

"Lincoln. Where have you been? Where are your brothers at?"

"I've been looking at the machine. If they don't get the right drill bit here right now, that boss man's gonna make them start with the wrong one. Then, either the mechanic will have to run it slow, or the boss man will make him run it fast, and it'll break down."

"Oh, you got it all figured?"

"I do."

As his father, John Jefferson Henry, locked gazes with Lincoln, Mr. Vandenberg climbed to the top of a set of three stairs, fired a pistol in the air, and bellowed, "Ladies and gentlemen, may I have your attention? The New Haven Steam Drill Company is proud to welcome you to this Race of the Century between Man and Machine. The New Haven Steam Drill Company is so confident of the superiority of its product that today we will give one hundred dollars in gold coins to the champion steel driver of the Richmond and Nashville Railway if he is able to drill farther into this rock face than our steam drill."

A roar went up from the crowd. A few other pistols were fired into the air, and the group of steam drill customers, now boisterous and even more red-faced than Mr. Vandenberg, launched a few beer mugs toward the rock face. The mechanic fired up the machine and began building pressure in the steam chamber.

A few voices could be heard over the din of the machine calling out support for one side or another.

"Two dollars on the machine!"

"No Yankee machine is going to beat a good southern buck."

Mr. Vandenberg read out a series of glowing testimonials on behalf of his machine, written by learned professors from universities in the northern states and as far away as Germany. Then the mechanic told Mr. Vandenberg that the machine had reached a suitable steam pressure to begin.

Lincoln's papa brought the hammer to his shoulder.

Mr. Vandenberg fired his pistol again and yelled, "The race is on!"

Papa began to swing his hammer, connecting squarely on the drill with each blow. Lincoln expected to see sparks fly from the drill but then realized that Papa's blows were landing too precisely for that.

It was not that he was swinging rapidly or throwing extra weight into his swing. What made his hammer blows so effective was their clock-work regularity and the efficiency with which he struck the drill at the full extent of each swing, bringing the nine pounds of the hammer head onto the steel with all the force that a six foot man with broad shoulders could muster. And because of the efficiency of his hammering, Papa did not appear to be exerting himself.

Lincoln's optimism suffered a blow when he looked at the machine. It turned and turned and gave no indication that it was anywhere close even to the half speed the mechanic said was the best it could do today. The rhythms of its piston, its shafts and gears, seemed almost unhurried. They were also inhuman. If Papa could be said to wield his hammer "like clockwork," this thing truly was clockwork. It knew neither tiredness nor hunger nor time. As long as it had a supply of hard, black anthracite—and Lincoln saw with dismay just how large that pile was—it had no reason to ever abate.

But rock faces are hard, and neither strong men nor inhuman machines can dent them easily. To Lincoln's eyes, neither drill appeared to be doing much of anything, although there was no denying that there was some kind of mark forming in both places. Lincoln noticed a small pile of rock dust forming at the base of the cliff below the machine's drill. Clearly, it was grinding this ancient mountain, which had sat there since before Adam, into a pile of dust. Then he noticed the slightest cloud of dust in the air near his papa's drill bit. The resounding impact of each hammer stroke was turning the rock little by little into puffs of dust so fine they floated in the air like flour on bread-baking day.

The crowd continued to shout. The customers continued to drink beer. In the distance, a few voices were raised in song. "Dixie," sung by those who did not believe a Yankee machine could beat a man of the South, even if he was a free colored man. In time, the cheers faded out, and the songs changed to popular barroom ballads, most of them with words so off-color, Mama would have washed his ears out with soap if she'd known he'd been able to hear them above the hammer and piston.

There were a few new notes. Ringing sounds of hammer blows landing just off target and setting off sparks. Odd echoing noises coming from the steam engine, indicating pressure escaping through a widening gap where the cylinder was misshapen. A strange huffing sound, which may have been Papa's lungs or the steam hissing out of the pressure valve.

Now there was no denying that both drills were advancing into the rock. And there was certainly no denying that the machine's drill was deeper. If the machine could keep this pace, Papa could not possibly win.

If. Lincoln stared at the drill shaft as he counted revolutions per minute. He had no pocket watch but counted nonetheless, thinking of the rhythm of seconds when Miss Cadbury had first taught him to tell time on the school's clock. The machine was going at forty revolutions per second. He looked at where the drill dug into the rock wall and saw not just the pile of rock dust below but a cloud of rock dust in the air, like that forced up by his father's hammer blows.

Only this was not a cloud of dust. This was smoke. He thought for a moment and watched the cloud grow thicker. He counted the revolutions of the wheels and saw numbers in his head to represent the heat of the metal, the weakening of the iron.

At the same time, his papa was also showing the strain. His shirt clung to his back, sweat dripping onto the dust at his feet. His shoulder had a new hitch to it as it shifted back to begin the arc of the hammer. His eyes were red, his mouth hung open, his hair waved limply with each motion.

This could not last much longer.

Lincoln's attention was drawn back to the machine as its motion changed pitch, from the high whine of a mosquito to the rattling hum of a bumblebee. The mechanic had slowed it down. He was now looking underneath at the gears that turned the drill bit and wiping sweat from his forehead. Papa must have noticed that change in tone, too, because he picked up his own pace and began hammering faster again.

A roar arose from the crowd that was cheering for the man from the South.

Lincoln noticed Mr. Vandenberg charging toward the mechanic, even more red-faced than before. His top hat now gone, his cravat hanging loose on his shirt front, he shouted at the mechanic and pointed at the machine and at Lincoln's papa. The mechanic's lips moved, but Lincoln could not hear. He was sure the mechanic was telling the machine's owner that the machine could not keep up forty revolutions per minute any longer without either the shaft binding or the piston fusing to the red-hot interior of the cylinder. The owner shouted some more, and the mechanic returned to his controls, and the machine again began to make its high-pitched mosquito whine. Only now, it was a sickly mosquito, off-balance, flying in circles with one wing broken.

Still, even sickly, the machine made fast progress at forty revolutions per minute.

Lincoln's papa had to keep up his own fast pace, a fast pace he had started a short time earlier when it appeared that the machine was on the verge of breakdown. Somehow, his hammer did not slow, even though every swing seemed to involve a different group of muscles jumping into action in a different order. His shirt now clung to his back, and the disks of his spine seemed to jump this way and that.

A vision burst into Lincoln's eyes. His papa's heart, the numbers all out of balance as it tried to force more blood faster than the vessels inside could handle it. His papa's lungs, stretched thin like a soap bubble until they burst from the effort of taking in air. A new farm was not worth losing Papa. Lincoln would tell him to stop. But before he could, Lincoln heard a new note in the symphony, an off-key whistling from the machine. The owner still shouted at the mechanic, who looked only at the controls and did not seem to hear. Lincoln counted quickly. Fifty revolutions. Numbers again raced through his mind. The turning of the wheels and the gears, the teeth of the drill bit generating heat. He saw a new pattern emerging in the turning of one of the flywheels. A new thickness in the clouds of smoke. The machine was nearing the breaking point. And at the speed with which it was turning, it would break with a mighty explosion, perhaps even killing the mechanic and the red-faced Mr. Vandenberg.

This race had to stop.

Before he knew what he was doing, Lincoln had jumped over the rope and was grabbing the mechanic by the shoulder and pointing to the flywheel at the front of the machine.

"It's turning too fast. It's gonna burst on you."

"Get that boy out of here!" shouted Mr. Vandenberg.

The mechanic looked at the wheel and at the smoke and apparently heard a few words as Lincoln tried to explain the patterns of the numbers he had seen in his head. The machine could not take much more of this,

Lincoln said. In a flash, the mechanic understood what Lincoln was saying about the sound and the smoke and the rhythms of the flywheel. The pressure was building inside in a way that was not linear but logarithmic. It would reach dangerous levels in—

Lincoln watched a brief hissing jet of hot air burn the mechanic's back. If he had still been at the controls, where he had been before Lincoln had shown up, he would have been blinded for life, if not killed.

He grabbed Lincoln by the back of the shirt and hauled him toward his employer just as the machine shuddered and burst open. A group of firefighters, instructed to remain at the ready just in case, reacted with buckets of water and shovels filled with sand, while the mechanic shielded Lincoln from flying debris.

Papa was knocked to the ground by the force of the blast. Regaining his feet, he saw Bessie, Thomas, and George sitting a safe distance away but could see no sign of Lincoln. Papa crawled toward the mechanic.

John Jefferson Henry embraced Lincoln, then tried to walk with him toward Bessie and the other boys, but no part of his body would obey his brain's commands. It was Lincoln who put an arm toward his father and led him away from the destruction and heat of the machine so he could rest.

Lincoln's father lay panting with his arms wrapped around all of his loved ones. All those who still lived.

"You won, Papa," Lincoln told him.

"Hush," said Bessie.

Behind them, they heard a voice call out, "John Henry, three feet, two inches. Steam drill, three feet, three inches."

From the crowd came a groan.

Then the voice started up again. "But since there is still thirty minutes left in this race, John Henry can resume hammering, and of course the steam drill can resume drilling if repairs can be made in that amount of time."

A roar rose through the crowd.

"No you don't, John Henry," Mama said. "That hammering's gonna kill you."

The steel driving man pulled himself up, smiled at his family, and lifted his hammer. "I only got to do a little more than one inch in a half an hour, and I win us one hundred dollars in gold. Bessie baby, I can see that free state land now."

He walked to the wall and, as the mechanic and the steam drill's owner watched from the wreckage of the machine, John Henry hammered his way into legend.

8

"FAITH AND BEGORRAH, 'tis just like the Auld Sod, is it not, Seamus O'Finnigan Flanagan?"

Daniel looked up from the bucket of seed potatoes and saw Segal grinning at him. The wiry, dark-haired boy placed his hat over his chest, gestured to the rows of potatoes awaiting planting, and proclaimed, "Me Oirish heart loves me spuds."

Roth and Wiseman guffawed at Segal's performance. Daniel's supposed Irishness was a frequent subject of mirth with the three. Segal often cracked jokes at Daniel's expense, telling the boy to throw a brick of turf on the fire, or asking to borrow Daniel's shillelagh. Daniel took Segal's mockery as a playful expression of friendship, but he also knew Segal directed Irish jokes his way because Daniel was a safe target. The other Irish boys at the reformatory banded together as the Brickbat Boys and were the fiercest gang in the joint, so this was Segal's only opportunity to tell Irish jokes without sparking a gang war.

Daniel had been barred from admission to the Brickbat Boys shortly after arriving at the reformatory when one of the gang members recognized Daniel from his time living on the streets of the Five Points. "Watch out for this one," the boy had said. "If he's as crazy as his ma, he's after biting you like a dog."

Daniel, just starting to grow out of his little boy's body at age fifteen, had pounced on the larger boy and bloodied his nose before the other Brickbat Boys could intervene. That had attracted the screws, who arrived just as Daniel's tormentor produced a shiv, made from a sharpened, straightened bedspring wrapped with old rags for a handle. The boy with the shiv, one of the leaders of the Brickbat Boys, got a week in the hole and a month of extra duty. When he came out, he pronounced Daniel a snitch.

That might have been the beginning of a very difficult time at the Yonkers Industrial School for Boys, a time punctuated by slips on the stairs and accidents in the woodshop and by trips to the infirmary, if Segal hadn't come forward and announced that Daniel was in fact his long-lost cousin Hyman, last seen when he was kidnapped by Gypsies in Ruthenia. As such, Daniel came under the protection of Segal, which didn't count for much, and of Roth and Wiseman, which counted for a great deal more, given Wiseman's massive physical presence and nickname "The Giant" and the reputation of Roth's fists, which, combined with his cold, unblinking eyes, had given him the nickname "The Cobra." Realizing the protection Segal's story gained him, Daniel had given thanks for his dark hair and brown eyes—the combination often referred to as "black Irish."

Privately, Segal explained that he'd seen Daniel with Mrs. Kleinschmidt and figured, Irish or not, anybody who had an in with the Queen of the Fences was worth protecting.

Being under Segal's protection did not spare Daniel from Segal's lacerating humor, as he had been reminded throughout the morning's labors in the potato fields. In truth, Daniel didn't mind the Irish jokes. On such a grim, gray morning in early March, as they worked a mulch of straw and manure into the cold, heavy soil and buried hundreds of seed potatoes, anything to lighten the mood was welcome.

"When Oi was one and twenty," Segal warbled, in imitation of an Irish tenor, "Oi rambled 'cross the bog. But Oi ate a bad potato, so Oi stopped to drop a log."

"You want to be a singer when you get out of here, Segal?"

Segal grinned. "Naw. Any old stiff can sing. I'm gonna be the master of ceremonies. The guy that keeps the show going, tells jokes between acts, keeps everybody buying drinks, having a good time. He's the guy who makes or breaks a show. He might even end up owning the joint."

"I'll let Missus Kleinschmidt know that. Maybe she'll set you up."

"Yeah, but tell her no Bowery dive. I want a place with crystal glasses and a French maitre'd."

"We can hire Thibault when he gets out."

Thibault was the leader of a small gang of French boys from upstate, third and fourth and fifth sons of woodcutters and millworkers from the Little Canadas in the northern reaches of New York and New England. They were universally distrusted because they spoke to one another only in French, and in the tense atmosphere of the reformatory, every gang feared that the French boys were plotting against them.

"Okay, but I select the wine list. I wouldn't trust that pea souper to know champagne from cherry cordial."

"Let me write that down. I'll tell Missus Kleinschmidt next time we get together for tea and knishes."

Daniel's closeness to Mrs. Kleinschmidt had become a running joke between the two boys after she failed to show up once for a visit in his first six months of residence at the Yonkers school. By this point, Segal and Daniel had become friends, so Segal still maintained the charade of a family connection in front of the other inmates.

Wiseman's deep bass rumble interrupted Segal's and Daniel's banter.

"Can it. We gotta finish this field, or it'll be the hole for the lot of us."

Although the reformatory was called the Yonkers Industrial School for Boys, and it did have a small woodshop, the education it offered consisted of working in the farm fields that surrounded the sprawling brick compound. Working in the fields was meant to assist in the rehabilitation of the boys, most of whom were orphans or castoffs who had been picked up by the leatherheads for minor crimes. Their labor, Father Kennedy reminded them every second Sunday, was intended to impress upon them the important Biblical lesson that man, in his fallen state as a result of Eve's temptation, must earn his food by the sweat of his brow.

Farm work was therefore an opportunity to meditate on Original Sin.

On the other Sundays, the Methodist Reverend Buchanan, being of a more modern cast of mind, extolled the virtues of farm work for inculcating in the boys a sense of accomplishment and allowing them to develop habits that would stand them in good stead when they left the industrial school and attempted to become productive citizens.

From the point of view of the governors of the school, and of the Assemblymen of the State of New York, putting the boys to work in the fields had the fortunate effect of relieving the State of New York of the requirement to buy food for this collection of urchins and street Arabs. More welcome still, to the superintendent of the school, the fields and gardens could usually be made to produce a surplus, which could easily be hauled to a market in Yonkers, where the owner asked no questions about the merchandise.

Daniel set to work planting, using his short spade to create small depressions in the loosened soil every foot, then covering the seed potatoes with an inch or so of dirt. The soil was a heavy clay and took a lot of working to prepare it for planting. The school's grounds weren't ideal farm soil, but Daniel knew that he and his friends would be held accountable for the harvest from any field they'd planted. It was going to be a long morning.

A mighty exhalation alerted him to the presence of Wiseman, who worked the farm's fields like a two-legged ox. Wiseman's blast of air coincided with him breaking up a heavy earthen lump the size of a horse's head. Working ahead of Daniel, Wiseman thrust his shovel into the mass of clay and mixed it with straw and pungent manure from the dairy cows. Wiseman worked tirelessly, preparing the ground faster than Daniel could keep up with the easier job of planting.

In the next row over, Roth was distributing manure over a swathe of worked-over clay. He held his shovel high on the shaft, as if wanting to avoid besmirching his hands. The boy treated his hands with the delicacy of a surgeon, and those who had seen him operate on the Bowery toughs the previous winter, when they'd conspired with a Jew-hating screw named Hutchinson to corner Segal far from Wiseman's aid, would know that the comparison was an apt one. The boys were meant to learn a trade at the school, but it was clear to all who'd seen the damage Roth inflicted on the Bowery toughs that he'd already mastered the trade of pugilism.

Segal let it be known that a farm laborer's life was not for him. He spent as much time juggling seed potatoes as he did planting them. Given the chance, both could earn their keep entertaining the masses from New York to Baltimore to St. Louis—one with his fists, the other with his words.

Daniel smoothed over another planting and straightened himself in order to move his bucket of potatoes forward. As he did, he saw a dark shadow move across the field. Hutchinson. The screw had a particular dislike of Daniel, whose association with Jews seemed to strike him as a betrayal of Judas proportions. It particularly galled him that Daniel went along with Segal's fiction about the Ruthenian cousin, Hyman.

"It's Hutchinson," Daniel hissed. "Get busy."

Wiseman kicked up a cloud of dust as he broke apart a cannon-ball-sized clod of earth. Segal stopped juggling and began scooping out depressions and filling them back in with seed potatoes. Even Roth got his hands dirty. But Hutchinson wasted not a glance on the state of the field. His scarred face puckered up with distaste as he addressed Daniel.

"McCormack. Get your skinny, bog-trottin' Irish arse down to the superintendent's office."

"The superintendent's?"

"You got mud in your ear, bog boy?"

Daniel shook his head. Hutchinson turned and began walking toward the compound before Daniel could ask what to do with his wheelbar-row. Not wanting to incur any more of Hutchinson's wrath than he had already, he left it and its contents where they were and began running after the screw.

He wondered what he had done that warranted a trip to the super-intendent, which was usually the prelude to time in the hole. He had no contraband. He hadn't been in a fight. He hadn't broken any school property. All he could imagine was that somebody, probably one of the Brickbat Boys, had placed incriminating evidence in his bed. He hoped whatever time in the hole he was given would turn out to be brief. He'd heard stories of spiders and cockroaches swarming the dank pit, providing meals for the rats, which, according to the boys who'd been there, were the size of cats.

Daniel suspected some of the veterans of the hole had exaggerated its terrors, but having seen boys after they were taken out of the hole, he knew that not all the stories about the place could be made up.

There was one other possible reason for a visit to the superintendent, but Daniel did not even consider that on the grounds that hoping for the remote possibility of good news could only lead to heartbreak.

It came as a shock, then, to walk down the dank corridor that led to the boys' dormitories, past the mess hall with its aromas of half-spoiled meat and sour milk, and then make the left turn toward the superintendent's office, where the opening of the grand oak doors revealed a lady in a high lace collar and a blue bonnet with more bustles and frills in her dress than Daniel had holes in his cotton trousers.

The lady turned to Daniel, smiled, and said, "Daniel, my little lamb chop. There you are."

Mrs. Kleinschmidt smiled again when Daniel only stood with his mouth agape, unable to reply. She gestured for him to enter farther into the room.

"Your uncle and I are so delighted to find you at last," she said.

Daniel turned to see a large, bearded man whose brown gabardine suit stretched awkwardly over wide shoulders. Big Jim narrowed his eyes and nodded.

The superintendent clearly didn't believe Mrs. Kleinschmidt and Jim were Daniel's aunt and uncle, but for the sake of appearances, they maintained that fiction throughout the discussion that followed. Quite by coincidence, Mrs. Kleinschmidt had settled on an account that bore some resemblance to Segal's Gypsy-abduction story.

"My poor sister. For years I told her 'come to America, we have plenty of room on our ranch.' Finally, she decides to join us, she takes that long trip across the ocean, and just when she arrives in America, those gangs of scoundrels on the docks steal her little boy. Of course, she's desperate, out of her mind with fear and grief. By the time I reach New York to help her, it's too late."

Mrs. Kleinschmidt uttered a strangled noise and paused. She dabbed her eyes with a lace handkerchief while pushing her final words out between sobs. "The poor girl just could not live without her dear Daniel. An oysterman pulled her body from the Bayonne marshes."

The superintendent looked awkwardly about the room as Mrs. Kleinschmidt launched into a series of panting wails. Big Jim remained impassive, and Daniel was still frozen with amazement. The superintendent directed his attention at Daniel. "Don't just stand there, boy. We've taught you better than that. Comfort your aunt."

Daniel stepped forward and put his arm on Mrs. Kleinschmidt's shoulder. "It's good to see you, Aunt...." Not knowing what name she was using, he added, "Auntie."

Big Jim let out a loud sigh and rose from the horsehide sofa. "Now that we've had our reunion, perhaps we can move on. My wife and I wish to return to our ranch in the West."

Mrs. Kleinschmidt stood, her breathing back to normal, her eyes clear. The transformation from grieving aunt to practical businesswoman was complete. The superintendent rose and stepped out from behind his massive cherry wood-topped desk.

"I believe everything should be in order," Big Jim said to the superintendent, who looked down, as if inspecting his and Big Jim's shoes. Big Jim laid a hand on Daniel's back and ushered him away from Mrs. Kleinschmidt and toward the door.

The three exited the school through the grand front doors, adorned with polished brass fixtures, which were used only by the superintendent himself and the state inspector of schools. Daniel looked back over his shoulder at the school grounds, hoping to catch a glimpse of his friends in the potato field, waving an arm by way of saying farewell to Segal, Roth, and Wiseman, thanking them for their protection and, even more importantly, for their friendship. His farewell wave was cut short when Big Jim ushered him into a carriage, whose driver tossed a cigar butt into the mud and picked up his whip.

As Daniel sat in the back beside Mrs. Kleinschmidt, he looked across at Big Jim and waited for an explanation. He had dozens of questions churning through his brain but rising to the surface of them all was one that had been prompted by Mrs. Kleinschmidt's dramatic story of her fictional sister, found dead by suicide in the brackish water of the Bayonne marshes.

"Do you know where my mother is, Missus K?"

"Daniel, honey, you better get used to it. I'm your mother now."

Daniel directed his words to Big Jim. "Is she out of the bughouse?"

Big Jim sighed. "You know what a million is, kid? That's how many people there are in New York. You know how hard it is to find one person in a million?"

"You found me."

Mrs. Kleinschmidt put an arm around Daniel's shoulders. "Daniel, honey. Sometimes it's better not to know. You heard what I said to that goniff back there, the story I told him. You want me to tell you that was a true story?"

"Was it?"

Big Jim slammed a fist against the door of the carriage. "That's enough. We sprung you. You ought to be grateful."

"You ought to be grateful I spotted that trap at the docks. You could have been pinched too."

"You want us to turn around, boy?"

Daniel knew better than to call Big Jim's bluff. He rode in silence as the carriage turned off the main road to New York and wound through a birch forest to a clearing around a small stone farmhouse, trees growing through its collapsed roof, the remains of a barn beyond it little more than a pile of rotting wood overgrown with grasses and thistles. A bench sat in the clearing. The bench was covered in empty bottles. Beyond the clearing, largely hidden by trees, stood a small cabin of split logs. Daniel looked in dismay at this seemingly abandoned farm. What about the ranch out west?

Big Jim opened the door and stepped out, leading Daniel into the clearing. Suddenly, Big Jim plunged a hand into one of his pockets and, in one action, flipped a small rock toward Daniel, who caught it.

"Remember the day we met?" he said. "The way you threw those rocks? Let's see if you can still do that." He handed Daniel two more rocks and then directed the boy's gaze to the bench adorned with bottles.

Daniel looked up at Big Jim and down at the bench and then at the rocks in his hand. In a flurry of motion, he launched three rocks at the bottles, shattering three in a row with the rapid rhythm of a drummer tapping out a tattoo on a snare.

Big Jim allowed his features to crack a smile. "We sprung you because we've got a job for you."

Daniel's training began immediately. Big Jim led him into the cabin. In the middle was a bare kitchen table. The carriage driver followed. Carrying a wooden crate, he set it on the floor beside the table. Big Jim began to empty its contents onto the table.

"Walker Colt," he said. "Navy Colt. Army Colt. Webley Bulldog. Lift them, handle them. Feel them against your skin. Imagine pulling one of these out of a holster as fast as you fling those stones at those bottles. Sight down the top of the barrel. See where the bullet's going to go by looking at this piece of metal. It marks the spot."

Big Jim watched as Daniel held the pistols. It took him two hands just to lift the long-barreled Walker. The Navy Colt was lighter but still awkward. The Army Colt was manageable. The snub-nosed Webley fit easily in his hand.

Daniel went through the procedures for loading the weapons, the differences between the various sizes of bullets the pistols required, and which of them would stop a charging buffalo. He learned about the gases produced inside a pistol when it fired and how those gases could cause dirty deposits that, in time, could cause a weapon to misfire, even make it explode in the hand of the shooter. Big Jim gave him the tools for cleaning the barrel and chambers. In the days to come, he said, Daniel would practice until a pistol felt like part of his hand, and keeping it clean would be as natural as washing his hands. Then he looked at Daniel's hands, saw that they were still dirty from digging potatoes, and sent the boy to the well with instructions to "scrub his filthy paws."

When Daniel returned, shaking water from his clean hands, Big Jim reached into the crate and produced a wide leather belt with a pocket for holding a pistol. Big Jim instructed him to fill the rotating cylinder of the Army Colt with six bullets and place it in the holster, then led him back out to the clearing, where Daniel saw that the broken bottles on the bench had been replaced.

It dawned on Daniel that Big Jim was counting on him to have the same fast hands and unerring eye with a pistol that he had with a stone. The pistol was heavy, but its polished wooden handle felt as natural against his skin as a smooth river pebble did. He raised the pistol and held his arm out to its full length, looking down his arm to the barrel and the target at the end of the polished steel.

He squeezed the trigger and felt the impact race up his bones to his shoulder as the recoil drove his forearm back and up. The bottles remained standing, intact. Big Jim had said soldiers called this pistol "thumb buster." No wonder.

Daniel said, "Let me try the little one."

Big Jim handed him the Bulldog. "It's fine as a pocket pistol, but with that short barrel it's no good for accurate shooting."

Daniel sighted down the stubby barrel and squeezed the trigger. The bottle exploded. He pulled back the hammer to cock the pistol, aimed at the other bottle, and shattered it as well. Daniel smiled. He could do this. This was not so different from throwing a rock. He looked at Big Jim and Mrs. Kleinschmidt, both staring intently at him. They needed him. Whatever they were up to now, the stakes were higher. They needed their own gunman.

Daniel put the Bulldog down.

"What are you doing, boy?" Big Jim said. "Hitting a couple of bottles doesn't make you a marksman."

Daniel swallowed and took a deep breath. "What job's so important you'd spring me from the reformatory?"

Mrs. Kleinschmidt stepped forward. "Daniel, I missed you."

"You need a gunman. You figure I'd be a good one. What do you need me for?"

Big Jim drew himself up to his full height, puffed out his chest, and clenched his fists. It was a display of physical menace that had brought countless fully grown men to heel. Daniel faced it without flinching. He would not be a simple tool, an ignorant watchdog.

"It won't be the reform school if this goes bad," Daniel continued. "It'll be prison. So, I need to know."

"You need to know what happens if you don't shut your yap, boy."

Mrs. Kleinschmidt stepped between Daniel and Big Jim and placed a hand on each.

"Daniel. You're a good boy. You never put your nose where it didn't belong. You have a good head on your shoulder. So, you know Mister McGuire and I, not everything we did before was kosher. And the worst thing I did was bring in a good boy like you and make you work with our gang."

Mrs. Kleinschmidt had never spoken to Daniel like this. Even her voice changed as she spoke directly to him. "I only did this because Mister Kleinschmidt left me with nothing. He went off to Montana with all his big talk of striking it rich and coming back to New York with a fancy private coach and money for a big house up in Harlem. But he never came back, and I was left all alone."

Mrs. Kleinschmidt appeared overwhelmed by the memory. She slumped against a tree, unsteady on her feet. Big Jim stepped forward and placed an arm around her. Daniel regarded Mrs. Kleinschmidt in a new light. She was like his mother, left all alone with no husband to help her.

With a deep breath, Mrs. Kleinschmidt stood straight, stepping away from Big Jim's supporting arm. "They say America is a land of opportunity, but they don't say the people who got here before you had the opportunity first. They got the land, built the railroads, started the banks. And the people who come later fight over what's left. After I come to America, I do some reading, and I find out that's what they call capitalism. Nice Jewish boy from the old country writes a book all about it. So, when we have our close call and you get put away, I think 'time to do something about capitalism.' I'm not going to work for myself anymore. I'm going to work for all the people like us who have nothing. Jim and I, we have a new life organizing workers to stand up to the capitalists."

She smiled bravely. Daniel thought it was a lot to take in. He recalled that Mrs. Kleinschmidt had been generous with credit for her customers at the dry goods store. And Big Jim had, like Robin Hood, taken from the rich. Perhaps this talk of fighting for the workers was sincere.

"Why do you need me?"

Big Jim and Mrs. Kleinschmidt exchanged glances. Mrs. Kleinschmidt shrugged her shoulders and gestured to Big Jim, who picked up Daniel's Bulldog revolver. It looked like a child's toy in his meaty hand.

"We need you because the capitalists won't just hand over what they owe to all the little people. We go out to organize the workers, the owners are going to fight back."

"You want me to kill them?"

Big Jim laughed. "If you shoot that thing the way you throw stones, a demonstration should do. No killing necessary. But I need to know now that you're with us. I'm leaving tomorrow to get this thing going. You'll meet up with me in a couple of weeks when I've made some contacts."

Daniel took the heavy Colt from his holster and examined the intricacy of metalwork—the smoothly rotating cylinder, the precise motion of the hammer clicking back into cocked position. In a single motion, he raised the heavier pistol and squeezed the trigger, and the remaining bottle vanished. Each pistol was a thing of beauty, in its way, and also a tool for killing.

He had seen death when a fever would sweep through the poor quarters of the city like the old man with his scythe. Once, he'd heard a mother's keening when her child ran into the street in front of a brewery wagon. Daniel had no illusions about the painful reality of death. He had also heard death threats, both on the streets and in the reformatory. He'd seen men and boys who claimed to have killed, boasted about it, told jokes about it. Daniel had no desire to be such a man. And yet, those men who would use others' fear of death to work their will over them—who could stand up to them but one who was prepared to deal in death? Would it be possible to use this tool only to defend Mrs. Kleinschmidt from such men?

No, not for Mrs. Kleinschmidt alone. Daniel would not take up this tool for killing just for her.

"I can do this for you. But you've got to do something for me. Find my mother."

Big Jim began to scowl. Mrs. Kleinschmidt cut off any response. "Such a good boy he is," she said. "It would be a mitzvah... a good deed, to help him find his only mother."

In the following days, Daniel remained at the abandoned farm, where he learned to shoot and care for all the firearms in the crate, even the heavy Walker, which required him to use both hands and had such a powerful recoil it knocked him flat on his back when he first tried it. He still preferred the smaller Bulldog but after a few days felt almost as comfortable with the Army Colt.

Daniel also learned to shoot with a lever-action Henry repeating rifle and a 12-gauge shotgun and learned how to take the weapons apart, clean them, grease them, and reassemble them. He practiced quick draws with the pistol. He looked at illustrated dime novels about the pistoleros of the West and attempted to mimic their styles. He tied the holster low on the hip, so that the end of the barrel hung down to his knee, and he tried tucking the pistol into a sash with the butt backward and drawing across his body in the style of Wild Bill Hickok, a western mankiller he'd seen pictured in a dime novel stolen from one of the screws at the reformatory. He tried using his left hand to fan the hammer for rapid fire. He tried filing the hammer for rapid and easy thumb-cocking. Within a few days, he was able to shatter an entire row of bottles in one quick draw.

In between lessons with the guns, Daniel walked to a neighboring farm, where Mrs. Kleinschmidt had paid the owner of a quarter horse to let Daniel learn to ride. Mrs. Kleinschmidt told Daniel he'd need to be an expert rider if he wanted to pass for a pistolero out west, so he'd better practice mounting and dismounts, saddling the horse and riding her bareback, directing her with and without the reins. Mrs. Kleinschmidt, who knew little more about horses than which end the oats go in and which end they come out, insisted on this part of Daniel's education.

One day, as Daniel entered the neighbor's yard for his riding practice, he noticed that the farmer's son had his nose buried in an illustrated story about Jesse James. The boy told him Jesse James was the Robin Hood of the West, a brave outlaw who stole only from the rich and gave to the poor farmers to help them keep the banks from repossessing their land.

Daniel asked to borrow the book when the boy was done with it and spent the next few nights piecing together the words as best he could by lantern light. With the help of the book's illustrations, he followed the outlaw's exploits as he held up trains and made a point of stealing only from those in expensive suits. He read about times when James and his gang, on the run after a robbery, would shelter in the home of a poor sodbuster, who would later discover a stack of gold coins hidden under the bedding. Daniel had met enough thieves and robbers in his young life to be skeptical, but at the same time he wondered if it might be possible to redistribute some small amount of America's wealth in this manner to those who needed it more.

When he wasn't learning to be a gunman, Daniel tried to grow physically into his new responsibilities. He ate plentiful portions of stew and beans, bread and cheese, and washed them down with pitchers of milk. He needed to put some meat on his bones if he was going to be any use to Mrs. Kleinschmidt. After two years in the reformatory, the food was a delight to the senses and to the stomach. Daniel left not a spot of any of the food and drink he was offered.

With each day at the farm, Daniel felt himself gaining strength.

While he was learning to be a gunman, Mrs. Kleinschmidt was investigating the whereabouts of the boy's mother. Each day, when she visited the farm, she would provide a progress report. Each day, the sound of the carriage would prompt Daniel to put down whatever weapon he was studying and run to ask Mrs. Kleinschmidt for news. And each day she would shake her head. After a week of this, Mrs. Kleinschmidt left for several days, during which Daniel's burning desire for knowledge of his mother kept him awake long after the candle was extinguished.

When she returned and Daniel ran to see her, she said, "Tomorrow. I'll take you to her."

There was no doubt in Daniel's mind, judging by Mrs. Kleinschmidt's facial expression, what that meant. Still, it would be better to know than not to know.

Early the next morning, the sound of a horse's steps woke Daniel before first light, the murky gloom giving the dark horse and the carriage and the bald-headed driver a spectral air. Daniel bundled into the back, where Mrs. Kleinschmidt sat with a thick woolen blanket over her lap to ward off the early morning chill. They traveled in silence along the road to New York, bumping over ruts carved by farm wagons hauling food to the ever-ravenous city. Here and there, they passed a factory, steam already belching into the lightening sky, rhythmic pounding pouring out from the gates. Teamsters' wagons grew thick on the road as they hauled raw material—coal and iron, flax and cotton and grain—one way and finished goods—farm implements, tools, furniture, clothing, blankets, beer—another. The city's appetite had devoured Daniel's mother just as it was devouring old farms all the way up the Hudson. Someday, it would spit these factories and their workers out, just as it spat out Daniel's ma.

Before they arrived at the city, they left the turnpike and trotted down to the river, which Daniel smelled long before the iron-hued water came into view. Swamp gas mixed with coal oil and creosote, and beneath it all lurked a smell of death. At Mrs. Kleinschmidt's signal, he disembarked and felt the mud suck at his feet as he walked toward a dock jutting into the water. From the weathered wooden dock, the far bank was hidden by a long finger of fog curling up the river from New York harbor. All color was drained from the scene before him. The mud, wood, water, and sky were all shades of gray. Out of the fog, the prow of a ferry emerged, the sound of its churning paddle wheel breaking free of the muffling effect of the clouds, a ragged man holding onto a railing.

As it approached the dock, its cargo came into focus—two wagons pulled by teams of draft horses, each piled with gleaming, brass-handled coffins.

After the coffin wagons were unloaded, Mrs. Kleinschmidt's carriage driver flicked his whip and drove onto the ferry. Daniel walked over a gangway to a row of benches just below the pilot's cabin. The pilot himself was only a shadowy presence, largely obscured by the film of filth on the cabin window, a red glow from his cigar his only sign of life. A weathered deckhand, face lined by a life of exposure to wind and sun, limping from some long-ago injury, unsecured the thick, oily rope, and the paddle wheel began to break the surface of the water, reversing the ferry into the main flow of the river. The ferry was powered by a steam engine connected to a single wheel on one side of the vessel opposite the pilot's cabin. A black man, shirtless in the chill of the morning, stoked the boiler, singing a new song about a steel driver, dead of a burst heart after beating a steam drill in a race.

"Pay the ferryman," Mrs. Kleinschmidt said and handed Daniel a silver dollar.

As the current caught the boat, it began to turn and drift downstream. For a moment, the wheel stopped, then after an explosion of steam, it began again, stronger, in the other direction, and the ferry aimed directly into the fog bank, and the stoker filled the firebox with more of the cheap, foul-smelling coal. Mrs. Kleinschmidt's horse whinnied and began to step back and forth nervously as the ferry seemed to be swallowed up in an off-white void.

Just when it seemed the horse might harm itself or damage the carriage, the ferry emerged on the other side of the fog, and the New Jersey shore came into view. The limping deckhand stood at the prow, holding the railing, the rope in his hand. As the pilot brought the ferry to the dock, the man jumped off, secured the boat, and lowered the ramp. The horse needed no prompting to leave the boat, and it took the driver some effort to stop it so that Daniel and Mrs. Kleinschmidt could climb inside.

The road on this side of the river was much like that on the other—farms and orchards transformed into factories and mills, and beside them rows of workers' houses, here and there a saloon already open and selling cheap beer to mill hands. The largest of the factories squatted behind a gate on which wrought-iron letters announced "New Jersey Coffin Manufacturing Company."

Soon, tenements began to crowd right up to the doors of the factories, and crowds grew thicker on the street. At a word from Mrs. Kleinschmidt, the driver turned the carriage away from the river road and along a murky creek, used as a rubbish tip by industries and homes. They stopped before a clearing, a pockmarked piece of uneven and overgrown ground bristling with wooden crosses, some new, white, and standing straight, others weathered, ashen, and leaning. Before some of the crosses were mounds of freshly piled earth. Others stood behind sunken depressions. Weeds grew taller than some of the crosses.

A stoop-shouldered, thin man with splotchy pink cheeks scarred by shaving with a dull blade emerged from a stone hovel, carrying a thick leather book. He led Daniel and Mrs. Kleinschmidt along the rows of crosses, each marked only by a number, none decorated with flowers. He stopped before a new, white cross, though on closer inspection this cross was already showing signs of wear. Painted on the cross was the number 289. Beyond it, the numbers continued to 303. Beyond that was space for occupants yet living.

"I hear you're looking for your mother." The stoop-shouldered man held out a book—rows of numbers and names with the signatures of witnesses. He pointed a talon-like finger at the entry for number 289. "Margaret Anne McCormack. That her?"

Daniel saw the name and the date of her death and burial. It had happened not long after he was captured at the docks and sent to the reformatory. Behind him he heard Mrs. Kleinschmidt's voice, the same throat-clearing sounds Daniel came to know from shabbos dinners. He felt he should do something, make the sign his mother had taught him so long ago, a finger to his face, then to the center of his rib cage, his heart, ending on the opposite side of his chest. Mrs. Kleinschmidt turned him and held him in her arms.

He tried to cry, tried to force moisture from his eyes. He called up memories of his ma before the bad times, when she'd dance and sing in their room. He had trouble painting the details of her face into the pictures in his head. As he struggled to recall his ma, he looked up at Mrs. Kleinschmidt, who gave him a calculating eye.

"I'm sorry for your loss, Daniel." She gave the thin man a handful of coins and waited while he walked away. "That's our end of the bargain, then. We've found your ma."

Daniel thought of his life with Ma, even in the good times, spent between the narrow grimy walls of tenements in the Five Points. He thought of the cramped confines of the reformatory. Every picture in his mind was of enclosed spaces, walls and gates, smoke and steam, bricks and iron. The faces in his mind were blurred—fruit vendors, hot corn girls, beggars and pickpockets, leatherheads and thieves, screws and Brickbat Boys. Only Big Jim and Mrs. Kleinschmidt had clear images in his thoughts. And Segal, Roth, and Wiseman.

In this potter's field in New Jersey, he would bury his old life.

"I'm ready. I want to go west now."

Mrs. Kleinschmidt pulled back from the hug, rearranging her features into those of the one-time Queen of the Fences and the newly minted benefactor of the victims of capitalism.

"From your lips to God's ears."

"What's wrong?"

"Recruitment has been… slow. Turns out 'go west, young man' isn't such a great sales pitch after all."

"Who else do you have?"

She pointed at the cadaverous driver. "Moishe says he's too old to take the trip, and he's got a point. But the others have read too many dime novels. They've decided they'd rather roll sailors on the docks than get scalped by Indians. So, now I need to find some others who want to come in as partners, maybe the Whyos or the Brickbat Boys."

"Not the Brickbat Boys."

"You're fast, but you're going to need some other men on your side."

Daniel thought of the men Big Jim had worked with in the past. Big Jim hadn't trusted any of them. They'd been as likely to steal from Mrs. Kleinschmidt as to steal for her. They were loyal to nothing and nobody. They'd been cruel and cowardly, and a few of them had looked at Daniel and licked their lips like fat men in an oyster house.

All Daniel knew about the West was that it was a place where men fought for everything. To survive there, he would need allies he could trust, allies he knew and liked, who knew and liked him. Maybe even allies who owed him gratitude.

"I got three guys who'll fight with me," he said. "They're young, but two of them are as tough as any grown man. The other one's skinny but real smart."

"And where are these Samsons and Davids hiding?" Mrs. Kleinschmidt asked.

"In the reformatory."

9

"**S**TRIP HER DOWN and dress her up with a nice shiny coat o' grease."

Those were Mr. McTaggart's instructions when he set Lincoln loose in the yard at the New Haven Steam Drill Company's Virginia depot. Here the company cleaned and overhauled machines that resembled little more than inert masses of grime and coal dust. As Mr. McTaggart's apprentice, Lincoln coaxed seized engines into life with a combination of lubrication and cleaning, a task sometimes accomplished with a mallet and chisel when heat and pressure had given the dirt the density and imperviousness of tarmacadam. Occasionally, he came upon moving parts that had fused together in the intense heat. These he identified by shape and placement and, if visible, part number, so that new parts could be ordered from the foundry in New Haven, a place of mystical wonder in his imagination.

When it was time to rebuild an engine with clean new parts, Mr. McTaggart would invite him to hold the tools and feel the amount of pressure needed to tighten a nut, the amount of tension needed for a belt to run smoothly without slipping but not wear out under constant stress. He would ask Lincoln to turn his mind to calculations of forces with names like torque and shear—measures of the strength of a machine and the point at which the machine might break down just as his father's heart had broken down after winning his race against the broken steam drill.

Lincoln looked out at the work yard, where three steam drills awaited major overhauls.

"There's a mess of cleaning to do today, Mister McTaggart."

"Aye, Lincoln. More o' these blessed contraptions comin' back bunged up every day."

Mr. McTaggart had been complaining with increasing frequency about the tendency of the company's steam drills to overheat and break down under pressure. In the immediate aftermath of losing the race with Lincoln's father, it had seemed that the company's equipment sales were likely to suffer. But as word had spread about the race—spread up and down the Appalachian mountain chain and well beyond by a network of saloon story-spinners and cookhouse gossip—orders had begun to pile up.

"Blessed dirt scratchers haven't the sense to keep the movin' parts oiled. It's no wonder they can't keep their blessed machines runnin'. If I didna have my young apprentice, Lincoln, I would never keep up wi' the work."

Lincoln's cheeks warmed with pride at the compliment. He had learned a lot these last few months, but it hadn't felt like learning. Not like memorizing names of presidents and kings in Miss Cadbury's class, nor like memorizing Bible passages at church. It was more like the way he figured out angles and shapes by looking at a spiderweb or the roof beams in the church. Lincoln knew it was wrong to feel proud about working on engines. He knew he should hate machines and mechanics. He knew that people sometimes pointed to him and whispered that he was the boy whose father had been killed racing a steam drill.

But Lincoln could not feel anger at the machine. He knew that it was nothing but geometry drawn in steel. The machine that raced against his papa could no more be blamed for John Henry's death than could John Henry's hammer. Nor could Mr. McTaggart. All he had done was stoke the boiler and watch the steam gauge. If anybody could be blamed, it was the owner of the New Haven Steam Drill Company for tempting Lincoln's father with a hundred dollar wager. Or perhaps it was the construction bosses on the Richmond and Nashville Railway for paying him so little that he felt compelled to accept the wager.

Thinking of money made Lincoln think of his mama and her locked money chest. She was still saving for the family's future but no longer saving up for a homesteading fee and farm equipment. Lately, she had been talking about buying a boardinghouse, a good quality home for traveling men on business and unmarried schoolmasters. Tomorrow was a payday, and Lincoln would bring his wages home to Mama, and he would ask her how close she was. Mama wouldn't want to talk business with a loose-limbed adolescent boy. Instead, as always, she would want to test him on the schooling that Mr. McTaggart had been giving him in between engine overhauls, one of her conditions for permitting Lincoln to work as an apprentice.

That agreement had not come easily. After the race ended in disaster for the steam drill, Papa had shuffled away like a sleepwalker, then dropped into the shade of a pine tree. Other workers had rushed to cheer, calling out his name and seeking to raise him on their shoulders and parade him through the camp. He'd waved them off, and Mama had shouted at them, calling them fools for disturbing a tired man's rest. Papa ate nothing that night and, after being brought back to the family's tent in a buckboard, he'd lain, face gleaming with sweat, for the rest of the day.

Mama had sat with him all night listening to his shallow and rapid breathing and attempting to spoon a bit of soup into his mouth. In the morning, she'd sent Lincoln for the doctor, and by the time Lincoln returned, Papa's condition had worsened. The doctor had placed a kind of listening bell on John Henry's chest and had looked grave as Mama had sent the boys outside to play. The broken steam drill had been hauled down to the camp by this time, and as he supervised George and Thomas, Lincoln had watched Mr. McTaggart's efforts to salvage the undamaged portions of the machine. Lincoln had been drawn to the machine and was on the verge of asking Mr. McTaggart a question when he heard his mother's lamentations.

Now, a cry from Mr. McTaggart brought Lincoln back to the present day and the repair yard. His mentor stood beside one of the steam drills, wrapping a handkerchief around his knuckles and muttering a string of angry but unidentifiable words as blood dripped onto the oil-covered ground.

"It's gettin' worse, Lincoln," he said, shaking his head and eyeing the damaged machine with disgust. "When I first started workin' on these machines, they just needed a wee bit of cleanin' and adjustin'. But now the parts are like as not to snap off in your hands when you try to loosen them. It's that Vandenberg's doing. Penny wise, pound foolish, he is, makin' the factory use steel that's closer to tin. Aye, he'll save a few dollars on each machine, but what good is that if the mines and railroads stop buying the blessed things?"

Mr. McTaggart showed Lincoln a bolt that had sheared off and sent him to the storeroom to find one the same size. He also instructed the boy to return with a bottle of solvent to remove the accumulated grime that was binding a flywheel. Lincoln looked at the broken bolt and envisioned the pressure exerted on it by the compressed air in the engine's mighty combustion chamber. He saw as if it were happening in front of him. He felt the heat in the chamber as he made the calculations Mr. McTaggart had taught him to determine how heat would increase the pressure and how the metal would expand when heated.

"Reckon them inventors never thought of how things grow when they get hot?"

"No, Lincoln, I don't think they thought of that."

"How 'bout if there's a fan here, blowing cool air on that hot metal? Might could be you could run a belt from this flywheel here, and it'd turn that fan for you."

Mr. McTaggart studied the machine and then eyed Lincoln from head to toe as if trying to confirm that he was in fact only a boy and not a grown man with a decade's worth of experience in a machine shop.

"Lincoln my lad, I will say it once again. You have a gift."

That's what he'd said to Lincoln's mama after the funeral. The minister had preached from the Bible about man needing to earn his bread by the sweat of his brow. John Henry, he'd said, had earned his every bite of bread. He'd worked and suffered to feed and clothe his family. He'd borne his burden across this Vale of Tears, but now his Savior had called him to lay that burden down. And some day, the minister continued, they would all lay their burdens down on the other side of the River Jordan. The minister had led the congregation—the colored workers and their families—in a chorus of "Shall We Gather by the River?" Then six of Papa's fellow workers had carried the pine box from the cook tent that served as a church to the sad little patch of ground where Lincoln's baby sister lay. At the sight of the freshly dug hole beside Annabelle's, Mama had finally burst into tears, requiring the efforts of the minister and another of the worker's wives to keep her on her feet. Lincoln remembered standing by the graveside and wanting to hold Mama's hand but seeing both her hands occupied by Thomas and George. He remembered walking back to their tent. He remembered Mama handing money to the coffin maker and the minister and the doctor. And he remembered looking through the opening in the tent canvas to see Mr. McTaggart, the lone white face at the funeral.

"The boy has a gift," Mr. McTaggart had said to Mama after making the offer of an apprenticeship.

"This blood money? Your steam drill killed my husband, and now you make it better?"

"No, ma'am. This will nae make it better, I ken that. But you've three young ones still to feed. I had to work meself at his age for much the same reason. Your boy's nae cut out for workin' underground or driving steel. He's safer if you give him leave to work as my apprentice."

Mama had hated the prospect of Lincoln working on the machine that had killed her husband, but she hated that less than the thought of John Henry's son following him into the same early grave. A doctor's bill and funeral costs that ate up the one hundred dollars John Henry had won in his race had also helped her come around. She'd given her blessing and allowed Lincoln to leave, then followed with George and Thomas when the opportunity arose to go to work cooking at a railroad camp closer to the New Haven Steam Drill Company's Virginia yard.

It took a long day's efforts to free the jammed parts on one of the steam drills in the yard. When Lincoln returned to his hammock in the storage room at the back of the machine shop, his entire body ached.

Tired as he was, his mind kept running faster than any steam engine. His brain sketched out new designs for steam engines, techniques for cooling, dissipating pressure, reducing bulk, balancing forces. What would happen, he wondered, if an engine had two or four or six cylinders? Would it be possible for them all to be timed to fire one after another so that the power could be generated smoothly? What if there were valves inside the engine to inject lubricating oil to keep it from heating? What if cooling liquid could be circulated throughout the engine, pumped by the power of the engine itself?

Lincoln wished he could travel with Mr. McTaggart to the foundry in New Haven to see how the parts were made. He wished even more that he could travel to those wondrous cities described by Mr. McTaggart, where every second man was a skilled mechanic—places like Glasgow, Belfast, and Liverpool. How much he could learn from these men, about metal and fuel, about physical forces and the almost magical things that happened deep inside everything in the world to make materials come together or pull apart.

Mr. McTaggart had taught him the words for the subjects that fascinated him so completely—physics, chemistry, engineering. He thought of the big special schools where people spent all day figuring out things like that. He knew when he died he'd need no pearly gates or angel's wings. Working out physics and chemistry and engineering all day would be his heaven.

The next day, Mr. McTaggart went into town for an errand and set Lincoln to work on one of the other steam drills. It was even more of a mess than the one they'd been working on the previous day. Not only was it bound up with rock dust and sand, but it was visibly malformed in places where the cheap and shoddy steel had bent or stretched under the heat and pressure. At best, it could be used for spare parts. More likely, it was simply scrap metal. Just as Lincoln felt the sudden loosening of a bolt he'd been working on all morning, he heard an unfamiliar voice at the entrance to the shop.

"Is there a McTaggart here?"

Lincoln looked up and saw a man in a shiny silk vest, a long coat, and a black bowler hat. The man held papers in his hand and was accompanied by an older man wearing a top hat and a morning coat with long, striped trousers. Standing behind them was a large man with a shiny star on his shirt front. The first man called out again.

"McTaggart!"

Lincoln scanned the shop to ensure that there was nobody else to answer this visitor. He set down his wrench and walked to the entrance.

"Mister McTaggart ain't… isn't here."

"I can see that, boy."

The older man, the one in the top hat, shook his head in apparent disgust.

"I see now the diligence with which this firm managed our capital. I wish we'd taken action months ago."

The first man leveled his gaze at Lincoln.

"Listen here, boy, we need to know where McTaggart went and when he's coming back." He turned to the man with the star on his shirt front. "We should probably start with the saloons."

"No, sir," Lincoln said, obliged to defend his mentor and friend. "Mister McTaggart just had to go into town. I expect he be back presently."

"And he left you here to do his work for him?" the older man said. "There's the reason for all the breakdowns. The only man working here is a little colored boy."

Lincoln knew there were plenty of other reasons for equipment breakdowns at the New Haven Steam Drill Company, but something told him these men would not appreciate being corrected by a grease-spattered colored boy. He felt he should return to his work but feared that would be rude. Manners surely were a bothersome thing.

The younger man in the silk vest took charge at this point and invited the older man to rest his feet on Mr. McTaggart's chair, then delivered a series of orders to the man with the star on his shirt. Lincoln didn't catch all the words, as they were spoken too fast in a Yankee accent. But at the end of his instructions, the man with the star took a mallet and a paper from a bag and attached a notice to the front door of the shop. The fast-talking Yankee walked around the shop with a paper in one hand and a pencil in another, reading the names of tools and equipment off of a list and searching for the items on the floor and shelves. As the men had stopped paying attention to Lincoln, he returned to his task and was working on removing a set of seized gears when the fast-talker stopped him.

"See here, boy, what do you think you're doing?"

"Mister McTaggart set me to work on this engine, sir. I'm supposed to have it all apart by the time he comes back."

"Put that down now. This is no job for an ignorant child."

Lincoln set down the gear he held in his hands.

The man examined the partially disassembled steam drill Lincoln had been working on. He looked into the firebox. He looked into the steam chamber. He looked into the cylinder. Then he looked at his sheet of paper.

"Is this a steam drill?"

"Yes, sir."

"Model A?"

"No, sir. Model A has the cylinder on top of the steam chamber. This is a Model B. It has the cylinder on the end of the steam chamber."

The man gave Lincoln a disbelieving look, then compared the location of the cylinders on two of the steam drills.

"How about this 'variable speed angle grinder?' Know where I'd find that?"

Lincoln directed the man to the back of the shop where the massive grinder sat. It was a terrifying but also satisfying piece of machinery that showered the shop with sparks when a machine part had to be trimmed down to fit into place. The man inspected the machine and made another check mark on his paper, then pointed to the next item on this list and recruited Lincoln to help him find it. Lincoln glanced at the man's list and led him around the shop, pointing out all the items that the man needed to have identified.

As they approached the bottom of the list, the older man, exasperated by his wait, called to both of his colleagues that he had wasted enough time for one day.

"If you've made your inventory, we can simply padlock the place. I've no need to speak to this mysterious Mister McTaggart."

"Very well, Mister Henderson. I had hoped we could speak to McTaggart to get a better idea of the value of this operation."

"I can tell you the value of this operation, Mills. Eighty percent less than when my bank invested in it. Now, come along."

The two men left the building after the younger man, Mills, directed Lincoln out the door. Outside the building, the man with the star—Lincoln now realized he was a sheriff—stoked the red coal of a cigar beside one of the signs he had tacked up. It read *REPOSSESSED* in large letters at the top, followed by a long block of type. The younger man handed Lincoln a dime for helping him find the items on his checklist and then directed him to wait for Mr. McTaggart and inform him that Mr. Henderson at the Shenandoah Valley Bank would like to speak to him.

Then he and Mr. Henderson climbed into a black coach, and the sheriff mounted to the driver's seat and whipped the horses into action.

Lincoln was still seated on a log out front of the shop when Mr. McTaggart arrived, beaming, with a rolled-up paper in his hand. Lincoln ran down the road to catch him before he could see the signs on the walls.

"Mister McTaggart, three men came in and locked up the door and put up signs. What does 'repossessed' mean?"

Mr. McTaggart laughed, then laughed again when he read the sign.

"Lincoln, my lad, this day has been comin' since Vandenberg bought the company. All flash, that carnival barker. His shoddy approach to business was bound to fail sooner or later."

"So, are we out of a job?"

"We are, Lincoln, we most certainly are. But only temporarily."

"Are we gonna get another job?"

"Lincoln, I've been down at the telegraph office. The owner of what will likely become the richest gold mine in America has sent us a message. He's a forward-thinking man who knows the value of modern machinery and mechanics."

"Are we gonna fix his machines?"

"More than fix, lad. We're goin' to invent new ones."

He paused to let the words sink in, and Lincoln thought for a moment about being able not just to repair broken-down machines but to design new ones, better ones, machines with more power and more graceful, fluid movements. Machines made with beautiful angles that made better use of the power of numbers to do wonderful things. He thought of Mr. McTaggart's personal project, the sketches the mechanic had made of a self-propelled steam-powered wagon that would allow people and goods everywhere to move with the speed of a train, without the need for rails. It would take plenty of money to put some flesh on those sketches, but the owner of the richest gold mine in America would have that.

"This mine. It far away?"

"Aye. But he'll send us train fare."

"Can my mama come?"

"Of course. There'll be a braw new company house for your mama."

A new house. Not a tent in a railroad camp. Mama and George and Thomas would be able to live with him while he went to work and learned how to be a mechanic and an inventor. It was Lincoln's vision of heaven.

"Where are we going?"

"The Dakota Territory. Deadwood."

10

---◦◆◦---

THE TRACKS LED north through the sand hill country toward a pair of jagged spires, an isolated outgrowth of the convoluted red and white rock formations known in the territory as badlands. Rock or grass, it was all bad land, as far as Josiah Stuart could see, a land of cactus and meager forage presided over by wolves and heathens. But soon this wilderness would be brought within the circle of Christendom. The heathens were on the run, many of them hiding out across the line in Canada. And the wolves would soon follow, their numbers depleted both by the loss of the buffalo and by Josiah's traps and poison.

Soon, sheep would safely graze even here in this heathen desert.

The thought of sheep transported Josiah to the church in Lynchburg. It was the big Episcopal church with padded railings for kneeling and dark, intricately carved, high-backed wooden pews. It even had stained-glass windows displaying the story of the birth, crucifixion, and resurrection of the Lord. It was nothing like the simple Presbyterian church in the hills where Josiah's grandfather preached and where a young Josiah had tried so hard not to fidget during the long sermons on Original Sin and Justification by Faith Alone.

His mother had taken him to Lynchburg to hear a choir sing, and he had stayed with her in her house in the city, something Josiah's grandfather would not normally have allowed. It must have been near Christmas. Perhaps it was her final Christmas. He remembered the sound of the organ, those growing, reverberating notes that seemed to emanate from the walls and the roof joists, and the choir singing with many voices that, together, sounded as beautiful and terrible as the voice of an angel. Each verse began the same way. "Sheep may safely graze and pasture."

He'd whispered to his mother, "Why are they saying that?"

She had shushed him, and when he asked again, she said, "Because when Jesus returns, He'll get rid of all the wolves, I suppose."

For now, though, that was Josiah's job. He dismounted and crouched beside a patch of moist earth that retained several sets of prints. They were finely detailed. The largest was nearly as wide as his hand. He followed the line on foot, watching the smaller tracks meander back and forth around the large set. A small twist of rabbit fur embedded in wolf scat caught his eye. A sniff of the fresh scat told him the fanged demons had recently passed this way. A glance at the size of it told him they hadn't eaten much.

There were four of them. A bitch and her three cubs. Those fools in the territorial government only paid half price for a cub's pelt. As if a wolf cub doesn't grow into a full-size stock-eating demon. But the money was mostly incidental for Josiah, aside from keeping him in provisions and poison.

The wolves were probably looking for small herds of stray buffalo. One adult female wasn't going to bring down a cow, but where there was a herd, there might be a young calf that could be separated from its mother. They would follow a seasonal creek, temporarily flowing with the spring melt, to whatever prairie might serve as the meeting place for the herds. That way, they might flush an elk calf from the creekside brush on the way. His best chance would be to take a shortcut to a point farther down the nearest creek and place his traps there. To figure out how to get ahead of the wolves, he decided to head straight for a pair of jagged points, the highest on the horizon. From there he might be able to see the dust of distant herds or at least trace the path of whatever creeks crossed this wilderness.

His horses balked when he spurred them on, but they knew better than to protest too vigorously. His gelding picked up the pace to a trot. The old mare packhorse followed, and the feet became yards and miles. But distances were deceiving in this treeless country, even after years of hunting buffalo and wolves on the equally treeless Kansas plains, and the spires turned out to be higher and farther off than Josiah expected.

It took a full hour to reach the high ground. In the late afternoon light, he scanned the horizon with his spyglass. The land dropped to the north, and lines of willows and a few tall cottonwoods provided evidence of water. The creek would meander northeast, winding its way toward the Moreau River.

If he made a straight path in the direction of the Moreau, he could get ahead of his quarry and place his traps. If he pushed hard, he might make it to the creek before dark.

But first, Josiah would give thanks. He opened a saddlebag and removed a parcel wrapped in oilskin. He unwrapped the oilskin, opened the Bible it protected, and reflected on an engraving from Harper's Weekly of General Thomas Stonewall Jackson, which he'd placed inside for safekeeping. During the war, the general had read the Bible to the men of the Second Corps and dwelt on the similarities between the invading Yankee army and the idolatrous Philistines of old. Josiah, who had carried his own Bible in his haversack through three years of march, bivouac, and combat, had marked every passage the general had read in his deep, booming voice that was so reminiscent of Josiah's grandfather.

Josiah recited Ezekiel 25:16 to the whistling wind, "Behold, I will stretch out mine hand upon the Philistines...."

The wind raised its voice. Something in these lifeless hills was listening, wailing, and gnashing its teeth. Josiah remembered what a half-breed scout had told him—that in these parts was a point of high land called Crow Buttes, where many years ago the Sioux had besieged a war party of Crows. The Sioux had surrounded their enemies and, instead of attacking, had waited for thirst on this isolated hilltop to finish them off. Then they had scalped the Crows and held a celebration, dancing to their demon god into the night. The next morning, though, the victorious Sioux began dropping like trees in a Carolina hurricane because someone among those dead Crows had carried smallpox.

The protest of the wind dropped to a sigh of defeat. The Lord had begun clearing out the Philistines even before the arrival of Christendom. The heathens were soon going to be gone.

But the wolves remained. Josiah spurred his horse toward the distant creek. He had a job to do.

It was fully dark by the time he placed his traps and poison baits along the creek. Josiah led his horses away from the water for the night, not wanting the smell of his camp to alert the predators. He let the animals pick their way through a prairie dog town by the light of a half-moon. Once they were clear of the maze of holes and mounds, he stopped and hobbled them. He would make no fire tonight. Neither light nor the smell of cooking would betray his presence. He rolled out his blankets and ate some hardtack and jerky and washed his meal down with foul creek water. It was a Spartan camp, but in truth he preferred to sleep without a fire. Where other men saw comfort in a campfire, he saw a reminder of that northern Virginia battlefield known as the Wilderness. But fire or no fire, that orgy of bloodshed would haunt his dreams.

No sooner had he closed his eyes than he was transported back to the spring days in 1864 when the Yankees had charged the Confederate lines in a thick forest of willow and alder, wild rose and devil's walking stick. Josiah and his comrades had repelled the charge, then left their cover to chase the retreating bluecoats all the way back to the Potomac if they could. He'd joined with the others, raising his voice in a triumphant Rebel yell as they approached the Yankee line, and then the world erupted in fire and thunder as the enemy's cannons poured out canister shot.

Images of bloodied bodies flashed through his sleeping mind, and the night's true horrors began as he relived the fires that had been lit by the cannon blasts. Men, northern and southern, living and dead, burned up in the fierce blaze. Josiah, running blindly, dodged flames and gunfire and escaped the battlefield and the war and the whole fallen world that had brought such punishment upon itself. And he kept running until he fetched up on the treeless plains of the West.

Those plains glowed with the first light of morning as Josiah awoke and the wolves saluted the fading darkness with their infernal chorus.

11

A NOTHER STOP FOR Stanislas's Circus of Wonders, another Dakota farm town, another standing ovation for Sparky's knot-untying.

Uncle Stanislas had moved Lily to the closing spot more than a year earlier, and, while she'd added plenty of tricks to her act since then, she still used the rescue as her finale.

With the audience already making their way to the exit flap, Uncle Stanislas thanked them for their patronage and wished them a safe trip home, then turned on his heel and made for the back exit. By the time Lily had thanked her dogs, led them to the wagon she shared with Madame Mystere, and fed them, the other performers were gathered around the fire by Uncle Stanislas's wagon, concern etched on their faces.

Uncle Stanislas stood in the firelight with the cashbox in his hands and counted out the evening's take. He hadn't even paused to change out of his costume or remove his greasepaint.

Lily listened in the shadows as the conversation moved around the circle.

"Better money back east," suggested Arnold, one of the tumbling midgets.

"But more competition," added Tommaso Largo.

"Money's no good anywhere." In contrast to the fool Mr. Szabo played in his act, once he removed his costume and greasepaint he could always be found reading a newspaper and holding forth on politics and world affairs. "It's been getting worse ever since the bank panic in '73. Roads are lined with men looking for work, and those who have work are holding tight to their money. This is why I say we need a policy of free silver that will allow the common man to crawl out from under the heel of the bankers."

The other performers groaned. They knew that Anton Szabo could carry on about free silver and bankers for an hour if given the chance.

Madame Mystere said, "This may be true, but our little circus does not have the power to tell the president of the United States of America what to do. What can we do until the president sees the wisdom of free silver? That is the question."

"We must find virgin ground," Uncle Stanislas said. "Opera houses, Chautauqua, circuses with elephants and lions! Is too much competition for small circus like us."

"We have Lily," replied Hymie, the other tumbling midget. "Not even Barnum has an act like her."

"Lillian the Lycanthrope is one act, not whole circus," said Uncle Stanislas. "Problem is, where is place where people think all of us look special like Lillian?"

Lily was shocked. All the performers were special! She'd had three years in the circus but still had not lost the wonder she felt every time she watched Tommaso defy gravity, or Uncle Stanislas make birds magically appear from underneath a silk scarf.

"But you're a wonderful magician, and Tommaso is so brave on the high wire," she said. "And Mister Szabo and Madame Mystere—"

"Grazie, bella," Tommaso said. "But I am growing too old for the high wire. My balance will soon tell me arrivederci."

"Tommaso is right, Lily," Madame Mystere said. "Every circus has a fortune teller and a clown. We're all good enough for these backwater towns, but you're the only act we have that could make the big time."

Uncle Stanislas continued, "And Anton also is right. America is having too many men with no work. No work means no money for circus. So, we must go where is work. I believe we must go west to the mining towns. Many men working there, not so many circuses."

Mr. Szabo nodded. "Where do you mean?"

Uncle Stanislas told a story of a city built on a mountain of gold—an empty canyon in the wilderness in 1875, a tent camp with 5,000 men in 1876, and a growing city of brick buildings by the spring of 1877. Men starved for entertainment would run to spend their takings from the placer works or their wages from building the new underground mine. The new class of professional men—lawyers, merchants, bankers—would bring their families, eager to show their wives that they had not dragged them beyond the boundaries of civilization. The circus could play for weeks, filling the tent every night. And after that, word would spread throughout all the western mining towns, south to Telluride and Silverton, north to Bannack and Helena City, and west all the way to Virginia City and California.

All they had to do was get to Deadwood, in the heart of the Black Hills.

That name was in the air for days to come as the circus made its way westward, first taking the Great Northern Railroad to the end of steel in Bismarck, then bumping over wagon roads leading through the increasingly arid and empty country beyond the Missouri River. As they put the growing towns and rich bonanza farms of the tall-grass plains farther behind them, the picture of prosperity Uncle Stanislas had painted began to fade.

The expected wagon road from Bismarck to the Black Hills, established a few years earlier by Colonel Custer's Seventh Cavalry, was already being reclaimed by the wilderness. Occasional ruts made by wagon wheels in patches of sandy soil were the only evidence they were still on the road. The absence of civilization brought images of bandits and Sioux raiding parties ever more frequently to mind. Deadwood was known to be a lawless place, where not even the legendary gunslinger Wild Bill Hickok was safe from an assassin's bullet, and it was known to be surrounded by tribes of warlike Indians who had been fighting the United States Cavalry for many years.

On the third night out from Bismarck, little Arnold the tumbler put the question to Uncle Stanislas. "What chance does a wagon train of misfits and freaks have against Jesse James and Crazy Horse?"

"Please. Is no reason for fear," Uncle Stanislas implored the group. "Sioux are back on reservation or in Canada. Jesse James is licking wounds after Northfield robbery. We are safe as a baby in its mama's arms."

"It doesn't look safe from where I sit," said Madame Mystere, who had attempted to convince Uncle Stanislas that audiences in Quebec were as starved for entertainment as those on the western frontier.

"Fear is good for us. Every other circus is too afraid of the dangers of the Wild West. We have all the money of the miners to ourselves. Because we are brave. We are circus folk. Our job is to have no fear. Tommaso, are you afraid of the high wire? Arnold, Hymie, when you do your tumbling, do you fear that you will land on your heads? Michelle, my mysterious one, do you fear that you will be unable to see into the minds of your audience? No! We live by bravery. Bravery will reward us!"

He reminded the group of the great wealth in the mining towns and assured them that, though the trail was not heavily traveled, it was still secured by cavalry patrols. When his words were answered by the distant cry of a prairie wolf, he raised his walking stick in the air as if wielding a saber and uttered a favorite phrase made famous by the Emperor Napoleon. "Toujours l'audace! Always bravery!"

Madame Mystere raised herself from the padded chest that served as her camp stool and began her slow walk to her sleeping wagon. "Did Napoleon say that before or after Waterloo?"

Uncle Stanislas produced a flask of brandy from an inside pocket and quoted Shakespeare as a toast. "'The coward dies a thousand deaths. The valiant only taste of death but once.'"

A thousand deaths, unfortunately, sounded to some in the circus too much like the treatment the Sioux might mete out to their prisoners.

Despite Uncle Stanislas's efforts, the atmosphere of fear failed to lift. By day, all members of the small wagon train scanned the horizon for indications of dust kicked up by war parties. By night, they pulled the wagons in an increasingly tight circle, and the men took turns guarding the small camp with Uncle Stanislas's old cap-and-ball Springfield rifle.

On one such night, one week out from the Missouri River, Lily awoke to an urgent warning, felt rather than heard, from her dog Sparky. "Wolf! Wolf!"

The little Chihuahua burrowed its nose under Lily, digging frantically at her blankets, as if trying to create a tunnel in which to hide. Sparky's tail, such as it was, pointed directly downward between his hind legs. His flesh bounced like water in a soup pot as nervous twitches overwhelmed him. Lily poked her head out of the wagon to see where Lancelot and Galahad should be keeping night watch. Neither was there. In the moonlight, she saw Mr. Szabo seated on a saddle blanket, his head slumped forward, the Springfield rifle leaning against a wagon behind him.

The night breeze carried Galahad's and Lancelot's growling voices her way. "Go away," she heard, or rather felt. "This is ours."

A third, unfamiliar voice blended with theirs. And in that other voice she detected a question. "Who are you?" And a demand. "Go away."

Without stopping to put on shoes, Lily climbed down from the wagon and ran barefoot through the jagged dry grasses. She felt something sharp enter the bottom of a foot but kept running. She burst into a flattened clearing in the grass and found herself standing between Galahad and Lancelot and a large gray wolf, the long hair on its shoulders standing up, its ears pointing back, its upper lip raised in a snarl.

"Please," Lily said. "We mean no harm."

An uncertain note entered into the wolf's growl. It flicked its ears toward Lily and sniffed, trying better to understand.

"We are just passing through. We aren't going to hurt you." Lily stepped back and gestured to the dogs. "This is Galahad, and this is Lancelot. Don't worry, they're friendly." She turned and looked back to her dogs, hands on hips like a schoolmistress. "You two be nice."

The wolf was now moving back and forth, sniffing the night air and listening for night sounds and trying to get a better sense of the situation, still on its guard but no longer prepared for an immediate attack.

Lily turned toward the wolf and smiled. "You have a den near here, don't you? Is your mate out hunting for your cubs? I bet he's going to bring them something good."

Lily felt the wolf's aggression fading. Even somebody unable to communicate with wolves would have seen in the animal's posture and muscles that it was no longer on the defensive. Yet she could still feel fear in the animal's thoughts.

"Bad man. Killer man."

"Don't you worry," she said. "We're not killers."

"Coming this way."

Lily felt the wolf's terror. The bad man was something from a nightmare, a force of evil and hatred and agonizing death.

"Don't you worry," she told the wolf. "If we see the bad man, I won't tell him I've seen you."

The wolf seemed reassured by this and trotted a few steps closer, poking its nose toward Lily's hands. She stood still, allowing the wolf to sniff, then felt the unexpected, sandpapery surface of its tongue. She responded by hesitantly placing a hand on its shoulder, causing it to flinch. After a moment, it moved closer again and allowed her to run a hand from behind its tall, pointed ears to the corduroy pattern of its ribs.

Then the wolf yipped a goodbye, turned, and sauntered off into the grasslands. Galahad and Lancelot responded with subdued barks and wagged their tails.

The land through which they traveled grew drier, and the gentle rolling of prairie sand hills became increasingly broken by tall, flat-topped hills. Mesas, Mr. Szabo called them. They had long left behind the tall grasses of the eastern Dakota Territory, which in summer could rise to a horse's withers. Here were short grasses, some still brown and dead from the long winter, others soft and green with the spring rain. A silvery leafed plant called sagebrush perfumed the air, as did the first golden flowers of a bush called wolf willow, which grew along creeks in the dry land. On sunbaked, exposed southern flanks of hillsides, a ground cover of small pincushion cactus made travel difficult. The cactus needles could not pierce a horse's hoof, but the draft animals were reluctant to expose their ankles to the needles. In places, vast tracts of land were pounded down hard and level as paving stones, where a herd of buffalo had grazed everything in sight and moved on. Elsewhere were networks of small mounds, created by dirt hauled out of holes by small, plump, dun-colored creatures. At intervals throughout the collection of mounds, the little creatures stood guard on their hind legs, letting out alarm calls when the circus wagons came too close. Prairie dogs, Mr. Szabo explained. Lily tried to speak to them and quickly realized that they were dogs in name only.

Once, the party came to a remarkable cliff of clay and sandstone. They all left their wagons to look. Below them was a valley, devoid of trees, filled with rocks of all shapes. Some were narrow like pointing fingers. Some looked like stone mushrooms, with flattened caps balanced atop stems. Ridges jutted into the valley with walls of red, yellow, orange, and white. Nothing grew in the valley.

"The land God gave to Cain," said Mr. Szabo.

A few days later, a dark line across the southwest horizon provided their first glimpse of the Black Hills. The circus wagons stopped at a shallow creek to water and rest the horses. Lily climbed down from the wagon and took the dogs to a bluff overlooking the creek in order to practice a new trick for the act. Just as she was explaining to them that she intended to hand out cards to audience members, she saw a terrified expression break out on their faces and in their bodies. Was this another wolf? She looked toward the wagons and around at the grasslands below and saw a rider approaching, leading a packhorse and headed by a pack of dogs.

The rider made for the wagons and hailed Uncle Stanislas and Mr. Szabo, who had been conferring beside the lead horse team. From a distance, the rider appeared to be questioning the circus folk, but his conversation was cut short by an interruption from his dogs, which burst into a run and charged up the rise toward Lily, their voices raised in barks and snarls.

Lily tried to read the thoughts of the stranger's dogs but only understood, "Hate, hate, hate."

"There's no reason to fight," she said. "We're just passing through."

"Hate, hate, hate."

Galahad and Lancelot stood on either side of Lily, their fur standing and teeth bared, ready to protect her. Sparky stood between her feet, making sounds that expressed equal parts anger and terror.

The rider called to his dogs and, when they did not come, he spat and spurred his horse.

"Worthless stupid mutts," he said, then noticed the way the dogs were pointing at Lily. "Strangest thing," he continued. "That's the way they bark at a wolf. You ain't been around wolves lately, have you?"

Lily sized up the man, noticing only now that his horse's hindquarters were draped with the silver and gray of wolf pelts. Steel traps jangled on the back of the packhorse alongside a pair of pack boxes. The man was dressed in black and, despite the spring warmth, had a cloak of fur over his shoulders. He gave off a feral smell of sweat and blood and meat left too long in the open air. A long rifle hung from his saddle in a leather scabbard, and from his belt dangled a pistol and a fearsome long knife.

"No," she replied.

"No? These mutts of mine may be stupid, but their noses ain't. Be mighty surprised if they think they smell wolf on you and they're wrong."

"Maybe I sat down in the grass where a wolf had been resting. I imagine there are a lot of wolves out here in the wild prairie."

The man laughed mirthlessly and spat again, then opened his blackened cave of a mouth and inserted a plug of tobacco. "Not so many wolves out here now, little girl. That's my doing."

He paused, staring intently, as if gauging Lily's reaction. Lily winced as she imagined the pain and terror of the wolves caught in his traps.

"You want to make this country safe, don't you?" he continued. "You don't want some big, bad wolf coming into your camp some night and killing your little doggies, now do you?"

The man grinned. Lily felt the taunting and challenge in his voice.

"I'm not afraid of wolves."

"You should be. You know how them demons kill? A group of 'em will chase a calf, taking turns nipping at its heels, just enjoying the sport of it. Then one of 'em will bite the calf's hamstrings, make it fall so it can't get back up. While it's down, they'll bite it in the guts, rip out its intestines, and pull them out and play with 'em while the calf's bleating on the ground, slowly bleeding to death. They'll eat the liver while the thing's still alive, then maybe take one or two bites of the choice bits and leave the rest to rot."

Lily thought of the wolf she met and the strength of its desire to feed and protect its young. She knew the wolf was a hunter. But not a monster.

"I don't believe you."

"And I don't believe you, little girl." He spurred his horse again and called to the dogs to follow as he resumed his course along the shallow prairie creek. He turned and spoke over his shoulder. "I hope you know that those who bear false witness are an abomination in the eyes of the Lord. If I see you again, I trust you'll speak the truth."

The encounter with the wolfer darkened the mood of the circus. Even the horses felt it. They became restive and stubborn. It took longer to harness them, and they required additional coaxing to continue dragging the wagons onward. Uncle Stanislas kept his old Springfield within reach on the wagon bench and frequently ran his hand along the smooth wood of the stock, as if calling upon a talisman for protection. There was no doubt now that the little wagon train had reached lands beyond civilization. You didn't need the fortune-telling ability of Madame Mystere to see that danger lay in wait.

The evening after the encounter with the wolfer, Lily's gaze was drawn to the circling flight of a vulture. It was not the first she'd seen, but seeing this one gave her heart a jolt that had not occurred when she'd seen the others. She had a powerful foreboding that the vulture was connected in some way with the wolfer. The vulture appeared to be circling just beyond the nearest hill. The others were busy setting up camp for the night. Lily had half an hour to investigate before her disappearance would be noted.

"Sparky, stay here. I don't think you're fast enough for this."

She called Galahad and Lancelot to her side and, checking over her shoulder to make sure she wasn't being observed, set off up the hill. It was a longer climb than it looked. When she reached the top, she looked down on a narrow creek winding along the center of a wide, flat valley floor. The moist soil near the creek supported a narrow band of cottonwood trees just beginning to turn green. The vulture circled lower near the center of the valley, watching something along the edge of the wood.

"Lancelot, Galahad, go ahead and see what it is."

The dogs bounded over the grasses and the sagebrush. Lily followed, struggling down the loose clay of the slope. As the slope flattened out, she began running toward the trees.

As she approached, she heard her dogs barking. It was the wolf. It was still alive.

Lily came upon the wolf, which had apparently been lured by a carcass attached to a stake. The wolf's right hind leg was trapped in jagged iron jaws, blood darkening and thickening where the teeth had bitten into the flesh. The animal chewed at its leg, licked its wound, and pulled on the heavy iron trap, which was securely anchored to a tree.

Pain and fear were evident in the wolf's voice and face but also something else. A different kind of fear. Lily realized it was fear for the wolf's cubs that she felt. She heard whimpering from a thicket of wolf willow. The cubs had been traveling with their mother, possibly on their first hunting expedition. Lily took a step toward the wolf willows to see them and heard the trapped wolf growl at her.

"I'm here to help you, wolf. But I'm going to need you to trust me. You're here with your cubs, aren't you?"

The mother ceased growling, still eyeing Lily suspiciously.

"I'm going to try to open up this trap, but it might hurt a little."

She approached the wolf slowly, placing first her hand and then her whole body within biting range. So far, the wolf seemed to trust her. She got down on her knees near the wolf's hind leg to get a better look. Slowly and carefully, she reached out a hand to touch the leg. The wolf jumped. She reached out and touched the leg again, and this time the wolf only shuddered. She ran her hand down the leg toward the teeth of the trap. Had the trap broken the wolf's leg? She didn't think so, though it had cut deeply. Placing one hand on each jaw of the trap, she attempted to pry it apart. It didn't give. She looked more closely at the trap and saw a handle near where it was connected to the chain that held it in place. She placed a knee on the handle to press it down, while using both hands to pull on the jaws with all her strength. The wolf shuddered again as the teeth pulled out of her flesh.

Once the trap was open, Lily examined the injured leg again. "This might hurt, wolf."

She held the wolf's paw in one hand and leg in another and gently pivoted the ankle bone. The wolf closed its powerful jaws around her arm, with a warning pressure that would not break the skin. The injury might be serious.

"Stay here, wolf."

Lily climbed down to the creek, which ran clear and cold over a gravel bottom. This would be good for the wolf's leg. She ripped off a length of fabric from the bottom of her skirt and soaked it in the cold water, then returned to the wolf and carefully scrubbed the wound. She repeated this process until the wound looked clean. Then she ripped off another length of fabric to create a longer bandage, which she wrapped around the leg to provide it with support and protection. Tight enough to protect the leg but not so tight as to cut off the circulation of blood. She secured the clean bandage with the wet length of cloth, hoping it would stay in place long enough for the injury to heal.

"Now, don't you take that off before your leg is better."

The mother wolf stood on three legs. She attempted a few test steps around the forest edge near the trap. It was obvious to Lily that the wolf could barely walk and certainly could not run or hunt.

How long, she wondered, would it take for the wolf to heal? Would riding in the wagon for a few days help?

"Wolf. Do you trust me? Would you come with me?"

The wolf eyed her with uncertainty.

"My people can protect you while you get better."

To demonstrate the sincerity of her offer, Lily untied the chain from the tree and pulled it farther away from the wolf. She used a stick to spring the trap closed again, so it would endanger no other creatures, and tossed it in the creek. When the wolf saw that the trap was gone, it yipped gently toward the willows, and out came a litter of three cubs, still sporting their fluffy newborn coats but beginning to take on the dimensions of the long-ranging predators they would become.

Two cubs stepped forward gingerly. The third, however, was overcome by curiosity and ran forward to inspect Lily, Galahad, and Lancelot, wagging its tail and poking all three with its wet nose.

"Oh, you're a playful one," Lily said as the cub's sniffing nose tickled her legs. "You listen to your mother. There's plenty of danger out there."

While the brave cub began to jump and roll with Galahad and Lancelot, Lily looked the mother in the eyes and felt the animal's gratitude. The mother yipped at the cubs to bring them to heel and, as Lily and her dogs began walking across the valley to return to the wagons, the mother wolf limped behind, keeping a careful watch on her cubs all the way to the wagons.

The arrival of a family of wolves in the circle of wagons caused a sensation among the humans and spooked the horses. The tumbling midgets were understandably leery since they were the size of a wolf's appetizer. Mr. Szabo cautioned Lily against thinking that domesticating a wolf could be an easily accomplished task. Tommaso Largo noted that the party would be hard pressed to provide a family of voracious predators with enough meat, especially to allow for the rapid growth of the cubs. But Uncle Stanislas smiled widely.

"Tommaso, you see only today," said Uncle Stanislas. "I see future. I see crowds lining up to watch Lillian the Lycanthrope with her pack of trained wild wolves."

Lily meant to protest that she had no intention of including the wolf family in the act but thought it wiser to remain silent. She led the mother wolf to her wagon and filled one of the horse's water buckets, setting it down near a rear wheel. Then she removed a portion of salt beef from the food stores, broke it into pieces, and distributed it to the entire family. The wolves ate hungrily, calming Lily's concern that the carcass that had lured them to the trap might be poisoned. She trusted that the wolf's injury was not beyond recovery. The fear she'd heard in the animal's voice had been focused entirely on its cubs, which she took as a sign that the injuries were not as deep as they had at first appeared. Fear would drain strength from the wolf, so she would stay up all night to assure her that her cubs were safe, just as Lily's mother had stayed up all night with her when she'd been stricken with some childhood fever.

The next morning, when the circus folk began preparing for another day's journey, the mother wolf struggled to her feet. The night had brought no healing to her wound. There was no question of her leading her litter away to safety on this day. Uncle Stanislas cleared a space in the back of Lily's wagon and propped up a board for use as a ramp, placing a portion of salt beef at the top.

"Come, Wolf Girl, call your friends into wagon."

It took some coaxing, but Lily was able to convince the wolf that the wagon offered safety for her cubs. As the wagons jolted into motion, Lily remained in the back with the wolves. Over the course of the day, she discovered that the wolves found her voice soothing, so she continued to speak and sing to them as they bounced over the prairie. She was in the midst of yet another chorus of "Green Grow the Lilacs" when Mr. Szabo, who was driving the wagon, told her to shush. Over the jolting sound of the wagon, she heard Tommaso's voice call out, "Riders coming." Moments later, the wagon jolted to a stop.

"Tell Lily hide. Hide."

Mr. Szabo turned and tossed a robe over Lily and told her not to move. The cubs, sensing fear from the humans, crawled under the robe with her. Lily felt the wagon grow darker as he tied a piece of canvas over the back of the wagon as if preparing to weather a storm. The robe muffled sounds from the outside world, but Lily felt she heard approaching hoofbeats, followed by human voices making sounds she had never heard before. They were met by the voice of Uncle Stanislas, though his words were indistinct. Soft, running footsteps penetrated through the canvas wall and the robe. So did Uncle Stanislas's voice, now louder and closer.

"We carry nothing but the tools of the circus. You are welcome to some food—"

The noise of an impact was followed immediately by a cry of pain from Uncle Stanislas.

Light flooded into the wagon, reaching underneath the robe that hid Lily, and the mother wolf emitted her fiercest growl. Again the human voice uttered a string of sounds the like of which Lily had never heard, even though she'd learned words of Polish, Hungarian, and Italian in the circus and heard plenty of Swedish and German from the Midwestern audiences. More of the voices converged on the wagon, and suddenly Lily felt the robe lifted from her. She looked up to see a dark face with high cheekbones and dark eyes and long dark hair underneath a blue cap. She pushed as far back in the wagon as she could, the wolf cubs climbing over her and hiding behind her. The mother stood on all fours, hair raised, shoulders hunched, teeth bared, protecting her litter and Lily.

The warrior addressed Lily directly in English. "Girl, out."

Hesitantly, she crawled out and around the mother wolf, jumping down from the wagon onto the prairie grass. The warrior pulled her away from the wagon so that his comrades, both mounted on shaggy Indian horses, could look her over. She returned the scrutiny.

One of the mounted men trained an army repeating rifle on Mr. Szabo, who was holding the old Springfield with its barrel pointed to the ground. The other held a feathered coup stick in his hand and, judging from the blood flowing from Uncle Stanislas's nose, he had just used it. Both of the other men deferred to the man with the stick. All three were attired in a way that told of their participation in the battle the previous summer with Colonel Custer's Seventh Cavalry. The man on foot, who held Lily by the neck of her dress, wore a blue cavalryman's forage cap atop his dark hair. The man guarding Mr. Szabo wore blue trousers with a yellow stripe down the side of the leg. The leader wore a cavalryman's tunic over his buckskin breeches and carried an officer's saber at his belt and had a long lance lashed to his saddle.

As Lily focused on the man in charge, she came to realize that dangling from the end of the lance was a collection of scalps, at least two of which, judging by the hair color, had belonged to white men. She had heard whispers of what Sioux warriors might do to a captive and hoped that, if she were meant to die, it might happen quickly.

The man with the lance spoke and gestured with his coup stick at the wagon. Lily looked back to see the mother jumping awkwardly, landing on three feet only. The cubs in the wagon looked over the edge at their mother, who hobbled up to Lily to take a defensive position in front of her. A second string of words from the warrior, which was followed by laughter, alerted her to the arrival of the bravest of the wolf cubs. He'd joined his mother in a defiant posture. The leader dismounted, continuing with his speech, and walked soundlessly through the grass to where Lily stood, frozen in place. More words followed. Then he paused and looked toward the companion in the forage cap, who translated.

"He says wolf is hurt. He asks how."

"She was caught in a trap."

Another string of words.

"He asks, did you free wolf?"

Beyond the Indians she saw Uncle Stanislas, holding a cloth to his nose, mouthing the words, "Be careful."

"I freed her. She was hurt."

The leader dismounted from his horse and slowly bent toward the wolf's injured leg. Then he straightened and walked toward Lily, producing a handful of dried bark and berries, wrapped up in grasses and a strip of rawhide. He handed it to Lily, pointed to the wolf's leg, and mimed the action of tying the bundle to the leg.

"He says wolf's leg is hurt bad. Needs powerful medicine to heal. Tie this to leg and give plenty water and meat."

"We don't have meat. Just a bit of salt beef."

The leader spoke again, and the translator continued. "He says wolf needs good meat of his brothers buffalo and elk. You must feed her. He tells you his name is Dreams of Horses."

Dreams of Horses and the young English speaker mounted their horses, and the three warriors continued riding northward, showing no indication that they were interested in the wagons.

When the Indians were gone, the rest of the circus performers looked at Lily in a new light, as the girl who had saved them from murder, scalping, or fates worse than death. Even Uncle Stanislas was unable to summon up his usual forceful personality. The blow from the young Indian had deflated him like an old balloon. It took all the strength he had left to call for the wagons to be arranged in a circle. Fires were kindled, and some of the last of the flour was measured out to make a batch of biscuits. Mr. Szabo produced a bottle of brandy and poured a dram for each member of the company, Lily included. Madame Mystere, who had previously cast covetous eyes on each piece of salt beef given to the wolves, called out for all in the company to let the wolves take that night's portion of meat, and no voices were raised in dissent. The sun set on a silent company.

The next morning, as they were un-hobbling the horses, Lily noticed something odd. In among the aged, plodding old plow horses they had bought to pull their wagons was a sprightly young paint, brown and white with a long mane that grew all the way back to the rawhide Indian saddle on its back.

"Lillian, I think your friends left you a present," Uncle Stanislas called.

As Lily admired the animal, cautiously extending a hand to let it learn her scent, Mr. Szabo noticed something hanging from a branch of a nearby bur oak and called Lily to inspect it. The freshly killed hindquarters of an elk hung by a length of rawhide from a low branch. Jutting from the trunk of the elk was something else, something shiny and deadly. The man who had brought the wolves this gift of meat had given Lily the cavalry saber, still marked by the blood of the elk. It was a generous portion of meat and would be enough to feed the wolves—with a taste left over for their two-legged companions—until the caravan reached Deadwood, where the performers could again earn their meals through acts of wonder and amazement.

12

GEORGE AND THOMAS were fidgeting, as if they had ants in their britches. Truth to tell, Lincoln felt powerfully pent up as well in the small corner of the wagon the three boys shared as they bounced their way from Cheyenne. After the speed of the Union Pacific Railway, two hundred and sixty miles behind a team of draft horses might as well have been forty years of wandering in the desert.

Lincoln had begun whittling parts for a small toy wagon the previous day, figuring it would give him some way to pass the long journey. He planned to make two of them for his brothers to keep them from getting on Mama's nerves. She'd been getting more short-tempered as the days wore on and the bouncing of the wagon sent jabs of pain up her backbone and into her head. Maybe he could take a look at the underside of the wagons and see if there was something that could be done to make the ride a little gentler. Maybe when they stopped for the night. Right now, he had to concentrate on fashioning a pair of axles for his toy wagons.

Tools and supplies for the toy-making project were the least of his concern. The train of five wagons was loaded to near the breaking point with all manner of metal-working equipment, as well as lengths of steel rod and sheet metal, springs, steam-engine parts, and a box of Mr. McTaggart's books on chemistry, physics, and engineering.

Many of the goods had arrived by train with them, while others had been stockpiled by the Cheyenne business agent for the Homestake Mine and its owner, Mr. George Hearst. It was the business agent Mr. McTaggart had been telegraphing in the days and weeks before their departure for the West, as there was not yet a line to the new mining town of Deadwood in the Black Hills. It would have been simpler, Mr. McTaggart said, to work on their special project back east and bring it in completed form to their employer. But Mr. Hearst appeared to be a man who liked to keep things he valued close to him. He wanted to watch their project take shape.

And so, after their arrival by train, Mr. McTaggart and Lincoln had spent a few days taking inventory and watching Mr. Hearst's hired teamsters load the wagons for the long, slow trip across the dry plains of eastern Wyoming.

It wasn't just the monotony, the cramped space, or the rough ride that made Lincoln's mama tense. The moment she saw the armed men who would accompany them to Deadwood, she pulled all three boys close.

"Don't you boys be talking to any of those men," she'd said. "I think I've seen their type before."

With their rifles, swagger, and Southern accents, the guards for the wagon train did seem familiar. Lincoln had seen plenty like them when he was still a schoolboy in Tennessee. He remembered hard-eyed white men riding their horses down the road by the colored church, making old folks and women with babies step aside. It was hard to imagine that these men were here as protectors.

Lincoln completed the two wagons and gave one to each boy. Then, knowing the toys would only keep the boys busy so long, he started another project.

He'd learned that music follows the same rules of numbers as anything else, that the pitch of a vibrating string depended on the thickness and length of the string, that the amount of sound depended on the space the string could vibrate over. With that in mind, he'd borrowed five lengths of wire from the supplies for Mr. Hearst's project, plus some screws and a short length of flat wood.

Now, he began assembling the pieces to make something that he hoped would hold his brothers' attention until they reached their destination. If only he had something with a hole that could go under the strings to raise up the sound.

That evening in camp, Mr. McTaggart watched as Lincoln plucked at a wire, increasing and reducing the tension and holding it to his ear. Lincoln then watched Mr. McTaggart walk away from the firelight where Lincoln sat and return a short time later with an empty cigar box.

"This may serve your purposes," he said.

"Don't you need this for your cigars?"

"Ach, 'tis a dirty habit anyway."

Lincoln worked with his new materials until it was too dark to see.

The next morning, they'd been traveling only a few hours when one of the armed guards raised a hand to stop the wagons. He conferred with the other guard and spurred his horse to a gallop up the trail. A half an hour later, as the other guard watched, finger on the trigger of his Winchester rifle, the man returned and called for the wagons to continue.

As they rumbled along the trail, Lincoln stood and balanced himself on the bed of the moving wagon and caught sight of a red shape in the featureless prairie. Soon, it grew and resolved itself into a stagecoach, minus its team of horses. A group of men leaned against the shady side. A short distance from the men lay what looked like a rolled-up carpet.

Mr. McTaggart jumped down from his seat in the wagon directly in front of Lincoln's family, then ran back, waving his arms to tell the teamster to stop.

"Missus Henry," he said. "I think ye'd best keep the boys inside."

Mama, seated in front of Lincoln, blocked Thomas and George's ability to exit out the front of the wagon.

Lincoln peered over her shoulder.

"You heard the man, Lincoln. Sit yourself down now."

"It's no sight for children, Lincoln," Mr. McTaggart added.

Lincoln had seen plenty in his short life that he shouldn't have. But there was no point letting George and Thomas do the same. He turned back to his brothers, tightened the wires around the screws, then used a screwdriver to make the wires nice and taut, while George plinked on the wires. When he guessed it was close enough to tuned, he handed the boys their new cigar-box banjo.

"Now we gonna have us a time!" George said, striking the strings.

"Now, why'd you go and do that, Lincoln?" Mama said. "Hard enough to get these two thinking about their schooling without you giving them this distraction."

"Don't worry, Mama. I can teach them how it works. Music's nothing but numbers you can hear. If they learn this, they can learn all their sums and figures."

"They'd better. I didn't raise my boys to stand on the street corner and play for pennies."

George and Thomas took turns strumming on the banjo, and Lincoln showed them how they could hold the wires down at different points along the instrument's neck to create different tones. Meanwhile, the conversation outside the wagon came to them in murmurs. Lincoln strained to hear, even as he showed his brothers the use of the banjo.

"How many?"

"You see where they went?"

"Damn fool tried to be the hero."

"Nothin' we could do."

"Sent our fastest man back to Deadwood on foot."

"How long?"

"Got any water to spare?"

"Wish I'd never heard of this godforsaken hellhole."

"He's gettin' rank. I ain't haulin' him back to town."

"Got a shovel?"

"Mama, I got to go."

This last was George. The toy wagon and then the banjo had kept him distracted for a time, but he could no longer put off the effect of last night's beans and this morning's bouncing along on the road.

"You just wait. This is no place to get out of the wagon."

"Mama, I can't wait."

"You should have thought of that before we started."

"I didn't need to go then."

"Mama, I got to go too," said Thomas.

"All right. You boys just step over the boxes and stand at the back end of the wagon."

"It ain't that kind of going, Mama."

"Don't worry, Mama," Lincoln said. "I can take them."

Lincoln led his brothers out the back end of the wagon, facing away from the horseless stagecoach, and walked an appropriate distance for privacy where they could drop their drawers behind a clump of sagebrush. While they ducked behind the bushes, Lincoln watched the stagecoach.

Two of the men who had been sitting beside the stagecoach now stood beside what Lincoln had thought was a carpet. One swung a pickaxe to loosen the hard-packed soil. The other placed a foot on a shovel and began to dig. Judging by the distance the men stood apart from one another, their project was a hole about six feet long. The digging was slow work, and the men had made little progress by the time George and Thomas were done. Lincoln walked the boys back to the wagon, keeping up a stream of talk about the magical mathematics of music. He helped the boys up and then said, "Sorry, Mama, now I got to go."

It was a sin to lie and a bigger sin to lie to your mother, but Lincoln felt he had to know. He caught Mr. McTaggart's eye, and the mechanic came his way.

"Who's the dead man?" Lincoln asked.

"I wish you hadna' seen that, Lincoln."

"I've seen worse, Mister McTaggart."

"He was the shotgun guard for the stagecoach. Bandits... they call them road agents out here... took them by surprise two nights ago. The blackguards shot him, stole what money they had, and took the horses."

As Mr. McTaggart spoke, a group of riders rounded the hillside, coming full speed from the direction of Deadwood.

"Are they coming back?"

"I expect this is what they call a posse, Lincoln."

In the lead was a thick-necked, barrel-chested man with a pair of pistols on his hips and a shotgun slung over his shoulder. The man veered away from the stagecoach and trotted up to Lincoln and Mr. McTaggart. As he approached, Lincoln imagined a shaved bear in men's clothing.

"You must be McTaggart," he said, spitting a wad of tobacco into the dust.

"Aye. And you are?"

"Boone May. Hearst sent me to make sure you get in all right. Didn't want the same welcoming committee coming for you as came for the stagecoach. Damn road agents. Every stagecoach leaving Deadwood is like to get robbed by men thinking it's loaded with gold. Every one coming to Deadwood too. Road agents figure it's got the mine payroll inside."

"And this one? Gold or payroll?"

The sound of an argument drifted their way. The men digging the grave shouted at the posse members who looked down on them from their mounts. Evidently, the victims of the robbery weren't pleased with the level of help offered by the posse.

"Neither," May said, eyeing the stagecoach and its passengers. "Just some busted-out prospectors and a dry goods salesman. Now, load yourselves up. We're going to get you into Deadwood."

Mr. McTaggart asked, "What about the stagecoach?"

"We sent word back when we met their runner. They'll have fresh horses by tomorrow. Now, let's hit the trail. We're burning daylight."

"Should we not wait until the man is buried so we can pay our respects?"

"He kin of yours?"

"No."

"How 'bout you, boy? He your kin?"

"No, sir."

"You stick around Deadwood, you'll learn. A dead man ain't nothin' you change your plans for."

The big man laughed and inserted a fresh plug of tobacco in his mouth. He took in the heavily loaded wagons and turned back to Mr. McTaggart. "I heard something about what you're doing for Mister Hearst. Now you know why he's so fired up to put you to work. You better be able to build what you say you can. He ain't a man to disappoint."

13

S EGAL HELD A card out, back facing Daniel, and flashed him the
front side as quickly as his fingers would allow.

"What card was it?"

"Not again, Segal."

"What? You got some place to go? An audience with the president?"

"We've been doin' this since Chicago."

"Pardon me for trying to make the most of our time. Such a terrible
fate it is to have a friend who tries to help you develop your talents."

Segal flashed two cards at Daniel, who sighed and pushed his new
hat down over his eyes.

"If I tell you, will you let me sleep?"

"Such a question. Of course I'll let you sleep."

"Nine of hearts and jack of diamonds."

Segal turned the two cards face up. Daniel was right.

"And the first one?"

"I thought you'd let me sleep."

"Tell me, kid. The first one."

"Six of clubs."

Segal flipped over the card he'd flashed a minute earlier. Correct. The
skinny youth, his dark hair glistening with pomade that he'd somehow

managed to acquire immediately upon being sprung from the reformatory, leaned in toward Daniel and whispered, "Now listen. There's a
game in the club car. Ten dollar buy-in. I can stake you. You just gotta
use those eyes of yours."

"I can't see through paper."

"But I'm betting you see every little nick and crease in the back of
each card. So, you just gotta remember when they show their cards what
the backs look like. After a couple of hands, it's like they're playing with
their cards facing you. Then you bet big and win us a bonanza."

"And get myself shot."

"Roth and Wiseman will stand outside the door. They'll be your
protection."

"And you?"

"I'll teach you the game. It's been sixteen hours since Omaha, so from
the look of this endless steppe out here, we've got another six months to
Cheyenne. Plenty of time to make some money."

"You want to explain to Missus Kleinschmidt when we get thrown
off the train for cheating at cards?"

Segal shook his head and sighed, evidently disappointed by Daniel's
lack of imagination and ambition. The older boy had become increasingly
impatient the farther west the train had traveled. Daniel knew Segal was
nervous about his new life in the West. When he wasn't coaxing Daniel to become a card cheat, he cracked jokes about scalping parties and
rattlesnakes or laughed at the absurdity of a gang of young desperadoes
named Segal, Roth, Wiseman, and McCormack. He'd dubbed Daniel
the Kosher Kid.

"So, you think it's fine to use your magic eyes and hands to become a
gunfighter, but using them to make money at cards is beyond the pale?"

"Big Jim says I'm not going to be a gunfighter. I just need people to
see me shoot in practice, and I won't have to draw on anybody."

"Kid, you're a babe in arms, so I'll go easy on you. But you and Jim
are both crazy if you think the world works that way."

For a moment, Segal dropped the cynical clown mask he wore when
joking his way through an argument, and Daniel saw that his friend

had thought deeply about how the world works. In the reformatory, Daniel had come to rely on two Segals. The wisecracking Segal had kept Daniel's spirits up when thoughts of his mother had dragged them down and had given Daniel courage when the Brickbat Boys menaced him by word and gesture. The philosophical Segal had taught him a kind of acceptance that allowed him to bear a life that had taken him from a tenement to the streets to the reformatory. He'd done this by teaching Daniel to disregard what half-remembered scraps of moral lessons he'd picked up as a child. The world was not overseen by a kindhearted Sunday school teacher with a beard. There was no heavenly scorekeeper recording who deserved happiness and love and who didn't. Segal had taught him that the best way to endure suffering was to abandon thoughts of fairness and justice and that expecting nothing from your fellow man was the best way to avoid being disappointed by him. That's probably why Segal had been struck speechless when Mrs. Kleinschmidt and Big Jim had sprung him, Roth, and Wiseman from the reformatory. In apparent defiance of the bleak wisdom Segal had taught him, Daniel had returned kindness with kindness.

"Listen, kid. When this crazy business falls apart, we're all gonna need a little something of our own. So do it for your friends."

Daniel saw that Segal wasn't joking. Segal didn't trust Big Jim or Mrs. Kleinschmidt or their big talk about organizing workers into unions. Maybe it was a bit of a long shot. Maybe more of a long shot than the poker game in the club car. He shrugged and gestured to Segal, who opened the door of their compartment and led him back to the club car near the caboose, where gamblers played their way across the Great Plains. The two youths bounced along the rocking aisle, past families bedding down for the night and porters delivering blankets and pillows. They stepped along the covered walkway between cars and felt the cool night air of the western plains and breathed in the sagebrush and knew themselves to be far from the world of their slum-bound youth. Ahead they saw Roth and Wiseman attempting to look casual, Roth rolling a cigarette and Wiseman staring at a fixed point on a page of a three-day-old edition of the Kansas City Star. Roth gestured with his hands as he rolled his smoke, and Daniel saw the light from the card room at the back end of the smoking car.

Daniel had no idea how a new player entered a game but felt that if he stopped now to inquire, he'd lose his momentum. He'd study the room, see how many were playing, and wait to see if the opportunity to join presented itself. Through the smoke-darkened glass pane in the door, Daniel peered at the men gathered around the table, a mix of dandies, sober-suited businessmen, and men dressed for riding the range. A large pile of chips in the middle of the table testified to the stakes of the game.

Daniel placed his hand on the door and took a breath.

But then he noticed the giant man with the eye patch. The loss of an eye had little changed the man's appearance. He still had the same flattened nose and massive, single eyebrow, and his yellowed, uneven teeth still looked like something fit for a great carnivorous beast. The giant—Bull, Daniel recalled—stood with his back against a wall behind a card player whose face was not visible.

Daniel recognized the man's long, agile fingers, though, for he had seen them dance along a tabletop with a trio of walnut shells. The man was better dressed than Daniel recalled, and had longer, thicker hair that Daniel now realized was a wig for vain, bald men. The man turned briefly to talk with a fellow card player, and Daniel caught a glimpse of the man's nose, bent at the bridge where a rock had caught it three years before, and his mouth, filled with brilliant, false teeth of ivory that gleamed in the lamplight.

The man—Mr. O'Donnell—smiled at the neighboring player, and Daniel felt the same chill he'd felt when he'd looked up from Bull's grip at the man's cold smile in a Five Points alley.

Daniel spun on his heel and shot past Segal, Wiseman, and Roth, not pausing until he reached the safety of his compartment. Roth and Wiseman entered, creating an instant sensation of overcrowding. Segal stood at the door and inspected Daniel's face. Wiseman sat beside Daniel, who felt his own breathing tighten, as if the mass of Wiseman took oxygen from the room. Roth, who sat opposite, reached under the seat and produced a loaf of dark bread. He ripped it down the middle and tossed half to Wiseman.

"I guess he ain't playing," Wiseman said, nodding toward Daniel.

Segal appeared to find his answers in Daniel's face. "He's saving himself for Hickok."

"I thought you said Hickok was dead."

"He's saving himself for the new Hickok."

Daniel watched the glow of moonlight on the endless Nebraska plain. The ground had become drier and increasingly barren as the train had chugged its way west from Omaha. Settlements had become more widely scattered. Farms had become fewer and larger, and fields of grain had given way to unbroken pastures and herds of cattle, whitefaces from the East and longhorns driven north from Texas. It was a landscape where hiding from a fight would be impossible. And there would be no hiding behind Big Jim, who had gone on ahead weeks ago to lay the groundwork for organizing the miners. Daniel needed to warn his friends.

"The big man with one eye and the dandy with the false teeth. I did that to both of them. I expect if they see me again, I'll have to kill them."

Roth stopped chewing his bread and studied Daniel.

Segal secured the door and pulled the blind, sat beside Roth, and ripped off a chunk of the bread.

"Like I said, saving himself for the new Hickok."

A gnawing anxiety tugged at Daniel's innards. It didn't add up that Mrs. Kleinschmidt, seeking to go straight and escape old enemies in New York, would travel to the very edge of white settlement and become some kind of friend of the working man. What could a New York dry goods merchant know about gold miners? And not for the first time, he wondered what it said about organizing workers that it was a job requiring recruitment of a new gang.

Daniel attempted to set his doubts aside. He had given his word that he'd work for her if she found his mother, and she'd kept her end of the bargain. He closed his eyes and let the rhythm of the train rock him to sleep.

As the train swayed and clattered over the short-grass plains, Daniel saw a woman dancing and singing in a tenement room. Her dress was simple but clean and new. The tenement room was also clean, with bright light streaming in from a south-facing window. The more Daniel looked around the tenement room, the more it became a normal house. Bigger, brighter, cleaner than the tenements Daniel had lived in with his mother. A child's laughter broke into the dream, and a boy on a stool clapped his hands in time with the woman's voice.

Daniel realized that he was looking at himself as a boy and wondered why he was seeing the scene as an outside observer rather than through the eyes of the boy. Was this a sign that he was now a different person?

The woman turned and smiled and was no longer Daniel's mother. She was one of the hot corn girls from the Five Points, grown up and married. The boy was a consumptive beggar child Daniel had seen the leatherheads haul off to the orphanage, now filled out and rosy-cheeked. Daniel was aware he was dreaming. The consumptive beggar boy had probably long since died at the orphanage. And the hot corn girl was unlikely to grow into a married woman with a big, clean house.

Now, the scenery of the dream changed. Daniel faced a row of bottles on a fence rail, an array of pistols placed in front of him. The bottles exploded in clouds of dust, gun smoke, and shards of glass. Daniel's hands barely moved, yet somehow he fired off bullets faster than a Gatling gun, hitting his target every time.

Yet no matter how many bottles he struck and shattered, each time he looked up he saw more approaching. It was up to Daniel to stop the bottles from advancing, but there were so many of them, and he was growing weary.

He awoke in a darkened compartment. Wiseman's snoring created a counterpoint rhythm with the huffing of the locomotive. Daniel felt moisture on his shoulder below Wiseman's steadily trickling open mouth. Removing himself from Wiseman's bulk, Daniel rose to his feet and threaded his way through the nest of legs on the floor of the compartment. He opened and closed the door quietly and slipped out into the narrow hallway. Noticing a breeze from the back door, he followed the circulating air to the covered walkway between cars. In the light of a match, Daniel saw Mrs. Kleinschmidt light a cigar and gaze out at the featureless night, black now with the setting of the moon. As silently as Daniel moved, she sensed him coming and turned.

"You caught me with my bad habit," she said. "Such a terrible example I set for a healthy young man."

"Sorry. I couldn't sleep."

"A boy like you should sleep like a baby."

Daniel watched as Mrs. Kleinschmidt took a deep breath on her cigar and exhaled into the swirling, crisp night air.

"I'm thinking, you said all I got to do is show people how fast I am, and I'll never have to shoot anybody. That ain't really true, is it?"

"Such a good boy you are. Such a good heart. You don't want people getting hurt."

Mrs. Kleinschmidt patted Daniel's cheek, then passed her fingers through his hair to smooth the knots of sleep. "I read the newspapers. Special ones from Europe the exiles bring with them. There are terrible battles coming. Workers gather in groups to demand more money, safety, better houses. Owners don't want to pay, so they send out men with guns. Then, the workers get their own men with guns. Soon, there are dead men everywhere. What we do, we get in between the workers and owners before the war, prevent all the killing, see?"

Daniel understood about the anger of hungry, desperate men. He'd seen it as a child in the Five Points. If a war was coming, he didn't see how he could stop it, no matter how fast he pulled his gun.

"But what if they're so angry, or the owners are so stingy, they don't want us in between them?"

"Then we make sure they know what you can do."

"But that won't stop everybody, will it?"

Mrs. Kleinschmidt said nothing at first. She looked out at the dark plains, a vague sensation of movement created in the blurred blackness all around. "When I was a girl," she said, "there was a farmer who had apple trees, but he also had an angry bull. He put up a warning sign so everybody knew. 'Dangerous bull.' But sooner or later, some putz comes along and thinks he can run faster than the bull."

As Daniel took in the implication of this in silence, he noticed a distant flash of lightning along the northern horizon. Somewhere up there, the plains of Nebraska shrugged up into the hills that were the expedition's destination. Another flash lit up the sky. Mrs. Kleinschmidt tossed her cigar butt onto the tracks and opened the door.

"Cheyenne this morning, Daniel. Then the stagecoach to Deadwood. Soon enough you find out if people think they can outrun the bull."

14

"THEY WEREN'T JOKING with the name, were they?" Segal asked as he and Daniel looked up at the steep-sided hills, covered with dead trees from a recent forest fire, which hemmed in the mining town of Deadwood on either side. Two long, narrow streets defined the town, with cabins and false-front sheds thrown up on either side, along with new clapboard buildings erected in such haste that the uncured planks were already warping. What wood wasn't standing dead in the burnt forests was stacked beside numerous building sites where men hammered and sawed at all hours, conjuring up a town rumored to house ten thousand souls out of what had been nothing more than a string of camps the year before.

The two boys stood at the entrance to the Bellevue Hotel, one of the growing city's more affordable lodgings thanks to its location in the Badlands, the district at the northern, downhill end of Main Street otherwise occupied by saloons and houses of ill repute. Beyond the Badlands, the town proper ended as the camp occupied by Chinese laborers began.

Looking up the street toward the more reputable precincts brought a view of mercantile and dry goods shops, banks, law offices, and other such businesses. Beyond them, the road bent with the valley and continued to the neighboring town of Lead, where George Hearst and half a thousand men were busily carving out the Homestake Mine to bring to the surface deposits of gold comparable only to the mines of King Solomon himself.

"Lotta workers here," Segal said. "Wonder how they feel about being organized?"

They would find out soon enough. The workers' advocates had arrived on the two o'clock stage and taken time only to set up in the Bellevue Hotel and pick up a letter for Mrs. Kleinschmidt at the post office. Once she had absorbed the information left for her by Big Jim, their work would begin.

The door behind them opened, and Mrs. Kleinschmidt entered, accompanied by Roth and Wiseman, the latter still hobbling after seventy-two hours of fitting his bulk into the tiny bench atop the stagecoach.

"Boys," Mrs. Kleinschmidt said, "time to unite the working classes."

Roth and Wiseman handed leaflets to Daniel and Segal, and the group stepped into the mud of the street. Dodging horse droppings, they made their way toward Lead. Along the way, they handed out leaflets—announcing the arrival in town of the Brotherhood of American Miners—to everybody whose muddy boots and grimy dungarees indicated membership in the laboring classes. They stopped en route at a law office, where Mrs. Kleinschmidt introduced herself to a young lawyer. They then entered the office of the *Deadwood Herald*, where Mrs. Kleinschmidt asked for the editor, one Mr. Eustace Bly.

"Mister Bly is out," said a young girl, who had been bent over a case of type. "May I take a message?"

Mrs. Kleinschmidt handed over her business card, identifying her as an agent for the Brotherhood of American Miners, and wrote the name of her Deadwood hotel on the card. "Tell him to call if he wants the most important news this town has ever seen."

The girl's eyes lit up, and she grabbed a notepad and pencil.

"You're here to organize the workers? Let us run the story, and I can guarantee you top of the front page. Seven-column headline."

"Such an enterprising girl," said Mrs. Kleinschmidt. "Boys, you could learn a lot from this one." To the girl, Mrs. Kleinschmidt said, "We're not ready for a public statement, young lady, but we will make sure to work with our friends in the press."

Before leaving the newspaper office, Mrs. Kleinschmidt bought copies of the last two editions. She handed Segal a few coins and directed him to a dry goods store to pick up a pot of glue and a pair of scissors. Daniel glanced at the headlines on the front page. A stagecoach robbery, a drunken stabbing at the Bella Union, a public health warning against the opium dens of the Chinese camp—the news from Deadwood did nothing to dispel the town's reputation.

Segal caught up with Daniel and the others a few minutes later as they continued uphill to Lead. They reached the entrance to the mine just before the day's work was done. Mrs. Kleinschmidt stationed the boys along the road, each with a stack of leaflets, and as the workers left company property, she announced the presence of the Brotherhood and recited some of the numerous slogans printed on the papers. "Workers of the world, unite! You have nothing to lose but your chains!"

It took only minutes to bring about a response from the mining company. In short order, a half dozen broad-shouldered and meaty-handed brawlers came their way, led by one particularly thick-necked individual whose unblinking gaze, from gray-green eyes flecked with yellow, marked him as the leader of the Homestake wolf pack.

The big men brushed Segal and Daniel aside without visible effort. When they raised their hands toward Wiseman and Roth, the boys stepped backward while maintaining attitudes of defiance. Mrs. Kleinschmidt stepped in front of the company thugs to announce that the representatives of the Brotherhood wished neither for violence nor surrender.

"We are not here to fight, and you are not here to fight an old woman, are you?"

The workers watched this exchange as they filed out of the mine's property. Among them was a tall, bearded, Irish-looking man whose handlebar mustache had been incorporated into a tangle of whiskers. Daniel noticed that Big Jim carried himself like a leader among the miners, even though he had only been in Deadwood a few weeks. Big Jim's gaze passed over Daniel so quickly that nobody but Daniel would have seen the glimmer of recognition in them.

Mrs. Kleinschmidt backed down the road, directing the boys away from a confrontation with the mine's muscle.

When they were out of earshot, she turned to Daniel and Segal. "The big one with the funny eyes, he's the one we want. You know what to do."

That night, Daniel lurked in the shadows beside a stack of logs down the street from the hotel where Mrs. Kleinschmidt and the boys were staying. In his hand, he held a rock the size of a goose egg. A string wrapped around the rock attached a piece of paper. Using letters cut from the newspaper and glued in place, it said, *LEAVE DEADWOOD OR ELSE.* Wiseman stood guard beside Daniel, creating a deeper darkness.

One block farther into the Badlands, Segal stood watch outside a house of ill repute, into which the man with the gray-green eyes had disappeared some time ago. As Daniel understood it, Big Jim had gotten word to Mrs. Kleinschmidt that the leader of the Homestake Mine's guards, Boone May, was known to frequent this particular establishment. The afternoon's encounter with May and his cronies had been a ruse to ensure that witnesses would see him confronting Mrs. Kleinschmidt. All they had to do now was wait for May to finish up.

Furtive steps alerted Daniel to Segal's arrival.

"He's leaving now," Segal said.

A heavy, unsteady tread caught Daniel's ears. May had been drinking. That was good. He would be slow to react.

Daniel held the rock at the ready and looked up at Mrs. Kleinschmidt's window, which May would pass in a few seconds.

"You've only got one chance," Segal whispered. "Don't miss."

Daniel let the rock fly and heard it shatter the window glass.

15

Readers tantalized by news that a workers' organizer has sought to swear a complaint against Mr. Boone May, shotgun guard for the Homestake Mine Company, will be forced to suppress their appetites for detail for at least one month, pending the unexpected illness that prevented Judge Granville G. Bennett, Jr., from hearing the complaint Wednesday last at the Deadwood Territorial Courthouse.

Vera Bly's pencil soared across the page of her notebook as she attempted to write her dispatch on the proceeding and, at the same time, look over the shoulders of the men who crowded the front rows of the courtroom.

On one side sat a squadron of men in dark suits, mostly lawyers for George Hearst's gold mine, carrying bulging Gladstone bags filled with legal documents and law books. Not all the men on the bench appeared to be lawyers. A few thick-necked specimens, obviously employed to protect the company's interests in a more direct fashion, leveled menacing glares around the room and specifically upon the complainants who had the audacity to press assault charges against the leader of their employer's Praetorian Guard.

Vera recognized a few as shotgun guards for the mining company and the stagecoach, including Boone May, whose sleepy expression belied his reputation for fast shooting. Conspicuously absent this morning was Hearst himself, which prompted no end of curiosity in Vera. Maybe he was washing his hands of May, who was rumored to have thrown a rock with a threatening message attached through the complainant's hotel window. Or more likely, Vera thought, maybe the mining magnate knew that the judge would be absent today. Had he some hand in arranging the judge's absence? Vera's father had written about Judge Bennett's ambitions to run for Congress and the likelihood that Hearst would support him in the election next year. Keeping away from inconvenient cases against the Homestake Mine could well be the price of Hearst's support.

The complainant, Mrs. Hedda Kleinschmidt of the Brotherhood of American Miners, wore an old-fashioned mourning dress with a stiff, high, black collar. She'd been less formally attired a few days before when she'd sought an audience with Vera's father. Her solitary, young lawyer looked frequently at his pocket watch throughout the wait for word on the whereabouts of Judge Bennett and alternately smiled at his client and mopped his forehead.

Vera had never seen the young lawyer before and presumed him to be a recent arrival in Deadwood. Like the representatives of the Homestake Mine, Mrs. Kleinschmidt had a retinue of protectors, although they were a posse of juveniles around Vera's age. Vera recognized them from the brief encounter at the newspaper office. Two of them matched the older guards on the other side of the room for physical presence. They lounged on the stiff-backed courtroom benches, responding to the glares of their opposite numbers with half-lidded eyes and expressions of contempt and boredom. One was a giant, his shoulders straining at the seams of his coat, the other trim but with the look of a resting panther about him. A tall, thin boy seemed to have great trouble keeping still. He frequently whispered in the ear of the fourth young man—boy, really—whose head was too small for his hat. His collar rode up on his neck. He resembled a child playing at being an adult, and yet he was taking the game very seriously indeed. It was obvious from the tall and thin young man's demeanor that whatever he was whispering to the boy was meant to be amusing, but the boy steadfastly refused to crack a smile. It looked, in fact, as if he was biting the insides of his cheeks to suppress laughter.

When the court clerk announced Judge Bennett's unexpected illness, Vera determined that she would learn more about this strange case. This might pose a challenge, as technically speaking, she was not employed as a journalist. Her attempt to insert a one-paragraph item on the arrival in town of an organizer for the Brotherhood of American Miners had been caught by her father at the last possible moment. Aghast at the danger of a confrontation with George Hearst and his armed retainers, and at the thought of his daughter pursuing a career among his own ink-stained brethren, Eustace Bly had pronounced his edict as head of the household and editor-in-chief of the largest-circulation newspaper in the Black Hills.

Vera Bly was banned forthwith from the newspaper.

Rather than spending her free afternoons in the office, she would learn to comport herself as a young lady in order to marry well, thus heading off the perils of a future of consorting with criminals, reprobates, deviants, and journalists.

In order to write her new article on the court appearance, Vera had engaged in a level of subterfuge worthy of a criminal or journalist, if not of a reprobate or deviant. That morning, she had struck a bargain with the son of a Swedish miner at the one-room school where she assisted the teacher, Miss Pringle. In exchange for twenty-five cents and a piece of pie, Henrik Larsen swallowed a spoonful of Dr. Hathaway's Digestive Ease Syrup, a concoction intended to allow the patient to expel harmful humors of the stomach. In other words, to vomit.

Henrik had promptly run from the schoolroom, leaving a noxious pool on the steps, giving Vera the opportunity to volunteer to take the boy home to his cabin, which just happened to be two miles up the valley. Two miles uphill, two miles down, and a credible hour in the cabin waiting to make sure the boy was fine before returning to the school gave Vera three and possibly four hours to watch and report on the proceedings in court. Surely when she showed him her work, her father would not only decide to run this shocking piece of information on the front page, but would see that his daughter was cut out to be a journalist.

But now she had nothing to show for her deviousness. Worse still, with a delay in the proceedings of at least one month, Vera would not be present when this case resumed. She would, instead, be far to the east in Kansas City at Mrs. Cramp's Finishing School for Girls, where she would practice the piano, paint pictures of flowers, and learn to converse in French—skills considered essential in the pursuit and capture of the son of a banker or senator. The only chance to avoid such a fate would be to get the story without waiting for the court appearance, directly from the complainants and the management of the Homestake Mine.

As soon as the postponement was announced, the Homestake guards massed around May and the company's lawyers and moved like an unstoppable phalanx across the small courtroom and out into the street, scattering all bystanders. There would be no interviews with them today. The complainants had remained seated during the departure of the Homestake team, with the exception of the youngest member of the group, who had followed the Homestake group out into the street. She watched as the lady in mourning dress, Mrs. Kleinschmidt, conferred with her twitchy, squirrel-eyed lawyer. The two menacing young men maintained their casual poses, while the gangly one, his face sporting a wispy mustache, appeared to be whispering to himself, occasionally smiling widely in admiration of some private joke.

Vera and Mrs. Kleinschmidt's eyes met, and Vera decided to introduce herself.

"Excuse me. I'm terribly sorry to interrupt. We met at the *Deadwood Herald's* office. You left a message for my father, Eustace Bly. You said you'd work with us to tell your story. I was wondering if you'd like to tell me about your complaint against Boone May. Our readers would be very interested."

"Such a confident girl you are," Mrs. Kleinschmidt said. "And so polite. A blessing it would be to have such a child."

If this woman with the old country accent was afraid of Boone May and the Homestake Mine, she kept it well hidden.

"Your complaint, ma'am? Did Mister May threaten or hurt you?"

The woman patted Vera's arm. "Aren't you kind to ask? But what Mister May did or did not do to us is unimportant. What is important is what the Homestake Mine does to its workers every day. It sends them into that death trap of a pit and pays white Americans a wage that would insult a Chinese coolie. And that is why the Brotherhood of American Miners has sent me here to organize the mine workers of Deadwood. Together, we will win better pay, better working conditions, and a better future for the children of the Dakota Territory."

A union in Deadwood. Fighting for better pay and working conditions. That would be news across the country. And Vera was the only reporter to know about it. She just needed some specifics.

"Your court case about Boone May... did he try to stop you?"

"Do rocks have wings? Do poison pen letters just write themselves?"

Vera's pencil flew. Now she would need to make her way to the Homestake Mine to ask George Hearst for an interview. She felt a weight settle into her stomach as she contemplated approaching the mine owner and feeling the cold scrutiny of his protector. She imagined herself facing the bottomless depths of those reptilian eyes.

"What rock? What letter?" she asked.

Before Mrs. Kleinschmidt could answer, the youngest and slightest of her party returned, brushing his long hair out of his eyes.

"Rifleman with a Springfield buffalo gun on a rooftop up the street. Also, they got a hay wagon with a shooter inside a block down the street."

Mrs. Kleinschmidt nodded. "Hidden in the hay, Daniel?"

"There's a hole on the side. Just big enough for a rifle barrel and a bit of light. You step out the front door, and they'll have a clear shot at you."

The fidgety boy said, "They're going to shoot us in the middle of the main street?"

"The champions of the working man can't hide in the courthouse all day," Mrs. Kleinschmidt said.

"I'll take care of it," said the boy named Daniel. "Boone May's watching from the porch in front of the saloon down the street. I'll have a talk with him."

The group walked to the entrance of the courtroom and waited as the boy named Daniel stepped into the street. Vera crept to a window, cracked it open, and poked her head out, hoping that the gunmen the boy had mentioned wouldn't mistake her for a member of the complainant party. The boy adopted a more youthful posture and pace, kicking rocks down the street and seeming to stumble over his feet like an awkward adolescent. He walked in this manner until he stood directly in front of Boone May.

The boy doffed his hat and cast his eyes downward, looking like an errand boy sent to pass on a message. Vera saw May laugh and bark out a remark, which brought dismissive laughter from his friends. They were still laughing as the boy dropped his hat. Before the hat had even reached the ground, a pair of pistols materialized, one aimed at May, the other at the man on May's right. Vera saw the boy's jaw move.

May raised his hands, prompting the others to do the same. The boy's jaw moved again, and Vera heard May shout, "McCullough! Come out of the wagon! Glass! Get down from the roof!"

A moment later, hay fell from the box of the wagon, and a man emerged, stalks stuck to his hair and clothing, a rifle in one hand. At a command from May, the man dropped his rifle and joined the group clustered in front of the saloon. The boy edged to his right and gestured up the street with one of his pistols.

"You heard me, Glass!" May shouted again. "Get down!"

Vera poked her head out the open window, craned her neck, and saw a man on the roof of Star's Mercantile, holding his rifle out to the side. He dropped the rifle to the street, then lowered himself from the roof and dropped the remaining eight feet or so. He collapsed upon landing and bellowed curses that reached Vera at the courthouse.

Walking his captives to the injured man, the boy holstered one of his pistols, bent to retrieve the man's rifle, and left the man crumpled against the side of the mercantile. With the injured man's rifle in one hand and a pistol in the other, the boy led May and his group across the street to the courthouse.

Mrs. Kleinschmidt and the others stepped out. As the young gunman covered the Homestake group with his pistol, the gangly, laughing boy patted them down and removed a small arsenal of weaponry.

Vera sneaked in behind the gathering, pencil and pad in hand.

May addressed Mrs. Kleinschmidt. "Can your pistolero shoot, or is he just a fast hand?"

Mrs. Kleinschmidt laughed. "What do they say about curiosity and cats?"

"Good one, Missus K," said the tall boy, laughing as he unloaded a pistol confiscated from one of May's men.

"You'll get your toys back, Mister May," Mrs. Kleinschmidt said. "Thieves, we aren't."

Her two physically imposing young protectors took positions in front of and behind her, and the group began down Main Street toward the Badlands, while the gangly, laughing boy carried an armful of captured weapons and the young gunman covered their departure.

The young gunman spoke again. His soft voice had traces of the East and a slightly musical lilt.

"Is there a rat catcher in this great heap of mud?" he asked. He gestured with his forehead to the crawl space of the saloon, where a rat had just emerged from its nest. With his right hand still holding a pistol covering May and the captives, he drew his other pistol with his left and fired, and the rat's lifeless carcass bounced in the dirt.

Vera assessed the boy. Barely five and a half feet tall and not a grain over 110 pounds. Not quite as young as he looked from a distance, perhaps sixteen, but with smooth cheeks and an upper lip that could allow him to pass for twelve. Pupils that seemed unnaturally large, set in eyes that never rested. It would be extremely difficult to take this boy by surprise.

She also examined his hands. She did not think she had ever seen hands so still. As she watched, in one fluid and silent movement, the boy spun his pistols and placed them inside his coat in what Vera could now see was a pair of holsters hanging just below the arms. She suddenly realized that the pistols he carried were small ones. Not the long-barreled handguns that were usually seen on the streets of Deadwood. She realized, as well, that in his constant visual assessments of the scene, the boy had noticed she was watching.

"Who are you?" she asked.

"Nobody you'd want to know."

The boy carrying the captured weapons had stopped to watch the shooting demonstration.

"You want to know who this is, Miss? We call him the Bulldog Kid."

"No, we don't," the boy said.

"On account of the deadly Webley Bulldog pistols he carries. But we could call him the Peacemaker Kid just as easy. Or the Henry Kid because you ought to see what he can do with a Henry repeating rifle."

"Put a sock in it, Segal."

"Well, you never liked Kosher Kid."

"I never asked for a name."

The taller boy, evidently named Segal, raised his voice as if to address the entire town. "You want a story for your newspaper, Miss? This kid is the fastest gun on either side of the Mississippi. Son of an old Southern gentleman, taught to fire a dueling pistol before he was six. Family went bankrupt when carpetbaggers took over their plantation, and now he works as a private security guard for the Brotherhood of American Miners. There's a trail of dead men, all shot in self-defense, who'll show you how effective he is with rifle or pistol. Or a rock."

Segal addressed the captives directly. "Today is your lucky day. The Bulldog Kid slapped leather at you, and you're going to see another sunrise."

"That's enough," the boy said. "Let's go."

The boy—or, thought Vera, the Bulldog Kid—turned and walked down the street, apparently unafraid to expose his back to his enemies. Segal winked at Vera and, as the Bulldog Kid caught up to him, placed an arm around the young gunman. Before they were out of earshot, Segal called out over his shoulder, "You tell the world, Miss, there's a new legend in town."

16

DANIEL TOOK A seat on the bench beside Segal and inspected his friend's plate.

"Should you be eating this?"

"What?"

"I think Missus Kleinschmidt would call this *trayf,* right? You shouldn't eat it."

"What do you mean? It's delicious."

"It ain't kosher, Segal."

Segal signaled to an old man stirring an enormous pot on a woodstove and pointed at Daniel. The man ladled a mass of vegetables and meat onto a plate and carried it out from the tent that served as the kitchen and plopped it in front of Daniel, causing a wave of sauce to spill onto the crude platform that served as a communal table for the boys and other customers. The number of men breaking their fast attested to the quality of the food, or perhaps to the fact that Deadwood's non-Chinese establishments adhered more faithfully to the town's Sunday-morning closing rule. Daniel inspected the plate, attempting to figure out its exact contents.

"I think we get a pass on this kind of food, Kid," Segal said.

Daniel picked up his fork and began shoveling the oddly spiced stew into his mouth.

"When the Celestials are cooking, the usual rules don't apply," Segal added. "You can't talk to them to ask what's what, and you've got no way of knowing what's on the plate. So, it ain't my fault if it's not kosher."

"Segal, there's a pigpen just the other side of that fence."

"Circumstantial evidence, Kid. They might keep pigs to take care of the garbage."

Daniel grinned, shrugged, and kept eating. Whatever it was, it was good. And he hadn't had much of a chance to relax since hitting town. Mrs. Kleinschmidt had kept him close, especially since the encounter outside the courthouse, and he was feeling restless from staring at the walls of the hotel. Segal had been free to explore, since his presence wasn't needed to protect Mrs. K.

"Good idea coming here," Daniel said. "I was getting pretty sick of the restaurant at the hotel."

"Glad you like it."

"You got a taste for this stuff? Is that what brought you to Chinatown in the first place?"

"That and her," Segal said, pointing to a girl walking past the huts, chicken coops, laundries, and pigpens of the Chinese quarter. As she neared them, Daniel got a closer look.

She was about their age, blond, wearing a patched dress. A shawl half covered her head, and she carried a bag over her shoulder. She walked with a determined stride down the middle of the lane, but Daniel could see her eyes darting cautiously side to side, as if she was trying to make sure she wasn't being followed. He could see, as well, a deep, calm intelligence in her eyes. And he noticed something else—the shiny tip of a blade sticking out from underneath her cloak. Wherever she was going, she was going there armed.

"Who is she?"

Segal reached into his jacket and took out a handbill, an advertisement for a traveling circus that had set up in Deadwood, while Mrs. Kleinschmidt was holed up awaiting her court date and holding late-night meetings with Big Jim. Daniel, who had been working on his reading since being sprung from the reformatory, puzzled through the description of the acts. She wasn't a clown or the fat lady or a tumbling midget. She didn't look like a Tommaso Largo. She could be a Lillian.

"What's a ly-can-throppy?"

"I've got no idea, Kid. But I'm going to find out soon as they open their show."

"I don't think—"

"Shh. Watch where she goes, Eagle Eyes."

Segal grabbed Daniel by the shoulder and pulled him away from his breakfast. Daniel watched as the girl tiptoed up to the back door of a shed, adjacent to a pigpen, knocked lightly, and held up a hand with a few coins in it. A Chinese man stepped forward and took the coins and handed the girl an animal carcass—it looked like a piglet—which she dropped into the bag she carried on her shoulder.

As she walked away from the shed, a stray dog ran out of an alley, nose up, sniffing the dead animal. The dog's fur stood up on its neck, and its yellowed fangs glistened with saliva, but the girl merely glanced at it and spoke a few words, and it walked away, following its nose to some other food source.

Daniel, whose attitude toward dogs was formed by his experiences with strays in the alleys of the Five Points and later by the warden's German shepherd at the reformatory, whistled in admiration. "She's got a lot of sand, whoever she is."

He kept watching as she left the last of the houses behind and entered the pine forest down the valley. She walked with the stride of one with an important appointment and spent no time searching for trail markings. This trail had become so routine, her feet knew the way on their own. "She's going to visit somebody."

"And bringing a dead pig as a little friendly gift?"

"Maybe she has a dog of her own up there."

"And she can't keep it in town?"

"She's staying in a hotel that doesn't allow pets?"

"That's good. I can talk to her about my love of man's best friend after the circus."

"Segal, I don't think you can go to the circus."

"Us, Kid. You're comin' with me."

"You know I gotta watch the street."

"Nobody can watch the street all the time. All that staring'll make you go blind."

Daniel finished his plate of stew, breaking off pieces of bread to soak up the brown sauce with its hot and smoky spices, and gestured back toward the hotel. Deadwood was wide awake now. Construction sites lay idle, and roof joists poked into the sky above the frames of new houses, stores, and saloons. For a change, no teamsters drove ox carts or wagons through the muddy streets.

But the streets were filling up with a different kind of traffic. Uphill, in the better blocks of town, men with brushed suits and polished boots accompanied wives and children to church. All manner of conveyances, from sleek, polished Rockaway carriages to rough buckboards on creaking axles, carried families to the Episcopal church, in the case of the former, or the Methodist church, in the case of the latter.

Downhill, in the Badlands, gamblers calculated the odds on a turn of the cards, while barkeeps poured gassy beer for men who had already waited too long for the taps to reopen. A hired killer could easily hide in plain sight amid these throngs, unseen by all save those with a gift for seeing. Daniel took in the scene, and his brain picked over the details that stood out. A rifle, but it was in the scabbard of an express mail rider who, from the freshness of the dust on his saddlebags and the lather on his horse, had just reached Deadwood. A shotgun propped against the sidewall of a farmer's buckboard, likely kept there in case the family had the good fortune to come across a turkey on the way home from church. Even if the farmer was in the pay of Hearst's mine, his weapon posed no danger beyond its short range.

A man lounging across the street from the hotel with an obvious bulge under his coat was the most likely candidate to be a threat, so Daniel gave him a wave and opened his own coat just enough to reveal the grip of one of his Webley Bulldogs. Daniel could tell from the movement of the man's eyes that he had heard of the kid with the small pistols and fast hands, even if nobody apart from Segal used the term "the Bulldog Kid."

He and Segal arrived back at the hotel just as the restaurant opened for the day. Daniel ran up the stairs to be ready for Mrs. Kleinschmidt to go to breakfast. Roth and Wiseman stood watch at the door to her room.

"Sorry, boys," Daniel said. "Just checking out the crowds. One man watching across the street but nothing else."

Wiseman said, "Boss is still in a meeting."

Daniel knew that Big Jim had been planning to visit the hotel in the morning to make final preparations for the afternoon's meeting with the mine workers. It was a Sunday, and the men would be free after church, and Jim had had several weeks to establish himself as a man to look up to at the mine.

Listening at the door, Daniel heard a male voice but not the low, ominous rumble of Jim's.

"Did Jim bring any other miners with him?" Daniel asked.

"Nope," Wiseman replied.

"Then who's in there?"

Wiseman looked to Roth, who said, "Is this information that'll make your gun hand move faster, Kid?"

Daniel knew an answer was not forthcoming, so he leaned against the wall and removed the circus leaflet from his pocket. He'd never seen a circus and found his mind racing in anticipation. Would there be elephants?

The sound of chairs scraping along the floor in Mrs. Kleinschmidt's room brought him back to attention.

The door opened to reveal a tall, white-bearded man in a scruffy brown tweed coat and dented derby hat, shirt collar askew and tie lopsided. Daniel thought he must be a mine worker, dressed up for the afternoon's meeting.

"This has been a very informative meeting," the man said, bowing slightly toward Mrs. Kleinschmidt. "You will have my answer within days."

The man turned and faced the hallway and Daniel. "You're the boy who bested my men outside the courthouse," he said.

"Sir?"

The man reached into a pocket and produced a gold coin, which he handed to Daniel. "I like to reward talent when I see it."

He turned, tipped his hat toward Mrs. Kleinschmidt and Big Jim, and made for the stairs leading to the back-alley exit.

Big Jim shut the door as the meeting continued.

"Me? If I owned as many mines as George Hearst, I'd buy a new hat," Segal said. "Maybe go crazy and get a whole new suit."

"That was Hearst?" Daniel asked. "What's he doing here?"

"Negotiating with Jim and Missus Kleinschmidt, I imagine."

"He's giving up already? The workers haven't gone on strike or anything."

Segal gave Daniel a pitying look. "You gotta learn to pay attention, Kid. We're running a short game here. We get the miners excited about the Brotherhood and barking like a pack of fighting dogs, ready to sink their teeth into May and the rest and go on a strike. Then, Hearst gives us money, and we hand over the ringleaders. Strike's over before it starts."

Daniel ran a hand through his long hair as he felt uncertainties and doubts. It made a certain amount of sense.

"Get outta here," Roth said. "This ain't a short game. It's a long game. You think Missus Kleinschmidt and Big Jim would go to all this work for one payoff?"

Segal wasn't buying it. "Why's Hearst paying a visit, then?"

"They want him to know we ain't busting our asses for the mine workers is all. Listen, you're right, there ain't gonna be any strike here. That much is obvious. But we're working on a much longer game. We're gonna organize the miners who work for Hearst, and we'll get Hearst to toss them a few pennies so they feel we got 'em something. Hooray for the Brotherhood, right? Workers all vote to give us a dollar a week in dues to help all the widows and orphans and cripples. Missus Kleinschmidt looks after the money and sets up a regular skim for us. We move on to Colorado or Virginia City, set the same game up there. A little bit here, a little bit there, and in a few years we're living like kings in San Francisco."

"Why's Hearst going along with it?" asked Daniel.

"Because he reads the newspapers. He knows what's going on over in Europe with the anarchists and the socialists. He knows he's gonna get some kind of Brotherhood here someday, so it's better for him when it's us."

Daniel's schooling had been brief and patchy, and reading a newspaper article about revolutions in Europe was too much work for him. But he applied what knowledge he had to Roth's argument. It had cost thirty dollars each just to travel by stage from Cheyenne. The rooms were two dollars each per night, and meals were ten dollars per week. That was a big investment for Mrs. Kleinschmidt, and it had to be eating into whatever she had left after she left the business of fencing stolen goods in New York. She'd be crazy to spend that kind of money for a one-time payoff to prevent a strike and help the mine round up troublemakers.

Daniel thought of the workers he'd seen in Deadwood—thin, ragged, bent-backed, and scarred. And he knew those with jobs were the lucky ones in a country where an army of men wandered the streets and rail lines looking for handouts, offering to clean out pigsties for meals. Mrs. Kleinschmidt and Big Jim planned to milk the suffering of these men and their families, to offer them hope of additional dollars and give them pennies instead.

The door opened again, and this time Big Jim emerged and smiled at the four youths.

"Boys, here's where you start to earn your pay. You are serious-minded young soldiers for the cause of the workers. You need to play that part so the men feel safe to come forward."

He directed his attention to Daniel and reached down to take hold of the boy's right wrist. He brought the hand up to display to the others.

"The men are talking about what happened by the courthouse. They're impressed. These magic hands of Daniel's are going to reach into the pot of gold and pull out a handful for us."

Big Jim let Daniel's hand go. He then placed a cloth worker's cap on his head and departed by the front stairs.

When Mrs. Kleinschmidt emerged from her room, she was again wearing her black mourning dress with the hoop skirt and high collar. This time, she also had a black hat with a veil that partly obscured her face. She held out an arm for Roth, who took it and helped her negotiate the descent to the street. Daniel stepped out, held the door, and searched up and down for any changes since his hasty inspection.

"To the Episcopal church, boys," she said, and the group walked up the street to the more refined section of town.

They arrived as the service was starting and walked Mrs. Kleinschmidt to a pew near the front. The boys took seats in the back. Daniel had sat through plenty of church services at the reform school, but the sermons had always been simple. Depending on the preacher, the boys had either been subjected to lectures about the Last Judgment and warnings of the fate awaiting the damned, or hopeful stories about the Prodigal Son whose return inspires his father to kill a fat calf. This preacher's sermon wandered back and forth from the Bible to America.

The preacher talked about a rich farmer in Bible times, who left his workers in charge of his spread when he went away. When he came back, the man asked the workers if they had looked after things for him. When one of the workers told him he'd taken the rich man's money and used it to make more money for him, the rich old man was happy and announced that he'd give this worker a reward. The message of the story, the preacher said, was that God wants all his children to be good workers.

After the sermon, the collection plate went around, and Mrs. Kleinschmidt placed a stack of greenbacks on it. The congregation stood for the final hymn, which Daniel recognized from the reform school as "Crown Him With Many Crowns."

"What else are they gonna crown him with?" Segal whispered as the hymn came to an end.

Mrs. Kleinschmidt shook hands with the preacher on the way out of the church. "A lovely sermon, Father, but I kept waiting for a rich man, a camel, and a needle," she said, loud enough to be heard by others in the congregation.

While the bells announced the beginning of a free afternoon for the children of the town, and the resumption of legal alcohol service, Mrs. Kleinschmidt led the group down the street. They soon left the respectable zone, passed through the Badlands and the shacks of the Chinese camp, and approached a clearing where a large stand of pines had been cut to create lumber for the growing town.

Amid the wreckage of stumps and slash was a scattering of tents and lean-tos and a few partial cabins consisting of low log walls and roofs made of canvas stretched over frames of lodgepoles. A few hollow-faced children watched them approach from the openings of their tents or played listlessly with sticks, which they used to beat a reddish mound of pine needles and sand that housed a kingdom of ants.

Smoke rose from a few fires, but Daniel could smell nothing cooking. This miserable camp was home to men and families worse off than the Chinese coolies—unemployed miners who had either lost work to injury or failed to secure jobs in the first place. Daniel knew that they slept for free under canvas, and each morning the men and boys walked through Deadwood and uphill to Lead in hopes of a day's work hauling rock or timbers. It was a rare day when more than a few found work.

Daniel looked back and saw a stream of men approaching from town, singly, in pairs, and in groups.

Big Jim, clad in the worn gabardine suit like a workingman in his Sunday best, led the ragged day laborers to greet workers from town and lead them to a firepit around which stumps and logs were arrayed in a series of circles. The seating area was half occupied, and arriving miners threaded between the legs of those already seated. Many of the men were dressed in ragged, patched, and threadbare workingman's clothing, in many cases hanging loose on wasting bodies. Among the crowd were men carrying crutches or exhibiting angry red burn marks on their faces. Others had the red faces of anger. Some wore the heavy blue overalls of working miners. Still others were dressed like Big Jim in the churchgoing outfits of men who toil in the pit six days a week, then give thanks on the seventh for their meager pay.

Daniel scanned their waists and pockets for hidden weapons. He searched their faces for the eyes of assassins and watched their hands for movement. Big Jim slapped backs and shook hands with men from both groups and introduced the men to Mrs. Kleinschmidt. He directed Daniel and the boys to benches on opposite sides of the seating area, where they would be able to keep watch, and led Mrs. Kleinschmidt to a space beside the firepit. He cleared his throat and said, "Brothers, thank you for coming today."

"Where else we gonna go?" asked a voice from the back, to a smattering of laughter.

"Well, I appreciate you giving over your Sunday afternoon to this
meeting. To those of you who don't know me, I'm Jim McGuire, and
I'm a workingman like you. I'm a pick-and-shovel man down on level
three in the pit, breaking my back for two dollars a day."

"That's more than we get!" shouted one of the ragged men from
the camp.

"We'll get to that, don't worry. Brothers, I know what it's like not to
have work. Like a lot of you, I lost wages when the Panic hit in '73, and
I never got them back."

A few men in front applauded, and one shouted, "Me neither, Jim."
The men who had laughed earlier now nodded in solemn agreement.

"I never had a lot of schooling, but every day I have learned a lesson
about how this world works. That is, them as have, gets, and them as
don't have, give. What I have seen, whether pounding spikes on the
Union Pacific or sweating blood in the ironworks in Pittsburgh, is that
everything in America is owned by somebody with a lot more money and
power than you and me. They squeeze the little man out and leave him
fighting for scraps at the bottom. That's how I felt when I met this lady
here, Missus Hedda Kleinschmidt. Talking to her has got me thinking
about the power of brotherhood."

"You talking about a strike, Jim?" a man shouted. "Hearst has the
money to break a strike."

Big Jim held his hands out to ask for quiet. "That's right, brothers.
Hearst has plenty of money. And because of that money, when his workers
organize into a brotherhood, he can hire unemployed men like the men
in this camp to take their place. That's why we're holding this meeting
here. That's why we're bringing together the men who have jobs and
the men who don't have jobs. The big bosses want you to be on opposite
sides, so they can play you against each other. Men with work won't fight
for more money and better conditions if they know there are men with
no work who'll take their place without a raise. But what if you were all
together on the same side?"

A ragged man, clearly one of the unemployed workers, stood up. "Are you asking us to sit on our hands if Hearst offers us work? I've got a family to feed, and I'm not going to let them starve just to help men who aren't grateful with what they've got."

A murmur arose among the other unemployed men. Daniel now saw that the crowd was evenly divided and had sorted itself in two. On one side were the men in rags. On the other were the men in work clothes, dirty but whole. On one side, clothes hung off shoulders and fluttered like clothing on a line. On the other side, muscles hardened by pounding rock showed through sleeves.

Mrs. Kleinschmidt stood up. "No, he is not asking you to sit on your hands. Mister McGuire is asking you to realize you are on the same side. And he is asking you to help one another. We propose that the men with work pool their money now and we create a strike fund that will help both men with and without jobs to survive a strike. This way, the unemployed men will have no excuse to break the strike when it begins."

Silence greeted her proposal. Daniel saw the questioning faces on both sides of the divide as men figured in their heads how much money they could afford to pool into a strike fund and how much would be needed to keep a strike from breaking.

"I know it's a lot to ask," Mrs. Kleinschmidt continued, "but it's the only way the workers of Deadwood will be able to take on the capitalists."

One of the ragged men stood up. "Brothers, I tell you, this makes sense. I worked in George Hearst's mine, and I've seen that he doesn't give a tinker's damn for the lives of his men. I've seen men maimed and killed by cave-ins and explosions. I've seen so-called mine engineers skimp on timber supports in order to save George Hearst a few dollars, and I have seen the price paid in lost lives. I was lucky to get out of that mine alive the day the timbers collapsed around me. Now, I want to work again if my back ever lets me, but I don't want to return to that kind of death trap. So, those of us without work have every reason to support a strike by those who do have jobs."

Men on both sides of the divide applauded.

Mrs. Kleinschmidt joined in the applause. "That's the spirit. But

I need to warn you, this is a long battle. We cannot just start a strike and force George Hearst to his knees. We need to sign up as many of the mine workers as we can and set up a chapter of the Brotherhood of American Miners. We need to establish weekly dues and build a strike fund and a fund to pay for injured workers and the widows and children of men killed in the mine. All of this will take time, but when we have this in place, we will be strong enough to fight George Hearst, and we will have proven our worth to all of the workers in Deadwood, who will rush to support us."

Subdued cheers followed. The men had not counted on this being such a lengthy process.

Big Jim said, "You think Rome was built in a day? You've been slaves your whole lives. We're telling you it's going to take some work and planning to win your freedom. What did you think?"

This time, the cheers were louder. Men stood and applauded. However, one man wasn't about to give up. He took off his crushed hat and brushed his long, greasy hair from his eyes and called out to the crowd, "What about Boone May and his shotgun guards?"

"What about them?" Jim asked.

Jim's chest looked ready to burst through the buttons of his coat. His eyes glowed with a dangerous fire as he looked at the lank-haired man, who opened his mouth to speak again but seemed to think better of it.

Mrs. Kleinschmidt smiled sweetly at the workers. "I won't take up any more of your time with my little thoughts. I hope you agree to work with the Brotherhood, but this is for the workers of Deadwood to decide. I just have to tell you that it breaks my heart to see the suffering of the little children. I hope you don't mind, but I've brought a little something that might put a smile on the faces of the little angels. I'll be over by that tent, and if any of the children want to come along, they can have a treat."

She led Wiseman and Roth to a tent where a colored woman and two boys had recently arrived carrying baskets covered with cloth. Mrs. Kleinschmidt lifted the cloths and opened the cheesecloth inside, and at the smell of cornbread, children, attracted like ants to honey, came running from all directions.

The injured worker who had supported Big Jim proposed a round of applause for Mrs. Kleinschmidt, and when it died away, Jim's booming voice sounded out again.

"Look at how happy they are to have a piece of cornbread. A piece of cornbread. That ought to make you angry. It makes me angry. A poor child shouldn't be so hungry that a piece of cornbread makes a day seem like Christmas. Is it right that children in this great nation should feel that kind of hunger? How many of you fought to keep this country together? How many of you saw your friends blown to pieces so that bankers and railroad men could get rich off of war profits? Is this the America you fought for?"

The crowd was mesmerized now. Big Jim was feeding their anger and feeding off it himself. Daniel had never heard him speak with such fire.

"That lady there, she's giving us a chance to work for a better country for every miner and mill hand in America. Somebody asked, 'what about Boone May and his shotgun guards?' Well, there's a handful of them, and there are thousands of workingmen in these hills. It's time to show George Hearst and his goons who's stronger."

The crowd broke out in applause that grew louder when Big Jim signaled to a pair of workers who approached the crowd carrying jugs.

"Did you fellows think we only brought presents for the little ones? Get your mugs, and let's toast the future of the Homestake Mine and the men who work it."

17

THE RED DEVILS came out of the earth after the hounds took
off in pursuit of the wolves' scent. The first one stood up in front
of Josiah and aimed a cavalryman's Springfield carbine at him.
Riders galloped his way from either side, weapons at the ready. Escape
was impossible, even if Josiah managed to draw his Colt and shoot the
standing gunman. The Indian ponies were obviously faster than his horse,
worn to the bone from the Dakota plains with their meager pastures.
The Indians would run Josiah down in minutes.

He had refused to give up the trail of the wolf bitch and her litter and
had eventually returned to the site where he'd crossed paths with the
circus wagons. Following the circus had brought him to a place where
the scent of the wolves intersected with that of foreigners, then to a
rendezvous between the wagons and three unshod horses.

Josiah looked at the two riders, who now had him boxed in on the right
and left, and to the man on foot, whose pony was no doubt hidden on the
far side of a hill, and realized the Indians he faced were the same who had
met the circus. The man on the ground gestured for Josiah to place his
hands in the air, while his partners swooped in and drew the Sharps buffalo
gun from Josiah's rifle scabbard and slipped the Colt out of his holster.

With Josiah disarmed, the Indians were drawn to his packhorse.

They untied the pack boxes and the bundle of pelts and rummaged through them.

"I have no whiskey if that's what you're after, but I have a few bags of beans and a sack of flour if you're hungry."

They slit the bag of beans and dumped the flour on the ground.

The oldest in the group, the apparent leader, who had sprung the ambush by appearing as if conjured by a demon, lifted the lid on the box that contained Josiah's traps. A babel of grunts and bloodthirsty cries followed as he lifted traps into the air and showed them to his followers. Then he untied the binding and unrolled the wolf pelts and held one up to its full length, the thick, shiny hide of a powerfully built male that had not yet shed its winter coat when Josiah killed it along with its mate and spawn. The Indian rolled up the hides and returned them to the back of the packhorse, placed the traps in the pack box, and secured the box in its place.

The youngest Indian, the one who had disarmed Josiah, now said, "Off horse."

He punctuated his command by gesturing with the barrel of Josiah's Sharps, which at this range would tear a hole in his chest big enough for a cannonball.

"We take your horses today," the Indian continued. "You come back, we take your life."

Josiah dismounted. A slight gust of prairie wind brought with it the barking of his hounds, still in pursuit of the wolves' scent. The oldest Indian jumped onto Josiah's horse and grasped the reins of the packhorse, and the three Indians rode off in a whirlwind of dust and sweat. Josiah calculated the hours it would take him on foot to reach the nearest habitations. It would take three days to walk to one of the ranches near Belle Fourche.

He had taken long and arduous walks before and was prepared for another. With the money he had hidden in his sock, he would be able to acquire a horse at Belle Fourche. That would place him a day's ride from Deadwood and the circus folk who had sheltered the wolves and loosed these devils on him.

Three days on foot and one on horseback wasn't too long to travel for justice.

18

ANXIETY CLOUDED LILY'S mind and muddled the performance of her backstage duties as she waited to take the stage. She forgot to put Uncle Stanislas's magic panel box in the correct place, forcing him to improvise some close-up magic with coins and hand-kerchiefs while she wheeled it into its spot. And she mistakenly filled Mr. Szabo's fire bucket with actual water, instead of confetti, prior to his exploding-cigar routine. That turned out to be a happy accident, as many in the audience had seen confetti-filled fire buckets used in other clown acts. When Mr. Szabo stood shocked with water and greasepaint dripping down his face, it brought the house down.

Lily registered her mistake and the audience reaction, but her thoughts quickly passed over it. Try as she might, Lily could not stop thinking that the wolfer was somewhere out there, stalking the wolf, and perhaps her as well.

Part of her had expected the wolfer to follow the circus ever since the encounter on the Dakota plains. But with each day, as she settled into the routine of practicing her act, leaving leaflets in the town and secretly feeding the wolves in their hidden canyon, she had managed to set thoughts of the killer and his hateful hounds aside. Such thoughts now burned through her like a prairie fire.

Working the ticket booth for the evening's performance, talk about the wolfer's close call from a band of scalp-collecting savages had been on the lips of every citizen in line. Some speculated that this was the beginning of another round of the Indian Wars, perhaps the vanguard of Sitting Bull's force returned from their winter's rest in Canada. Others pointed out that the victim was only a single wolf trapper who had been robbed of his belongings, not killed.

"Wolfers are a brutish bunch," one man said, reassuring his worried wife. "No doubt this was some private enmity."

A private enmity indeed. When her spell in the ticket booth was over and she took her place backstage, Lily's dogs sensed her emotions. Lancelot and Galahad stood beside her like a pair of sentinels with muscles coiled, ready to strike. Sparky, the little Chihuahua, puffed out his chest and paced in front of her, confronting all the hands and performers backstage with his bulbous eyes and daring them to fight. Lily realized it was time to help Madame Mystere into her costume and lead her to the stage to tell the audience's fortune.

Madame Mystere, surprisingly quiet for a woman of her bulk, was already there.

"You were preoccupied. I asked Tommaso to button me up."

"Sorry, Madame. I was just going over the routine with—"

Madame Mystere dismissed the attempted lie with an imperious wave. "You were thinking of a man. A mysterious figure. Perhaps one who represents an element of danger. I see a weapon. A rifle? Or perhaps a pistol. Yes. And your fate will be linked with his."

Lily felt a wave of nausea break over her. She wasn't convinced that Madame Mystere could see the future, but there was no denying her intuition. She must have sensed out on the plains that the wolfer had marked Lily as his enemy. The narrow valley of Deadwood Creek was not big enough for the two to coexist in peace. Nor were the vast plains of the West.

"Please, Madame, there must be some way to solve this."

"Solve? There is no solution to being in love, my dear."

Lily's face froze in place, her mouth agape. "In love, Madame?"

"Yes, my dear. I have seen these young cowboys and express riders, with their leather chaps and gun belts and legs like marble sculptures from gripping the flanks of a horse all day. A well-brought-up girl like you, growing up with no boys your own age, why it's only natural that one of these saddle tramps would catch your eye. I was like you at one time, drawn to every young cavalier who appeared mad, bad, and dangerous to know. But do not fear, Lily. It will pass."

With that, Madame Mystere cocked her head to listen to the final words of Uncle Stanislas's introduction, then stepped through the parted curtain to the applause of an audience still lapping up a long-awaited feast of entertainment.

On the far side of the tent, behind the backs of the audience, Tommaso Largo climbed silently to his perch in order to begin by flying dramatically over the crowd as soon as Madame Mystere was finished. Lily watched him climb and felt her spirits perk up at the sight of the brave little man. If he could set aside his fear of dying night after night to perform his feats of balance high above the ground, surely she could push the wolfer from her mind long enough to go through her routine with her canine friends.

With a renewed sense of purpose, Lily opened her mind to let her thoughts mingle with those of Galahad, Lancelot, and Sparky. For the remaining minutes, she shared their perceptions of the sounds and scents in the big tent. She felt again the boundless excitement of little Sparky, the loyalty of Galahad, the love of Lancelot. These canine feelings washed over her and left her renewed and hopeful, so that when Mr. Szabo crashed the cymbals to mark the successful conclusion of Tommaso's act, she was able to stride confidently into the ring.

Lily worked the dogs through several new opening routines. First, she sawed out a few tunes on the fiddle and led the dogs through a round of social dances—a waltz and a schottische. She ended with a rousing square dance. Then she changed the tune to "Hail to the Chief," while Mr. Szabo and Tommaso moved a pair of flag-draped podiums into place and brought out the appropriate costumes, and Galahad and Lancelot took turns barking at one another in imitation of the Lincoln-Douglas debates—Lancelot adorable in his stovepipe hat. As the applause for the debate faded and the podiums were moved backstage, she laid out a baseball diamond in the ring and positioned Galahad and Lancelot in the outfield and little Sparky behind home plate. Then she called out for volunteers. The word was barely out of her mouth when a tall, fidgety young man was on his feet. Enthusiastic volunteers were often trouble, but this young man didn't appear drunk, and the dogs, who normally sensed trouble, gave her no warnings. She gestured him forward.

"Welcome to Stanislas's Circus of Wonders. What's your name, sir?"

"Segal. Myron Segal."

He stepped forward with none of the hesitation or awkwardness volunteers usually exhibited. Without being told, he turned and cheated his body positioning so that he appeared both to face the audience and Lily. His arms rested comfortably at his sides, with no nervous groin-covering or hand-hiding. A frisson of fear ran through Lily. Had she chosen a would-be actor who would attempt to commandeer her performance?

"Thank you for helping, Mister Segal."

"Forget about it. My mother always dreamed I'd run away and join the circus."

He could project, no doubt about it. And he got a laugh.

"And where are you from, Mister Segal?"

"Odessa originally, but I grew up in New York."

"Well, Mister Segal, you speak like a native-born New Yorker."

"Thanks. It wasn't easy, I tell you. Especially growing up with my mother. I think I was ten years old by the time I learned that 'you're still here?' doesn't mean the same thing as 'good morning.'"

Another round of laughter.

"Do you like sports, Mister Segal?"

"You bet. Back in the old country, my family never missed a game of kickball. They had to be there. They were the ball."

Yet another outburst of laughter. His delivery was good. He had a way of setting up a joke and then taking it in an unexpected direction. His humor had an edge to it. He was mocking himself but in a way that, if you were in on the joke, mocked other people more. It was the opposite of the clown humor of Mr. Szabo. Segal wasn't invoking pathos. There was none of the gentleness that Mr. Szabo's pratfalls and pranks had at their core. Segal's jokes felt like an American kind of humor, a big-city humor, something that grew out of the streets of New York and Philadelphia and Chicago. Still, Lily had to nip this in the bud. She placed a hand on the young man's shoulder and leaned him forward so she could whisper in his ear.

"This is my act, Mister Segal. Don't make me regret picking you."

He turned a shade of red and cast his eyes downward.

"As I was saying, Mister Segal, do you like baseball?"

He nodded and then stammered out a "Yes."

"Very well. We're going to play a game here, Mister Segal. Lancelot and Galahad are playing in the field. Sparky here is doing double duty as the catcher and the umpire. You're the pitcher, and I'm the batter. When we get started, you'll pitch the ball to me, not too hard, and I'll see if I can get a hit. How does that sound?"

"Good."

She handed Segal the ball—a soft ball made out of rags with a sewn-on leather cover—and took her place at home plate. As she stood at home plate, she noticed movement in the audience. She first thought that a disappointed audience member was leaving early, something that rarely happened. Had Segal affected the performance that much with his jokes? But then she realized it wasn't a departure that was causing the disturbance. It was an arrival. Segal's first pitch came while she was still looking at the movement in the darkened back of the stands. Sparky jumped in the air and caught the soft ball in his tiny jaws, jolting Lily out of her distraction.

The little dog set the ball down and barked once, a sharp, short bark.

"Oh. I forgot to mention. Sparky will call balls and strikes. That was a ball."

A scattering of laughter welcomed this explanation, though usually it brought much more laughter. Lily's timing was off.

"Sparky, why don't you demonstrate what you say if the pitch is a strike?"

Sparky let out a longer, higher-pitched, more sustained bark, then walked to the pitcher's mound to deliver the ball. While the Chihuahua trotted back to home plate, Lily glanced at the movement in the stands and, for the first time, caught a glimpse of the late arrival. It was the wolfer. She imagined she saw his eyes radiate hatred from across the tent.

The ball passed in front of her.

Sparky jumped again, caught it, and this time barked out the longer, high-pitched call for "Strike!"

Galahad and Lancelot flexed their muscles into attention, sensing the need to defend Lily, aware that something had gone wrong.

Lily looked at Myron Segal, smiled nervously in an attempt to reassure him, and gave the bat another practice swing. She stepped back from the batter's box, closed her eyes, and concentrated on calming thoughts to send to the dogs. She didn't want them feeling her fear. And she didn't want them feeling the anger now flooding her breast. The deep wells of rage in her heart came as a surprise to Lily, who could not erase the image of the mother wolf with her foot caught in the cruel jaws of the trap. If she accidentally communicated that feeling to Galahad and Lancelot, they would tear the wolfer to pieces. Satisfied that she had calmed herself, she resumed her position at home plate, but as the pitcher prepared to throw the ball, a movement in the audience caught Lily's eye, and she turned to see the wolfer stand up on his bench in the back row, feigning the limbering stretch of one who had been seated throughout a long performance.

Again, the ball sailed past Lily.

Again, Sparky caught it and called it a strike.

Mr. Segal looked at Lily with lines of concern forming on his youthful face. Lily opened her mouth to speak, but nothing would come out. Sparky began to bark but not the practiced "ball" and "strike" barks. Galahad whimpered in fear, in sympathy with the fear he felt from Lily, not knowing Lily was afraid of her own emotions. A low growl rumbled from the back of Lancelot's throat. The crowd's murmurs reached Lily's ears, but when she tried to form words, the image of the wolfer and his angry hounds came to her mind. He was a killer, and Lily realized she could be one as well.

In the wings, Lily saw Uncle Stanislas and Mr. Szabo frowning, worried. This wasn't the great finale she was supposed to deliver. Lily looked toward the young man and nodded her head. She was ready for one last pitch.

This time, as the young man wound up for the pitch, Lily heard a whistling from the back benches, followed by the familiar hate-filled sound of the wolfer's hounds calling for blood—that of her dogs or the wolves or her own. Instinctively, she turned to face the threat, wielding the baseball bat as a weapon, just as the ball sailed past her. In the outfield, Lancelot and Galahad bared their fangs and faced the wolfer.

The first scattered boos emerged from the crowd. Whatever her act was supposed to be, it didn't look like much of anything to the paying customers.

"Strike three!" called a rough voice. "She's out."

The young man turned to the crowd. "I think that's two strikes and two balls."

Sparky, who had failed to catch the ball because of Lily's strange behavior, ran to retrieve it, delivered it back to the young man, and uttered the long, higher-pitched bark that meant "Strike."

Another audience member cried out. "Listen to the umpire! She's out!"

As Lily struggled to free herself from this spell of fury and terror, the young man did something unexpected. He stepped toward Lily, put one hand on her temple, and snapped the fingers of his other, exclaiming, "Pinch hitter!" He winked at her, then he turned to the audience.

"Ladies and gentlemen, I suppose I should explain myself. I am a mesmerist. I practice the ancient arts of mind control. Earlier this evening, I met Lillian before the performance and placed her under my power. That's why she picked me to volunteer and why she's behaved so strangely tonight. I've seen her act in Dodge City and Abilene and, believe me, she never lets a pitch get past her. 'Pinch hitter' is the magic phrase that releases her from her mesmeric spell. Isn't that right, Lillian?"

He gave Lily an imploring look, urging her to run with his cover story.

"Well, I remember meeting you earlier and, yes, you did say something about being a mesmerist. Did you just mesmerize me?"

"You don't remember me pitching you the ball four times? And you let all of the pitches go by?"

"I did that?"

The young man turned to the audience and rolled his eyes. "Women. And they say we're forgetful. Am I right?"

The men in the crowd laughed, as did a few wives who had had to find their husbands' ties for them earlier that day.

Young Mr. Segal stepped toward Lily and announced to the crowd, "Now, I'm going to examine my subject to ensure that she has fully emerged from her trance. This is a process that requires a careful observation of the pupils."

He leaned forward with his nose inches from Lily's and tilted his head so that his lips were hidden from the audience and his head blocked the view of her face.

"What's the problem?" he whispered.

"A man. A very bad man. In the audience."

"Big guy in the back? Came in during your act?"

She nodded. "I can't talk to my dogs when he's here."

"Then let me take care of everything."

At that, Segal smiled at Lily, then turned and addressed the crowd.

"Ladies and gentlemen, while we're waiting for Lillian to completely recover from my mesmeric spell, I would like to introduce you to my good friend, the Bulldog Kid." Segal pointed to a thin youth in the front row, who began to shake his head and mouth words of resistance. "You may know the Bulldog Kid from his amazing feats of marksmanship at Wild West shows and Chautauquas from Virginia to Montreal. Bulldog and I recently set off for California to launch our own show in the Golden State and, on a whim, we made a detour to your fine community so we could see what the fuss was all about. Now, surprisingly, for the fastest gun on either side of the Mississippi, Bulldog is shy. But I am certain we could entice him to provide us with a demonstration of his shooting prowess if we all put our hands together."

Segal began to clap, slowly and gently, and increased both the force and rate of his applause as audience members joined in. The thin youth, one eye nearly obscured by a loose strand of his long brown hair, his wrists poking out from the cuffs of a worn coat he had outgrown, took the stage.

In her years with the circus, Lily had heard a great many discussions of other acts on the circuit. Trick shooters were not uncommon, and in fact Uncle Stanislas had proposed prior to the trip west that a shooter would be a good addition to the show. But she had never heard of a skinny, young fast-gun artist known as the Bulldog Kid, nor a mesmerist named Segal.

Lily could see Uncle Stanislas watching the two young imposters. He took a step out when the Bulldog Kid began to ascend the stage, then appeared to change his mind. He stopped and turned to restrain Mr. Szabo from entering the ring. Apparently, his businessman's instinct to end this unexpected and unrehearsed interruption lost out to his showman's desire to see magic in the moment.

"Kid, show 'em the Bulldogs," Segal said.

The thin youth glared at Segal and reddened, either in anger or embarrassment or both.

"What? Are you waiting to be mesmerized?"

A gasp arose from the audience when they realized the Bulldog Kid now sported a short snub-nose revolver in each hand, though none had seen the hands reach into holsters or pockets. At the same moment, Segal produced a deck of cards from his inside coat pocket.

"Now, ladies and gentlemen, I am going to give you just the briefest indication of the remarkable shooting talents of the Bulldog Kid."

Riffling through the deck with the deftness of a card shark, he produced a pair of face cards and flourished them to the audience. He handed the cards to Lily. Then he returned to the side of the Bulldog Kid, asked his friend to follow him, and led the young gunman to a place on the back bench beside the wolfer.

"In a moment, ladies and gentlemen, I will return to the middle of the ring to provide the Bulldog Kid with a target. Don't worry, we have not recruited the lovely and talented Miss Lillian to undertake this hazardous task."

From the distance, Lily could see Segal and the Bulldog Kid engage in a short stare-down, after which the tall youth stepped to his left and placed his lips next to the ear of the wolfer, still standing in the back row. The wolfer turned quickly to look at Segal and the young gunman. But any confrontation was prevented when Segal turned and ran back to the ring.

"I gotta tell you, ladies and gentlemen, I've been trying to teach Bulldog to play poker, and it's been kind of like trying to teach a pig to sing. It wastes your time, and it annoys the pig. It was enough of a challenge just teaching him to identify the different kinds of cards."

At this, he produced the deck from which he had removed the two cards he'd handed to Lily. He quickly pulled the other ten face cards from the deck and held them up, fanned out, toward the audience with one hand. With the other, he reached for the two cards Lily held.

"Those of you seated in the front row will see that Lillian here was holding the two one-eyed jacks. And I am now going to shuffle them in with the remaining face cards to create a deck of twelve cards—kings, queens, and jacks. Lillian, if you would like to place these twelve cards in any assortment you would like, facing up on the ground here in the ring, that would be most appreciated. I will block the Bulldog Kid's view of the cards. He will have no way of knowing where the various kings, queens, and jacks have been placed."

Lily was becoming intrigued by the impromptu performance and could see that the audience's attention was riveted. One way or another, they were in for something unexpected. Either they'd see a great feat of marksmanship, or a ridiculous fraud, which in its own way they might find even more entertaining.

Segal removed his coat and held it out like a cape and directed Lily to lay out the cards in the area below and behind it, where the trick shooter would be unable to see them. When Lily finished, Segal directed her to move to the side. He asked audience members seated directly under the path a bullet would take to move to either side.

"On the count of three, I am going to move out of the way, so that the Bulldog Kid can see these cards. He will then shoot the two one-eyed jacks, but only the one-eyed jacks, and he will do so immediately after I move. Audience, are you ready? Bulldog, are you?"

The Bulldog Kid, a revolver in each hand, let out a sigh that was audible throughout the tent, otherwise quiet as a tomb. Segal stepped aside, and immediately a pair of gunshots echoed through the tent, prompting a chorus of gasps and several shrieks. With a cloud of gun smoke drifting through the air of the tent, Segal bent and picked up two cards. He handed them to an audience member in the front row, then bent and picked up the remaining cards.

"Can you tell the audience which cards the Bulldog Kid hit?"

The audience member stood, held out the cards, and said, "The jack of hearts and the jack of spades."

"And those are the one-eyed jacks?"

"Guess so."

Segal turned to the audience, lifted the cards aloft so all could see the hole driven through the face in each, then directed his right hand toward the marksman and announced, "Ladies and gentlemen, I give you the one and only Bulldog Kid."

When the applause died down, he stared pointedly at the wolfer and said, "I tell you folks, I'm glad he's my friend. I wouldn't want to be his enemy. Or the enemy of a friend of his."

The wolfer glared at Segal and Lily and crept out of the tent. Lily heard the barking of his hounds recede into the distance. She looked to the side of the tent, saw Uncle Stanislas beaming, looked at the smiling and astonished faces in the audience, and mouthed her thanks to Segal and his dangerous friend. Then she publicly thanked the great mesmerist, Myron Segal, and his colleague, the Bulldog Kid, opened her mind to her dogs, and closed the show with a well-executed round of canine baseball.

She still had an enemy in Deadwood, but she had made a friend. Two of them. And Deadwood seemed to be a place where you needed friends.

19

THE CHALLENGE, AS it had always been, was getting the weight down while making the steam wagon powerful enough to carry guards and gold and durable enough to survive hundreds of miles of rough travel. Lincoln looked again at the plans Mr. McTaggart had treasured since seeing his first steam wagon up in Canada.

"You're lookin' at the future here, lad," the old mechanic had said the first time he unrolled them.

The simple steam engine in its original form, demonstrated years before at a fair in Quebec, was easy to maintain but inefficient. With each injection of steam, the cylinder heated up, and with each exhaust cycle, it cooled down. As a result, too much of the potential energy in each chunk of coal ended up being wasted, heating up steam instead of turning the drive shaft.

Mr. McTaggart had stolen hours here and there for years to adapt a compound steam engine for use in a self-propelled wagon. The compound engine's multiple cylinders were designed to operate at multiple temperatures, so that the still-hot exhaust that was vented from the main cylinder powered the next cylinder. It was a more complicated design, and more work to keep it tuned up, but because it was more efficient, it allowed for a smaller boiler and firebox.

Saving weight was vital if the steam engine was to be capable of traversing the steep hills between Deadwood and Cheyenne. It became even more necessary because of Mr. Hearst's top design priority—that the steam wagon be fully enclosed and bulletproof.

The additional weight resulting from the steel shell covering the driver had required extra strengthening in the frame, which in turn made the wagon heavier and demanded still more power. Mr. McTaggart had also modified the original design to allow a feature that hadn't been present during the demonstration he'd witnessed a few years after the war—brakes.

The weight of the overpowered, bulletproof wagon meant that the brakes were likely to burn out between Deadwood and Cheyenne, possibly the first time the operator pointed the bow of the land ship downhill. All that weight also meant the wagon would bog down in the first patch of mud it had to cross. Lincoln knew how Deadwood's Black Hills soil became sticky as a mustard poultice after the spring melt or a summer storm.

It was Lincoln who had solved this dilemma.

He had watched workers maneuver a heavy drill into place in the mine by placing logs in front of it and rolling it forward, then, after it had passed over them, placing the logs into position again. The workers were making a road for the drill as they moved it.

A vision had come to Lincoln while watching the men—a steam wagon that made its own road as it moved. He ran to the workshop and sketched out an image of a continuous loop of steel cleats running on a series of wheels. As the wheels turned, the cleats would be driven backward and would push the wagon forward. The numbers swirled in his head, and he saw how this continuous steel loop would allow the weight of the steam wagon to rest on a much larger surface area. Instead of sinking into the mud or sand, the heavy wagon would ride along on the surface, just as the trappers who headed into the mountains in winter stayed above the snow by strapping wide wood-and-rawhide platforms to their boots.

As he worked through his idea with Mr. McTaggart, Lincoln showed him how the steel cleats would also solve the problem of burnt-out brakes.

A steel wagon running on a continuous loop of cleats would break its own downward momentum instead of accelerating like a wagon with free-rolling wheels.

But Lincoln's innovation brought its own challenges.

The loop of steel and series of drive wheels that propelled it made the steam wagon even heavier. More weight demanded greater power. A larger steam engine. A bigger pile of coal. A bigger supply of water to turn to steam. He and Mr. McTaggart had brought the weight down by ordering steel components from a mill in Pittsburgh, where a new kind of furnace made steel lighter and stronger. But that only went so far.

Lincoln looked at the plans and looked at the wagon he and Mr. McTaggart had built and let his eyes go blurry and his thoughts go hazy. The steel structure broke up into little pieces in his head and turned into swirling lines and angles, numbers and ratios and patterns of curves and colors. He visualized the strain on the steel beams in the frame in flashes of red. He saw the wagon in movement, saw the lines of force pushing or pulling at every rivet and weld. He saw the power locked into the pile of hard coal, dug out of a pit in Wyoming Territory and hauled by horse-drawn wagons, and his mind turned that power into heat and smoke at a god-awful pace.

There was only so much power locked in a ton of coal, and it didn't seem like it was going to be enough.

"I don't mean no disrespect… any disrespect… but this isn't hauling any gold to Cheyenne," he said.

"Aye. Burns too much coal, doesn't she?"

"Because it weighs too much. 'Cause of all that steel."

"Can we tune her up? Make her run more efficiently?"

"Don't think we can. I think we need a different kind of engine. One that burns kerosene, so you can get more power with less weight."

Lincoln and Mr. McTaggart had had this discussion before. Mr. McTaggart had been curious about Lincoln's drawings for a new kind of engine, one in which burning fuel in a cylinder inside the engine moved the drive shaft directly instead of heating water for steam to turn the shaft. And he'd encouraged Lincoln to work, in his free time, with kerosene to see if there might be a way to use the liquid fuel as a lighter, purer alternative to heavy, dirty coal.

"We've got coal just across the line in the Wyoming Territory, lad, but kerosene has to be hauled all the way from Pennsylvania. We've got to find a way to work with what the Lord gave us."

Mr. McTaggart produced a thin knife and cleaned out his pipe. Lincoln knew it was the same as the young apprentice letting his eyes go all hazy to bring the numbers to life.

"What if we build a proper road?" Mr. McTaggart asked. "With a solid surface? And we blast away the steepest climbs?"

Lincoln knew Mr. McTaggart was getting desperate. Watching the blasting crews in the mine to get a sense of the numbers and lines all locked up in a stick of dynamite, Lincoln could look at a hill or a mountain and see where the sticks would have to go and how many it would take to blast all that rock and dirt into a loose pile. And he knew—and he knew that Mr. McTaggart knew—that even Mr. Hearst and the Homestake Mine Company couldn't afford all the dynamite it would take to make a smooth road all the way to Cheyenne.

"Take years to make a road like that, Mister McTaggart. What's Mister Hearst gonna pay the men who build that road and dig out all the coal to run this steam wagon? I'll eat my hat and call it cornbread if that's not a whole lot more than all the stagecoach robbers this side of the Mississippi steal."

Mr. McTaggart sighed and scratched his head. "Aye. You're right on that, I'm afraid."

"Reckon Mister Hearst will believe that this just can't be done?"

"No, Lincoln, I don't think Mister Hearst is a man who takes kindly to words like 'can't.'"

Lincoln sighed and slipped on his cap, stuffing rebellious shoots of hair underneath it. He removed his goggles from his pocket and placed them over his eyes and lay on the wheeled board he used for inspecting the undercarriage of the steam wagon. There was nothing to do but keep looking for something that could lead to a breakthrough.

He then rolled from one end of the wagon to the other, cleaning joints and lubricating couplings as he went. As his eyes moved along the undercarriage of the wagon, they removed struts, thinned columns, reconfigured the arrangement of the structural skeleton. And every time he made these changes in his mind, he saw the wagon collapsing under the weight of the engine, coal, water, and steel shell. This steam wagon was already as strong and light as it could be.

The day was getting late, and Mr. McTaggart would soon send Lincoln home to his mama. Maybe in the night, some idea would break through like a new seedling.

The steam wagon worked, there was no disputing that. He and Mr. McTaggart had driven it around the walled compound, observed only by Mr. Hearst. They had shown how the continuous loop allowed the wagon to climb over obstacles and move forward on rough or boggy ground. That in itself was an impressive accomplishment. But Mr. Hearst had set them to work to build a self-propelled wagon for transporting gold, a moving fortress that couldn't be stopped by gunfire and, unlike an armored stagecoach, wasn't vulnerable to attacks against horses or barriers of logs placed across the coach road.

The growing numbers of desperate men roaming the West, following the example of the James and Younger brothers by robbing trains and coaches, made this look like a promising idea when Lincoln and Mr. McTaggart had first set to work. Now Lincoln wondered if there had been something more to the project right from the start.

He cast his mind to those tests they had done in the walled compound. He thought of a smile on Mr. Hearst's face as he watched the wagon roll out of the shed for the first time. It was a dangerous sort of smile, he now realized.

Lincoln thought of the fenced compound, located in the trees and watched over by Mr. Hearst's armed guards, and he thought of the strict orders for secrecy Mr. McTaggart had been given. Why was it necessary to keep this project hidden? Wouldn't it be to Mr. Hearst's advantage for robbers all over the West to know that the Homestake Mine was working on a way of transporting gold in bulletproof, unstoppable steam wagons? If they knew about the steam wagon, wouldn't the robbers decide to stay put and keep rustling cattle down in Texas instead of taking the long journey north?

Lost in thought as he inspected the drive wheels and saw them turn and turn, Lincoln did not at first hear the men as they entered the shed. When he heard their voices, he turned his head and saw three pairs of boots. He heard Mr. McTaggart call his name and rolled out from underneath the wagon and saw even more men—surly, unpleasant-looking men carrying shotguns, with pistols in their belts.

He recognized one heavyset, sour-faced lump of muscle and bone as Boone May, the leader of the men sent to escort their wagons into Deadwood. He knew now that May was the lead shotgun guard for the mining company and a man with a reputation for shooting first and not bothering with questions at all.

"The little monkey's playing at being a mechanic," one of May's men said, pointing at Lincoln's legs as they jutted out from underneath.

"Mister Henry is my apprentice," said Mr. McTaggart.

"See, boys?" May said. "Mister Henry's learning a skilled trade. Unlike you lunkheads."

The men guffawed, and May said, "Get up here, Mister Henry."

Lincoln lifted himself off the ground and brushed away some of the dust on his clothing.

"I'd lay odds you also know how to drive this thing," May said. "Am I right?"

"Yes, sir."

"You can't take Lincoln with you," Mr. McTaggart said. "He's just a boy."

"I reckon we can take whoever Mister Hearst wants us to take, seeing as how he's paying us all."

Lincoln saw the concern on Mr. McTaggart's face. These men wanted to take the steam wagon for a test drive. Probably Mr. Hearst wanted to see how the wagon performed with a party of guards inside. Maybe he also wanted to give his guards the experience of traveling inside the cramped, noisy space with the echoing roar of the engine reverberating off the walls.

It was strange that they wanted Lincoln to drive, though. Maybe Mr.

Hearst knew weight was a problem and he wanted to save the seventy or so pounds Mr. McTaggart had on his apprentice.

"I'll go and get some of those twists of cotton for everybody's ears," Lincoln said.

"No, Mister Henry, you and your boss here get this thing ready. Make sure it's got enough coal and water."

"We don't need but a couple buckets of coal to ride around this yard."

"Who said that's what we're doing?"

Boone May ordered three of his men to grab shovels and buckets and load up the steam wagon's tender. He sent the other two men to open the big barn door that led to the testing yard, then the big gates in the outer wall, which hadn't been opened yet. So, they wanted to take the wagon for a longer test.

Despite his misgivings, Lincoln was excited. This could be a way for him to see how the wagon might be improved. And if not, it might convince Mr. Hearst that the wagon needed to be redesigned from scratch with a new kind of engine.

Lincoln stepped up inside the wagon and started the pretest inspection. He placed the big gear shift in neutral. He checked the water level and closed off the steam vent to build pressure. He checked the exhaust pipe to make sure there were no leaks that could poison the crew.

"She's all ready to roll," he said.

Mr. McTaggart stood on the floor of the shed and looked up at Lincoln, worry lines carved into his forehead. "Lincoln, come out here. I think you should bring along a spare Murphy gear just to be safe."

Lincoln opened his mouth to ask a question but saw something in Mr. McTaggart's eyes that stopped him. "Yes, sir."

"I'll go to the supply closet and get you one."

Mr. McTaggart turned and walked to the little back room where they stored tools and spare parts and where Lincoln kept a cot for nights when he worked too late to go on home to his mama. Moments later, Mr. McTaggart called to Lincoln to join him in the supply closet. Somebody, he said, had gone and moved those blasted Murphy gears again.

"Sorry, Mister McTaggart. That must have been me."

Lincoln hopped out of the cabin and felt Boone May's curiosity as he ran to the closet and saw Mr. McTaggart waiting for him, his hands squeezing the life out of his cap.

"I'm sorry, lad, but I don't think this is just a test run," he said. "I don't want you to be part of this. Run on home to your mother."

"But why?"

"I think Mister Hearst has something very different in mind now for his steam wagon."

The door to the storage burst open, and Boone May stood there glowering. He spat a stream of tobacco juice on the floor and narrowed his eyes at Mr. McTaggart.

"What are you hens cluckin' about?" May said.

"I told Lincoln he's not needed today. I think it would be best if he went home."

"That boy ain't goin' nowhere 'cept inside that war wagon."

"You don't need him to drive the wagon."

"I don't need you, Scotty. It's gonna be a tight fit inside there, and I don't need you gettin' in the way. You're gonna stay here with one of my men to make sure you don't go blabbin'.'"

Boone May placed his hand on Lincoln's shoulder and dragged the boy toward the wagon, while another of his men came forward and directed Mr. McTaggart to follow. The shotgun guard and two of his men bundled inside, along with their weapons, while Lincoln and Mr. McTaggart went through the final starting procedures. Lincoln poured some paraffin oil on some wood chips and started a fire, then squeezed the bellows to make it heat up as he added small pellets of coal. Then he flooded the chamber so that the water could heat up and start building steam pressure.

The largest of Boone May's men took the stoker's position and, once the fire was roaring in the box, began to feed it. Lincoln watched the steam gauges, though in truth he could feel the heat and in his mind see right through to the steam chamber to tell when there was enough of a head built up.

He knew without even checking the gauge when it was time to slip the machine into gear and felt it glide into first gear smoothly, thanks to his regular ministrations with the oil can. The steam wagon—war wagon Boone May had christened it—lurched into movement.

As frightened as he was by the armed men and Mr. McTaggart's warnings, Lincoln could not suppress his joy. He had driven the wagon around the practice yard before, but nobody had ever taken it beyond the wall. Now, as it roared through the gate, every turn of the drive wheels took it farther than a continuous-loop steam wagon had ever gone before.

Every bump in the road, every rise and dip, was a new test for his and Mr. McTaggart's invention, and it passed every one.

"Can you stop this thing?" Boone May shouted in his ear.

"Yes, sir."

"Do it."

Lincoln slipped the engine into neutral on a flat stretch of trail just before town.

"I want you to show me how to drive it."

Lincoln looked nervously at the big man. Could he learn to operate the machine under test conditions like this? It was a big, heavy piece of machinery and would destroy anything in its path if the driver wasn't careful. And for all the power in its engine, it couldn't just race over or through every obstacle. Lincoln had figured in his head the maximum angle the wagon could climb without getting stuck or flipping over on its back like a turtle, and he had a sense of how much brush the wagon could push through without becoming stuck like a hound dog in a briar patch.

Boone May didn't look like he'd tolerate any back talk, so Lincoln quickly went through the driving controls—the two levers that controlled power to the left and right tracks, the brake lever, and the turning technique involving making one track move faster than the other.

Turning was the trickiest part of driving, and Lincoln remembered how he had zigzagged across the practice yard when he'd first taken the wagon out. He didn't much like the idea of Boone May zigzagging his way through the town of Deadwood.

After driving along a short, straight stretch of the trail, the guard told

Lincoln to take the controls again. Maybe he realized it was too much
to learn all at once.

"Point it right down Main Street, boy!" he shouted.

Lincoln drove the wagon past the big houses of the merchants and
lawyers, past the assay and law offices and the doctor's surgery, past the
dry goods store and the milliner and shoemaker and tailor shops, past
the business hotels where the drummers and government men stayed,
then past the cheaper hotel where the circus folk were bedded down,
and finally through the Badlands, where the rumbling, rolling thunder
of the wagon was such a distraction it caused the most dedicated of
drinkers to stagger away from the bar to watch it pass. Men, women,
and children ran from the path of the wagon, horses reared in terror,
crows squawked.

Peering out the porthole, Lincoln saw enough to realize that the
wagon was a sight of terror and wonder. To the folks in town, its rumble
and roar was one of the Bible's seven trumpets of the end times. With
this long drive, Mr. Hearst wanted to strike fear into the hearts of any
robbers who might think of attacking his gold wagons, even if the wagon
couldn't travel all the way to Cheyenne.

In the back of the cabin, one of the guards panted as he shoveled
coal from the shrinking pile into the firebox. The heat in the cabin
took on weight, heavy as a blacksmith's apron. Lincoln, sweat pooling
in his hair and running down his spine, pondered a system of fans to
blow cool air into the cabin. How much power would they require?
His mind drifted so deeply into pictures of fans and arrangements of
drive shafts that he almost didn't hear Boone May's shouted instruction.
"Turn left here!"

They had reached the Chinese camp beyond the Badlands. All the
houses in the valley were behind them now. Why did Boone May want
the wagon to travel into this wasteland of logged forests and played-out
mine claims?

"Now, turn right."

Lincoln turned to the right and directed the wagon down a well-worn
path. In the distance, in the fading twilight, he saw the glow of a fire.

"We best turn soon, Mister May. We might damage the wagon driving it in the dark."

"Keep it going, boy."

The wagon continued to rattle down the trail, grinding up the trailside moss and grass under its steel cleats. Lincoln could now make out the shapes of people casting shadows with the dancing fire behind them. Some stood to face the approaching wagon. Others ran toward the scattering of tents spread around the central firepit. Those who remained closed ranks, presenting a wall of bodies to block the wagon.

Lincoln eased back on both throttles and slipped the transmission into neutral.

"What are you doing, boy?"

"We go any closer, we run these folks over."

Boone May pushed Lincoln aside and placed a hand on the gear shift lever.

"That's the idea, Mister Henry."

The gears shrieked, and Lincoln pictured teeth flying off at all angles. But then they clinked into place, and the wagon lurched, juddered to a stop, and lurched again as Boone May pushed both throttles forward.

The men forming a line in front of the wagon broke away to the sides as the wagon resumed its collision course.

Panic broke out. Lincoln saw shouting—though no words penetrated the steel hull of the wagon—and one big man in a brown suit, his blue cheeks and deep, dark eyes illuminated in the crackling flames, pointed to the wagon. Lincoln heard the sharp, clanging impact of rocks as they bounced off the steel armor and saw men reach down and pick up projectiles to throw.

"These slackers think rocks will stop us? Boys, we'll show these malcontents and radicals what's what." Boone May pushed one throttle control forward while pulling back on another, and the wagon lurched immediately to the right.

In moments, it tore through the nearest tent, temporarily blinding the occupants as the fabric covered the porthole. Boone May stopped the wagon and backed it up, and the tent fell away. In the half-light, Lincoln saw the crying faces of a woman and her children, two young boys, and a little one about the age his sister Annabelle got to before the fever took her.

A sharp pinging sound echoed through the cabin. Boone May turned the wagon and directed it toward the men who had been blocking its path moments before. Lincoln saw flashes of light and realized that somebody was shooting at the wagon.

Lincoln reached for the throttle levers.

"Mister May, we gotta go."

"Quiet, boy."

"Mister Hearst will be angry—"

A meaty paw caught Lincoln in the chest and threw him against the back wall. The boy's head whipsawed back against the wall, and he collapsed to the floor. Breathless from the shock of the violence as much as from the impact, Lincoln took a moment to come to his senses. He was brought back to awareness by a deafening roar.

Two of the guards stood at shooting ports near the front of the wagon and emptied both barrels from their shotguns, filling the cabin with acrid smoke. The pinging of bullets and thud of rocks abruptly ceased.

Lincoln felt tossed to the side as Boone May put the wagon through another sudden high-speed turn that became a complete hundred-and-eighty-degree reversal. As the wagon bounced through the turn, Lincoln pulled himself up high enough to look out one of the ventilation holes in the back and saw, in the light of the campfire, a lady older than his mother, wearing what looking like a black mourning dress, holding the bleeding body of the tall man in the brown suit.

"Good shooting, boys!" Boone May shouted. "Now give her some more coal. We're heading home."

Lincoln, who had endured the destruction of his family's crops without crying, thought again of the power locked in the numbers that flowed like spring water just under the surface of the whole world. He had unlocked the power in a pile of anthracite coal, a tank of water, and a couple of wagon loads of steel. And that power had come down on people with no more ability to fight back than his family had. Tears that he'd forced back then and in the years since burst out, and he fell back in the corner of the cabin as Boone May drove toward the Homestake Mine Company machine works.

"What are you blubbering about, boy? Your precious war wagon passed the test."

20

R OTH POINTED OUT Daniel's limited career options.
"You got one talent that puts you above everybody else, Kid. I
say you use it."

Daniel explored the hard faces of Wiseman and Roth, who had pulled
him to the back door of the saloon and out to the alley, which provided
a view of the hog yards and laundries of the Chinese camp. Both faces
were set in grim expressions of defiance. Were they looking for revenge
or resigned to the only choice life had ever offered them?

"Face it. Big Jim didn't spring you from the farm so you could put
on a circus show."

Inside, in the Bella Union, Big Jim lay in a pine box, dressed in a new
coat to replace the one that had been torn to shreds by buckshot. Miners
gathered at the bar to drink whiskey, paid for by Mrs. Kleinschmidt,
while an Irish tenor sang of sadness and the determination to right
wrongs, starting with, "Well, Father, dear, the day will come when on
vengeance we will call."

Mrs. Kleinschmidt had insisted on a proper Irish wake for Big
Jim. She'd hired the coffin maker, rented the saloon, and spread word
among the miners. Many of the survivors of the attack on the camp
had been afraid to show their support for Big Jim, even after his death,

but those with the most powerful thirst had set aside their fear of the Homestake's killers and their war wagon, and the gathering had grown increasingly rowdy.

Daniel had spent most of the afternoon slumped in a corner with his back to the wall. He'd waved away Segal, Wiseman, and Roth, and they'd let him sulk alone until eventually Segal had brought him a glass of whiskey, which tasted to him like a mix of patent medicine and India ink.

After an initial sip, the glass stood untouched on the table beside him as Daniel pictured the smoking, roaring, steam-powered dragon the miners had described. Bullets bounced off it. It crushed everything in its path. And it breathed fire and buckshot.

Would things have turned out differently, he wondered, if Segal hadn't convinced him to sneak away to watch the circus? Two hours, it was supposed to take. What harm could befall Big Jim and Mrs. Kleinschmidt, Segal had asked, when they were surrounded by their allies in the miners' camp and when Hearst himself was in on their plan to prevent a strike?

Though nobody got a good look at it in the chaos, the armored wagon must have had shooting holes. For Daniel, placing a bullet through one of the holes would have been as easy as shooting Segal's one-eyed jacks at the circus.

Mrs. Kleinschmidt had apparently read his thoughts. She stood beside him, still in her mourning dress with the high collar.

"I know you're feeling bad, my boy. But there was nothing for you to do."

"We don't know that."

"So, maybe you could have shot one of the men in that cursed thing. And maybe they could have shot you."

"At least I'd have done something."

"Listen. A dead boy who did something, I don't need. I need a young man who can go ahead with the plan. For Big Jim's sake."

She'd left him with that thought in order to watch the bartender and make sure he wasn't overcharging her account for the rounds of whiskey. And then, with Mrs. Kleinschmidt and Segal busy at the bar, Wiseman and Roth had hustled him outside.

A roar went up from the miners as the tenor finished his song. Somebody called out for "A Nation Once Again." The more the liquor flowed, the more Irish the miners seemed to feel, even the Poles and Hungarians. A bigger roar went up when a new contingent of miners, their late shifts done, trooped in to pay their respects.

"What about Segal?" Daniel asked as Roth crowded him, waiting for an answer.

"He'll come with us if we say. What else is he gonna do?"

"He's sweet on that Lillian."

"Lillian never watched his back in the prison farm."

Daniel realized that Roth's argument applied to himself as well. Without his two bodyguards, his time in the Yonkers Industrial School for Boys would have been far tougher, and he'd have been at the mercy of the Brickbat Boys. He realized, as well, that he was far from any place that might pass as home. He was jobless, penniless, and now dependent on a gang whose members were all still too young to legally drink the whiskey that flowed like water.

"What kind of gang do you think we'd make? You two can barely ride. Segal's no better."

"We'll learn. Look at all these schmucks on their horses. How hard can it be?"

"Maybe we should wait and see what Missus Kleinschmidt comes up with."

"This is what Missus Kleinschmidt has come up with."

Daniel heard another miner begin a funerary oration. The man's voice carried through the closed back door, though the sense of the words did not. Still, Daniel could guess what was said. Jim McGuire was a champion of the workers, a man of courage who had faced down the fire-spewing mechanical beast of the Homestake Mine. The workers of Deadwood owed loyalty to his memory. Daniel shrugged and sighed and looked up at his friends. "So, we're going to steal the workers' money!"

"Hey, why don't you shout it a little louder?" Roth said. "The Chinaman over there sloppin' his hogs didn't hear."

Finally, Wiseman spoke up. The giant boy yawned and opened his half-lidded eyes a little wider. "I smell food. Let's go before those bums from the camp eat it all."

The door closed, and Daniel was left in the alley. It had been a long time since he'd had any solitude, since those days in the Five Points, searching for scraps of food and dodging the leatherheads. Sometimes, in fact, he missed it.

He missed having his choice of paths to take every day, idling away the hours watching the traffic in the street, sneaking in the back doors of saloons to listen to bawdy songs if he was in the mood for entertainment. But, of course, he realized that he only had that freedom because of his ma's sickness and, when he thought of her, he wished his childhood had not been so free, that he'd had to listen for his mother's voice calling him home in the evenings, that he'd had chores to do and lessons to practice to earn her kiss good night.

He'd heard men in Deadwood, new arrivals from the East and from overseas, talk about how much they relished the freedom of the West. But Daniel, alone in the alley, with the music playing on the other side of the saloon door, felt that freedom was overrated.

He returned to the saloon and saw Wiseman and Roth have a close-up talk with Segal, who looked over their shoulders at Daniel. No doubt they were explaining his new job to him. He didn't look too happy about it.

Mrs. Kleinschmidt, with her mourning veil drawn over her face, sat in a chair directly opposite Big Jim's coffin. She saw Daniel and erupted into waves of emotion, real tears visible beneath her mourning veil.

"Daniel, my boy," she called, and Daniel felt hands at his back pushing him toward the keening woman. Mrs. Kleinschmidt enveloped him in a suffocating hug. Her perfume, powder, and the musky aroma of her sweat nearly overpowered him. She pulled back and held his face in her hands, giving him a meaningful stare before she let him go. She placed a hand on each of Daniel's shoulders and set him to the side, gathering her composure with visible effort. She turned to the assembled miners, and a hush descended on the saloon.

"Friends, brothers, thank you for coming to pay your respects to a great man and a champion of the workers. I've only known Jim McGuire for a few days, but since arriving in Deadwood, I have come to regard him as a great friend.

"Many tears have been shed today, and many more tears will be shed tonight before this wake is finished. But I believe our tears are not enough of an expression of respect for Jim McGuire. Jim McGuire was a man of action and a man of courage. The best way for us to remember him and to pay tribute to him is by carrying out the dream he had for Deadwood and for the workers of America."

One of the drunken voices called, "Strike! We'll go on strike in tribute!"

A chorus of cheers erupted from the saloon.

"That's the spirit. But we need to plan this carefully. It's no tribute to Jim to launch a strike that gets broken after a few days."

Men began to pound fists on tables and chant, "We won't break! We won't break!"

Mrs. Kleinschmidt raised her hand, asking for quiet. The saloon returned to a dull roar.

"You have courage, I don't doubt," she said. "But you have families, and Hearst has the money to wait and starve you out. We can't go on strike without the supplies we need to survive. So, what I propose is that we take up a collection, right now, to create an emergency strike fund. Every man here put all you can into the fund. Round up every man who isn't here tonight and get what you can from him. Then bring that money to the church tomorrow. As soon as we've buried Jim and paid our respects, we take that money and buy food and medicine to prepare for a strike."

Another cheer went up.

"And I've got a little surprise for George Hearst. Instead of buying supplies in Deadwood and paying the gouging prices charged by his friends, we go to Cheyenne, and we buy what we need there and haul it back ourselves. Every dollar in our fund will go at least twice as far, buying goods from right off the railroad. And Hearst won't know what we're doing. We'll be ready to go on strike and stay out as long as we want, and Hearst won't know what hit him."

Men drained their glasses and called for more. Individual voices vanished in the din. Order was restored long enough for one man, a well-respected old miner, one of the first to find color in the waters of Deadwood Creek, to be elected to accompany Mrs. Kleinschmidt on the stagecoach to Deadwood.

Once agreement was reached, Mrs. Kleinschmidt signaled to the bartender to quit pouring free beer. From here on, the men could pay for their own drinks.

21

LILY HAD NEVER seen so much mud. Mounds of it grew beside a broken crosscut-saw blade mounted cutting-side down outside the hotel so that guests could scrape their boots clean. Wagons plowed it into furrows in the streets and with each turn of their wheels spackled walls of buildings and the faces of walkers who were foolhardy enough not to turn away.

The hillsides themselves, denuded of vegetation by men seeking lumber for building or for shoring up mine tunnels, appeared ready to bury the town in wet clay.

Deadwood and its neighboring shantytowns were waking from their slumber after the night's deluge. In an hour, the valley would be swarmed with activity like an anthill stirred up by a cruel boy. For now, a few early risers had the streets to themselves.

Maids threaded around streams of runoff to reach the new grand homes up the hill where they would soon be locked in combat with muddy footprints. The first of the miners, dressed in heavy overalls caked with grime, walked stiff-legged up the street like unhorsed knights in armor. A young lawyer, who rented a room two doors down from the one Lily shared with Madame Mystere, stepped carefully over streams of rainwater and animal waste, trying to keep his black trousers and coat clean. Farther down the hill, in the Badlands, the growing army of fortune hunters, card sharps, fancy men, and dancing girls still rested from their night's activities.

Lily turned from the window, looped the strap of a sack around her shoulder, and, with another look around the room to ensure that Madame Mystere had not wakened, lifted her cavalry saber out from underneath the bed. She placed the saber belt around her neck and draped a shawl over her shoulders, more to hide the weapon than to ward off the morning chill.

Though the sun was beginning to climb over the hills, some men were just finishing their night's drinking. She hoped none would see her sneak out the back door but felt better with two feet of sharpened steel at her side. There were few women in Deadwood, and fewer still out and about this early.

Horses at the livery stables nickered as they caught her scent—probably still scented with traces of wolf—and she hurried down the valley toward the Chinese encampment. Her regular supplier was up, shoveling pig manure into a wheelbarrow. She caught his eye, held up a coin, and waited while he disappeared into the barn.

A moment later he was back with a small, dead piglet in his hands. He handed her the piglet, took Lily's coin, and returned to his shovel. Lily placed the piglet in her sack and resumed her journey to the edge of the town and beyond, toward the forested hollow where she hoped to meet the wolves.

Her feelings were mixed as she wound her way toward the narrow canyon that led to the thicket where she had left the mother and cubs. Part of her hoped they would be there so she could play with the cubs. But a larger part of her hoped that they had put Deadwood and its mining districts far behind them.

Deadwood was not a town where a family of wolves was likely to be safe, especially not now that the wolfer was back. Lily had heard that the year before, not long after the defeat of Colonel Custer at the hands of the Sioux, the town had paid a bounty for the head of an Indian, killed by men who suspected him of stealing horses. No doubt the town would also pay a bounty for a collection of wolf pelts. She hoped that the mother had healed sufficiently to take the cubs away and teach them how to hunt their own prey and survive in the wild.

Uncle Stanislas had hoped the wolves could be tamed and incorporated into Lily's act. A howling wolf pack would certainly be quite a spectacle. He had proposed dressing Lily as a Daniel Boone and having her fight the entire pack bare-handed. Or she could perform a scene blending Roman mythology with popular melodrama—Lily as an orphan raised by the mother wolf, then, kidnapped by a top-hatted villain and tied to a railroad track, calling the wolves to vanquish the foe and come to her rescue in the nick of time.

Neither seemed possible to Lily, who had discovered that she was able to communicate with the wild animals but was unable to train them to perform. She had no doubt they would come to her aid if she truly needed help but was certain that they would not pretend to help her.

They had an independence of mind her tame dogs did not possess. They enjoyed her company, respected her even, but they did not look up to her as their mistress. This was made obvious when she had attempted to give them names. However fitting each name seemed to Lily, the wolves ignored whatever name she added to a sentence.

Just the day before, Uncle Stanislas had given Lily the news. Since the wolves were proving untrainable, the circus could no longer afford to feed them. Buying dead pigs and bones from the Chinese encampment was not a great expense, but the circus could ill afford any additional outlay of money while still paying off the cost of getting to Deadwood. Now was the time to let the wolves go into the wild.

Lily had determined to trek once more to the hiding place to give the wolves the news. And since she didn't want to come empty-handed, the dead baby pig was her goodbye present.

Making sure nobody was following, Lily turned up a narrow gulch that had been abandoned by prospectors when their sluices yielded no color. She picked her way up beside a stream, currently running high with the rains and mounds of gravel dug up by prospectors.

After a quarter mile, she turned up a small hollow on one side that was choked with willow and alder. She had sought out a hidden place near town after the circus arrived and every hotel and stable they sought out refused to allow the wolves inside—even after Uncle Stanislas insisted that they were "purebred Swedish wolfhounds."

Lily was relieved that no business owner would allow the wolves indoors, as she knew the animals would refuse to be locked inside anyway.

In a clearing behind the trees was the hidden den she had hollowed out in the forest duff. As she approached the wall of willows, she removed the piglet from her bag and held it out so the wolves could catch a sniff. "Wolves, it's me, Lily. I've brought you something."

No movement answered. A puff of wind stirred a downy feather, and Lily noticed more feathers scattered throughout the bushes. Where they were thickest on the ground, she saw the feathered wing of a chicken and a pile of bones and flesh. Lily had never brought the wolves a chicken.

She ducked low underneath the branches, now filling out with the bright green of spring, and followed the narrow path the wolves took to go in and out of their safe place. When she reached the den, she realized the wolves had not killed the chicken. And she knew who had brought it. Three wolf cubs lay motionless in the den, no rise or fall detectable on their chests. Dead. Poisoned.

Lily heard a hoarse, choking sound and realized the mother was still alive, trying to empty herself of the poisoned chicken meat. Lily heard no thoughts from the wolf, save pain and unbearable sadness and thirst.

Water seeped from the rocks up the gully from the hiding place. Lily ran to the seepage, removed her boots, and filled them. She clambered barefoot over rocks, barely feeling them, and dripped water onto the lapping tongue of the suffering wolf.

The wolf drank, then vomited up more poison, drank again, vomited again. At last, Lily was able to give the wolf water that stayed down.

She had no idea of the time that passed as she sat with the unhappy mother. After a time, the mother was able to rise and sniff the carcasses of her young. Lily knew the wolf was weak and in need of nourishment, but when she offered her the piglet, the wolf did not even sniff it.

"You must go," Lily said. "The wolfer will be back."

She did not add that the wolfer would be back so he could skin the bodies of the cubs.

The mother stood like a stone sculpture. Her ears pricked up to a slight movement in the undergrowth. Then her muscles snapped into movement like a bowstring. She shot through the narrow tunnel in the willows, chasing a jackrabbit. Lily's last sight was of a streak of gray fur as she soared over fallen logs leading up hill.

Lily looked at the three dead cubs. They had grown during the last few weeks. Lily could lift one, or even two, but she knew she could not carry all three back to town. So, she dragged them to a place of flat, clear earth and constructed a pyramid of dry twigs. Then she lit a fire and nursed it until it was large enough to act as a pyre and placed one cub after another in flames. When the flames worked their way through the flesh of the cubs, she added what was left of the poisoned chicken carcass to make sure no other animals met the same fate.

As the stench of singed fur and feathers became unbearable in the close air of the gully, Lily noticed the barking of dogs and a familiar chorus of anger and hatred in their canine voices.

The walls of the gully were too steep, and the only way out was the way she had come, the way the wolfer was coming now.

The wind from the hilltops carried the smoke and the smell of burning flesh down the gully. The dogs must have detected it. They became louder as they grew closer. Then they burst into the clearing, snarling hatefully at Lily. She realized she still had the carcass of the piglet in her sack and tossed it to the hounds in hopes of confusing them or making them fight one another for food. They ignored it and tightened their circle around Lily. Heavy footsteps soon told her that the wolfer was running, that he must have smelled the fire by now.

"What are you doing here, girl?"

"Visiting friends. What about you?"

"I'm doing what I always do, ridding this territory of foul devil dogs." The man's eyes widened as he approached Lily and the fire and was able to see what she'd done. "Those were mine!"

"They're nobody's."

He ran past her and attempted to remove the smoldering carcasses from the fire, grabbing one by the unburned end of the tail, putting a stick into the mouth of another in order to push it from the heat. The other was too consumed by flame for even that measure. It would soon be nothing but blackened bones.

The wolfer stood to his full height and faced Lily. "Twice now you have cost me money, girl."

Lily attempted to back down the trail. "My people are expecting me back."

"You aren't going until you pay me back, Lillian."

Lily shuddered at the sound of her name emerging from the mouth of the wolfer.

"Call the wolf bitch back," he said.

She stared in disbelief.

"You can talk to animals, girl. Call it back."

"I can't do that."

The wolfer removed a handbill from a pocket of his jacket, spat, and read in an echoing, preacher's voice, "'See Lillian the Lycanthrope communicate with canines of all kinds. Does she speak their language or read their thoughts? You decide.'"

"My Uncle Stanislas wrote that. He's expecting me back."

"I have already warned you, girl, that bearing false witness is a sin against God. But you don't seem to have any compunction regarding the breaking of the Lord's commandments. You break the Eighth Commandment regularly, and you've also broken the Seventh at least twice."

The circus folk attended church services when they happened to be stopped in any particular town for a Sunday. It was necessary to dispel the bad impression proper folks had about them. Lily was usually too tired on a Sunday morning to remember much of what she heard, so she strained to recall which Commandment was which.

"The Seventh Commandment," said the wolfer. "'Thou shall not steal.'"

"I don't steal."

"Silence, girl! You stole my trap and a prime adult wolf pelt and three cub pelts. Your savage friends stole my horses. And now, after I found this den, you stole their pelts again. You stole from me as surely as if you had reached into my pocket with your thieving gypsy hand and taken out a fistful of dollar coins."

"I did not steal."

The dogs, sensing their master's anger, edged closer, snapping their powerful jaws at Lily.

"Wolves don't belong to you in the first place," she added bravely.

"They belong to Satan. And it is my mission to send them back to Hell."

Lily remembered something from church. "All creatures great and small. The Lord God made them all."

"Yes, God made the wolf and the serpent and everything else that torments man for his transgressions. And He gave man authority to rule over them." The wolfer closed his eyes and recited from memory. "'And God said, Let us make man in our image, after our likeness, and let them have dominion over the fish of the sea, and over the fowl of the air, and over the cattle, and over all the earth, and over every creeping thing that creepeth upon the earth.'"

Lily thought of her conversations with the learned Mr. Szabo, who took as great an interest in the behavior of animals as he did in that of politicians and bankers.

"My friend says the buffalo and elk need wolves to keep their herd healthy and to keep them from eating up all the grass. He calls it the balance of nature."

"Oh, your friend. One of your gypsy thieves and conjurers."

"He's not a thief or a conjurer. He's a kind man."

"He is a false prophet. 'Beware of the false prophets, that come to you in sheep's clothing, but inwardly are wolves.'"

As he quoted the Bible, the wolfer's face became a brighter red. Lily noticed that another change had come over him as well. His eyes focused on a distant place only he could see. His voice became deeper but with a gravelly top note in weird harmony, so that he sounded like more than one man. It was as if, when he began to preach, he was overtaken by a different being, a prophet.

Lily feared this prophet more than the wolfer. "I'm sorry about lying to you. But not about burning the pelts."

The wolfer returned, the prophet fading from his voice and face. "There's still the bitch. You can help me find her."

Lily began, hesitantly, to walk toward town, hoping the wolfer would call off the dogs as she approached them.

"And there are hundreds of other wolves out there," he said. "You can pay off the rest of your debt by helping me find them."

Lily turned back to the wolfer and saw him take a stride forward with a new expression on his face. She knew it was the face of a man who enjoyed the harm he inflicted, whether on a litter of wolf cubs or on a girl who stood in his way.

As she took in his thin smile and the cold fire in his eyes, a flame burst to life in her heart. It was the sudden rage she felt, secondhand, when she saw dogs fighting over a scrap of food. Heat flushed through her skin, and the sound of her own heartbeat roared like a hailstorm on a tin roof.

The man reached out a hand toward her but stepped back when she drew the saber from its place beneath her shawl. It would be the simplest thing in the world to run the man through and hack him and his hounds to carrion. She held the point at the man's throat. Its finely honed edge glinted in the sun, which had just broken through the morning clouds.

"Get away from me!"

"You don't want to do that, girl."

"You don't want to come closer, wolfer."

"Touch me with that, and my hounds will rip you to shreds."

"You won't live to see it."

Lily directed a harsh command to the dogs, and something in her voice, some new power, made them stop snarling and take a step back. Holding the saber to the wolfer's throat, she reached her left hand forward and removed the pistol from the man's holster. She had never before held a gun. It was surprisingly heavy.

He said, "You know how to use that?"

"Don't need to," she said, gesturing with her eyes to her saber. "I have this."

Still holding the pistol and the saber, she edged away from the wolfer, backing down the trail, now open since the chastened dogs had backed away. The tide of rage began to ebb within her and with it the speed and strength that had taken the wolfer by surprise.

"I knew you were a thief, girl. That pistol cost me fifteen dollars."

"I'm just borrowing it. You'll find it beside the trail next to the Chinese camp."

Lily walked crabwise down the trail, careful to avoid turning her back on the dogs or their master. As she reached more even ground and began to run, she heard the wolfer's voice acquire the deep bass rumble and gravelly top notes of the preacher as he said, "I know what a lycanthrope is, girl. A creature that uses sorcery to transform into a wolf. And I know what the Bible says about sorcery. 'Thou shalt not suffer a sorcerer to live.'"

22

"THAT GIRL ROBBED me of fifty dollars!"

Josiah watched as Sheriff Seth Bullock lower his copy of the *Cheyenne Advocate.*

"Fifty dollars in greenbacks? Or gold dust?"

Bullock leaned back in a pressed-wood chair that had made the long journey by train to Cheyenne and by freight wagon to the Black Hills. To his right, the remains of a morning fire smoldered in a woodstove, cutting the morning chill that could make Deadwood feel wintery even in the springtime. The smell of newly milled lumber filled the sheriff's office.

Josiah's dogs barked from the hitching post outside, where he had been ordered to tie them, lest they shed all over Bullock's new carpet.

Josiah raised his voice to be heard over the din. "I spent three days following those wolves. They were mine. And she freed them. Then I found them again in that hollow, and just when I was ready to skin the little demon dogs, she stole them again and burned them."

"No law against that, no matter what you say their pelts are worth."

"And she stole my new pistol!"

"That one you're packing on your hip?"

"She threatened me with a sword, and she sent those Indians after me."

Bullock stood and walked the few paces across the room to a window that looked out on Main Street. He gestured for Josiah to follow. It was a Monday morning, the time of the week when, by mutual agreement, the wives and daughters of respectable men remained in their homes so they would not encounter the working girls who left the dance halls and saloons and theaters in order to shop for new dresses and hats, attend to business at the bank and post office, and enjoy the fresh air. The girls walked in twos and threes, some with linked arms like schoolgirls.

Many, in truth, were no older than schoolgirls. Female laughter gave the street a holiday air, though the sounds of hammering and sawing from half a dozen new buildings being erected drowned out much of the laughter. Across the street, the men working on a new hardware store paused long enough to watch a trio of the younger, fresher girls pass. One even tipped his hat.

Bullock pointed to the busy street scene. "Mister Stuart, I don't know if you understand the complexity of a sheriff's job in a town like this. In addition to miners and merchants and captains of industry, these hills have drawn every thief, every fancy man, every card shark, every bush-whacker within a thousand miles. I am only one man. In order to keep the peace, I need to maintain the respect of the citizens of this community so that I can be assured that they will back me up when I need to raise a posse. I cannot do that by taking positions that the people of Deadwood will consider ridiculous."

"Ridiculous?"

"This is a slight little girl we are talking about. Do you seriously believe I would stand in front of a jury and attempt to argue that, in my professional judgment as a lawman, I believe that this orphan, this waif, posed a threat to a wolf hunter accompanied by a pack of hounds?"

"She is not a little girl. She is a conjurer. She is doing the devil's work."

"Well then, she is surely outside of my jurisdiction, seeing as I am only sworn to uphold the laws of man."

Bullock sat back in his chair, leaving Josiah to watch the passing parade of fallen women. Josiah turned to see that Bullock had resumed reading his newspaper. Bullock raised his voice and read out loud, "Here's the article I was looking for. 'A Glorious Day for Baseball.'"

"Sheriff Bullock, there's law and there's justice," Josiah said. "I wouldn't expect a Yankee to understand."

"I am an American by oath, but I am not a Yankee. I was born in Her Majesty's Dominion to the north, a place sadly lacking in this exciting new sport." He held the newspaper out toward Josiah, gesturing at the article about Cheyenne's new baseball team. "Do you think I could convince the Homestake Mine to sponsor a baseball team? It would give the young men of the town something healthy to do with their spare time."

Josiah ignored the newspaper. He certainly did not have time to talk about a child's game played by grown men. The wolf was somewhere out there in these hills. He would find it if he had to lay poison baits all the way to the Belle Fourche River. He turned and walked to the door.

"Stay."

Josiah redirected his attention to Bullock, who was stacking gold coins on his desk. Josiah counted five coins.

"You are an uncommonly dedicated wolfer, aren't you, Mister Stuart?"

"I take my work seriously."

"I believe you consider it something more than work. A calling, perhaps?"

"God gave man dominion over the earth."

Bullock reached into his desk and produced another handful of coins. He stacked five more. Josiah approached and saw that they were ten-dollar eagles.

"How's your Latin?"

"My Latin?"

"My father insisted I practice my declensions." Bullock put his hands to his temples as if massaging his memory. "Accusative, nominative, vocative... and... the others."

Josiah knew no Latin, except sic semper tyrannis, the words uttered by John Wilkes Booth when he shot Abraham Lincoln.

"Homo homini lupus est." Bullock removed a pipe from a vest pocket and filled it. He struck a lucifer and, between puffs on the pipe, repeated, "Homo homini lupus est. Man is a wolf to man." He then gestured to the vacant seat, which Josiah had refused on first entering the office. This time, Josiah sat.

"Four-legged wolves are a nuisance, to be sure," Bullock continued. "But for civilization to establish itself in these hills, we need to do
something about the two-legged variety. There are a half dozen gangs of
cattle rustlers, horse thieves, and stage robbers working the Cheyenne
Trail, and they will only become more brazen as the Homestake sends
out ever larger shipments of gold. I can raise a posse after a robbery, but
what I need is a tracker who can tell me where these gangs are before
they strike. I need somebody who can follow a trail and who won't give
up when the trail gets cold. Somebody who takes his job personally. Do
you know anybody like that?"

Josiah considered Bullock's words. Were thieves two-legged wolves?
The Lord forgave the thieves on Calvary. But He was filled with righteous
anger when His house was made into a den of thieves. Den of thieves.
His grandfather had called that Episcopal Church a den of thieves. He
didn't approve of its stained-glass windows and church organ. He'd been
angry when Josiah's mother had taken Josiah there to hear a choir sing
that song that still sometimes rattled around Josiah's head, the one that
went, "Sheep may safely graze, where a good shepherd watches them well."

Josiah pushed the jumble of memories aside. "You want me to track
these gangs, Sheriff?"

"I want you to take your wolf hunt down the Cheyenne Trail, and
wherever else I hear these men are hiding out. And I want you to join
them. Don't take this the wrong way, but you look like a disreputable
sort. It won't be hard for you to convince them you're a wolf too."

Bullock pushed a stack of five coins toward Josiah. "Here's fifty dollars
for your lost wolves." He pushed the other stack beside the first. "And
here's another fifty to get you started. If you provide information on
the whereabouts of these men, I can authorize two hundred dollars for
every man we are able to kill or capture as a result of your assistance."

Josiah put his hand on the gold coins, lifted them, felt their heft and
smooth coldness.

"And you're still welcome to the bounties on any wolf pelts you bring
in," Bullock added.

23

---◆◆◆◆---

HER FINAL ARGUMENT with her father echoed in Vera's ears over every rocky mile of the wagon road to Cheyenne. "A newspaper is no place for a woman," he'd said, turning his back on her and storming into his office, leaving her standing beside the compositor's desk with her story in her hands. "And it's certainly no place for a girl."

Eustace Bly ought to have known his daughter would not accept such an argument. She had followed him into his inner sanctum. "You never said that when I helped you with proofreading."

"I was wrong to let you. It gave you ideas."

"And ideas don't belong in the head of a woman. And certainly not in the head of a girl."

"Now you're being obstreperous."

"Fifty cent word! Replace with stubborn!"

She was nearly certain that had brought a hint of a smile to her father's face since it was what he'd say to a junior reporter putting on linguistic airs. At any rate, it changed his tone, made him more conciliatory. He'd closed the office door and led her to the upholstered armchair he reserved for important advertisers.

"Vera, a strong will is a good thing. You'll need one to raise a family in this changing world. But there's a difference between being strong and simply being... stubborn."

"But, Father, I know this is what I want. And I know I'd be good at it."

"Because you wrote a piece of sensationalist hero worship about a young bandit with a pistol? I could place an advertisement in the Chicago Sun, and next month I would have a dozen young men breaking down my door with this kind of 'fastest gun in the West' foofaraw."

"But my article is the truth. I saw how fast he was at the circus. And I was there in court too."

"All the more reason to get you out of this town now. Vera, I was wrong to bring you here in the first place. This is no place for a young woman. And the fact that you were able to wander out of school in order to consort with these self-styled pistoleros proves that."

And with that, he had shown her the tickets he had purchased for the stagecoach to Cheyenne and the train from there to Kansas City. Vera knew what going to Kansas City meant—enrolling as a student at Mrs. Cramp's Finishing School for Girls. It was a threat he had made before, but Vera had always assumed it to be an empty one. She'd clenched her fists to keep from crying, nearly drawing blood as her nails bit into her palms.

The argument came only two days before the journey, and so the following days were filled with packing and preparations. On the day of departure, her father had seen her off at the stage station in Deadwood. Without the spare manpower to run the newspaper in his absence—and in fact Vera wondered who he would get to correct his spelling now that she would no longer be available to proofread—he asked the housekeeper, Mrs. Franklin, to accompany her to Cheyenne and see her safely onto the train.

Vera knew that Mrs. Franklin would guard her like Cerberus until the train departed. And an official from Mrs. Cramp's Finishing School for Girls would meet her at the platform in Kansas City and in all probability be another mythological beast. Short of jumping off a moving train, Vera could see little opportunity to escape a year of elocution lessons, conjugating French verbs, arranging flowers, and sitting through piano recitals.

Would the fall hurt too terribly much?

A sudden bump that nearly tossed Vera out of her seat put thoughts of jumping from moving trains out of her mind. Caught between the impressive bulk of Mrs. Franklin on one side and the compartment's other female passenger, Mrs. Kleinschmidt, whom she recognized from the courthouse, on the other, Vera felt the air empty from her lungs in one strong gust. Then, as she struggled to gain breath, the pain from her back communicated itself to her brain.

"Goodness, this is a bumpy ride," Mrs. Kleinschmidt said without even acknowledging the meaty elbow that had dug into Vera's rib cage.

Vera's chaperone directed a withering look through the ceiling of the coach but kept her mouth shut. Vera knew that Mrs. Franklin, descended from free colored folk in Philadelphia and accustomed to being able to express herself with considerable fervor, had not found her footing since arriving in Deadwood and finding the town awash in Southerners, many of whom had fought for the Confederacy. The driver's incompetence would be the subject of a monologue later, with Vera as the audience of one.

Mrs. Kleinschmidt obviously felt no such reticence. She hammered on the ceiling with a meaty fist and opened her door to remind the driver that passengers had paid good money to ride in comfort.

"Ain't the driver's fault, Missus K," said another passenger, a wizened old miner who appeared to have scratched the earth at every set of diggings since the '49ers hit California. "They's under orders to keep their speed up. Make the road agents work at stopping us."

Vera forgot about her discomfort. "I thought the road agents were all chased from the territory."

That was certainly the impression left by the article her father had written about that spring's stagecoach robbery, an article painfully lacking in dramatic detail in Vera's point of view. Her father's article had focused mostly on the assurances of the Board of Trade that travel in and around the Black Hills was now as safe as anywhere east of the Mississippi. Her father had steadfastly refused to follow up on rumors that bandits had killed a man and had accepted Boone May's assurance that his posse had pursued the guilty party all the way to Montana.

"Well, maybe they was and maybe they wasn't, Miss. All I know is they hitched an extra pair of horses to this team. Now, maybe the stage company just wants to give us uncommon good service, or maybe they got a reason to think they need extra speed."

Mrs. Kleinschmidt reached across the narrow space separating the seat and slapped the old miner coquettishly on the knee. "No need to alarm the poor girl when we have you as a protector, Mister Stubbs."

"Have you encountered road agents before, Mister Stubbs?" Vera asked. She might not be back west again, and this could well be her last opportunity to speak to men who had witnessed the violence of the frontier.

Mrs. Franklin harrumphed. "Don't indulge the poor girl's foolishness, Mister Stubbs. She's already got a mind filled with road agents and Indians and pistoleros and anything else not fit for a young lady. Now, Miss Vera, you know your father wrote a long article in the newspaper about how Boone May and Sherriff Bullock are driving all the ne'er-do-wells out of the territory. We are as safe as children in their beds."

"Quite right, ma'am," said a well-dressed man seated beside the old miner. "I would think there are many possible explanations for harnessing an extra pair of horses. Perhaps the road is muddy. Perhaps the stage company needs to shift some horses to the other end of the line. I would caution against jumping to any conclusions."

The old miner apologized, smiled at the womenfolk, then lowered his hat over his eyes and fell into a sudden sleep.

Mrs. Franklin leaned toward Vera and whispered in her ear, "Road agents! If someone had behaved like a young lady instead of gallivanting around town with criminals, we'd be snug in our beds."

Vera wasn't sure whom to fear more—the nameless bandits hiding out in the darkness or the housekeeper who had raised her since her mother had walked out six years earlier. Mrs. Franklin, who had moved into the Bly home after the departure of Vera's mother, had brought stability to a home turned upside down by Eustace Bly's frantic attempts to find his wife and keep his business afloat and by Vera's reaction to her mother's disappearance.

Eleven-year-old Vera, nearly bald from vitamin deficiency and a nervous habit of hair pulling, had withdrawn into her room and spurned food. Cooks were brought in to prepare special tempting meals. Doctors were consulted, including an alienist who looked Vera over through his pince-nez, felt the bumps and ridges of her skull for abnormalities, and asked her a series of puzzling questions in a heavy Parisian accent.

But ultimately, it was Mrs. Franklin who got her to eat again simply through the force of her own personality. Mrs. Franklin expressed no doubt about the fact that the girl in her charge would eat and would regain the weight she had lost. Vera was simply swept up in the housekeeper's momentum.

Harsh words from Mrs. Franklin still carried a special and heavy weight with Vera. Perhaps she had been selfish and unreasonable in disobeying her father. It certainly was true that Deadwood was full of unsavory characters, even compared to the other towns where her father had launched newspapers in a desperate effort to gather intelligence about his wayward wife. And while she did believe that journalism gave her the opportunity to exercise her natural abilities as a writer, observer, and investigator, perhaps other exciting paths would present themselves to an educated young woman in a changing world.

A year of finishing school at Mrs. Cramp's wouldn't hurt her, and she might well acquire subtle skills that she could put to use in journalism or even the legal profession. The world was changing, and there was no telling what a young woman might dream of now.

As she was coming to terms with a different, less rough-and-tumble approach to her future career, her concentration was shattered by a series of echoing cracks and the simultaneous lurching of the stagecoach to a precarious angle. Once more, she was crushed between Mrs. Franklin and Mrs. Kleinschmidt, but this time Mr. Stubbs was thrown forward from his seat and propelled onto the laps of the three women.

A voice called out from the gathering dark.

"You all put down the shotgun! We done got you covered."

The driver shouted out an urgent, "Don't shoot."

"Don't do nothin' stupid, you dang polecat."

The voice, Vera thought, sounded familiar. But when she'd heard it before, the speaker had not been using that ridiculous Southern accent and those comical backwoods expressions.

Inside the coach, the passengers held their breath and maintained silence, as if they hoped to escape unnoticed. The well-dressed man, who had been so certain that the harnessing of extra horses was not in any way a sign of greater danger, produced a small pocket knife and made a slit in his seat cushion, in which he stuffed his billfold, pocket watch, and cufflinks.

"You with the shotgun! You want to know how we stopped you? We got a sharpshooter who can hit the rim of a moving coach wheel. Take a look-see. Very slowly. You-all want some more proof? Watch this."

Another shot rang out, and the driver and guard uttered oaths of astonishment.

"If my sharpshooter can hit the rim of a wagon wheel, what do you figger's gonna happen if he aims at your ugly belly? So, drop the guns and step down. Passengers too."

Vera heard the guard's shotgun land on the ground and felt the shifting of the coach as the two men stepped down. The miner then reached across the well-dressed man and opened the door and disembarked, hands up. At the sound of a fierce throat-clearing from Mrs. Franklin, the little man reached back and helped the two older women down. Vera followed on her own, searching for the source of the voice as she did so.

"I think there's still one more in there."

Slowly, the well-dressed man stepped down, leaving his valise, Vera noticed, on the seat.

A masked figure stepped out from behind a tree but remained largely obscured by the shadows of the forest. Two other figures, also masked, emerged from the darkness. One of them made a massive black shape as he moved through the dark forest. They checked the men for weapons, removing a knife and an old cap-and-ball pistol from the belt of the old miner. Then they climbed to the back of the stage and began untying bags and cargo, opening cases and searching hastily through clothing. They closed the cases and set them aside.

The thinnest of the three bandits looked inside the coach and picked up the well-dressed man's valise and inspected its contents, running his hands along the lining as if feeling for hidden jewels.

The big one climbed to the top of the stage and began to struggle with the locked strongbox. His partner returned to the shadows and then rejoined him with a canvas bag, a hammer, and a short pry bar, and together they began working on the hinges of the heavy metal box, bolted in place on the roof of the coach.

"This might take a while," the talkative one said, his Southern accent gradually fading, "so don't nobody move. And keep your eyes pointed my way. My pardners have stage fright."

Vera heard the sounds of arduous labor, grunts and heavy breathing, and the impact of the pry bar being driven into the lockbox.

"Looks like I have a captive audience. You folks like riddles? Why did the sharpshooter with the Henry repeating rifle cross the road?"

The passengers looked nervously at one another. The guard and driver looked down. The young masked man pointed at the well-dressed passenger.

"Come on. You know how riddles work. Ask me. Why did the sharpshooter with the Henry repeating rifle cross the road?"

The well-dressed man looked side to side, as if confirming that he was indeed the person being singled out. He opened his mouth to speak and let out a hoarse, dry sound. The poser of the riddle moved his hand in a "get on with it" gesture. The man cleared his throat, then tried again. "Why did the sharpshooter with the Henry repeating rifle cross the road?"

"I dare you to ask him that." The talkative one laughed, then assessed each member of his audience as they stood still and silent.

"Come on. That joke would have killed in dear old Alabamy."

The hinges of the strongbox yielded to the repeated hammering and prying. Vera chanced a look up and saw them remove a small valise.

"Anything good?" the riddle-maker asked.

"Got the money."

Mr. Stubbs spat at the riddle-maker's feet. "That ain't yours to take."

"That's kind of what makes it a robbery, old-timer."

The old miner's fist shot forward with speed that belied his age and caught the young man on the jaw. His two accomplices raced to the scene and grappled with the man as he snarled in defiance.

"Filthy rat! Stealing food from the mouths of widows and orphans!"

"Shh, Cyrus," Mrs. Kleinschmidt said. "They have guns. Don't get yourself killed."

"These cowards can shoot me before I bow to them!"

The younger, larger men had their hands full with the red-faced Mr. Stubbs, who thrashed and cursed, spittle flying from his lips. The larger of the two men looked uncertainly toward the riddle-maker, who was rubbing his jaw and shaking his head.

The sound of footsteps from the darkness drew Vera's attention to the arrival of a fourth robber, a slight man with his hat pulled down low on his forehead and, like the others, a scarf covering all but his eyes. He carried a repeating rifle that seemed too large for his delicate hands.

The sharpshooter approached Mr. Stubbs and pointed. "What?"

The man ceased struggling and stared at the sharpshooter.

"The money you're stealing. It doesn't belong to George Hearst or the bank. Every miner in Deadwood pitched in so this lady and I can go to Cheyenne and buy food and medicine. You steal this money, and families go hungry."

The other robbers, still holding firmly to Mr. Stubbs, fixed their gaze on the sharpshooter. Expressions of concern turned to outrage when he strode to the pile of luggage, lifted the valise, and set it back inside the stagecoach. One of the larger robbers called out in alarm.

"What the hell are you doing?"

The sharpshooter ignored the question.

"Make sure this gets to the families, old-timer."

The taller of the two robbers holding Mr. Stubbs took a step toward the sharpshooter, who responded by opening his coat, his right hand hovering at his waist.

Vera felt the clearing become a collection of statues.

"So, boss. Is there anything we can take?" asked the larger robber.

The rifleman stepped up and glanced quickly into the stagecoach.

"There's a slash in the seat cushion, and the fancy man's sweating more than anybody else. Check if he stashed his money."

While one of the men searched for the hidden money, Vera set aside caution and her fear of the wrath of Mrs. Franklin and addressed the rifleman. "Take me. I'm a writer. I want to tell your story. I'll pay you. It's not much, but I have fifty dollars hidden in my skirt."

The riddle-maker held his hand out, and Vera produced the money. "No offense, Miss," he said, pointing toward the rifleman, "but you ain't starving, and my friend's charity only goes so far. Anyway, you already got fifty dollars' worth of story tonight."

24

F ROM THE TOP of the ridge, Cedar Creek Station lay spread out
in the valley below. The station offered meals and beds to weary
travelers on the way to or from Cheyenne, while the adjacent
barns and corrals sheltered the fresh horses that would be exchanged
for the next leg of the journey. The stage line maintained several such
stations at intervals along the route. They made it possible for travelers
to cover the Cheyenne Trail in as little as three days. Each was an isolated
outpost of civilization in the hostile and empty barrens, protected by
periodic cavalry patrols from Fort Laramie, but otherwise at the mercy
of heathens, wolves, horse thieves, and high plains northers.

As Josiah descended on the rutted stage road, he made out two men
hitching a team of horses to a dusty stagecoach in front of the station,
while a boy led a pair of lathered, stiff-legged horses toward the corral.
No doubt the manager of the station and the driver of the coach, assisted
by the manager's son. Josiah felt a certain kinship with the manager of
the station, a man who would stand alone against the wilderness. His
interest today, however, lay in a complex of buildings a hundred yards
west, built to take advantage of proximity to the station.

Since the stage was stopped at the station, the Cedar Creek Saloon—known around the Black Hills as the Bucket of Blood—would

have customers this morning. If what he had heard was true, the Cedar Creek Saloon was the reverse of the Cedar Creek Station. Rather than an outpost of civilization and godliness, it was a concentrated potion of wanton barbarity, worse than the godless wilderness because it was the product of men fallen from Christendom. It existed to serve the worst vices of stagecoach passengers, drivers, and guards, offering up rotgut whiskey, gambling, and fallen women, who lured men into sin in the half dozen shacks clustered behind the saloon.

Among the reprobates drawn to the saloon, or the servants of Satan working in the establishment, he would find the eyes and ears of the robber gangs.

Josiah dismounted and hitched his horses to the railing. He had a moment of doubt at the front door of the saloon. What would his grandfather say? Entering a saloon and a house of ill repute? Pretending to be a robber and thief? He recalled then a sermon of his grandfather's on the topic of the Last Judgment. "The Day of the Lord so comes as a thief in the night."

Yes. Even the Lord masks His intentions and sneaks up on the unworthy. Josiah would do the Lord's work, even if he had to pretend to do Satan's.

A burst of laughter brought him back to the present. Men were gathered inside, no doubt sharing their vulgar, blasphemous stories. Josiah braced himself for the worst and opened the door.

"So, this man walks into a saloon." A thin youth stood against the wall to Josiah's right, his face in profile as he addressed men to his right. He looked up suddenly, and Josiah recognized him as the mesmerist from the circus, the friend of the sharpshooter.

The youth batted his eyes and continued his banter, but it was obvious he recognized Josiah. "Whoa. Seriously, this man walks into a saloon. Howdy, stranger, have a seat. You know what we say in the West. A stranger is just a friend you haven't met yet... who's probably going to shoot you in the face and steal your horse."

The drunkards laughed at Josiah, egged on by the fast-talking whelp. Josiah crossed his arms and stood planted in his place.

"So, this man walks into a saloon and says to the bartender, 'Gimme a beer.' Bartender pours him a beer, he takes a sip and spits it out. Says, 'This beer's disgusting!' Bartender says, 'Sorry, I should have warned you, we're in a serious drought.' Man says, 'So?' Bartender says, 'So, there's no fresh water for making beer. We have to go down to the stable with a bucket and collect horse piss.' Man gets a disgusted look on his face and says, 'Fool, everybody knows you don't use horse piss.'"

The bartender barked out a laugh and slapped the hardwood, while two tables of stage passengers burst out laughing, one man spraying his beer on the table. Josiah looked on in wonderment. The thin, young man looked at him across the small room.

"Get a look at Jedediah over here," the young man said. "He's thinking 'what's wrong with horse piss?' Not a bad question if you've ever tried the stuff Sam calls beer."

The bartender's expression turned sour. "You said this would be good for business, kid."

"Hey, at least I haven't said anything about the food."

One of the drunk passengers shouted out, "Or the whores!"

The bartender surveyed Josiah from across the room. "What can I get you?"

Josiah appraised the saloon. The bartender was a fat, balding man with massive forearms and a jagged scar on one side of his face. The scar ran clean through to a maimed ear. He stood behind a rough plank that rested on two barrels. The plank held an array of clear bottles containing liquid of various shades of amber. Beside him was another barrel, with the lid removed, and a ladle hanging on the side. Josiah realized that the yeasty smell in the room was coming from this barrel.

The two tables of stage passengers were divided into first class and second or third. At one table sat a pair of men in bowler hats, dark suits, shiny in places with wear, and shirts with visibly frayed collars. Each of these men had beside him a large case of the sort carried by drummers, who hauled samples of their merchandise, medicines perhaps, or some sort of dry goods. At the same table was a man in a dark suit with a handsome brocade vest and a silk top hat. He, too, carried a case but a smaller one, perhaps full of legal papers. These three had glasses and a bottle of whiskey on their table.

At the neighboring table slouched four men in denim and corduroy, two covered with dust and spattered with mud from riding on the third-class seat exposed to the elements. They had mugs of beer on their table, and from the way they had directed their laughter at the barkeep during the youth's joke, the description of its origins had not been totally fanciful.

Josiah walked to the bar, uncertain of what else might be on offer. The youth had joked about the food, so he decided to give that a try.

"Got anything to eat?"

The barkeep gave him a puzzled expression. This must not be a question he heard often. Then he gestured to a jar on the other end of the bar.

"Pickled eggs."

"I'll take one."

He slid the jar down the bar to Josiah. "Ten cents, big spender."

Josiah looked at the murky liquid in the jar and placed a coin on the bar. He opened the jar, filling the room with an aroma befitting a den of Satan, and fished out an egg. He popped the rubbery morsel in his mouth, chewed and forced it down, then cleared his throat, stalling for time as he tried to figure out a way to start a conversation with the barkeep. He had expected the barkeep to be the most likely man in the saloon to have connections with road agents. Such a man would know when the stages come and go and how many shotgun men rode as guards. But discovering the sidekick of the so-called Bulldog Kid gave him different ideas. Now he only had to determine how to gain the young joker's confidence.

Josiah, accustomed to traveling alone on the empty grasslands, had no idea how to put up a false front, how to banter and boast and tell the lies that such men consider conversation. Laughing at a joke was challenge enough.

Before he could formulate an opening, the door burst open, and a man called out, "All passengers for Deadwood, coach resumes in five minutes."

The passengers downed their drinks. One of the drummers grabbed the bottle and stuffed it in a jacket pocket. Those with cases lifted them and made for the door. The barkeep stepped away from the wooden plank and gathered up the empty glasses and placed them in a basin of standing water.

As the men departed, the thin youth ran after them with his hat upside down, imploring coins. A few dropped nickels in the hat. He followed them outside, continuing to prattle on about anything in order to prompt a laugh and squeeze out one more coin.

"If you ain't drinkin', we're closing until the Cheyenne stage stops this evening," the barkeep said, not even looking up from his basin.

Josiah stepped toward the barkeep and placed a dollar on the counter.

"What's your pleasure?"

"Information. Who's the boy with the jokes?"

"Calls himself Sherman. Showed up two days ago asking to push a broom for food. He started telling jokes for tips, and I let him." The barkeep, no doubt accustomed to queries from lawmen and bounty hunters, narrowed his eyes. "He got paper on him?"

"None that I know." Josiah slapped another dollar on the wood. "I'm just wondering what he knows."

Josiah stepped out into the sun and the rising heat of the day. Unaccustomed as he was to saloons, he didn't know if it was unusual for a ramshackle hovel like the Bucket of Blood to have entertainment. He suspected it was. Which made it seem certain the joker's true purpose was to watch for the comings and goings of stagecoaches.

As he approached the youth, who appeared to be counting the coins in his hat, the boy looked up and held it out to him. "Support the the-a-ter, Mister?"

"I thought you were a big-time circus performer."

"Hey, the life of the artist."

"Where's your friend, the quick-draw artist?"

"Creative differences. I'm just working up a stake, and then I'm bound for the bright lights again."

Josiah appraised the youth more carefully—the peach fuzz on his chin, the bandy legs and arms. All in combination with a mouth that surely would get him into trouble. A boy like this had no business being alive in the West. It was inconceivable that he would have split with the gunman, just as it was inconceivable that anybody as quick on the draw as the Bulldog Kid would be satisfied pointing his pistols only at playing cards. This boy knew how to find his friend and would lead Josiah right to him.

Josiah dropped a dime into the hat and said, "I like a laugh as much as the next man."

"Who's the next man, Cotton Mather?"

Josiah began to scowl but worked to turn up the corners of his mouth. "You're sweet on that girl. The girl with the dogs."

The thin boy blushed. "Listen, Mister. Sorry about that night. She said you were disturbing the act."

"You told me to watch your friend with the pistols and I might learn something that could save my life. That sounded like a threat."

"Hey, it's the West. Always a good idea to know who the fast guns are, right?"

Josiah attempted another smile. "And now I know. I'll make a point of not facing down your friend any time soon."

"So, what do you do, mister?"

"I'm a wolfer."

"And here I was thinking something solitary and violent. First impressions. Whaddaya know? So, how's the wolfing business?"

"Not so good. I'm looking for another line of work. Open to anything."

"Have you considered digging for gold? I hear they do that around here."

"I'm looking for something where you could make more money faster. Got any ideas?"

"If I did, I don't think I'd be working for spare coins in the Bucket of Blood."

Josiah pushed out a laugh and mounted his horse. There was no point trying to convince the young man that he wanted to join the gang. Better to wait and follow him to their hideout.

25

"CRACK OF rifle fire shatters the silence of the night and the stagecoach crashes to a halt. What has happened? Has some murderous desperado assassinated the driver or the noble steeds that pull the coach? No, in a feat of marksmanship that would make Daniel Boone and Davy Crockett green with envy, a hidden sharpshooter has struck the moving wheel of the vehicle, thus bringing its journey to this abrupt termination. Passengers are thrown hither and yon as the coach lurches to its stop. The terror is immediately upon the lips of all inside—road agents! But which gang could this be? The Youngers are dead or imprisoned since their misadventure in Northfield, Minnesota. Jesse James has never strayed this far west. The wealth of California keeps Black Bart busy beyond the Sierra Nevada mountains."

Vera looked over her opening paragraph. A bit flowery, to be sure, but flowery seemed to be expected in dime novels. The clichés, on the other hand, had to go. She put a line through "green with envy" and changed the reference to "a feat of marksmanship that would shame Daniel Boone and Davy Crockett." She replaced "thrown hither and yon" with "tossed like flotsam" but thought better of it. Dime novels were meant to appeal to a mass audience. Flotsam might be too obscure a word for many. She tried "tossed about like rag dolls" instead. Better but still not perfect.

Vera shook her head. She needed to complete the story, not worry about individual words and phrases. And the only way to complete the story would be to get back on the Union Pacific, get off in Cheyenne, get a horse, and ride the Deadwood trail. But was it necessary to have the complete story now? Weren't most dime novels written with a series of sequels in mind?

Of course, she didn't have the entire story of the Bulldog Kid. The Kid had barely begun to live his full story. The story of his origins, or as much of it as Vera could infer from the words of his accomplices, might be enough by itself for a dime novel.

If it turned out that there were readers for the story of the Bulldog Kid's beginning, she could always return to Deadwood for the sequel.

She continued writing the story of the stagecoach robbery, massaging her memory for the words of her fellow passengers and the commands of the gang spokesman and his two musclemen. Then she turned to the speculative part of the story.

She wrote down the details of the confrontation at the courthouse, ending with the gangly, nervous joker who told her to tell the world that the legendary Bulldog Kid had arrived. At first, she had been impressed by the speed with which the young man had pulled out his pistols but had thought that alone didn't prove he could shoot. A blind shot at a moving rat across the street provided the first hint that the Bulldog Kid—and come to think of it, the Kid didn't seem familiar with, nor particularly enamored of, the nickname—could possibly become a legendary gunman.

More proof came a few nights later. She had been as spellbound as everybody else at the circus, when a mysterious young gunslinger known as the Bulldog Kid put on an exhibition of marksmanship. His remarkable shooting—a bullet hole in each of the two one-eyed jacks—suggested that the Bulldog Kid would be capable of hitting the spinning wheel of a stagecoach.

As for the gunman's origins, she doubted the story of the son of a Southern duelist brought up with a gun in his hand. But then, so long as she made clear in her dime novel that this was the story told by one of the gunman's friends, she could certainly use it. Attributing it to the young shooter's partner in crime allowed her to stay at arm's length from any falsehood.

It's not gospel, she reminded herself. It's only journalism.

Vera was intrigued by the young gunman's mercy to the old miner, allowing him to keep the money he said would be used to feed women, children, and the aged and infirm. A Robin Hood angle would help to sell the story. Everybody loved an outlaw who afflicted only the comfortable. If only she could learn what brought about his compassion for the downtrodden.

She continued writing until she'd used up everything she knew about the Bulldog Kid and the stagecoach robbery. By this time it was dark, and Omaha lay just beyond the horizon, and Vera's eyes and hand were sore. She would board the Kansas City Express in a few hours, and tomorrow at noon the train would arrive at her destination, where she would be compelled to board the carriage that would take her to Mrs. Cramp's school. That would give her the morning to work on sketches. She smiled, pleased at her foresight in bringing her good sketch pads and her shading pencil.

The next day, when her train pulled into Kansas City, Vera smiled and curtseyed and made a point of being on her best behavior as Mrs. Cramp's servant and the under-housemistress met her on the platform. She told them what a relief it was to be back in civilization after being surrounded by ruffians in the West, how delightful and *absolument Parisien* Kansas City appeared after the tents and mud of the Black Hills.

Perhaps she was spreading it a bit thick. Still, the under-housemistress didn't appear suspicious, and Vera was able to note the names of businesses en route to the school, including two printing shops and the office of the *Kansas City Enterprise and Civic Booster.*

If the newspaper wouldn't buy her story about the Bulldog Kid, she could take her spending money and publish it herself.

26

—————▶•◆•◀—————

THE TENT WAS folded, and the wagons were packed for the trip to Cheyenne, and circus folk were gathered in the dining room of the hotel to talk business. Uncle Stanislas, dressed in the dark frock coat, brocade vest, and striped trousers he wore for meetings with bankers and town councils, raised a glass and puffed out his chest as if about to introduce the next performance.

"Ladies and gentlemen, artists of the road, creators of magic, I am pleased to announce that word of our Deadwood triumphs has reached every gold and silver town from Montana to California."

Lily smiled to hear Uncle Stanislas speaking in the theatrical mid-Atlantic accent he used during circus performances.

"I have just received a telegram offering us bookings throughout Colorado... in Denver, Leadville, Colorado Springs, Telluride, Silverton. We will bring enchantment to the miners and their families until the mountain passes are covered with snow. And then we will travel to the Arizona Territory and spend the winter performing in the warm sunshine."

"But how did we do at the box office, Stanislas?" Mr. Szabo asked.

"Well enough to keep the circus traveling but not yet well enough for a general distribution of funds."

This news was greeted with a round of groans.

"Ah, the legendary 'general distribution of funds,'" Mr. Szabo responded. "What kind of triumph will it take for us to witness this financial unicorn?"

Uncle Stanislas held up a calming hand and took a sip from his drink. "Anton, you know that keeping food in our bellies and a roof over our heads is not cheap like borscht."

"Then we should charge more," urged Madame Mystere. "We debase our art and ourselves by performing for pennies."

This brought another chorus of agreement from performers who knew only too well how many of the seats in Deadwood had been filled with two-for-one promotions.

"We filled that tent every night for two weeks," protested Arnold, stepping up onto a trunk to make himself heard. "Every rube in this town came at least once."

"Is not possible to raise ticket prices when mining companies pay workers with a handful of kopecks," said Uncle Stanislas, losing his ringmaster's accent and voice. "Hungry miners have no golden-egg hen in coop."

"So we must return to the East!" Tommaso Largo shouted.

"But in the East, we are just another little circus. We have no elephants, no lions."

Mr. Szabo pounded on the table and stood. "Stanislas is right. America is the land of winner-take-all. In the East, we have Dan Rice and Barnum's American Museum and the fortunes they have built. They have money to cover every wall in America with posters and fill every newspaper with advertisements. What do we have? A few paragraphs from the *Deadwood Herald*. We must admit that a few clowns and tumblers, a high-wire walker, a magician, a fortune teller, and Lillian and her dogs are no competition. I hoped Lillian's friends would be that something more. Audiences from Boston to New Orleans would pay good money to see the Bulldog Kid, and I confess young Mister Segal could be trained to be an entertaining clown. Unfortunately, they appear to have vanished, along with our hope of acquiring a fresh act."

Mr. Szabo sank into his chair and bowed his head. The room was stilled, the silence punctuated only by sighs and the sounds of glasses being drained.

"So," Uncle Stanislas said. "Is nowhere to go for us but up. And up means Cheyenne and Colorado."

Uncle Stanislas called for another round, nodding toward Mr. Szabo, who shrugged and left the room. As the first of the new mugs began circulating around the tables, the quavering minor-key notes of an accordion could be heard from down the hall. The volume and tempo of the music increased as Mr. Szabo returned to the room playing a czardas.

As the clapping began and Uncle Stanislas joined in on his violin, Lily wandered into the night for a final look at the moonlit hills above Deadwood. She thought of the narrow gully, where insects had surely picked the charred wolf cub corpses clean, and of the man she had encountered there. She would be happy to put the Dakota Territory far behind her.

Two days later, as they approached the unmarked line separating the Dakota and Wyoming Territories, Lily felt a prickling sensation like wet skin in a lightning storm.

It was her dogs. Not the full-blooded terror they had felt in the wolfer's presence, but there was no doubt that they were on edge. Sparky chirped his sharp little barks, while Galahad and Lancelot jumped down from their wagon and stood with their noses in the air, their muscles tensed and their tails standing straight.

She had chosen on this journey to ride the pony given to her by Dreams of Horses. She put heels to the animal's side and trotted to the lead wagon, driven by Uncle Stanislas, and called for him to stop. When he halted the horses, she drew hers up alongside and peered at the approaching rider. She saw a lone horseman, male, with a narrow-brimmed city-style hat, riding a small paint, probably an Indian pony purchased from a rancher. He wasn't an expert rider, but he seemed to sit the horse tolerably well. She was relieved to confirm that the lone rider was not the wolfer, though if it had been that grim, black-garbed animal killer, her dogs surely would have sounded the alarm.

As he pulled up beside the horse team and reined in his mount, she realized she was face-to-face with the Bulldog Kid.

Uncle Stanislas was obviously delighted to see him.

"Greetings friend! Stanislas's Circus of Wonders is pleased to welcome you back. Do you wish you join us on our tour?"

The Kid's eyes widened in apparent surprise. He looked down at Galahad and Lancelot, who had approached cautiously, sniffing the air, and were now looking up at him in curiosity.

Lily was equally curious.

"My uncle was impressed by your performance. He was hoping you and Mister Segal would be interested in joining us."

"Joining the circus?"

"That's what we are, Mister Bulldog."

"Daniel. Bulldog Kid is Segal's *meshuggah* idea."

Like many circus folk, Uncle Stanislas knew a smattering of Central and Eastern European languages. *"Meshuggah?* What's so *meshuggah* about traveling freely across this great country and entertaining thousands of paying customers every night?"

Daniel appeared flummoxed by Uncle Stanislas's enthusiasm. His cheeks reddened, and he hastily removed his hat, as if he had just remembered a point of etiquette. He directed his words at Lily and Uncle Stanislas equally. "I'm sorry for getting in your way today, but I'm not looking to join the circus. I'm looking for Segal."

Lily's sharp intake of breath caught the attention of the dogs. They immediately became more watchful. "He's not with you?" she asked.

"I was supposed to meet him. But he didn't show up."

"What could have happened? Do you think Indians? Or robbers?"

"I thought he might be with you." Daniel pointed to a rise far enough away that a telescope would have been in order. "I saw you coming from the hill over to the west."

"Why with us?" Lily asked.

"I thought maybe, since he had so much fun helping you in your act, he might have met up with you and lost track of time. He's a good friend but kind of scattered."

Lily thought of the fast-talking young man and his joy in making the audience laugh. She thought as well of his willingness to help her when the wolfer derailed her act and the warning he'd given to that brute. She had seen the fury on the wolfer's face.

She turned to Uncle Stanislas and mouthed an apology and called to Galahad and Lancelot to join her as she raced ahead on the wagon trail. Daniel spurred his horse and followed her to the high point from which he'd seen the circus wagons.

When they reached the top, Lily dismounted first, and Daniel followed. "I need to talk to you, and I didn't want the others to hear," she said. "They don't know the whole story about the wolfer."

"You think he came for Segal?"

Lily filled Daniel in about her confrontation in the gully near Deadwood. "He strikes me as the kind of man who wants revenge. I'm always with the circus. Segal's safe when he's with you. But if you were separated, maybe that's when he caught up with him."

"Yeah, we were separated."

"So if we go back to wherever Segal was last—"

"We've done that. Nobody saw anyone take him."

"Maybe not, but we can track him."

"I'm not a tracker."

"Lancelot and Galahad are. I'll tell them to follow Segal's tracks."

Daniel gave her an appraising look from head to toe. "You can really talk to your dogs? Like, you can talk, and they understand? And they can talk back?"

"Everybody thinks it's some kind of trick, and I know it seems hard to believe, but I just—"

"You can do something nobody else can?" Daniel bent and picked up a pair of rocks, quickly tossing the first high in the air and then throwing the second so that it struck the first as it was falling to the ground. "People say I'm hard to believe too."

Lily examined the delicate hands that moved faster than any eyesight and the eyes that saw farther than a spyglass. "Uncle Stanislas says I'm a 'prodigy.' Which is sort of a nice way of saying a freak."

Lily smiled at her fellow prodigy. She'd been living with the big, strange family of the circus, surrounded by people who might have been considered freaks by many in the audience, but even still, she'd felt alone for a long time. It was nice to meet somebody who knew that feeling. As she smiled at Daniel, she realized her dogs were wagging their tails at him. They were still worried, but they weren't worried about the young gunman.

Daniel cocked his head at an angle and spied movement farther up the road. He waved and placed a foot in a stirrup, then turned to see Lily already atop her horse, waiting for him. They rode until they fell in with two other young men, one tall, trim, and broad-shouldered, the other built like a grizzly bear. The young men plodded along uncomfortably on surplus cavalry mounts. Daniel introduced his friends Wiseman and Roth. Lily looked back in the direction of the circus, approaching them along the trail. Her circus family would not let her leave with these young men on their dangerous errand. She dismounted and picked up a stick and wrote in the dust beside the trail, "Helping a friend. Will join you in Cheyenne."

"Make sure Mister Szabo and Uncle Stanislas see this," she said to Galahad and Lancelot. "Then, follow us." Then she climbed on her horse and set off with the other three for a place Roth called the Bucket of Blood.

As they cantered along the trail, she felt increasingly comfortable in the saddle. Uncle Stanislas had spoken of her father's trick-riding skills—his daring, agility, balance—and now Lily felt those same attributes had been passed on to her. She gripped the horse firmly yet lightly with her knees and communicated clearly by voice and gesture, and the horse took her where she wished to go at the speed she desired.

She felt none of the mind-sharing that she experienced when she communicated with canines, but knowing something of one animal intelligence, she knew that the horse had a mind and soul of its own. Somehow, this awareness, and the confidence it gave her and respect it generated in her, won the horse over. Perhaps when this was all done, Lily thought, she would try adding an equestrian element to her act.

Lancelot and Galahad soon rejoined her, and she was relieved to learn that they had carried out her request. Perhaps she could rejoin the group before they even reached Cheyenne.

Soon, they approached a ramshackle collection of buildings—a horse barn, a work shed, a ranch house, and, a short distance to one side, a larger shack with a collection of smaller sheds scattered behind it. On the roof of a ranch house, a man pounded nails into loose shingles, while another man—or perhaps a boy—could be seen emerging from the barn with a shovel and wheelbarrow.

"What was Segal doing here?" Lily asked.

Daniel looked embarrassed and guilty. He stared at the ground and muttered, "He had a job in the saloon. They let him tell jokes for tips and then clean up after the customers left."

Lily leveled a skeptical eye at Daniel. What kind of job was that?

She and Daniel tied their horses to a hitching rail and entered the saloon where Segal entertained. Only the bartender was present, sleeping with his head on the bar, and he woke with a start, mumbling something about not expecting customers until the next stagecoach.

As Daniel spoke to him, it was clear that he had provided answers earlier that day on Segal's whereabouts. It was clear, as well, that he didn't trust the thin young man. In the West, Lily was learning, young men and men of slight build were sometimes more feared than the largest bruisers because it was assumed that they would be quicker to use a firearm if slighted. She shivered as she realized that the shy young man she had ridden in with might well be the most dangerous shootist north of Texas.

As they left the saloon, a thought occurred to her. Working in a stage line station like this, where all north and southbound coaches stopped for water and fresh mounts, would be ideal for a lookout for a gang of robbers. And a talkative, outgoing joker might be the ideal person for such work, drawing out valuable information from passengers, drivers, and guards alike.

"Was Segal really just here to tell jokes?" she asked.

"It's what he loves to do."

"That's not an answer."

"When we find him, we ask him to join your circus. That's where he belongs."

"Not with you and your gang?"

Daniel opened his mouth, and Lily felt sure he was going to say that he didn't have a gang, but instead, he turned away and pointed to a shed in the back.

"Segal slept there sometimes, when it wasn't being used for, you know...."

Lily called the dogs, and together the four of them approached the shed. Lily opened her mind to Lancelot and Galahad and made sure that they felt how strongly she wanted to find the funny, friendly, gangly young man. She cautioned the dogs that he might have been captured by the wolfer, and so they might detect signs of the wolfer's hateful hunting hounds. They were not to risk a confrontation with the hounds. As she ended the communication, they ran off in circles around the saloon, noses to the ground, and quickly converged on a hitching post where Lily saw them both adopt a fearful defensive posture. With hair standing on their shoulders and teeth bared, the dogs pointed to the post, then turned and indicated the direction of the tracks.

"The wolfer was here," she said.

"With Segal?"

"Not right here. But somewhere around here. I'm sure he took Segal." She directed words out loud to the dogs. "Find Segal's tracks. See if the wolfer caught him."

Daniel and Lily stood in the hot Wyoming sun, in the treeless yard of the station, and watched the dogs follow traces of Segal's scent around the yard. Much of their movement looked as random as a busy anthill as they ran back and forth from the saloon to the outhouse, to the station, to the tiny shed. Then Lancelot caught a scent that led to a path leading up to the sand hills behind the station, and the two dogs began to race upward.

Lily mounted her horse and turned to Daniel. "It looks like he left by the back way. Almost as if he was sneaking away. Isn't that odd?"

Daniel said nothing but followed on his horse. They climbed through thickening willows that would have hidden Segal from anybody who happened to be watching. Lily could see bent and broken twigs indicating the passage of a rider, perhaps more than one.

From up ahead, on the downhill side of the sand hills, she heard the barking of the dogs. They had found something, and they wanted her to know, but she was not yet close enough to understand what they were saying.

She spurred her horse to trot up the last of the rise and down into the saddle below, resting between two tall hills.

She opened her mind to the dogs and saw what they saw—Segal, the wolfer, and the wolfer's hounds. She asked the dogs where they were going, and they set off north. Without waiting for Daniel to catch up, she hurried after them overland until, a few miles later, she came to a faint trail where the dogs turned. It was an old scout's trail, clearly little traveled now that the stagecoach company had built the main trail. It led east toward the Black Hills and Deadwood.

It took Daniel some time to catch up, and he was breathless from the gallop across the grassland when he reached her.

"I suppose a man who kills wolves for their bounty might turn to catching men with bounties on them, wouldn't he?" Lily said. "The wolfer has taken Segal back to Deadwood. I'll help you free him, but I need to know why he was taken."

Daniel looked as if he were about to be sick. His eyes had begun to water. He wouldn't meet Lily's eyes. Lily had heard preachers talk about shame a few times on occasions when the circus had attended some kind of fire-and-brimstone service. It had always been described as something a sinner feels standing before God. Lily had never felt it, but Daniel seemed to feel it in her presence.

"It's all my fault. If I hadn't given back the money, we could still be working with Missus Kleinschmidt, and we wouldn't have had to find another stagecoach to rob."

"Another?"

Daniel shrugged. "Let's ride, and I'll tell you all about it."

27

LINCOLN HAD NEVER been in the offices of the Homestake Mine Company, and he had certainly never dreamed of setting foot in the rich oak-lined private office of Mr. Hearst. He had read about kings and presidents, including the one whose name he bore, and he had always assumed such people lived in grand buildings surrounded by expensive furnishings. For all his ability to visualize the movements of machinery or the lines of strength and weakness in a cliff face or a building's frame, he had never actually imagined what these worldly palaces might look like.

More amazing still, when he stopped to think about it, was that all this finery should be here in Deadwood, hundreds of miles by trail from the rail line in Cheyenne.

That big polished wooden globe, with jewels inlaid for the great capitals of the world, those paintings of old castles, their frames plated in real gold, that rich, thick carpet with the pattern of colored threads and intricate knots that threatened to mesmerize Lincoln—all had been loaded onto trains in New York or Chicago and shipped to Cheyenne, then carefully but firmly strapped into wagons for the long trip to the Black Hills.

Most bewildering, perhaps, was the massive mahogany desk, with its intricately patterned legs thicker than Lincoln's papa's thighs and a surface area the size of some miner's cabin. Try as he might, Lincoln could not see how it could have been transported to Deadwood. It must have been delivered in pieces, but how?

"Have some more Turkish delight, Mister Henry," Mr. Hearst said. "I'm sure it's better for you than these cigars."

Mr. Hearst held out a burning wood chip to Mr. McTaggart, who leaned in and puffed on a cigar that seemed to be nearly the size of a corncob. Once Mr. McTaggart's cigar was lit, Mr. Hearst held the wood chip to his own cigar and puffed vigorously. The air turned blue with smoke.

"First things first, Mister Henry... Lincoln. I would like to thank you for your excellent work. And, of course, Mister McTaggart, thank you. But more importantly, I would like to apologize for the tragic events you witnessed during the test run. I assure you, it was never my intention for the steam wagon to be used in such a manner. I assure you, as well, that Mister Boone May has been disciplined for his misuse of the steam wagon. His orders were simply to take it out for a comprehensive test and, secondarily, as you guessed, to demonstrate to wrongdoers that the Homestake Mine Company is equipped with tools to make life difficult for both road agents and anarchists. He was not authorized to visit the radicals' camp. Of course, the radicals are ultimately culpable for the loss of life, since they were the ones who began shooting. There's a saying out here in the West. 'Never take a knife to a gunfight.' I would suggest that 'Never take a gun to a steam wagon fight' might be equally valid. Nevertheless, I deeply regret the emotional harm inflicted on a young man who, I understand, has already experienced more than his share of turmoil."

Mr. Hearst paused, his prepared remarks delivered, and sucked on his cigar. Lincoln watched in anticipation as the ash grew longer. Would Mr. Hearst allow it to fall on his expensive desk?

After taking in another mouthful of smoke, Mr. Hearst leaned back and blew a smoke ring, then gently tapped his cigar on an onyx ashtray the size of a cauldron. He looked toward Mr. McTaggart, as if inviting him to accept the generous apology.

"Aye, Mister Hearst, it was a terrible thing for the lad to see. That's why, I think, it might be best to find him an apprenticeship somewhere else. I have a friend in Minneapolis—"

"It does my heart good to know that such a talented young man has a protective mentor looking out for him," Mr. Hearst cut in. "But don't you think the best thing for Lincoln is to remain with the teacher who has helped him to develop his remarkable abilities? Not to mention the remarkable career benefits he enjoys having the resources of the Homestake Mine Company at his disposal. Your friend in Minneapolis may be a fine mechanic, but can he provide Lincoln with an opportunity to make mechanical history?"

Mr. Hearst stood and turned his back, preventing any reply. He walked to the window, looking out on the mine, and called for Lincoln to join him. From up here, the fault lines in the rock were visible, and Lincoln felt he could see where the layers of rich ore were most accessible. He watched men laden with tools climb into a wagon on rails to descend to the ore face. He watched others build the giant headworks where ore would be sorted and crushed before the addition of arsenic to extract the shiny, precious metal. It was a big place and getting bigger fast.

"You've probably never seen the scale of this operation, have you?"

"No, sir."

"You see that mountain there? My geologists tell me nearly the whole thing is ore, rich enough to keep mining for a hundred years. What do you think I'm going to do with all that gold, Lincoln?"

Lincoln had wondered just that. What does a man want with a mountain of gold? He'd heard a story of a king who loved gold too much and ended up turning his wife and daughter into golden statues. Lincoln had an idea that Mr. Hearst didn't feel like that about gold. It wasn't the sight of it or the heavy feeling of it in his hands he loved. But he loved the power it gave him.

"I don't know, sir. I expect that much gold makes you like Mister Carnegie or Mister Rockefeller."

"You mean rich? Powerful?"

"I think so, sir."

"But what's the point of being rich and powerful? You must wonder about that, don't you?"

"Not really, sir."

Mr. Hearst smiled. "I assure you, Lincoln, being wealthy and powerful is not just one long ice cream social. It is the way of the world, sadly, that he who achieves something will attract every manner of thief and parasite. Those who do not have the courage to rob outright will attempt to use extortion or the power of the mob in order to siphon off a taste. Soon enough, a man of wealth and achievement will be covered in tiny bloodsuckers, none lethal by itself, but collectively enough to bring down the strongest of men. Does that sound right to you, Lincoln?"

"No, sir."

"No indeed. And that is why I refuse on highest principle to yield to these bloodsuckers. And Lincoln, in protecting my wealth, I am not merely thinking of my own comfort. I intend to use my wealth... the wealth God put into the ground in the form of this ore... to create a new world. The America I was born in was a place of rutted, muddy wagon roads, dark forests teeming with man-eating creatures, malarial swamps, children coughing their lungs out in crude cabins incapable of keeping out the winter winds."

Lincoln knew this was supposed to be a powerful statement about the challenges Mr. Hearst had overcome, but it sounded a whole lot like the America Lincoln had always known.

"What I wish to do, Lincoln, is make a new America. A new world. A place of houses built to last a hundred years. A place where men and women and children have the freedom to travel this remarkable land of ours in a matter of weeks or even days. A place where the knowledge and cultural achievement of humanity reach into the humblest homes. This gold mine will provide me with the resources to bring that about. Lincoln, your mind will create the tools to make that new America. Beginning with a perfected version of your steam wagon."

Mr. Hearst's expression grew stern, and the light in his eyes dimmed. "And for that reason, I must insist that you both remain in Deadwood to fulfill the terms of your employment contracts."

Mr. McTaggart stood, placing a hand on Lincoln's shoulder. "But we didna sign contracts!"

"That is not what my lawyers say. My learned friend Judge Bennett takes a dim view of those who attempt to dodge their legal obligations."

Lincoln didn't know much about contract law or the politics of the Dakota Territory's judges, but he didn't need to apply his special talents to see the forces at play in the room. Mr. Hearst had all the money and power he needed to force his master mechanic and apprentice to do whatever he wanted them to do.

Mr. Hearst then issued his commands. Mr. McTaggart and Lincoln would set to work on modifications to the steam wagon to make it more effective in bringing order to Deadwood and the world beyond. They were to begin working on these improvements to the existing version of the steam wagon immediately. When these improvements were completed, they were to begin developing a new design that would address the steam wagon's shortcomings in terms of speed, weight, and operating range.

Since this project was so important to the future of the Homestake Mine and to that of America, it would be carried out in secrecy. Therefore, Lincoln and Mr. McTaggart would live at their workshop until further notice. Mr. Hearst's employees would see to all of their needs and, should it be necessary to visit Lincoln's family in Deadwood, they would act as chaperones for any visits beyond the guarded compound.

Mr. Hearst gave them each a bonus of two hundred and fifty dollars in gold coins and dismissed them.

After his meeting with Mr. Hearst, while Lincoln pondered escaping with his family to someplace far from Deadwood, Boone May rode up with two of his men, all wearing pistols. May carried his usual shotgun. They accompanied a wagon pulled by a pair of heavy draft horses. In the box was a stack of wooden crates of varied size.

"I hear Mister Hearst has a little project for you," May announced, dismounting and picking up a pry bar from the toolshed.

Lincoln watched with growing unease as May popped boards off the boxes, revealing straw packing and odd shapes of steel. He had no idea what to expect of these steel arms and tubes, but when May pulled what looked like a crank handle from one of the boxes, Lincoln heard Mr. McTaggart gasp.

"Oh my Lord!"

"What is it?"

Boone May smiled down at them from the box. "It's Mister Hearst's little plaything. He had this brought out even before you started working on your war wagon. A little something to have in case Sitting Bull decided to pay us a visit last year after he finished with Custer."

May directed his men to unload the pieces and place them on the ground. First, the men brought out a pair of wheels and a long box that looked like it might contain the axle assembly. Various plates and frames came next. Then, a curious collection of tubes all bundled up together.

"Get over here, McTaggart," he said. "This ain't no holiday picnic. You too."

As Lincoln approached, he began putting the pieces together in his mind. Mr. McTaggart glanced at a stack of papers May had handed him and gave out instructions to the men. Lincoln picked up a wrench to help but was surprised when Mr. McTaggart waved him off.

"Not for you, Lincoln," Mr. McTaggart whispered.

As he watched, Lincoln saw a two-wheel carriage assembly come together, then a platform with a freewheel that would allow forty-five degrees of side-to-side rotation. Then the collection of tubes was attached to the freewheel, and the crank handle was joined to the tubes using a gear assembly that allowed a turn of the handle to make the tubes turn. When it was assembled, Mr. McTaggart turned and directed Lincoln to stand farther back.

May's men lifted the wooden crates out of the wagon box and carried them to the wall of the compound, about fifty feet from where the wheeled device stood gleaming in the sun. When they returned, they stood beside May, who gripped the handle in one hand.

"Mister Henry," May said, glancing back with a narrow smile. "You may want to see this."

Fire leapt from the ends of the bundled barrels as May turned the crank. A deafening thunder filled the compound, along with a growing cloud of acrid, dark smoke. Splinters of wood and a haze of sawdust filled the air around the crate.

Lincoln shifted his gaze to the complicated mechanisms that rotated the bundle of barrels, loaded them, fired them, and extracted spent shell casings in a continuous motion. Somebody put a powerful amount of thinking into this—somebody who didn't much mind if a whole lot of people died.

May stopped turning, and the machine went silent, but the sounds continued to ring in Lincoln's ears.

"It's the new model," May said. "Light weight, short barrels. They say you could mount one of these on a camel and have yourself the deadliest cavalry in the world. But Mister Hearst doesn't have any camels."

Lincoln wasn't so sure about a camel sitting still for all that noise and smoke, but he knew better than to argue with Mr. May.

"What we got is the war wagon. Mister Hearst wants you two to figure out a way of fitting this inside the steam wagon."

He and his men mounted up and left them with what Lincoln now knew was a Gatling gun. The gate clicked shut behind them, and Lincoln heard the sound of a bolt being slid and locked in place.

"They locked us in, Mister Mc—"

"I know." Mr. McTaggart told Lincoln to make him a mug of tea.

Lincoln kindled a fire to bring the water to a boil. As he waited, he stood in the doorway and watched Mr. McTaggart loosen the bolts that held the gun assembly to the wheeled carriage.

Mr. McTaggart, who hardly seemed to be watching his hands, was in a powerful hurry to loosen those bolts. The wrench slipped, and Mr. McTaggart skinned his knuckles. He shouted a string of oaths and tossed his wrench to the ground.

Lincoln ducked back into the workshop and made the tea. As he handed Mr. McTaggart the mug, with his other hand he felt the fine millwork in the brass and steel components. It chilled his heart.

"This ain't... isn't... right," he said.

"No, it isn't, Lincoln."

"Reckon we can just say no?"

Mr. McTaggart uttered a short, bitter laugh and took a sip of his tea. Lincoln noticed the wrench lying forlornly in the dirt. Mr. McTaggart had never let a tool get dirty before. Lincoln bent and retrieved it and removed a rag from his back pocket to wipe it clean.

"We'd have to beat his lawyers in court. And then we might have to deal with Boone May and his men. All we can do is get to work."

Lincoln smiled, despite the ominous presence of the gun, at being included again. He helped Mr. McTaggart take the gun apart and then joined him at the door to the steam wagon.

"How on God's green earth do we get that diabolical contrivance in here?" Mr. McTaggart asked.

"I'll get my sketch pad."

Lincoln felt a hand on his shoulder.

"No sketches, no calculations, Lincoln. Nothing on paper. Let's see if we can do this one all in our heads."

"That seems a whole lot harder way to work."

"No doubt. But when we're done, all Hearst has is one of his precious 'war wagons' instead of plans to make a fleet o' them. And if he wants more, he'll have to ask us. That gives us a little more room to negotiate."

It was a strange way of working and forced Lincoln to concentrate hard enough to make his head pound. Over the next several days, as sheets and lengths of metal turned over and over in Lincoln's mind, he became aware of Mr. McTaggart's mental absence. Mr. McTaggart would start a piece of work or offer a suggestion at breakfast, but by midmorning, he would be seated at his desk with a mug of tea and a blank expression.

Working largely on his own, Lincoln developed a mount for the gun that would allow it to swivel. That wasn't the difficult part. The difficult part was figuring out what to do about all that smoke.

"Four hundred rounds per minute," Mr. McTaggart said. "That's a lot of burnt gunpowder."

Lincoln remembered choking on the smoke-filled air from a few shotgun blasts in the confined space. With the Gatling gun firing, everybody inside the steam wagon would soon be clawing blindly at their throats, drawing black, acrid poison into their lungs.

Mr. McTaggart set Lincoln to work on a design that would place the gun within an airtight housing, but the gun was so big the entire steam wagon would need to be redesigned. It might be possible if they had teams of metal workers and access to a foundry. But in the Black Hills, with the foundries of Pittsburgh and Cleveland thousands of miles to the east, they'd need a simpler solution.

Lincoln devised a fan, powered by a belt connected to a flywheel off the engine, that would suck most of the smoke from the gun out of the cabin. Long before Mr. McTaggart had tested the drawing power of the fan, Lincoln had seen the numbers fly through his head—the amount of gas released by each bullet, the amount of smoky air that would be drawn out of the cabin, and the amount of fresh air that would flow in through the shooting holes.

It would work. Lincoln saw that.

28

THE HEBREW WHELP had been getting on Josiah's nerves since before dawn the previous day, and now, with the sun setting and Deadwood still at least a day's ride away, it was increasingly difficult to keep from giving him a thrashing.

"What do you know? Beans," Segal said as Josiah filled a tin cup. "I love a nice mound of beans as much as the next man, but I gotta tell you, you know all those songs about being a lonesome cowhand? I think that problem might go away if you gave the beans a rest."

Josiah took the boy's cup and wolfed down the beans himself. "If you get hungry tonight, you can eat your jokes."

He scanned the sky, clear overhead with dark clouds far to the west over the Bighorn Mountains. Josiah had endured plenty of prairie storms, so the prospect of rain blowing in wasn't worrying. If anything, it was to be welcomed, since it might finally still the yapping mouth of his captive. He looked at the rope coiled on his saddle and pondered securing Segal for the night but decided it wasn't worth the trouble. Josiah was a light sleeper, and his dogs would alert him to any movement in the event Segal turned out to be stealthier than expected. Instead, he hobbled his horse and the Indian pony on which Segal had been riding when Josiah had intercepted him. Segal had been making his way to meet with his gang.

The boy had sand, Josiah had to admit. Surrounded by the baying wolfhounds and with the muzzle of a Peacemaker pointed into his face, he had concocted a lie that had led to a wasted day in a hidden gully. Segal swore it was the gang's hideout. After a day and a night with no sign of Segal's gang, Josiah had decided on his current course of action—taking Segal back to Bullock for his immediate reward and then watching the jail to see if that fast-gun Bulldog Kid would attempt to spring him.

Josiah had no illusions about his ability to outdraw the trick shooter, but then, he had no intention of getting into a Dodge City-style shootout with him. A Sharps buffalo rifle and a safe hiding place would be all he'd need to even the scales.

As the shadows lengthened into darkness, Josiah heard his dogs growl and rise from their light sleep. He peered into the shadows and strained to listen, then checked by the dim glow of the campfire to see that Segal was asleep, still propped against the tree where he'd left him. The boy hadn't alarmed the dogs. Somebody or something was out there.

The wolfer instructed his dogs to investigate. "Git!"

Josiah put a hand over Segal's mouth and woke him. Straining at the whisper of wind in the trees, and the rustle of night creatures in the undergrowth, Josiah relied on his years of hunting on the plains and hills to picture what lay beyond the circle of light.

Barking alerted him to a human presence. Josiah felt himself to be dangerously conspicuous in the illuminated clearing. The skinny, young Bulldog Kid possessed an uncannily acute eye—that much had been made clear in that demonstration at the circus.

Josiah ducked forward and kicked dirt on the embers, then pulled his pistol and grabbed Segal by the shoulder, pressing the muzzle against the young man's ear. He pulled his prisoner against the tree trunk and squatted beside him, hoping he was opposite the unseen intruder.

The barking grew louder. Josiah deliberately slowed his breathing to keep his aim true. If this was to be his time, he would take as many two-legged wolves as he could on his trip to judgment, starting with the Jew. Moments later, he heard a dog's snarl, followed by the whinny of a startled horse, then the roar of a shotgun, a high-pitched yelp, and a man's voice cursing.

"Call off your dogs if you don't want to lose 'em all!"

In the darkness, the sound of movement, the shotgun, and the man's voice seemed to come from all directions, distorted by the pounding in Josiah's ears, but he thought the voice sounded familiar.

"We've got you surrounded. Put your guns down and your hands up."

Two dogs burst into the clearing in a scurry of shadow. Josiah let go of his prisoner and holstered his pistol. "My name's Josiah Stuart, and I've been deputized by Sheriff Bullock. I'm taking a road agent back to Deadwood for my reward."

Segal shouted, "I'm an entertainer, not a road agent!"

Josiah swung the back of his hand against Segal's mouth and silenced him. The whicker of horses and crackle of movement through thick brush swirled around the clearing as riders approached from all sides. Josiah stood slowly and raised his empty hands.

As the riders emerged from the shadows, he was able to make out the thick neck and steamer-trunk torso of Boone May, who snorted and spat a glob of mucus that made a resounding splat and hiss as it hit what was left of the fire.

"Sheriff Bullock said he sent out a bounty hunter."

"I'm not a bounty hunter."

"What are you then?"

Josiah thought of answers a worldly man given to drink, gluttony, and the flesh would not understand. *A cleansing force. The hand of the Lord.* But he merely said, "Just a man trying to make his way through this world."

May dismounted and approached, and Josiah could see a smile on the big man's face.

"Let's see this road agent you got. If he's what you say he is, Mister Hearst will help you on your way."

"He'll pay for my dog too."

"Sorry about that. Damn mutt took a bite out of my horse."

May squatted beside Segal, reached into a pocket, and removed a lucifer, which he lit and placed beside the young man's swollen face. May then reached out and grabbed Segal's wrist and pulled it away from his nose and mouth, revealing lines of blood flowing from a recently broken nose and a red and bloody upper lip. He looked closely at Segal's blackened eyes and disheveled hair, then pulled the youth to his feet to take in his build and stature.

The flame burned down to May's fingers, and he shook the lucifer and dropped it with a curse. He turned his head toward Josiah, dug into a pocket, produced a gold coin, and tossed it to Josiah. "That's for your dog. Mister Hearst's gonna be happy with this road agent."

"Entertainer," Segal said, wiping the blood from his upper lip. "I make a living from my good looks, so this *putz* is gonna be hearing from my lawyers."

May laughed and shook his head. "You'll feel better in a day or two if you help us find your boss, the Bulldog Kid. Mister Hearst has heard all about him. Stole a satchel full of money and then gave it back when he found out it was for the anarchists. If there's one thing Mister Hearst hates more than a bandit, it's a bandit thinks he's Robin Hood."

Josiah didn't like the possessive way May and his men were acting around his prisoner. He wasn't about to give up custody or his claim on the reward from Sheriff Bullock. But if the owner of the Homestake Mine was prepared to offer a better reward, he could work with Boone May and his men. Given the possibility of Segal's fast-draw friend setting up an ambush on the way to Deadwood, it made sense to join forces with these other armed men.

Working with others didn't come naturally to the wolfer, but he invited May and his men to sit while he built up the fire and heated another pot of beans. They shook their heads at the beans but dismounted, hobbled their horses, and availed themselves of the firelight for rolling cigarettes, which they smoked while passing a bottle back and forth.

Swallowing his words of disgust at the smell of liquor, Josiah filled May in on his encounter with Segal and the sharpshooter at the circus.

One of the men at the fireside said, "I hear his father was an officer in the rebel cavalry. Taught him to shoot before he was five years old."

"I heard him talk," another man said. "He ain't no Southerner. He's a Yankee."

"You bums put a sock in it," May snarled. To Josiah he added, "Go on."

Josiah described his attempts to track the road agents after the stage robbery. Too much time had passed, and a summer hailstorm had obliterated both scent and tracks. Luckily, he'd come across the gang's scout at the Bucket of Blood saloon. When he caught up with Segal at night, sneaking into the hills behind the saloon, he'd attempted to extract information from him on the gang's hideout, but Segal had been a tougher nut to crack than expected.

"Looks like you damn near wore out your nutcracker," May said, eliciting a round of laughter from his men and a grim smile from Segal.

Josiah ignored this jibe. "I want to get him into Deadwood before his gang figures out where he is. I'm planning to get a couple hours of shut-eye. Half-moon should come up after midnight. That'll give enough light to travel."

May concurred with the plan and assigned his men shifts on guard duty while they waited for the light. As May and his men put down their bedrolls on either side of Segal, Josiah shifted to a new place at the other end of the clearing. It already felt too crowded. He thought of the dog May dispatched with a blast of his shotgun and felt a momentary sense of obligation.

The dog had protected him and helped him earn a living for three years, and a couple of times, when he'd been caught out in a prairie blizzard, it had helped to keep him alive by sharing its body heat. Perhaps he should find the body and try to protect it from the scavenging vermin.

Without a shovel, there was no question of digging a grave, but raising a cairn would be no more than an hour's work. He thought of his father and shook his head at such sentimental foolishness, mourning a soulless beast as if it were a child. That was the sort of thing his father might have done with his precious pack of foxhounds, before he'd had to sell them to pay his gambling debts.

He thought of his father's death and the simple wooden cross his grandfather erected. It was probably already moldering in the Blue

Ridge rains. Ashes to ashes, dust to dust applied to dogs and men. The two remaining dogs sniffed around him and curled up in the shelter of a young pine tree as the winds began whipping the upper branches.

The wind augured rain, and rain it did before the moon arose. Josiah felt the drops on his face and rolled up his blanket to keep it dry. He pulled on his long, black riding coat and his hat and squatted under the pine tree with the dogs as the rain turned to a late spring downpour. The clouds blotted out starlight, so the clearing was black as a tomb, illuminated only by flashes of lightning.

The horses shrieked their displeasure at the bursts of light and the pelting drops. Josiah hoped they were securely hobbled. Valuable time would be lost in the morning if it became necessary to search for them.

Clouds remained after the rain diminished to a sprinkling and then to nothing.

Josiah drifted off in his damp clothing and soon dreamed he heard paws padding around him but could see no animal. In his dream he turned his head to the left to try to determine the source of this sound of movement and was assailed from his right by snarls and growls, shrieks of pain, and the tearing of flesh. He turned his head to the right and saw nothing untoward, heard the same sounds from his left, growing closer. He tried to gain his feet and run, but his legs were unresponsive, so he extended his arms to their full length, grabbed hold of the ground, and began to pull himself forward. He pulled and clawed and felt the skin of his hands wear off on jagged rocks when, again, he heard the sound of paws and looked up and stared into the drooling jaws of a wolf.

Josiah woke with a start and saw that the clouds had parted and the three-quarter moon was shining brightly. It was clear enough to begin moving. If they caught a few hours on the sun, they could make Dead-wood by midday. The evening's rain would keep the sharpshooter from finding their trail. He rose to his feet, crossed to the tree where May's men and the prisoner were sheltered, and grabbed his prisoner by the collar.

"Up. Time to move."

Boone May and his sluggardly followers stretched and yawned and rubbed the sleep from their eyes. By the time they were on their feet,

Josiah had Segal on his pony, the pony secured to his own horse. He ignored May's curses and spurred his horse. If May wished to assist in bringing this miscreant to justice, he and his gang could put a little fire in their step.

The others caught up a short time later as the trail climbed land leading to Spearfish Creek. Little moonlight penetrated into the thick pine forest, so Josiah trusted his horse to find the way, and if his horse could not feel the true path, Josiah would rely upon the Lord. He had placed his fate in the Lord's hands before and survived. Behind him he heard May and the others take the Lord's name in vain as they rode headlong into branches and fallen trees or stumbled on the uneven surface.

Both the man of faith and the blasphemers survived the trial of darkness, and daylight found them at Cheyenne Crossing. Josiah grinned. From here it was a matter of hours to Deadwood.

29

THE GIRL DIDN'T scare easily, that was certain. If she was frightened when Daniel admitted to being an outlaw, she didn't let on, not even when the two of them joined up with Roth and Wiseman and she found herself riding with three-quarters of a gang of road agents. Now she was looking down on a likely ambush by lawmen and vigilantes and thinking things through, as if busting accomplices out of jail was her full-time job.

"If Segal's the bait, they're expecting you to come down there for him, aren't they?" she asked as they looked down on the narrow gulch where Deadwood lay spread out like so much wooden debris.

From here on the side of Mount Moriah, Daniel noticed the contrast between the bustling traffic on the main street and the curious lack of activity around the jailhouse. He scanned the rooftops and examined the angles pointing toward the front door of the jailhouse, considering which windows were most likely to house sharpshooters. He couldn't see any gunmen waiting in ambush but did notice a set of deep, patterned ruts leading to the closed door of a livery stable, one block from the jail.

"Yeah," he said. "They probably are."

"Because you're so good with a gun. You're the one they want."

"That, and I figure Boone May and the wolfer both have reason to hate me."

"You humiliated the wolfer at the circus. What about May?"

"Hearst gave me a dollar for getting the drop on May when we first got here."

"That must have stung."

Daniel thought of the big thug who'd lost an eye to a thrown brick back in the Five Points. Big, strong men didn't like losing out to skinny kids.

If only they'd caught up with the wolfer before the other riders joined him. But Daniel and Lily had been slowed by Wiseman and Roth, plodding along like sacks of potatoes on their surplus cavalry mounts.

Daniel cursed himself again for taking the time to meet up with his old reformatory bodyguards. Whatever benefit their fists provided, it wasn't worth the delay caused by their poor horsemanship.

Then they'd been slowed even more after a rainstorm washed out so much of the wolfer's scent. Daniel had to admit that Galahad and Lancelot were uncommonly smart dogs, but for a job like this, a less educated bloodhound with a cleverer nose would have been more help.

By the time they'd found the trail again, they'd lost another half day. Their hope of a quick and easy reunion with Segal was dashed when they saw that the wolfer was now accompanied by at least three other riders. Gunfire would endanger Segal and maybe this headstrong girl as well.

Sensing that he was leading the group into a trap, Daniel had left the trail before Deadwood and taken a roundabout route to the ridge above town.

Roth finally caught up with Daniel and Lily. "What do you see, Kid?"

"The wagon that attacked you. It has some kind of special wheels?"

"Nobody was lookin' at the wheels, Kid."

Daniel watched the stable, waiting for any telltale sign. And then he saw that the stable's chimney emitted no smoke. None would be expected on a late spring afternoon, but black smoke seeped out between the rough boards of the stable walls. Somebody was burning coal in there.

"The wagon's in there," he said.

Roth nodded and looked at Wiseman, who nodded back.

"Here's how it's gonna be," Roth said. "That wagon comes out of the stable, it's gonna be aiming straight south first. So, you get into a nice hidden spot where you can see the shooting holes on this side, the left, I guess. Me and Wiseman go in first, and we go in shooting. Just enough to make them bring out that thing. And you shoot through them holes and take out everybody on that side of the wagon."

"No. I can't—"

"That's no trouble for a guy can hit a moving wagon wheel."

"No, Roth."

"What? You thought you could do this without shooting nobody?"

"It doesn't matter if I kill the men in the wagon if that wolfer kills Segal."

"He ain't doing that, Kid. He kills Segal, he's got nothin' for bargaining."

Daniel felt the looming shadow of Wiseman blotting out the sun as the giant moved into position behind him. Ever since the robbery, when he gave the workers' money back to the old miner, he'd been expecting to wind up on the receiving end of a blow from Wiseman or Roth. Well, maybe he had it coming, but they could beat him black and blue, and he still wouldn't agree to a plan that was likely to get Segal killed.

As he braced himself for a punch, Lily squeezed between Daniel and Wiseman. "You two don't know the wolfer," she said. "He's not right in the head. You can see on his face that he's burning up inside. He wants to kill. He needs to kill."

"So, the Kid kills him first," Wiseman said.

Daniel felt sick. He remembered what it had looked like when he smashed the big man's eye a few years earlier. A red blossom. In his mind he saw another blossom emerge on the wolfer's chest. He'd do it for Segal, but he felt it would change him, make him a different person.

"Wait," Lily said. "Have you ever seen a magician at work?"

"Huh?" Wiseman said.

"My uncle's a magician. He does this all the time. You want to take something out of a box without being seen? You get the audience looking somewhere else."

Roth nodded, a smile of understanding spreading on his face. "We create a distraction. That what you're saying?"

"That wagon belongs to the mine, doesn't it? And you came here to organize the workers and make them fight against the mine, right? So, if there's some kind of disturbance in town that looks like the workers are getting ready to fight, maybe the wagon will come out from that stable and go up to protect the mine."

Roth and Wiseman discussed Lily's idea. Mostly Roth discussed, and Wiseman listened. Daniel kept watch on the scene below. He was certain that there were shooters hiding somewhere else, in addition to the wagon. If Roth and Wiseman could create a big enough disturbance, maybe they'd all leave. Then he'd only have to deal with whoever was still in the sheriff's office—with luck, only the wolfer and the sheriff. That made the odds of getting Segal out alive a whole lot better.

"We'll give it three hours," Roth said. "If we can't stir up those bums at the workers' camp by then, we'll have to go with our first plan."

Leaving Daniel to watch the jail, Roth and Wiseman mounted up and headed down the far side of Mount Moriah, aiming for the workers' camp. Lily sprung onto her Indian pony, whistled to her dogs, and said, "Galahad, Lancelot, go ahead and look for people on the trail."

To Daniel she said, "Wait for me here. I'm going to make sure your friends don't bump into any sheriff's deputies."

As he waited, Daniel watched for movement, flashes of sunlight on gunmetal, blurry figures in windows, anything that might reveal a hidden sniper. He watched the doors of the stable, the sheriff's office, and the neighboring buildings for signs that watchers might be changing shifts or getting tired of waiting. At length, he was rewarded by the sight of the sheriff's door opening. Out strode a tall, whiskered man, dressed more for business than for fighting drunks or pursuing road agents but wearing a silver star on his jacket, over his heart.

Sheriff Bullock had been pointed out to Daniel during his time in Deadwood, and despite the distance, he recognized the sheriff. His gaze followed Bullock as he sauntered up the street toward the commercial district. A few minutes later, he came back with a copy of the *Deadwood Herald* tucked under his arm and a checked-cloth-covered basket in his hands.

Bullock didn't look like a man who would die to keep a prisoner from escaping. Daniel had a feeling that whatever trap had been set was more Hearst's business. If Wiseman and Roth could get the workers riled up, there was a chance that everybody but Bullock and the wolfer would leave to take care of it.

When Bullock opened the door to his office, Daniel confirmed his and Lily's fear about the wolfer. As soon as the door had opened a crack, a barking dog lunged out, snapping at the sheriff, who jumped back and called to somebody inside. The dog continued barking as the wolfer stepped out, grabbed it by the collar, and hauled it back inside. So, two guns inside the office, probably three if the sheriff had a deputy with him.

As the minutes crawled by, Daniel detected, one by one, the gunmen who had been positioned to turn the street in front of the sheriff's office into a killing ground. The sun had traversed an hour's worth of sky by the time he heard Lily's dogs return to the hilltop, where he crouched behind a tree. A short time later, after securing her horse out of sight, Lily joined him, and Daniel told her what he'd seen.

"Three men up above, at least two in the sheriff's office, and that wagon," Daniel said. "They must really want me dead."

"You're special. That scares them."

"Segal would find a way to make a joke about that."

Lily laughed. "You make a good team. The fastest gun in the West and the fastest mouth in the West."

"He told me one time that his jokes might be a more powerful weapon than my guns if he uses them against people like Hearst."

"Maybe he's right. We've all got talents. We just have to find the best way to use them."

Lily stopped speaking and seemed to Daniel to go all thoughtful. He waited for her to say something, but nothing came out, so he returned to watching the sheriff's office.

"Maybe there's a way to use our talents to free Segal," she finally said. "A way that helps avoid killing and gives Segal the best chance of getting out."

"What do you mean?"

"Take a look to the north. Do you see any sign of action over at the workers' camp? You'll have a better view farther along the ridge."

She pointed a hundred yards along the hilltop to a large fir tree that blocked the view north. Daniel shrugged and ran in a crouching posture toward the tree. He wondered what he'd see. Were Roth and Wiseman planning to build a signal fire?

Before he reached the tree, Daniel heard hoofbeats and turned to see Lily racing her pony as rapidly as she could toward town, her dogs at her side. He ran back to his former position, considered giving chase but thought better of it.

Whatever she had up her sleeve, the odds couldn't be any worse than they already were.

30

LILY SLOWED HER horse to a walk as she reached the buildings of Deadwood. As she slowed, she panted several times, as if she had galloped all morning. She reached forward to pat the neck of her horse, mouthing calming words. It occurred to her that she should have covered herself in trail dust to complete the effect but decided she had taken on a generous portion earlier that day. The narrow trail she'd taken connected with the road to Cheyenne Crossing just a few hundred feet from the jail, and Lily knew she was now visible to anybody who might be watching.

Deadwood wasn't a place where young girls went riding alone. She knew she'd attract curiosity. She cast her eyes along the line of roofs on the north side of the street and at the windows on the back sides of the Gem Theater and Bella Union Hotel, both of which looked out on the streets leading toward her destination. She wished she had eyes like Daniel's.

She opened her mind to the dogs and allowed her feelings and perceptions to mingle with theirs. A familiar place. The scent of the dust. The high-pitched sounds of the piano drifting across the narrow valley. The savor of animal flesh roasting and hot fat bubbling in the big round pots in the Chinese camp. They were comfortable but wary. Muscles coiled. Tails slightly raised. Ears pricked up and cocking this way and that.

Then a trace of the angry, hateful hounds. Somewhere close. And the rank sweat and deathly odor of the wolfer. Galahad and Lancelot stopped and looked back the way they came, but Lily would not let them give in to fear. She fed them a taste of her anger, and they turned back toward the jail and resumed course. This time, she would not fear her own emotions. This time, she would not stand frozen as if mesmerized by the wolfer's hatred.

To reach the jail she would have to ride her horse right in front of the stable where Daniel had spotted the strange tracks. The wagon, whatever it was, must be something fierce, for she had seen the clouds that passed over the faces of Wiseman and Roth and felt for a moment that she could see this rolling nightmare as they had. She would not let on that she knew it was there.

The streets were deserted. At this time of day, people should be going about their business. Workers should be busy on the new hotel being built between the Gem and the Bella Union and on the new feedstore and blacksmith's shop just up ahead. Miners from the distant creeks, still hoping to find a placer claim that had not been played out, should be riding into town for supplies or to have nuggets and dust weighed and assayed.

She felt the weight of uncounted hidden gun sights on her chest as she spurred her horse to what she hoped looked like an exhausted trot. She had decided not to gallop for fear that a sudden movement would cause a panicked response in whoever was watching. As she trotted up to the jail, she saw the door open and Sheriff Bullock emerge.

Lily channeled all her anger at the wolfer, her sorrow at the death of the wolves, and her fear for that troublesome but kindhearted criminal Segal, and surprised herself by bursting into actual tears. "Help! Sheriff, help."

She dismounted and felt dizzy, her knees nearly buckling under her. The sheriff looked puzzled. Lily rushed toward him without even pausing to hitch the horses to the rail. "You've got to help us, Sheriff."

As she approached, he appeared to reach a decision and stepped forward to put an arm around her shoulders. He turned to open the door to the jailhouse, and as soon as the door was ajar, the wolfer's dogs dashed outside and charged at Lily. Galahad and Lancelot lowered their heads and hunched their shoulders instinctively in a fighting posture and began to snarl in a way Lily had never heard.

Lily felt the thoughts of the wolfer's dogs more powerfully than ever. "Hate! Hate! Hate!"

Only now, she felt her own dogs respond with rage. As the dogs prepared for a fight, Lily realized that the wolfer had lost one of his hounds since last she'd seen him.

Bullock reached out to grab one of the wolfer's hounds, but at that moment, the wolfer himself arrived on the scene.

"Call off your damn dogs, Stuart," Bullock shouted as one of the hounds turned its attention on the sheriff. The dog's gnashing teeth narrowly missed Bullock's hand.

The wolfer grabbed both dogs by their collars and began to haul them toward the hitching post beside the sheriff's office.

When the hounds were out of biting reach, Lily returned to her planned performance. She allowed her knees to fold up, and Bullock stepped forward to keep her upright. Bullock shouted over his shoulder for a deputy to run outside and hitch the young lady's horse and ordered the wolfer to keep his hellhounds outside. Then he led Lily into the office and behind his desk, where he sat her down on his own chair. Once she was seated, he turned toward Lily's dogs, sniffing their way around the room. One walked to the back, following a scent toward the three jail cells. The other stopped at the open door, watching the deputy hitch the horses out front.

"Water," Lily said. "Please, so dry."

As Bullock turned his back on her to walk to a sideboard that held a pitcher of water and a hamper with a loaf of bread sticking out from under a cloth, Lily made contact with Galahad and Lancelot.

She formed an image of a ring of keys. She saw in her mind the dogs picking up the key ring from a desktop or pulling it off of a hook on the wall. She imbued these images with a sense of caution and stealth. The dogs would understand, she hoped, that this meant they must wait until no eyes were on them but hers.

She leaned forward and panted, making terrible whooping cough sounds as she unbuttoned her dress at the neck to get more air. She needed time to think of a plan. As she did this, the deputy came back and took up a position at the window, where he sat with a Winchester in his hands.

Only then did Lily look toward the three cells, each large enough for a sleeping pallet and a slop bucket and enough room to stand. Two were unoccupied. In the third, Segal sat cross-legged on his pallet, the studied expression of boredom on his face a contrast with the swollen purple and brown around his eyes and the puffy, red nose with hints of dried blood around the nostrils. Her vision of Segal joined with one she had picked up from Lancelot, who had scented him immediately upon entering the room. Lancelot, a good judge of character, liked the tall joker. When Bullock turned back toward Lily to bring her a glass of water, Segal smiled, then quickly struck the pose of a stricken woman from a melodrama. He could tell she was faking.

As Bullock bent to hand Lily the glass, Segal fixed her with a parody of a mesmeric gaze and held out the fingers of both hands pointed at her, as if directing his mind control powers at her. Lily fought back a laugh, an act that, fortunately, looked like a brave effort to suppress tears.

The wolfer returned to the sheriff's office, having finished tying his dogs to the hitching post, where their angry sounds now contained a complaint at being constrained. Lily willed herself to ignore his presence and directed her appeal to Bullock.

"We have to go and help Mister Szabo. He's injured badly."

"Hang on, Miss. You tell me what's happened, and then we'll figure out how to help."

"But he's hurt."

Bullock handed her the glass. She took a long drink, shaking her hand and spilling water on her blouse as she did.

"We'll get the doctor and send out a posse."

"This is a ploy," said the wolfer. "She wants you to send men away so her friends can rescue—"

"Quiet, Mister Stuart. This is sheriff's business, and I remind you, you're a guest in the sheriff's office." To Lily, he said, "I do need to know what we're getting into. Start with who you are."

"Lillian Mandeville. I'm with Stanislas's Circus. We just finished our run in Deadwood, and we were moving on, and then they took everything. The robbers. They took all our money, every penny we made here."

"What robbers, Miss?"

"That Bulldog Kid. Him and his gang."

Bullock's attention focused sharply. As did the wolfer's.

Bullock turned toward the deputy who was watching the window. "Jim. Go tell May. He's going to want to hear this. Then round up the doctor and a wagon."

The deputy left his post and departed the room. Lily heard the sound of running feet. No doubt the deputy was running across to the stable where Boone May lurked with the wagon.

With the deputy gone and both men concentrating their attention on Lily, this was the chance for Lancelot and Galahad to search the office. Lily directed her thoughts to the dogs. Find those keys now. But quietly.

"Now, tell me everything," Bullock said. "When was this?"

"Yesterday. On the Cheyenne Trail."

"And they shot your Mister Szabo?"

A cruel smile spread across the wolfer's chiseled face. "So, your beau robbed your caravan of gypsies and heathens."

"He's not my beau!"

"My mistake. Your beau's the one in here."

Bullock appraised the exchange. "I guess I forgot that you two were old acquaintances. Miss Mandeville, I believe you owe this gent here an apology. He says his Colt hasn't worked right since you dropped it in the mud by the Chinese pigpens."

Lily turned and gave the sheriff a mortified look. She hoped the sheriff interpreted this as shame over her misdeeds. But it was not. She hung her head, wishing she had pulled the trigger when she had the chance. Then she directed a doe-eyed expression toward the wolfer, Stuart, she knew now, and offered an apology.

"I am terribly sorry, sir, but I misunderstood. I had been warned so many times about road agents and wild Indians and ravishers in these hills that I felt I had no choice but to disarm you. Your pistol was so heavy, and I was so frightened, I must have dropped it somewhere on the trail, but I am afraid I have no memory of that. If you help us to regain our stolen property, I will pay you back out of my share. I give you my oath."

"The Bible says swearing oaths is a sin."

"No oath, then, just my word as an American and the daughter of Captain Martin Mandeville of the Fifth Michigan Cavalry."

Stuart's scowl deepened. Lily had guessed that he'd fought for the Confederacy. His expression proved it. She wondered if, among those masses of men thrown into the cauldron of the war, Stuart might have been present at the battle where her father met his end. Could it be, perhaps, that he had fired the fatal shot that had left her fatherless, or was that a plot device from one of Madame Mystere's thick French novels?

"Were you at Gettysburg, Mister Stuart?"

"Fredericksburg. Chancellorsville. The Wilderness."

She saw the haunted look on his face as he made this roll call of slaughter and felt an undeniable urge to dig the knife in a little deeper. "So, only the battles where the rebels went on the defensive and cowered behind trees?"

Stuart took a step closer and raised a hand. Bullock stepped between him and the girl. Lily's cheeks flushed. Bullock looked back and forth between Lily and the wolfer.

Lily noticed with satisfaction that both men had their backs turned to the rest of the room. They were too distracted to pay attention to her dogs as they searched.

"Let's get back to the matter at hand, Miss. Who shot your Mister Szabo?"

"Nobody, sir. He set out with me to get help, but he had a bad spell. Some kind of fit. His skin was all white and clammy, and he had trouble breathing. I didn't want to leave him, but he said I had to ride into town to get help. It was the only way."

"So, he's somewhere on the trail between here and Cheyenne?"

The wolfer's expression again expressed his doubts. "Can't you see, Bullock? She's wasting your time."

"No. It all happened so fast, and I've been riding so hard. I'll start from the beginning. We were a couple of days out of Deadwood on the

Cheyenne Trail. We were going to play for a week in Cheyenne and then make our way south into Colorado. Uncle Stanislas said all the mining towns were starved for entertainment. And we'd been working up some new material—"

Bullock cut her off by frowning and waving his hand in a "speed it up" gesture. Lily apologized. The longer she took to tell her story, the more time the dogs had to find the keys.

In the corner of her eye she saw Segal pointing to a small writing desk near the window where the deputy had been posted. He'd figured out what the dogs were doing. Lily took a long drink of water, ostensibly to calm herself and gather her thoughts, while sending the dogs a mental picture of the desk drawer.

"There were three of them," she continued. "The Bulldog Kid and two of his partners. One was huge—a great big bear of a man but young with a little wisp of a mustache. The other was also young but older looking. He had a dark beard. Very dark eyes. Stern. Powerful shoulders but a narrow waist."

"Yes, Miss, we have a description of them."

Behind the sheriff's back, Galahad had quietly gripped the handle of the drawer with his front teeth. Lily hoped it wouldn't stick. As the dog began to pull, she increased both the pitch and volume of her voice, as if the story called forth greater fear and urgency. "They jumped out of the woods, Sheriff, and shouted 'Hands up!' Madame Mystere swooned. I thought she'd died of fright. I screamed, 'Don't shoot! Please, don't shoot!'"

Galahad stood on his hind legs with the open drawer in front of him and turned his head back toward Lily with a puzzled expression in his canine eyes. If the canine mind was capable of grasping the concept of theatrical criticism, Galahad appeared to consider Lily's acting to lack subtlety. Lily reminded him about the keys.

"They went through all of our things, looking for any money we had hidden, Sheriff. The Bulldog Kid had his pistols out and kept us from moving. We all knew how he could shoot."

Bullock held up a finger to stop her. "You know him, don't you? Didn't he do a shooting demonstration at your circus?"

"Yes. One night. I didn't expect—"

"And this one back here," Bullock said, gesturing over his shoulder at the jail cells. "You know him, too, don't you?"

"Yes. Yes, it *is* him. What's he doing here?"

Bullock didn't answer. Lily set her mouth into a snarl of outrage. She stood and directed a hateful stare at the prisoner. "Your friend is a no-good scoundrel, Mister Segal. They ought to catch him and take him to the top of Mount Moriah where everybody in Deadwood can see him and hang him. And you should go up there too!"

The sheriff placed a calming arm on her shoulder and sat her back down. "So, you're not old friends, then?"

"Of course they are!" the wolfer said, earning a shushing sound from the sheriff.

"I met them just one night," Lily said. "This one, Mister Segal, volunteered to help in my act. I'm not completely sure what happened, but he said he's a mesmerist and… well, the next thing I knew, he was introducing his friend, and they were putting on a shooting demonstration. And I felt powerless to stop it. Uncle Stanislas thought this was their way of getting a job with our circus. They wanted to show us what they can do. But then we never saw them again, until the robbery, that is."

While she talked, Galahad lifted the set of keys from the drawer. Lancelot carefully pushed the drawer closed and trotted across to Segal's cell with the key ring held in his teeth. Segal reached through the bars and took the key ring. He placed it in his pants, then smiled, winked, and mimed riding a horse.

"Sheriff, I feel better now. I'd like to get back on the trail and show you where Mister Szabo is."

"I don't think you're in any condition for that, Miss."

"Please. He's like a father to me."

Lily stood, adopting the expression and posture of a brave and determined young woman who would not be stopped in her effort to save a beloved mentor. She turned toward the door just as it burst open to reveal a thick-necked man whose deep-set eyes were an indescribable combination of yellow, green, and gray. Two other scowling men followed. All three had pistols in their belts. The man with the thick neck carried a double-barreled shotgun in the crook of his arm. His enormous hands and wrists made the weapon look as lethal as a broomstick.

"What's going on, Bullock?"

The sheriff addressed the leader of the men. "We need to find this girl's injured friend, May. Maybe we'll also find this Bulldog Kid's trail."

"No need," the wolfer said. "He'll be coming here. The devil looks after his own."

"That's as may be, but my responsibility is to save lives if I can. May, I need a couple of your men for a posse. Mister Stuart, I'd like you to come with me and bring your dogs. They might come in handy. Jim, you stay here and watch the prisoner."

The wolfer spat on the floor. "I will not go with you. This is my prisoner, and it is my responsibility to bring him to justice."

The two men faced off, and Lily noticed that the sheriff was the one who looked away. He must have seen what Lily saw, that the wolfer was not the kind of man to reason with.

"All right. Jim, you come with me. Mister Stuart will watch the prisoner. May, you coming with us or staying with your war wagon?"

The thick-necked man laughed. "If you had a war wagon, you wouldn't ask no damn fool question like that. 'Course I'm staying with the war wagon. Anybody comes to town to spring this boy from jail, he's in for a big surprise."

Lily looked around the group of men. The sheriff and his deputy and a few of May's men were out of the picture now. And if Segal acted fast, he could open his cell door and perhaps grab a rifle from the rack on the wall. But the war wagon was still there, and the thick-necked man and the rest of his men and the wolfer, whom Segal would need to overcome. The odds were marginally better than before but still not good.

"Please, Sheriff, we have to leave. Mister Szabo may be dying."

"All right. I guess you can come with us, Miss Mandeville."

May and his men turned and went out to the street, and Bullock and his deputy gathered up weapons, ammunition, and other supplies for a rescue mission or a fight with road agents.

Lily reached out and gave the sheriff a hug. She almost meant it. She broke off the hug and called her dogs and stepped out of the office. Now she needed to get the wolfer out of the office, and Segal would be all alone and able to use his key, arm himself, and make sure that nothing looked suspicious.

When Bullock and Jim left the office, Lily directed her dogs to approach the wolfer's hounds and bark as ferociously as they could.

"Mister Stuart!" she shouted as loud as she could. "Please, I think your dogs are getting loose!"

The wolfer stepped out, directed a withering gaze at Lily, and inspected the knots he'd tied in the leather straps. Then he turned and reentered the office, where Lily desperately hoped Segal sat behind an unlocked iron door.

31

A S THE SOUND of the retreating posse diminished into silence, Segal spoke up from his cell.

"They've all gone to the ball and left poor Cinderella behind."

Josiah ignored the guttersnipe's smug jibe.

"I told you all the way here, people might like you better if you washed."

The young man lay on his pallet, his hands folded under his head, and gazed at the ceiling. But for being fully dressed, with his boots and his coat on in the stifling late afternoon heat, he might have been preparing for a nap. Determined not to let the prisoner distract him from his thoughts, Josiah pulled a stool up to the window, placed his rifle against the wall, and scanned the street and beyond for signs of movement. His two hounds stood at attention on the porch of the jailhouse to better catch any sound or scent of Segal's would-be rescuers.

Patience was the special virtue of hunters. How many times had he waited patiently, silently, still as a statue, while watching a baited carcass? His grandfather had spoken of patience. The patience of Job, who was sorely tested, who suffered the loss of all he possessed and remained constant. Had Josiah not been tested like Job? Had he not suffered in body and mind? Mocked, detested, abandoned by men and women. There was a psalm about patience. Josiah remembered. He looked to the saddlebag he carried everywhere and brought out his Bible. His lips moved as he read, searching for the right one.

"Ah, he's praying!" the prisoner remarked. "A man of such holiness."

"Quiet!"

Josiah shut his eyes tightly and clapped his hands over his ears. He must blot out every sensation that fed his anger, his urge to unlock the door of the cell and gut that filthy street rat like a fresh-killed deer.

The rifle glowed in the corner of Josiah's field of vision. The Bowie knife on his belt vibrated against his skin. It would be so easy. And it would not spoil the ambush, for the rest of the gang would have no way of knowing it was too late to rescue their friend. But it was not up to Josiah to be the instrument of the Lord's justice. At least, not yet.

He focused on the book in his lap and found the passage he sought. A passage on patience, a passage on maintaining the faith to await one's reward, to await the punishments that would be meted out to the unworthy. He turned and read aloud, "Fret not yourself. It tends only to evil. For the evildoers shall be cut off, but those who wait for the Lord shall inherit the land—"

A burst of cynical laughter came from the jail cell. "Trust me, you're gonna wait a long time to inherit the land. And take it from one of the chosen people, get the date of possession in writing."

Josiah's hand reached out of its own volition and grasped a pitcher, which he hurled at the cell. The glass struck the bars and rained water and shards on the reclining figure, who rolled into a protective ball. As Josiah breathed deeply and slowly, clenching and unclenching his fists, the ball unrolled, and Segal rose to his feet, a trickle of blood running down one cheek. Josiah watched the prisoner's fingers move gingerly over his face. Then Segal turned toward Josiah and assumed his usual taunting smile.

Josiah slammed the Bible closed and gripped it like a brick. There were two ways of receiving the written word of the Lord, and if this heathen refused to accept it one way, he would have no choice but to accept it the other way. He pulled open the drawer where Bullock kept the keys to the cell and strode across the room, Bible in one hand, keys in the other. But before he could reach the cell, the prisoner pushed the door open and produced a rifle from beneath his blanket, pointing it at Josiah's heart.

"I'm no Bulldog Kid," he said, "but even I can't miss from this range."

Josiah's gaze alternated between the Bible in his hand, with its promises of eternal reward, and the dark orifice that offered an express trip to that destination. "You won't shoot me," he finally said.

"I'd say 'Want to bet?' but that's probably a sin, right?"

"If you shoot me, the men watching for your friends will kill you."

"So, I should stay here and wait for them to string me up? Listen, *putz*, you don't threaten a man who's got nothing to lose."

The keys in Josiah's hand took on an extra weight. He felt the cool of the metal, the smooth and solid heft of brass. Somebody must have unlocked the cell, smuggled in a rifle, and returned the keys to the desk. The girl. Bullock was a fool. He'd been only too keen to round up a posse and ride off to rescue the girl's circus friends, who, no doubt, were parties to this deception. It had been easy for the girl to deceive Bullock. Perhaps she used the same kind of mock-sorcery that attracted the idle and the idolaters to the circus, some quick hand movements and distractions that allowed her to unlock the door and pass the weapon to Segal.

Josiah's thoughts turned again to the trials of Job. Was he being chastised for his pride? Or perhaps for being insufficiently zealous, for misplaced mercy? This would not have happened if he had been an instrument of the Lord's justice when that girl first robbed him of the wolf pelts, or later, when she had the audacity to threaten him at sword point. He would not make such a mistake the next time he saw any of these lost souls.

He raised both hands above his shoulders.

"That's better," said Segal, holding the rifle one-handed while he reached out and removed Josiah's pistol from its holster. "Now, very slowly, I want you to step into the cell, close the door, and reach through the bars with one of those keys and lock the door."

The boy stepped aside, the rifle still pointed at Josiah. It took three tries to find the correct key, but eventually Josiah heard the bolt on the lock slide into place. Segal reached out and gave the door a tug to make sure it held, then took the keys from Josiah's hand.

Segal pointed to the Bible. "If it takes Bullock a while to come back, at least you've got something to read while you're waiting."

The boy backed across the room and picked up Josiah's long black coat and hat. He slipped the coat over his own and, even with the extra layer underneath, it still fit him like a tent. Then an idea seemed to dawn on him, and he looked through Bullock's desk until he found an inkwell and a small shaving mirror. He poured ink onto the sleeve of Josiah's coat and, holding up the small mirror, darkened his cheeks and chin.

Josiah sat on the pallet and opened up the Bible to the Psalms. He would read again about patience and the wait for the Lord's reward and the Lord's justice.

The boy paused at the door when he had his disguise ready. Then he turned back to Josiah and quipped, "If you have to time to finish reading that, don't tell me how it ends."

"It ends with you and all those like you in a lake of unquenchable fire."

Segal paused, hand on the door. "Naw. That's only in *your* version."

Then he stepped out into the street.

32

---◆◆◆◆---

I T HAD TAKEN days to refine the plan and days more to fabricate parts, starting at sunup and working by lamplight long after sundown. Lincoln looked at the fearsome beast he'd created and imagined how his life would have worked out if the riders had only let his family grow their corn back in Tennessee. Maybe, as Mr. Delacroix had told him long ago, he could have used his special talents to make the crops grow taller. He sorely wished he could have spent his time with plowshares instead of swords.

He and Mr. McTaggart had finished breakfast and were looking over the previous day's work when he heard horses approach. He and Mr. McTaggart had intended to carry out a test run of the newly installed Gatling gun and exhaust fan. But there would be no time for testing. The gate to the secret compound opened, and Boone May rode in at the head of a group of armed men, splattered with mud and disheveled from sleeping rough.

With no preamble, May demanded that McTaggart fire up the steam wagon. When Mr. McTaggart protested that the Gatling gun attachment and ventilation system hadn't been tested, May dismissed McTaggart's objections with a stream of tobacco juice.

"We got a gang of road agents riding into town," he said. "We need to protect innocent womenfolk and children."

"And splatter some guts," said one of May's men, laughing.

May drove the butt end of his shotgun into the joker's midsection, quelling all laughter.

"I need a driver for this thing," May said. "This ain't a request."

Mr. McTaggart stood still for a moment, his gaze shifting between Lincoln and May. He hung his head and placed a hand on Lincoln's shoulder. "I just need to get the boy some work. We might be gone for a while from the sound of things."

"No time for that," May said. "Hop in."

Mr. McTaggart reached into a pocket and removed a key, which he placed in Lincoln's hand. "I've given you so much work that I've neglected your education, Lincoln. There's a book in my desk you might want to read if I'm gone for a while."

Mr. McTaggart reached out—he no longer had to bend down—and placed his arms around Lincoln and urged him to be good to his mother and brothers. Then he turned and stepped into the cabin of the steam wagon.

Hours later, Lincoln sat alone in the shop, a sketch pad empty in front of him. He wasn't in the mood for reading, so he hadn't bothered looking for Mr. McTaggart's book. He had picked up the sketch pad because he thought it would calm the raging sea in his innards. It didn't work. He didn't want to imagine what kind of devilry Mr. Hearst's men were up to in town. He was just glad he didn't have to see it this time.

Whatever they were doing with the steam wagon and the Gatling gun, it was a watermelon social next to what they'd be able to do with the new kind of wagon once it had been built. Without his hand moving, the sketch pad filled up with lines, detailed drawings of the inner workings of a new petroleum oil-burning engine. And those lines turned to numbers that told him how many rotations its drive wheels would make and how those rotations would translate into speeds as fast as the locomotives on the Union Pacific or how they could gear down to provide power to climb steep hills or push through mud or crash through walls.

The imaginary lines that spread across the sketch pad turned into numbers representing the dimensions of the new style of wagon and then into other numbers representing the wagon's weight and, from there, into numbers that showed how much fuel it would burn and how far it would be able to travel without stopping to fill the tank.

Soon, the sketch pad in Lincoln's head filled with images of an entire fleet of these petroleum wagons, traveling a hundred miles or more on a tank of fuel, each one bristling with weapons, shotguns jutting out the firing loops on its flanks, and an enormous Gatling gun spouting fire from its mouth, like one of those fire serpents from the old-time tales Miss Cadbury had read to him back in Tennessee. He'd seen horrors in his young life, but he knew there'd be countless horrors if these visions were ever made flesh.

He put down his sketch pad. Maybe reading a book would get these thoughts out of his head.

Lincoln took the key from his pocket and unlocked Mr. McTaggart's desk drawer. It hardly budged as he tugged on the handle, but when at last he slid it open, papers spilled out—blueprints and sketches and, Lincoln was surprised to see, stacks of calculations made in his own hand.

Months of brain-taxing concentration had gone into those papers as he and Mr. McTaggart designed the steam wagon. And, since the great fuel thirst of the steam wagon had become obvious to him, he'd spent too many late nights staring into the circle illuminated by an oil lamp. And here it all was, locked away in one place. The only book he saw was a thick, well-worn leather-bound volume bearing the title *An Inquiry Into the Nature and Causes of the Wealth of Nations,* by Adam Smith.

It didn't look like much of a distraction to Lincoln.

He opened the cover and smiled to see that it was published in Edinburgh, Mr. McTaggart's hometown. "The Athens of the North," Mr. McTaggart had called the city, "and I'm not talking about the Athens in Tennessee or Georgia."

Lincoln flipped through the pages, and the book opened to a thick envelope addressed to him in Mr. McTaggart's handwriting.

It contained a stack of greenbacks, more money than Lincoln had ever seen, and a short letter. Even though he was alone, he read it aloud.

"Dear Lincoln. When I took you on as an apprentice, I imagined working with you for many years and seeing you grow into a man. I thought some day we might even be partners in our own manufactory and, to be honest, I imagined your brainpower would make me rich as together we devised new inventions for a growing nation. It has become ever more evident that our employer will never allow such a circumstance to come to pass.

"My conscience will not permit me to continue with the work we have been engaged in these last days. We know, since the attack on the workers' camp, exactly what Hearst has in mind for this more lethal version of the steam wagon, and we can guess what he would do with the new petroleum-fuel wagons we have been considering. We cannot allow such powerful weapons to fall into any man's hands, least of all Hearst's.

"I have been waiting for an opportunity to sabotage this development and, since you are reading this letter now, such an opportunity must have transpired. I ask you to take this money, which you have more than earned with your hard work, and run to your mother. Take all of the plans, drawings, and calculations I have gathered in this drawer and burn them. When he sees what I am about to do, Hearst will assume that it was I who destroyed them. If you leave immediately, you should be able to catch a stagecoach before Hearst's men are aware. Watching your mind at work has been a privilege. To be able to assist you in growing into the man you are meant to be has been an honor."

Salty drops landed on the letter and blurred the words. Lincoln wiped his cheeks and imagined Mr. McTaggart writing this letter late at night in the darkness of the shop.

His gaze landed on the writing in the book opposite where the letter had been hidden. The writing was small, and Lincoln had to squint to make it stand still for inspection. A line of text stood out from the rest. Again, he read out loud, "The desire of food is limited in every man by the narrow capacity of the human stomach, but the desire of the conveniences and ornaments of building, dress, equipage, and household furniture, seems to have no limit or certain boundary."

It took a bit of effort to ponder some of the longer words, but Lincoln figured that this Mr. Smith meant to say that some folks were never satisfied. That was Mr. Hearst all right. He had no limit to what he wanted.

Not so much in fancy living, though what Lincoln saw of his employer's private office was plenty fancy, and certainly not in fancy clothes, but in power over others, power represented by money and laws, and if those weren't sufficient, by armed men and weapons for enforcing his will.

Mr. Hearst would never be satisfied until his wealth and his weapons made him the most powerful man in America. Lincoln could not allow that to happen.

He gathered up all the papers and stuffed them in Mr. McTaggart's old carpetbag. He placed the book in a sack into which he stuffed his Sunday clothes and a change of underthings and slung the sack over his shoulder. Hoisting up the big carpetbag with both hands, he peered out the window to make sure no sentries had been left behind to watch him.

Not a soul stirred in the yard or at the gate.

He gathered up all the courage he had and used it to make himself look as calm and casual as if he was going fishing on a Sunday afternoon.

As he stepped out into the yard, he steeled himself for an angry voice to demand that he halt. When none came, he sauntered, or at least hoped he did a passable imitation of a saunter, to the gate.

A push on the gate told him that May hadn't locked him in.

Lincoln slipped out and ran to the nearest patch of forest thick enough to hide in. Then he ran as best he could with his burdens knocking against his knees.

Remaining in the cover of trees and bushes, he walked, ran, and at times crawled through the forested country between his worksite near the Homestake Mine and Deadwood. When he reached town, he took the back-alley route to the hotel where Mama worked cooking meals for people visiting on business.

He paused outside the back door leading to the kitchen and, when he heard his mama's voice, pushed the door open. She nearly dropped a casserole when Lincoln stepped into the kitchen in the middle of a workday.

"What's wrong, child?"

Words flowed out of Lincoln like spring melt water. He told her, for the first time, of his work on the steam wagon and his role in the attack on the camp and the even more deadly inventions he'd worked on since then. It all spilled out—the Gatling gun, his ideas for a petroleum oil wagon, Mr. McTaggart's letter, the money allowing Lincoln and his family to flee.

He told her of the meeting in Mr. Hearst's office and of the nonexistent contract that his employer claimed Lincoln had signed. He added that he and Mr. McTaggart had been locked into the work yard.

"You saying Mister Hearst want to keep you here like a slave?"

"Yes, Mama."

"Damn that man! Your papa didn't race that infernal steam drill so's you could be anybody's property, Lincoln. We gotta get."

"There some kind of big trouble today. Could be this is our chance to get away without being seen."

Mama called one of the maids to the kitchen and handed her an apron, instructing her to remove the casserole from the oven in one hour and chop up a pile of potatoes and onions in the meantime. Then she took hold of Lincoln's hand and led him outside.

Things had changed outside in the short time Lincoln had been in the kitchen. Angry voices drifted on the breeze. When Lincoln and Mama left the alley, heading toward the rental house in the poorer neighborhood where she lived with Lincoln's brothers, Lincoln saw a crowd marching into town from the direction of the worker-camp.

Men shouted and pounded on the walls and windows of saloons and shops as they surged into the main business district. Some brandished tools—sledgehammers and pickaxes and long steel pry bars. Other ragged men didn't look fit to swing a hammer or a shovel. Well-to-do walkers ran out of the way, and shop owners shut their doors and closed their shutters.

In the area called the Badlands, one group of workmen appeared to have taken a break from parading angrily about town and congregated on the street in front of a saloon, frothy mugs of beer in their hands. As they approached, Lincoln could hear them chanting Hearst's name and "String him up!"

When angry, drunken white men were in a lynching mood, it was best to make tracks. Lincoln and his mama ducked into the small home where she had rented a room. She gathered up a few possessions, including her precious box of savings and the only photo of the late John Henry. "We're going to Zeke's place. Walk fast, but don't run, and don't call attention to yourself."

Zeke ran a stable on the west side of town where Lincoln's brothers cleaned stalls in between lessons from the blacksmith who doubled as the colored children's schoolmaster. Zeke, the blacksmith, would know of any wagons set to leave for Cheyenne.

Lincoln and his mama stepped out and heard the mob again. Now it was on the move, but strangely, it was headed to the sheriff's office rather than the mine.

As they put greater distance between themselves and the mob, Lincoln heard a familiar mechanical rumble. He looked back and saw men running away from the sheriff's office.

When he realized the source of the sound, he pulled his mama against a back fence and made her crouch as he saw the steam wagon chasing the angry men back the way they came.

The wagon was followed by men on horseback, some of whom Lincoln recognized as Boone May's subordinates.

"Mama, we'd best hurry."

33

LILY SIZED UP Sheriff Bullock's horse and those of the other posse members. The sheriff rode a quarter horse, compact but well-muscled, shiny and brown with shapely, powerful legs. The same could not be said of the posse. Some of them rode plodding old nags that appeared to be only a few steps away from the glue factory. One rode a mule and another, a grossly fat man, dwarfed the little pony that staggered under his weight.

By the time they reached Cheyenne Crossing without coming upon the injured Mr. Szabo, she would have no choice but to make a break for it. Otherwise, she'd be under arrest for helping in what she hoped was Segal's escape.

Sheriff Bullock could ride, and his horse would have no trouble keeping up with Lily's. But as she watched him roll a cigarette, he gave off no hint of urgency. His trousers were new, his boots polished, and his hat freshly blocked. Lily doubted he would race through the underbrush to catch a girl who would soon join the rest of the circus in the Wyoming Territory, beyond Bullock's jurisdiction. Her freedom would depend on his lassitude and vanity.

As Lily and the posse rounded a corner on the road to the crossing, she glanced at a meadow up ahead and to the left. She could get a head start and build speed across the flat, grassy surface and then make for a draw between two hills leading south. As she prepared to spur her horse, she saw movement farther ahead on the road. When she focused on the distant sight, she realized it was the circus. Uncle Stanislas must have grown anxious.

She issued a sudden command and leaned forward and galloped straight ahead, waving as she did so.

Lily reached the lead wagon ahead of the posse, which, as she had expected, had been slow to action.

"Pretend Mister Szabo's hurt. You were robbed by bandits. Follow my lead when the others get here."

She raced on to the second wagon and addressed Mr. Szabo, directing him to lie in the back as if he had had a stroke. Hearing horses approaching from behind, she called out, "He's alive? Oh, praise God, he's alive!"

She climbed into the back of the wagon and held Mr. Szabo's hand. "Oh, Mister Szabo, I was so worried. I thought it might be a stroke."

She nodded her head at the old clown as if to say, "Now, your line."

"No, Lily dear," he said. "I just… it was just too much excitement, and I needed a rest."

Lily nodded and winked and raised her voice. "Oh, Mister Szabo, I was so terrified. I thought the shock of the robbery might kill you. Are you feeling better?"

She heard riders milling about at the open back end of the wagon. A horse snorted. Others stamped their hooves.

Bullock said, "This the injured party, Miss?"

"Ah, Sheriff," Mr. Szabo said, raising himself with a visible effort onto one elbow. "So good of you to look for me. It seems I swooned after the robbery. Too much excitement for this old heart."

Bullock gave a thin smile at Mr. Szabo's news and fixed a penetrating gaze on Lily. "I'll need to get full statements from Mr. Szabo and the rest of your people. Now, if you could come with me and show me exactly where this robbery took place?"

Mr. Szabo said, "It was somewhere along this trail. A few miles back. These forests and hills all look the same, don't they?"

Lily took her cue and picked up the story. "I was in such a panic. I might have been riding for hours to get into town, or it might have only been a few minutes."

"Well, we can just follow the trail until we see the bandits' tracks and start chasing from there. Can you tell me what kind of horses they had, and how many?"

Rather than answer, Mr. Szabo gasped and winced. He closed his eyes and began breathing heavily, as if working through intense pain. This seemed to change Bullock's mind.

"You'd better get to the doctor," Bullock said. "I'll ride with you."

There was no disputing this. Lily remained in the back of the wagon with Mr. Szabo, running through the likely outcome when a medical diagnosis confirmed the sheriff's suspicions about her story.

Her ruminations were interrupted by a whispered remark from Mr. Szabo. "Come closer, child. I need to tell you my last words."

Lily leaned in.

"Did you find your joker?"

She nodded.

"You're sweet on him."

She reddened.

"I'd say 'beware of vagabonds with no prospects for a stable life,' but...." He smiled and shrugged and gestured at his surroundings. "Are he and his friends bandits?"

She leaned in closer still. "I think so, but they're not bad, or not all bad."

"Lily, dear, in this country, the worst bandits commit their robberies behind a desk. But that doesn't mean every bandit on the road is Robin Hood."

The wagons bumped along the road to Deadwood, with the sheriff and posse riding as protectors or potential jailers. As they approached the town, Lily heard the sound of horses galloping hard. She peeked through the front of the wagon and saw Bullock conferring with a newly arrived rider who was gesticulating wildly, pointing back to the town and ahead at the circus wagons.

Bullock directed the members of the posse to join the rider, and they spurred their horses and quickly vanished around the bend. Bullock pulled up beside each wagon in turn and called for a faster pace.

Then Bullock turned his horse and trotted up to the back of Lily's wagon and called to her and Mr. Szabo. "Do you know the penalty for conspiracy to start a riot?"

"Goodness, Sheriff," Lily said, "I have no idea—"

"If you and your friends have anything to do with what's happening, if this is some attempt to free your friend, you'll be doing your tricks behind bars. The doctor will know if you two have been spinning a story. And if you have, I will charge both of you with everything I can think of."

Bullock ordered all the members of the posse, save his deputy Jim, to join him, and together they galloped straight away to Deadwood.

With the deputy riding alongside, the circus wagons clattered and splattered over the alternately rocky and muddy roads to the street of houses recently built for the community's new professional class. The doctor's house occupied a double-sized lot on the hillside above Main Street. The horses slowed to pull the wagons up the hill, then came to a stop, blocked by crowds of men milling about on the road.

The deputy had to ride ahead to clear a path.

When the wagon came to a halt in front of the doctor's office, Lily, Tommaso, and Uncle Stanislas helped Mr. Szabo down. Mr. Szabo played his part by stepping hesitantly, as if each movement required all the strength he had left in his body. He paused on the walk up to the door to draw laborious, wheezing breaths.

A crowd of men and women and children blocked the doorway. The deputy had to shout and pull several men by the shoulder to make room for Mr. Szabo and his helpers. "This is sheriff's business," he called to the backs of heads. "We've got a medical emergency here."

The doctor's waiting room was an enlarged parlor in the front of a new clapboard house made of freshly planed planks of Black Hills pine. The smell of tree resin fought with the mustard plasters and camphor-based unguents dispensed in the examining room on the other side of a curtain.

"The doctor's busy," shouted a man with a soot-blackened face and torn, filthy clothes, one of many in the waiting room who looked as if they had crawled out of their own graves to be there.

Some of the filthy men in the room were themselves bleeding. One had a length of soiled cloth wrapped around a dripping head wound. Another had an arm bound up in a burlap sack suspended in a sling made from a belt.

"What happened?" the deputy asked.

"That devil wagon came at us spitting fire. A dozen people got trampled trying to get away."

A blood-curdling shriek rent the air. The deputy squeezed through the crowd and made his way past the curtain.

Lily looked at Mr. Szabo, who, despite his best and most convincing performance, was clearly not as close to death as the patient behind the curtain.

The deputy returned, white-faced.

Mr. Szabo put on a brave face. "We must not distract the doctor with my... nervous affliction. I need only rest and quiet."

The deputy looked about the room, from the crowds of angry and injured men to Lily and Mr. Szabo. One of the workers bellied up to him and said, "What are you doing here with that tin star?"

"I'm here on police business."

"You should be out there," the man said, pointing. "Keeping Hearst's men from murdering us."

Another voice called out, "Murder, that's what it is. They already murdered one man with that wagon. Now who knows how many they're going to kill?"

The man with the blackened face drew a handkerchief from a pocket and wiped his face. He held a hand out to his side, as if to prevent his friends from attacking the deputy. "If you cared about catching crooks, Jim, you'd be up there at Hearst's office. He's the one sent that wagon after us."

A weeping woman on one of the chairs against the wall looked up. "The law don't care about us."

The bandaged man jabbed a finger at the deputy. "You tin stars did nothing when they attacked us unprovoked. Shot us down like vermin."

"Now, you all know darn well Sheriff Bullock has been investigating that incident, and there's evidence people in the camp fired first."

"We're nothing to them," said someone.

The man with the handkerchief nodded. "We'll just have to make the law care, won't we?"

The crowd roared its approval. One voice could be heard in the din calling out, "To Hearst's office!"

Powerless to silence the cries for revenge, the deputy was swept out the door along with the men chanting Hearst's name. Lily stepped to the window and watched as the swelling crowd on the street began to march into town. The deputy mounted his horse and raced ahead of the mob, leaving the circus folk behind with the seriously injured workers and their families.

When the way was clear, Uncle Stanislas turned to Mr. Szabo. "Show's over."

Mr. Szabo, refusing to break character, rose slowly and walked delicately to the door as if unsure that his legs would support him. "Perhaps it was just a simple case of the nerves after all," he said.

He took Lily by the hand, and they followed Uncle Stanislas out the door. The circus wagons were lined up down the street, and Lily could see Tommaso crouched beside the front axle of one. Below him, two pairs of legs jutted out from underneath the wagons. Lily recognized them as belonging to Arnold and Hymie, the tumbling midgets.

"*Cazzarolo,*" Tommaso said. "I feel she rattles too much coming into town, maybe hit a big rock. The axle is loose and maybe also cracked."

Tommaso uttered a string of what Lily took to be Sicilian curses. When his anger subsided, he added that the wagon train would need to buy more feed for the horses after wasting two days going back and forth along the trail.

"*Che palle.* But is maybe not too bad," he said. "I know a stable run by a good man, a man of honor."

The circus folk clambered aboard their wagons and made for the stable through streets that were ominously quiet in places and choked with angry men in others. Where possible, they detoured to avoid crowds that had gathered for no apparent purpose but to shout words of anger. This was not their quarrel, but they knew outsiders made convenient targets when men's minds were fevered. They also sought to avoid the sheriff's office, hoping the disturbance would allow them cover to complete a second, permanent departure from the Black Hills.

Without incident, they reached the rough-hewn log cabin that served as a blacksmith's shop and the double-sided lean-to that stood in for a barn at Zeke's Stable. It wasn't much of a place, Tommaso said, but Zeke was an honest man, and he hadn't overcharged when the horses needed shoeing after the long trip from Bismarck.

They pulled into the yard, and Tommaso and Uncle Stanislas consulted with the blacksmith, who was surrounded by colored children. After a short discussion, Uncle Stanislas handed a few greenbacks to Zeke, who gestured to the older children to hurry to the shed. The children returned, carrying a burlap sack between them.

While Tommaso helped them load another pair of feed sacks into the wagons, Zeke knelt and inspected the ailing axle.

"She ain't gonna take you to Cheyenne, not with that there axle."

"Can you change it? *Prestissimo*, very fast?"

Zeke crawled underneath the wagon. While they waited for his verdict, Tommaso and Uncle Stanislas conferred about the possibility of leaving one wagon behind for repairs while the others, with Lily and Mr. Szabo on board, left immediately.

"I won't leave you all behind," Lily argued. "I caused this trouble—"

"Hush, girl," said Uncle Stanislas. "You speak truth. You have caused enough trouble today."

Zeke hauled himself out from under the wagon and walked to the shed. He didn't look confident.

Uncle Stanislas ordered Lily to take her dogs and practice. He didn't want the dogs to get rusty, he said. But Lily knew he wanted to discuss the circus's predicament without her around.

She led the dogs away, concerned over the trouble she had caused her friends. Had it not been for Daniel's sudden appearance along the wagon road and her departure to search with him for Segal, the circus would be well on its way to Cheyenne, on the verge of a successful tour of the mining towns in the mountains.

Galahad and Lancelot sensed she needed sympathy. They took turns nuzzling up to her, rubbing their jaws and their flanks against her. Sparky seemed determined to cheer her up through force of will. The Chihuahua ran laps around her and spun like a top while chasing his nonexistent tail until he collapsed in a disoriented heap.

Lily laughed despite her anxieties. She looked back at the circus wagons and saw Tommaso and Mr. Szabo carrying cargo from the stricken wagon to another. Perhaps they hoped a lighter load would allow it to reach Cheyenne, or possibly they had decided to abandon it entirely. It was not her decision to make. All she could do now would be to make her act as entertaining as possible. To that end, she decided to investigate the blacksmith's shop further. She had speculated for some time about having armor manufactured for Lancelot and Galahad. A canine Knights of the Round Table might be a hit with audiences. She had been intending once the troupe reached Cheyenne to speak to a blacksmith about the idea.

As she approached the shed, she heard a boy say, "Lincoln says you can figure anything out by working out the way lines come together."

Another boy leaned over a group of children, all looking down at a small slate. The standing boy held a piece of chalk in one hand and gestured to a drawing of a triangle on a small slate.

Lily stood back and watched the boy quote "Lincoln," clearly a figure of awe among the children.

As she watched, a black boy about her age approached the stable. The younger children exploded with excitement.

"Lincoln! What you doing here?"

"Come to make sure you layabouts is... are doing your lessons."

"You ain't workin' today?"

"No, I *am not,* and you *are not,*" Lincoln pointed to two boys, including the one who'd been leading the lesson. "I need to talk to you two alone."

While Lincoln took the other two aside, Lily looked back to the yard, where the circus folk anxiously waited to see if Zeke could make the needed repair. A powerfully built colored woman, bent at the waist by the weight of a bulky carpetbag, addressed Uncle Stanislas. Her expression was both beseeching and proud. She appeared to be asking a favor but not begging.

Uncle Stanislas's head shook slowly. Whatever she needed appeared impossible. She held up a purse, apparently offering to pay. Did she want to hitch a ride? Lily heard the two younger boys respond to whatever Lincoln had whispered to them.

"We leavin' now? Why?"

"Never mind why, George."

"But we got friends here."

"Mama's going to find us a ride out of town. You'll make new friends when we get where we're going."

The dogs read Lily's curiosity about the boys, especially the older one named Lincoln. Sparky ran toward them and began to sniff about his ankles. Startled by the little Chihuahua, Lincoln traced the dog's path back to see where Lily stood against the wall of the stable.

"Sorry," she said, approaching and gesturing to Sparky. "I didn't mean to interrupt."

"That's no mind, Miss."

The boy's brothers bent and began to play with Sparky. The dog responded to the attention with his usual jumps and rapid running in circles.

Lincoln said, "He's sure full of beans, isn't he?"

"I think your mother asked my uncle if you could travel with us," Lily said. "I think he said no."

"We can pay."

"It's not a matter of money." Lily explained the problem with the axle.

A change came over Lincoln's face. He looked more hopeful and also more distant, as if he were suddenly deep in thought. "Let's see that axle," he said.

Turning his back on the younger children, he strode out the door toward the wagon, Lily following in his wake. He approached the wagon, took off his jacket, and crawled underneath, moving with such authority and certainty that nobody thought to question him.

As Lincoln lay under the wagon, Zeke returned to speak to Uncle Stanislas, saw feet jutting out from underneath, and called, "Who's that under there?"

The blacksmith's response when Lincoln emerged wasn't what Lily expected. Instead of telling the boy to get away from the wagon or play with the children, Zeke asked him for his assessment, as if he were a small-town doctor who'd called in a big-city specialist to consult on a difficult case.

Lincoln and Zeke both crawled back under the wagon and exchanged murmured observations.

When they emerged again, Tommaso asked what Zeke and his young apprentice were doing.

"Might could be we got a fix for your predicament," Zeke said.

The colored woman said, "You mean Lincoln got a fix for their predicament. That right, Zeke?"

The woman explained that her son had been apprenticed to a master mechanic and had a natural gift for building and repairing anything made by man. If the circus wanted Lincoln to fix their wagon, the price was passage for her family to Cheyenne.

"We don't even know if this will work," Uncle Stanislas said.

"Lincoln say it works, it works. You know that steam wagon shot up the workers' camp a couple weeks ago? My boy made that, but he wasn't the one decided to put guns in it. He can make anything he sets his mind to."

Lincoln bent and began drawing a diagram in the stable yard dirt, explaining as he drew the forces moving through a wagon as it bounced over the hills. His plan, he said, was to cushion the forces on the weakened front axle by bending iron staves to act as springs and at the same time to shift more of the wagon's weight to the stronger axle by tilting the wagon's bed slightly to the back.

"It's your best bet," Zeke said. "We can do this inside an hour. But it'll take me all day to carve a new axle for you and put it in place."

Uncle Stanislas conferred with Tommaso and Mr. Szabo, while Lincoln and Zeke began to work in the smithy.

"We'll give them an hour," Stanislas announced. "And you and your family may join us if this works."

Lily looked back at the town. A few tendrils of smoke rose over the rooftops, unexpected in the middle of a warm afternoon. The deep-bass roar of a shotgun carried on the wind. Things were out of control now, but how long until the authorities had things under control and came looking for the circus? She was the one the wolfer and the sheriff would want.

She needed to be on the road now. Or not on the road. In the forest, taking the hidden trails known only to Indians, robbers, and dogs.

She climbed into the wagon that held her belongings and found a coat. Then she rifled through the boxes of food and produced some beans, bacon, and flour. She stuffed all the items in a saddlebag and draped it over her horse. Then she reached into her special hiding place and removed the cavalry saber and rolled it into her bedroll. It might come in handy.

Mr. Szabo caught her in the act.

"When this riot is finished," she said, "they'll come looking for me."

"They will be busy with more urgent matters."

"You aren't safe while I'm with you. And I can't wait any longer."

Mr. Szabo's brow furrowed as he looked between Lily and the road leading back to Deadwood.

"You may be right. Every minute we wait, the risk grows that you will be caught. But if you leave on your own, how will you find us?"

"Galahad and Lancelot can find a way."

"They are dogs. Not wild animals. They do not know these hills."

"They haven't forgotten what it means to be wild. They can find a way. They can read the wind."

"Can they keep you safe? There may be bears in the woods, or bad men."

"They can protect me from bears. And the bad man I'm worried about is in town."

"Wait here. Say nothing to Stanislas yet."

Mr. Szabo turned and clambered into the wagon that carried his belongings. As Lily waited for him to return, Zeke and Lincoln approached the stricken wagon, carrying lengths of bent steel, a pencil tucked in behind Lincoln's ear. Zeke climbed underneath and placed the steel in position, and Lincoln handed him the pencil. Zeke emerged, smiling.

"That's gonna work fine, Lincoln. You can go talk to your Mama 'bout what you told me."

As Mr. Szabo disembarked from the wagon, he carried a rolled-up blanket. He approached Lily, gesturing with his head for her to join him over to the side, away from the group.

"I have a bedroll already, Mister Szabo."

"You need *this* bedroll." He unrolled the blanket just enough to reveal the butt of a revolver. "I bought it in Bismarck before we left for Deadwood. I don't like it, and I don't like to think of you carrying it, but I think perhaps you should have it."

She looked inside and saw a pistol, small like the kind the Bulldog Kid carried, and a box of cartridges. Lily stuffed the rolled blanket into the top of her saddlebag.

As she prepared to say her farewells, a disturbance caught her attention.

"What foolishness is this?" Lincoln's mother shouted.

"Not foolishness, Mama. It's for you and George and Thomas. They're gonna be looking for me soon as they get this trouble squared away. I'll cause you trouble if I stay with you."

"How are you going to leave by yourself? Have you got a wagon?"

"Mister McTaggart gave me money. Zeke's got a horse he can sell me."

"You ain't goin' off alone, and that's all there is to it."

Lily spurred her horse forward until she caught the woman's eye. "Maybe he doesn't have to go off alone."

She began to explain her plan, which brought Uncle Stanislas and Madame Mystere running over. Mr. Szabo strode into the midst of the argument and called for quiet. The two children had both played adult roles in the disturbances, he said. Now they had made their own decisions like adults, and those decisions should be respected.

A thick column of smoke rose over Deadwood. Something big was on fire.

"You two lookin' to get a head start, this a good time," Zeke said.

Their goodbyes were short, as the trail ahead was long.

Lily touched her horse's flanks, and she was off. Lincoln caught up in her slipstream. Time soared past, and the two spoke little more than an occasional "this way" or "careful, low branch." At times, Lincoln would call a stop, lose himself in concentration, and declare which direction was west and which south.

Trails crisscrossed the Black Hills, but none of them followed anything resembling a straight line. Trappers and prospectors had blazed pathways up every drainage in their search for furs and flecks of color. Colonel Custer's expedition a few years earlier had opened up wide trails leading south to Custer and Hill City and smaller branch trails in all directions where cavalry patrols had gone exploring. Outlaws had made their own trails, though they were intentionally hard to follow. Elk and deer created wide trails that might be easy to follow for a mile and would then disappear in a thicket of willow. A day passed and then another.

Without the dogs acting as scouts, Lily and Lincoln would have had to give up on their first day—if they had been able to find the way back, that is. But even with the dogs, progress was slow, and Lily despaired of reaching Cheyenne in time for the circus's opening performance.

More worrisome was the food supply, which was unlikely to last that long.

"What do you think?" Lily asked as the two riders came to a junction. She had learned that Lincoln had an internal compass. He kept track of the points of the compass no matter how many twists and turns the trail took.

"South-southeast's this way. So, the right turn, I reckon."

Lily heard the barking in her mind before her ears picked it up. Intruder. Threat. But not the hateful, fearful sound of the wolfer's approach.

There was something there, a presence, a consciousness. Something familiar. Galahad and Lancelot burst out of the undergrowth and stood at the feet of Lily's horse. Lily smiled.

"It's me," she called.

She heard a sharp, fearful intake of Lincoln's breath as the wolf emerged into the clearing.

"It's good to see you healthy again," she said.

The wolf sniffed the air and turned to circle Lily and Lincoln. She regarded Lincoln with caution.

"I am very sorry for your loss," Lily said. "This is my friend, Lincoln. He's afraid of wolves, but he means no harm."

Lincoln swiveled his head from girl to wolf and back again. "You're talkin' to a wolf?" It started as a question. He repeated it as a statement. "You're talkin' to a *wolf.*"

"I know this wolf. She knows me."

Lily felt something like friendship in the wolf's thoughts—a canine emotion, a fellow-pack-member feeling.

"Maybe she can help us," Lily said as she formed images in her mind of her destination. The high plains of Wyoming Territory, the rolling, dry, treeless lands beyond the Black Hills, the stagecoach trail to Cheyenne, with its series of stage stops and horse barns.

She saw the wolf ranging widely through the Hills and beyond to the land of the buffalo and antelope. She saw the wolf hunting fawns and rabbits and felt the wolf's desire to find a new pack. She saw the wolf following the setting sun into the high plains and knew there was a way out of this narrow, tree-choked valley.

The wolf turned and took the left-hand path.

"Good thing we met her," Lily said, touching her heels to her horse.

That night, the wolf bedded down in the tall grass beyond the feeble glow of their firelight. Lily and Lincoln shared a can of beans and cooked Indian bread by wrapping dough around a branch.

"These tricks you do in the circus, they aren't just pretend magic, are they?"

"Uncle Stanislas does the magic act. That's pretend magic, but don't tell him I said it."

"What you do. It's real."

"Yes."

"You've got something special, something nobody else got."

"It's not that...." Lily paused. How to explain it? Best to underplay it. "It's not that special. I've just worked a lot with my dogs, and I can tell what they're thinking by... by looking at their bodies, their tails."

Lincoln shook his head. He reached around and picked up the carpetbag that had never been beyond arm's reach since Lily met him.

"My teacher, Mister McTaggart, says we don't know half there is to know about how people think, what goes on inside people's heads. Folks might have all kinds of powers we don't know about. There are stories about folks hit in the head who are suddenly able to play piano or speak foreign languages. There are folks who have what Mister McTaggart called a photographic memory. They never forget a thing."

"I'm not like that, Lincoln."

"I am."

Lincoln opened his carpetbag and pulled out papers from inside. He showed Lily drawings of some kind of machinery, pages covered with calculations and drawings of angles and curves. "You heard I made that steam wagon. These here are the plans. I also made a plan for something worse, but I haven't written down all the details. I've been thinking about numbers and what I used to call come-togethers… geometry… since I was a baby. I never thought there was nothin'… anything… special about it. But I see how people look at me when they see what I can do. I'm like some folks you have in the circus, the bearded ladies or snake men. Freaks."

Lily looked at the papers. One of them showed a wagon with some kind of engine inside and smokestacks poking out. A wagon that could travel without horses would be a useful thing, and it would make somebody a lot of money. She'd heard about the steam wagon that attacked the striking workers. A steam wagon with a big gun, a steam wagon that could travel wherever its driver wanted to go, would make whoever owned it powerful.

"I kept this because I thought, if I have to, I can make a deal. Let my mama and brothers go, or I throw these in the river."

"We'll make sure they don't catch you, Lincoln."

"You and the wolf?"

Lily placed her thoughts in the wolf's mind and felt calm and comfort. The night was still, and no intruders disturbed the wolf's rest. Only the gentle movements of a rabbit, quarry in the nocturnal hunt to come, made the sleeping wolf's ears twitch.

"We're not freaks, Lincoln. We're prodigies."

34

SEGAL PUT ON a good show, walking out of the sheriff's office in the wolfer's big, black coat. Even from his hiding place on the edge of the forest, Daniel could see how his friend resisted the instinct to run, setting each footstep down as carefully as a man walking on ice. He'd certainly waited long enough to make his move. He must have wanted Lily to get far enough away to keep her from getting caught up in any action.

Daniel's guts had churned as he'd waited, hoping that the girl's plan—whatever it was—worked out. He'd watched as the wolfer left the office and tied up his dogs, then as Boone May and his men raced in. He had a feeling that growing up around circus folk had made Lily a fast talker, but he'd feared for her ability to keep a roomful of angry armed men spellbound.

With a big sigh of relief, he'd tracked the girl's departure with the sheriff, his deputy, and a few of May's men. And with a rising sense of dread, he'd watched the wolfer clench his fists and stride back inside. Lily's plan, no doubt, had been to make a jailbreak more likely by reducing the number of guards, but leaving Segal alone with the wolfer hardly seemed an improvement.

Now, Daniel could see the anxiety etched into Segal's face as he approached the hitching post where the wolfer's horse was tied. At least a hand taller than the paint Segal had been riding with the gang, the dark horse stamped its hooves as the strange young man approached dressed in the garments of its master. The dogs added to the horse's nervous reaction by launching into a chorus of barking and snarling. They, too, knew this was not the man in black they served.

With a mounting sense of fear, Daniel watched the stable doors. They remained closed.

He scanned the sharpshooters' stations and detected watchers eyeing Segal, but with relief noted, they did not have their weapons trained on him.

On his third attempt, Segal hooked a boot through the left stirrup and hauled himself onto the saddle. It wasn't the most graceful performance. He had to grasp the saddle horn and lean over the saddle to keep from sliding off, but at length he swung into position, pulled on the reins, and directed the horse to turn, placing his back to the stable.

The horse resisted the unfamiliar pull on the reins and shook its head, reared slightly, and stutter-stepped side to side. The dogs, tethered to the same hitching post, strained at their ropes, spewing clouds of spittle as they gnashed their teeth. It was only a matter of time, Daniel felt, before the watchers realized what was going on.

Before that could happen, Daniel heard gunshots in the distance. They echoed through the valley, but Daniel thought, and hoped, they came from the direction of the laborers' camp.

As Segal fought for control, men appeared farther up the street. Bearded, scarecrow thin, wearing patched dungarees and battered old farmer's boots split at the seams, many were the ragged men Daniel had seen on his first visit to the camp.

Leading the first few men were Roth and Wiseman, shouting and raising their fists in the air. The two familiar faces paused and waved successive lines of marchers forward as the crowd turned down a corner toward the sheriff's office.

Segal finally gained control of the wolfer's horse and spurred it into a gallop, heading straight west, as if the wolfer had belatedly decided to follow Bullock and Lily.

Before Segal was gone from sight, the doors of the stable opened, and the wagon emerged.

The men continued to chant and bear down on the sheriff's office until the appearance of the wagon froze them in their tracks.

Wiseman and Roth, still standing at the corner, a half a block behind the front ranks of the marching men, shouted and started forward, prompting a wave to begin in the middle of the crowd that pushed those in front closer to the mobile weapon. The wagon clanked and rolled and then paused, as if daring the men to continue.

Daniel noticed the bundle of barrels jutting from the front of the wagon. He'd never seen a Gatling gun, but he'd heard of the devil guns that pack the punch of an infantry company in the turn of a crank.

The wagon idled thirty feet from the leading edge of the crowd and from it the Devil's own fire erupted. The men vanished behind a cloud of dust and gunpowder as the Gatling gun drew a warning line in the dirt ten feet in front of the crowd.

Nothing could stand up to such a weapon. The ragged men knew that. As one, the crowd reversed direction. Men collapsed under the masses, seeking to escape the hellfire. The bodies of the fallen tripped others. Those frozen in fear were dashed to the ground by the wave streaming past them. Thick smoke shrouded the street. When it cleared, the street was empty, except for the injured, moaning in agony or struggling to regain their feet.

The wagon gave chase up the street, then turned to the west where the jailhouse road joined Main Street. As the wagon disappeared in the direction of the Homestake Mine, the rooftop sharpshooters abandoned their positions.

Moments later, Daniel saw that they, too, were chasing after the wagon. May and his men were obviously under orders to protect the mine and Hearst as their first priority, well ahead of stopping a jailbreak.

With nobody left on the road, Daniel mounted his horse, abandoned caution, and spurred it forward to chase down Segal. He had little trouble catching up to his friend, who still struggled with his unfamiliar mount. Daniel directed him back into the forest and up to the viewpoint on Mount Moriah, where they'd meet Roth and Wiseman.

When at last they were in cover and able to speak, Segal caught his breath and turned to Daniel. "I knew you wouldn't leave me to rot there, but why send Lily?"

"I didn't. She sent herself."

Daniel explained how he'd joined forces with the girl and her dogs and Roth's plan to stir up trouble among the workers to draw the war wagon away.

"Well, that part worked," Segal said. "But now we've got a new problem."

"Yup. Getting the hell out of the Dakota Territory before they put an end to this riot."

"No, Kid. I mean Lily. That was a real mitzvah, slipping me those keys. But now she's going to end up in jail when the sheriff figures out she was leading him on a wild goose chase."

Thrashing sounds in the forest made them cut their conversation short, and Daniel saw through the greenery the two young men who had sparked the riot. Roth and Wiseman smiled to see Segal with the wolfer's long black coat hanging off his thin frame.

"Ditch the coat, Segal," Roth said. "We gotta ride fast."

"I'm not riding anywhere. I have to make sure Lily's safe."

Roth insisted the four take advantage of the disturbance below to put as much distance between themselves and Deadwood as possible. Segal countered that Lily's bravery had saved his life, and he wasn't going to welsh on a debt. Things grew heated.

Daniel spurred his horse between Segal and Roth. "This ain't the time or place for arguing."

Roth said, "The Kid's right. We shouldn't be arguing."

He walked his horse a step closer and held out a hand toward Segal. Segal smiled and extended his own. As the two clasped hands, Roth turned to Wiseman and said, "Grab him!"

As Roth held Segal's right hand, Wiseman enveloped Segal's left arm in his iron grip. He brought Segal's right and left together and lashed them tightly in front.

Then Roth took the reins to the wolfer's horse.

"You... you four-flushers!" Segal sputtered. "You can't do this."

"I've already done it," Roth said. "Now, shut it, or the next step is we tie you to the saddle like a side of beef."

Segal turned to Daniel and implored him to help.

"Sorry, Segal," Daniel said, kicking his horse to trot alongside. He slapped Segal's horse on the rump, and it began to trot along the faint path leading south and east, down the far side of the hill. Daniel pulled on his own reins and dismounted. Something was gnawing at his insides, and it just about made him sick to think of it.

"Where you goin'?" Roth asked.

Daniel tied his horse's reins to a tree and pulled his rifle from the scabbard. "Unfinished business."

He crept back to the top of the hill and sighted his rifle on two furious hounds, still pulling and jumping, still howling and barking. If not for the riot, they'd have already prompted somebody to inspect the jail cell. And as soon as that happened, the dogs would have no trouble following the scent of the wolfer's coat, and his horse. Two distant rifle shots would hardly be noticed amid the chaos down there. He let his breath out slowly and squeezed the trigger, chambered another round, and squeezed again.

35

---◆◆◆---

JOSIAH LISTENED TO the disturbances beyond the jail cell walls. Sometimes, the jangle of breaking glass would penetrate, as if the mob was on the verge of bursting through the door. Other times, distant gunshots would testify to fighting far off in the direction of the mine diggings.

He hadn't heard the rumble of the steam wagon for some time, not since it had first filled him with hope and fear that Segal and the other bandits would be cut to pieces by the fabled Gatling gun. Hope, because that would be a just end for the smirking unbeliever and his accomplices. Fear, because he would not, therefore, be the bringer of justice.

He listened to the snarls of his hounds and felt satisfied that he would track these evildoers to the ends of the earth. For a moment, he imagined what it would be like if the Lord had given him the mind-reading magic that Satan had given that girl. He directed his thoughts through the walls at the dogs outside. *Hold still. Conserve your strength. Soon, we will be on the trail, and you will root them out for me.*

A pair of stifled yelps put an end to the canine barks and growls. Josiah had no doubt what had silenced them. A fast-draw *pistolero* who could hit the face of a playing card would have no trouble dispatching a pair of dogs.

Minutes crawled passed, and nobody entered the sheriff's office. He had faith that whatever disturbance had drawn away Boone May and the wagon had been planned as a diversion. Now the outlaws would have a head start, and without the dogs, Josiah would be on the trail for days. Weeks. But he had time, for he had no other purpose on this earth.

This realization brought a grim smile to his face. The Lord had selected Josiah to be His flaming sword. The years of eking out a living turning in wolf pelts for their bounty had been a long evasion of responsibility. His true calling was not to make war on Satan's representatives in nature, but among mankind. He turned to the appropriate passage from the Gospels and read it aloud, his voice booming through the empty room. "But I say unto you. It shall be more tolerable for the land of Sodom in the day of judgment than for thee."

Meditating on the vision of his enemies consumed by the fire that cleansed Sodom and Gomorrah of their sin, he lay on the straw pallet in the cell, closed his eyes, and drifted off to sleep.

He awoke to the sound of the key turning in the cell door. Sheriff Bullock shook his head, frowned, and looked down at him with pity and disgust.

"Bad dreams?" he asked.

Indeed, Josiah's dreams had again transported him to the bloody, burning forest at the Battle of the Wilderness.

"Never mind that, Sheriff. I need a horse and some good tracking hounds. The bandits are getting away."

Bullock laughed and turned his back on Josiah. A few long steps brought him to his desk, and he produced a key from a vest pocket and removed a ledger book from a locked drawer. As Josiah approached, Bullock flipped through the pages until he found the entry he sought, placed a finger on it, and spun the book to show Josiah.

"I advanced you fifty dollars on the grounds that you would help me to make the stage routes secure. Now, I see the man entrusted to your care has escaped and stolen a rifle belonging to this office. As far as I am concerned, you owe the town of Deadwood a substantial sum of money."

"I can't bring the bandit and his friends in without a horse and dogs."

"And I can't keep this town from burning down and Boone May from filling it with bloody corpses without some men of my own." Bullock reached into his desk again and this time brought out a tarnished brass star. "If this town is still standing in a couple of days, we'll talk about your horse and dogs."

Josiah gripped the back chair in front of the sheriff's desk hard enough to pop a wooden dowel from the seat. "The trail's getting cold. And that girl. She was in on it. We need to bring her in."

"My responsibility is to Deadwood," Bullock replied. "I am not going to leave this town in the hands of May and his war wagon. I don't want a massacre on my conscience."

Josiah pushed the chair aside with a snort. "Your conscience?"

"Watch your temper, or I'll add that chair to your debt. I can offer you a weapon and a horse, but I need you to promise you will help me to keep the peace here first."

Josiah glared at Bullock and the proffered star. Waiting felt like a denial of his duty. But he needed weapons and a horse and money to hire or buy dogs. He reached forward and took the star from Bullock's hand.

"Good. We'll see about the oath later. There has to be a Bible you can swear on somewhere in town." Bullock unlocked his rifle rack and handed Josiah a Winchester, noting the value of the rifle in his ledger. He then led Josiah out of the office to the hitching post, where Segal's little paint was tied up beside Bullock's horse. He gestured to the smaller horse and chuckled as Josiah mounted up.

"Looks like your prisoner and you did a little horse trading," Bullock said. "We'll adjust the stirrups later. For now, let's see what the hell that madman May is up to with that wagon."

Without waiting, Bullock spurred his horse, and his newest deputy had no choice but to follow.

They spent the remainder of the day patrolling Deadwood, chasing the sounds of gunshot, broken glass, and angry voices and riding between the two poles of the dispute—the Homestake Mine and the laborers' camp.

A gang of armed guards stationed behind an overturned wagon secured the road to the mine. Sharpshooters on the roof of George Hearst's office provided a second line of defense. At the laborers' camp, women and children, sheltered in tents, eyed Josiah, Bullock, and Bullock's deputy, Jim, warily. Always, it seemed, the rioters were just beyond reach of the sheriff and his deputies.

Though the war wagon posed a considerable threat, it couldn't be everywhere at once. The rioters, who had been dispersed initially by the fearsome roar of the Gatling gun, had adopted new tactics. Instead of massing for a march on the mine, they now gathered in small groups, many of them fueled by liquor, and launched hit-and-run raids. Drunken workers and layabouts directed their anger at their betters, who they saw as allied with their enemy.

Small groups emerged from the trees surrounding the town, like Indians of old, to toss rocks and flaming torches at the homes or offices of bankers and lawyers. The volunteer fire department, bolstered by citizens who feared the fire would not confine its damages only to Hearst's allies, organized bucket brigades. As night fell, a few of Boone May's men joined them in patrolling the well-to-do sections of town.

Warning shots resounded off the buildings, and rocks tossed blindly into crowds felled more than a few men on each side, but open warfare was kept at bay.

When it appeared that the rioters had exhausted their fury for the night, Josiah took advantage of his brass star to carry out investigations of his own. Bullock declared, sometime before sunrise, that it was time to turn in for the night. Josiah volunteered to keep the final watch. Once left alone, he rapped on the door of the hotel where the circus folk had been staying. Holding a lantern in one hand and pointing to his star with the other, he pushed past the hastily dressed innkeeper who greeted him. Upon learning which rooms the circus had occupied, he rifled through them, searching for anything that might tell him where the vagabonds were headed. He found what he was looking for in the third room. A wastebasket that had not been emptied contained torn tickets, obsolete handbills announcing the Deadwood performances, and one newer, imperfectly printed handbill announcing a week-long run in Cheyenne.

The poster, obviously thrown away as a misprint, was hard to read, but the date and time were clear—the next Saturday at one p.m.

The girl would be at a circus tent in Cheyenne that day, and Josiah was certain Segal would be there. And if Segal was there, so too would the *pistolero* and the rest of the gang.

Josiah stepped out into the gray predawn light. By now, the streets were quiet, Bullock's jail was full, two rioters lay on cots in the doctor's surgery with grievous wounds, and Deadwood was still standing. With no telegraph line, there was no chance to send out a description of the escaping miscreants. That meant no bounty hunter could steal the prize that was rightfully Josiah's, but it also meant he could count on no assistance against the guns of the *pistolero*.

He rode to the mine, woke Boone May, and asked to borrow a half dozen of May's men on sheriff's business.

"Nope," said May, placing a finger on a nostril and expelling the night's mucous onto the ground at his door. "Like to help you round 'em up, but the boss wants us to stay here. Keep things calm for a few days."

"A few days? The bandits will already be in Wyoming Territory by now. You want them to get to Colorado before you set off?"

"Hell, if they went that far, that'd suit Mister Hearst. He don't want them causing problems in Deadwood. Anyway, we got the war wagon, so we ain't too worried about road agents."

The war wagon. It was all these men could think about. Just because it could stop bullets and spray lead like a fire hose.

The war wagon! That gave Josiah an idea. He was one man against a gang of four—five, counting the girl—but that war wagon could even the odds. He made his way to look over the wagon but found it had been moved from its vantage point on the road outside the mine.

Josiah had heard the men talking about the wagon and the walled compound where a Scotsman and his colored apprentice had built it. Perhaps, after a day and night of action, the wagon had been taken back to the compound for some kind of mechanical treatment. He molded his face into a shape resembling a smile and approached the man who stood guard outside the compound. "They working on the wagon?" he asked.

"Nope, just trying to keep it safe," the man said.

"You think that rabble has the guts to come here and attack it?"

"Keeping it safe from the mechanic. Soon as the boys left him alone with it, the crazy coot doused it in coal oil. Tried to burn it. We got him locked up in his workshop."

Josiah used his star to gain entrance to the compound, claiming to be in need of a report on the wagon's condition. The wagon sat outside a small building with another guard outside. Josiah showed his star to the man guarding the workshop, entered, and woke the gray-faced mechanic, sleeping fully dressed on a pallet. "Need you to fire the wagon up again."

"Go to hell!"

Josiah placed his rifle's muzzle against the mechanic's forehead and lowered his voice to a whisper. "You first, Scotty."

"I'll not help you gun down innocent workers and their families."

"Those shirkers and bellyachers can burn this Gomorrah to the ground for all I care. I need to catch a couple of road agents on the way to Cheyenne."

"What kind of fool are you? The steam wagon won't survive a trip to Cheyenne."

"Then you'll get your wish. You wanted to wreck it. You can wreck it once I catch these road agents."

The mechanic explained that the wagon needed servicing. Lubrication. Cleaning.

"You've got till tonight," Josiah said, looking out the window at the compound. A wagon loaded with coal stood by the door. Other stacks of coal were piled on the ground beside it. "You got enough coal for this thing?"

The mechanic responded with a long speech about the steam wagon's powerful hunger for fuel. Josiah, whose head wasn't much for figures, tried to keep track of the numbers as he struggled to convert the miles the wagon had traveled putting down the riot into a proportion of the miles to Cheyenne. It just might work.

Josiah returned to the campsite he'd set up when he first arrived in town and lay down on his bedroll. He'd need to stock up on rest for the days ahead.

He slept through the morning and patrolled the streets with Bullock and Jim during the afternoon. There were still small spot disturbances to mop up and a temporary emergency ordinance against alcohol sales to enforce.

At suppertime, Josiah volunteered to work the night shift and make sure the riots didn't flare up under cover of darkness. He returned to his camp to get some shut-eye.

At midnight he relieved Bullock, who gave him instructions for the night's patrol. Then Josiah returned to his camp to gather up his bed-roll and a few cans of beans. The town was still quiet. Despite Bullock's concerns, the rioters were laying low.

He walked his horse to the mine stables, where he harnessed a freight wagon to a pair of draft horses. A teamster, awakened by the noise, came out to investigate, and Josiah showed his star and told the man he was needed to drive a wagon with important supplies for the defense of the mine. He directed the teamster to bring a second pair of draft horses and the necessary harnesses. He accompanied the wagon and the horses to the walled compound and flashed his star again to the man on guard duty and again woke the mechanic.

The wagon was ready. It was time.

Josiah called the guard and the teamster into the compound and pointed his Winchester their way. He directed them to load the team-ster's wagon with sacks of coal and harness the other team of horses to the wagon that was already laden with coal. He prodded the mechanic to fire up the wagon. The two horse-drawn wagons would travel first, with Josiah and the mechanic following in the war wagon.

"I'll say it again," the mechanic said. "You'll never make it to Cheyenne."

"I did a little figuring when you told me about the way this thing burns coal. I think with two wagons of it, I've got enough, unless you were bearing false witness yesterday."

Josiah approached the teamster and the guard with a pair of ropes. He directed the teamster to tie one around the waist of the guard and secure it to the bench of the wagon. Then he did the same with the teamster.

"If you men think you're going to scarper, just remember that I'll be right behind you with a Gatling gun."

36

LILY AND THE wolf were something to behold. If Lincoln didn't know he was considered unnatural by plenty of folks, he'd be inclined to think Lily employed some kind of witchery.

When they left the forests of the Black Hills behind, with the wolf's help, Lincoln became confident that he would see his family soon. He knew it would take some hard riding to make Cheyenne in time for the circus, but his horse was gentle, in part thanks to Lily's soothing.

"You talk to horses too?"

"I talk, but they don't answer."

"But you're good with 'em."

"That's just confidence and respect. I try to treat them the way I'd treat a dog, and they seem to like it."

They saw the last of the wolf on their second day out on the plains. She stood on a bluff, nose pointing to the south-southwest, then turned back to watch them climb toward her. As they approached the summit, she turned and headed northwest toward the distant blue line of the Rocky Mountains.

"Good luck," Lincoln said. "And thank you."

"It's her best chance to start again," Lily said. "She needs to find a new pack in a safe place where the wolfers won't get to her."

Lincoln thought of the government bounties on the hides of wolves and mountain lions and pictured the men who traveled the plains with rifles and traps and bags of poison. He knew it wasn't so long ago that men could get bounties for cutting the hair of the Indians who used to roam these plains as free as the wolves. And not so long ago, men in his home state made a living chasing down runaway slaves. Maybe, he thought, those bounties were what the preachers mean when they talk about "the wages of sin."

Once they were well and truly beyond the legal reach of the authorities in Deadwood, they decided they could take a chance on riding the stagecoach trail. They made good time, even though they took long detours to avoid being seen at the stations along the way. A day after joining the trail, they paused when Lily saw a figure in the distance.

"Daniel's eyes would come in handy about now," Lily said, sending the dogs ahead to scout. They came back a short time later, and Lily prompted her horse ahead. "It's a man walking. He seems unarmed."

As they approached, Lincoln noticed that the man was limping. Closer still, and he saw the man was shoeless. The man heard their horses and turned, waving his hands desperately. Lily pulled her horse up short.

"What are you doing here?"

The man hobbled in their direction. "You got any water?"

"Stop and tell me what you're doing here." Lily directed a growling noise to her dogs, and they cut off the man's approach. "I asked you a question."

Lincoln had not expected this hardness from the girl. He untied his canteen from his saddle horn, walked his horse forward, and handed the canteen to the man. The man unscrewed the canteen and held it to his lips, cast an appraising look at Lincoln, wiped the mouth with his sleeve, then drank deeply. An expression of deep relief came over his face as he took another pull on the canteen. He screwed it shut again and held it out to Lincoln.

"You're the little black boy built that Hell cart, ain't you?"

"Mister McTaggart built it. I was just his apprentice."

"That's what the Scotsman said, but I heard it was the apprentice did most of the figuring."

"You talk to Mister McTaggart?"

"He's with the wagon. And that crazy Bible puncher."

The man turned his attention to Lily, then to the dogs that did her bidding. "He's lookin' for you, missy."

The man, a teamster for the Homestake Mine, filled them in. He and another man, one of Boone May's guards, had been conscripted at gunpoint to drive coal carts in order to replenish the supply of what the man called the Hell wagon.

The other man had been set loose on the edge of the Black Hills when his supply of coal ran out, left bootless along the trail so he couldn't easily walk back to Deadwood to sound the alarm about the theft of the wagon.

Now it was just the mechanic driving the wagon and that demon-haunted madman with his hand poised on the crank of the Gatling gun. "Gonna be hell to pay if he sees you and your friends. I'd give Cheyenne a wide berth and make for Colorado if I was you."

"My friends are in Cheyenne. They're expecting me tomorrow."

As she and her dogs broke off from the teamster and her horse began to trot, Lincoln said, "Are we gonna leave this man to die here?"

"He won't die, but my friends might if we wait."

It was hot with no shade on the plain, and God himself would have been hard-pressed to say where the next water hole was. Lincoln looked at the hard ground and the man's tattered socks, one of which was stained with blood. He dismounted his horse. "We can't take you all the way, but you can ride for a while."

The man regarded Lincoln in amazement. He reached for the reins as Lincoln dismounted. Lincoln looked down the trail and saw Lily sitting her horse, a hand on her hip. He ran toward her, and she reached down to help him up.

"Mama says no reason you've got to return hurt for hurt in this world," Lincoln said.

Lily said nothing aloud but reached into her saddlebag and produced the pistol Mr. Szabo had given her. She tucked it into her belt so that the teamster could see. He tipped his hat to her and trotted up beside her.

They rode through midday until they found themselves on a hilltop from which they could see the distant walls and the flagpole of Fort Laramie.

"Thank God," the teamster called. "Thought I'd be left a pile of bones out there."

"Lincoln's going to need his horse back," Lily said. She removed the blanket Mr. Szabo had kept the pistol wrapped in and handed the blanket to the man. "You can cut this into strips and wrap up your feet. You'll be at the fort in a little over an hour."

The exchange complete, Lily uttered a short, sharp command, and her horse leapt forward in a gallop that made Lincoln struggle to keep up. They gave the fort an even wider berth, fearful that drawing the attention of the soldiers within would place Lily's friends in double jeopardy, between the Gatling gun on the wagon and the carbines of a company of cavalry.

With precious time running out, Lincoln and Lily pushed hard through the afternoon and past dark, pausing only for fear they'd wear out their mounts.

"Would you have used that pistol?" Lincoln asked.

"I don't know. Probably not."

"If you'd seen what I saw, you wouldn't make light of waving around a killing machine."

The next day, with rested horses, they put miles behind them, starting with first light until Cheyenne came into view. The country was now more heavily occupied. Isolated farmhouses were scattered across the grass and herds of cattle fattened in pastures. Another lone man staggering along the trail caught their attention. As they pulled closer, they realized it was Mr. McTaggart, breathing laboriously through a flattened nose, crusted blood in his hair. He stared at them with unfocused eyes until Lincoln touched him.

"Lincoln! Get away from here!"

Lily cut the reunion short, inquiring how far behind the wolfer they were, if the wolfer knew how to drive the wagon on his own, if they'd seen any trace of the circus or Segal and the gang. The mechanic's answers were confused, his ordering of events haphazard.

"We've got to get him help," Lincoln said, inspecting McTaggart's head injury. "That wolf hunter like to cave Mister McTaggart's head in."

Mr. McTaggart drained the last of Lincoln's canteen, then retched up the water and whatever was left in his stomach. Lincoln kept him from collapsing.

"Told him I wouldn't drive anymore." Mr. McTaggart groaned. "Said he didn't need me and tossed me out the door."

Lily urged her horse to its fastest gallop and left Lincoln to deal with the injured man. Lincoln let Mr. McTaggart ride and led the horse along the road. The man seemed decades older, pale, stooped, thin. Between his broken nose and the coughing fits that struck with regularity, he could hardly speak. It took all the strength he had left just to repeat his warnings.

"No, sir, Mister McTaggart. I made this mess. I've got to help clean it up."

He held the reins and helped Mr. McTaggart keep from falling as he led the horse to the nearest farmhouse, a one-room soddy built within sight of the new timber structures in town. Getting the injured man off the horse was no picnic. His feet flailed about in the stirrups, and he listed dangerously from side to side. A woman ran out from the house and saw the injuries and helped Lincoln bring Mr. McTaggart into the house. They led Mr. McTaggart to a bed, where Lincoln removed the mechanic's shirt and held his hand while the woman filled a basin with fresh water. As the woman bathed his wounds, Mr. McTaggart opened his eyes wider and grasped Lincoln's arm. "I didnae think the wagon would make it this far. You're too good a mechanic, son."

Lincoln left Mr. McTaggart with the woman, promising to return with a doctor. As he mounted up, he heard the sound of the Gatling gun spitting lead and death. Fire raged for five seconds. Then, silence. Lincoln raced toward the sound. Another burst of fire followed a few seconds later. Then, another silence. Then, a short burst of Gatling gun fire, one that stopped almost as soon as it started.

37

DANIEL HAD BEEN decisively outvoted when the gang members stopped to catch their breath after escaping Deadwood. Cheyenne, he'd argued, was the obvious destination for the gang—both the closest large town and the closest railway stop. That meant they should go north to the gold fields of Montana. Or anywhere, really, except where the sheriff and May and the wolfer expected them to go.

"What makes you think you get a vote, Kid?" Roth asked. "You're lucky we didn't bash your brains in after you gave back the money."

Segal had stood up for Daniel, noting that without his intervention he, Roth, and Wiseman would still be digging potatoes at the reformatory. But on the question of their immediate destination, he'd sided with Roth and Wiseman, who made it clear that they wanted to take the shortest journey possible to the railway and then take the first train east.

They rode south and east to Rapid City in order to put off any pursuers who might head straight to Cheyenne. Then, from Rapid City, after buying provisions with most of what remained of their thin takings from the stagecoach robbery, they set off for Cheyenne.

After Rapid City, they had just enough for train fare for three, not four. Segal prodded the riders to keep up the pace and each morning was the first to mount up. Daniel scanned the horizon from every high point they reached.

"Sorry I didn't stop them from tying you up, Segal," Daniel said one day as they paused to rest their increasingly fatigued and thin mounts beside a rare stream of sweet water.

"Save it till we know if Lily's safe."

"I can go look for her once I get you three to the train station."

Segal lifted his saddle and placed it on the tall black horse. "You want to make nice, Kid, why don't you lend me one of those noisemakers you carry? This thing I took off the wolfer nearly gives me a hernia when I try to lift it."

Segal reached into his saddlebag and removed the Peacemaker he'd stolen from the wolfer. Daniel wanted to ask his friend if he was prepared to kill a man, but he cut his own words short. The way things were going, Segal might well need to kill or be killed.

Daniel traded one of his Bulldogs for the Peacemaker.

Their horses rested and watered, they resumed their journey.

Trail days take on a rhythm that can turn an hour into a day or a week into an hour, Daniel thought. Sleep, eat, ride, water the horses, ride some more, eat, and sleep. After days of dust and saddle sores and sunburn, Daniel crested a rise on foot in order to look for signs of ambush or pursuit. He discovered that Cheyenne lay spread across the dry plains below. He spied the circus tent. Beyond the circus stood the Union Pacific station and past that, the marshalling yards where trains were assembled for the climb west over the Rocky Mountains.

And galloping into town from the north was a golden-haired girl who appeared born to ride, trailed by two dogs, one tall and shaggy, the other shorter and stockier.

As Daniel watched more intently, he saw that the girl held the reins with one hand and with the other held something close to her chest, which was revealed a few paces later to be the tiny dog that had played umpire at the circus. He heard the sound of hoofs from behind and saw that Segal had walked his horse to the hilltop.

"Get down!" Daniel told his friend, who squinted at the scene below.

"Somebody must be chasing her," said Segal, spurring his horse forward. "We gotta help."

Segal directed his horse on a path to intercept Lily at the circus tent. Daniel raced back to his horse, mounted up, and gave chase, leaving Roth and Wiseman with their older, slower horses behind. As he rode, Daniel scanned the rooftops and windows for signs of an ambush. After the riot in Deadwood, it might have taken some time for a posse to be assembled and sent after the fugitives, but more experienced riders might well have made up for the delay.

The tent flapped gently in the breeze at the end of a road on the east end of town, lined with pens for cattle being shipped east. Families filed in at the entrance to the tent. Banners proclaimed *"Grand Opening! Saturday! Watch and Be Amazed!"*

The circus appeared to be starting without Lillian the Lycanthrope. Was it possible, Daniel wondered, that Lily's race on horseback was just part of the act? He'd nearly caught up when Lily spotted Segal. She pulled her horse to an abrupt stop, and the two exchanged words. Daniel saw the alarm in her face. This was no act.

As Daniel came closer, Lily turned to him and shouted, "The steam wagon. It's here!"

Daniel had seen the Gatling gun fire its warning shots to disperse the mob in Deadwood. It had not chased them this far to shoot the dirt at their feet.

"Get out of the street!" he shouted as a mechanical rumble rose above the circus organ, the laughter of children, and the pounding of his own heart.

Daniel and Segal turned to see the wagon emerge from a side street. Daniel pulled his Henry rifle from his scabbard and placed it to his shoulder. As he did so, he saw Lily grab the bridle of Segal's horse and spur them both away, toward the shelter of a nearby barn. Then he sighted his rifle, looking for the viewing hole through which he intended to shoot the driver of the wagon. As he squeezed the trigger, a burst of flame shot from the wagon, and he felt his horse shudder and jump. His first shot went wide, and he attempted one more as his horse fell to the ground.

He saw flame and smoke, then blue sky, then momentary blackness as his head struck the dry, hard-pounded mud of the street.

Sounds raced through his head. The whistle of bullets passing directly overhead, and the thud of others striking the belly of his dead horse. Screams. Hoofbeats. The spitting thunder of the Gatling gun. The dying notes of the circus organ. The rumbling, unstoppable clank of the wagon's tread and the rhythmic hiss and boom of the steam engine.

The pain brought his mind into focus. The dead horse pinned his right leg to the ground. He twisted his body to place his left below the level of the horse's flanks so that it, too, was protected by the rampart of flesh. He leaned forward and pushed on the saddle, hoping to slide out from underneath, but he lacked the strength and the leverage.

As he attempted to extricate himself, he momentarily raised his head just high enough to see Roth and Wiseman ride into the battle, guns blazing, aiming at the side of the wagon.

He heard the Gatling gun momentarily stop and risked a look above his horse and saw the wagon spin in position as Wiseman and Roth closed in on it. If they could reach it before it had the gun aimed their way, perhaps they could climb on board and fire directly into a ventilation hole. But if not….

A sustained blast from the wagon cut off that hope. Roth and Wiseman were thrown from their horses by the torrent of lead. In that moment, Daniel saw where his rifle had fallen. It lay across the lifeless front legs of his horse. Reaching above the animal's flank and bending as far as he could, he hooked a finger on the sight at the end of the rifle barrel and pulled it an inch closer, then two inches. Then, as the steam wagon changed course and Daniel again found himself directly in the shooter's aim, he grasped the end of the barrel with his thumb and two fingers and pulled it to him.

He heard the machine rumble closer and knew he would have only one chance, if that, to stop it. From his position on the street, he couldn't see the viewing hole above the barrels. He was too low, the wagon too high, and Gatling gun barrels blocked the path a bullet would take to the hole. But, he thought, he could hit the rotating barrels. Maybe a lucky shot could jam the gun.

Daniel waited for the wagon to get closer and for a lull in the shooting. Turning that crank had to get a bit tiresome after a while, no matter how much the man inside was propelled by hatred and bloodlust. When such a lull presented itself, Daniel tensed his stomach muscles to raise his upper body just enough to bring the gun into view and squeezed off a shot at the source of the fire. He fell back down with the whistling of near misses in his ears.

He heard the wonderful sound of a stilled gun. Then, a door opening and footsteps, and Daniel knew now that the final shots would be man to man. He steeled himself to lean forward again and kill the man who had killed Roth and Wiseman and however many innocent circus-goers turning the red clay crimson behind him.

As he moved forward, Daniel heard a crack of gunshots, or perhaps one shot and a quick echo, and he saw the wolfer stand for a moment with a look of shock on his face. The wolfer dropped his rifle to the ground and turned away from Daniel and toward the barn, where Segal and Lily had sheltered. Then, he looked skyward.

Daniel heard the cries of the wounded and terrified and the hissing sounds of the steam wagon.

The wolfer, as he fell, heard something more. He smiled as he listened to the voices in harmony as a choir sang "Sheep May Safely Graze."

38

---◆◆◆◀---

LINCOLN ROUNDED A corner and saw the steam wagon, gun smoke pouring out of the ventilation shaft he had designed. He had done that, made it possible to fire the gun without being choked by the smoke inside. He cursed himself, wished he'd never seen numbers, never played with angles and shapes.

Beyond the wagon was a place of joy turned to a nightmare.

The circus tent beckoned from a vacant piece of land at the end of the street. Before it lay the shapes of people and horses struck by bullets from the Gatling gun. A tall brown horse, no rider in its empty saddle, galloped away down a side street. Screams emanated from the circus tent, and Lincoln could see black dots in the canvas, evidence of stray bullets that had passed beyond the targets and, at least some of them, lodged in the flesh of unsuspecting families seeking an afternoon of laughter and wonder.

The killing instrument he had helped to perfect had passed its test with flying bloody colors.

The door to the wagon opened, and Lincoln saw a man in black depart, in his hand a lever-action rifle. The man walked deliberately toward the scene of the carnage, toward a dead horse closest to the circus. Lincoln saw movement just barely visible along the horse's flank. He realized somebody was pinned under the dead horse and was struggling with his free leg and hands to emerge from under the heavy animal.

The man in black stepped close enough to see over the body of the horse and began to lift his rifle. Another shot rang out, perhaps two, perhaps one with an echo. The man stopped, his rifle wavering, then collapsed to the street. Lincoln looked to his left and saw Lily, a pistol in her hand. Beside her, a scrawny young man also held a pistol.

One threat had been eliminated. But a greater danger still lurked in the street.

Lincoln dismounted and climbed into the steam wagon. It was like climbing into a blast furnace. He could tell by the smell and the heat that the engine was dangerously low on lubricating oil. The labored huffing of the engine and the high-pitched whine, which reminded him of nothing he'd heard since the steam drill exploded long ago in Tennessee, told him that the steam wagon had been pushed to its very limit. He shoveled the remaining coal into the hopper, shut the steam release valve tight as it could go, and turned the throttle to full power. He put the wagon into gear and turned it one hundred and eighty degrees and pointed it straight down the road leading out of town.

After he had cleared the last buildings, with the metal-on-metal shrieking stabbing into his brain, he disengaged the drive wheels and let the machine coast to a stop. He jumped out and ran back toward Lily and her dead and injured friends, calling out to all who heard him to stay away from the machine.

He felt the explosion as much as he heard it and turned to see a second sun on a Wyoming afternoon.

39

L ILY LOOKED ASTONISHED.

"You mean you've never seen a baseball game?"

"I played stickball a couple of times when I was a kid," Daniel said."

Segal laughed. "Not a lot of baseball at the reform school. Good thing too. Every night, I'd pray, 'Don't let these Irish kids get their hands on bats.'"

Daniel watched the batters from the Cheyenne team step up to the plate, one after another, and swing at balls that weren't there. What was wrong with them that they couldn't do something as simple as hit a ball? True, the pitcher for the visiting team had a long arm and could get plenty of power into his throws. Lincoln had explained that already, with a lot of complicated numbers. But the ball wasn't moving that fast. Was it?

"The guys with the bats keep missing because the ball's moving too fast for them to see," Daniel said. "Right?"

"That's kind of what makes it exciting when they get a hit, Kid," Segal said.

Lincoln leaned forward and turned to Daniel. "Wait a second. You can see the ball?"

"Forget it."

Segal helped himself to Daniel's bag of peanuts and leaned forward to address Lincoln. "Didn't see *that* coming, did you?"

"God's truth" Lincoln persisted. "Can you *really* see the ball moving?"

Daniel shrugged, wishing he'd kept quiet. There were secrets you didn't even want your friends knowing.

"The pitcher's throwing the ball ninety feet, and it takes less than a second, so that's seventy, maybe eighty miles an hour," Lincoln said. "The ball's three inches across, and we're a hundred and fifty feet from the pitcher, and—"

"We get it," Segal said. "You're the numbers man."

"Sorry, I just don't see how anyone's eyes can work so fast."

"Some things you just can't understand, even with your numbers. The Kid's eyes and reflexes, Lily's thing with dogs, how I got to be so handsome and charming."

At last, one of the batters for the Cheyenne team made contact with the ball, but Daniel could see immediately that it was headed straight for the man in right field. If the batter had timed his swing better, it would have been the easiest thing in the world to send the ball into the space between right and center. Well, easiest thing in the world for Daniel.

Watching the runner try for first base, he felt a twinge of envy at the man's speed, and when the ball was caught in the air and the runner was declared out, Daniel continued to feel envious of the easy stride as the man loped off to his position in the field.

Daniel's right leg no longer caused him pain, but he still walked with a limp and knew it would be some time before he could run easily. He recalled how, while he was trapped under the weight of his horse, he didn't feel the crushing weight. The pain only came later, when the horse was lifted and he was pulled free. When Daniel was examined later, the doctor had warned him that he might hobble for life. The doctor hadn't counted on the special brace Lincoln had devised out of leather, springs, and thin straps of steel. It supported the damaged muscles in Daniel's leg, while allowing them to carry slightly more weight each day as they healed. Good thing, because Daniel didn't think he could afford the luxury of staying still for a long recuperation.

The doctor had said he was lucky, but thinking of the horror inflicted by the madman wolfer, he didn't feel that way.

He knew that as long as he lived, the image of Roth and Wiseman flying off their horses would never leave him. Nor would he forget the hatred on the face of the wolfer as the bullets struck him.

Daniel straightened his injured leg and rotated his ankle, determined to speed up his healing. "So, these guys really get paid money to play a game?" he asked.

"Not the team from Cheyenne," Lily said, leaning across Segal and reaching into Daniel's bag of peanuts. She casually shucked nuts without the trace of a shadow crossing her pretty features. "The locals are amateurs. But the touring players, sure. They travel around from town to town and put on a show. If the local competition is good, they play it straight. If it seems too easy, they'll mix things up a bit, do some funny stuff."

The touring team must have already decided that Cheyenne didn't offer much competition. After their lead batter reached second base on a hit straight up the middle, their second batter walked out to the plate. He carried a rocking chair. He sat and began rocking while waiting for the pitch. As the pitcher released the ball, the batter jumped up and took a swing and shot the ball down the third base line for a hit.

"So, they travel around, play baseball, and they make enough money to live?"

Segal reached into the bag of peanuts. "You lookin' for a new job, Kid? Being a hero ain't good enough for you?"

No, Daniel didn't think he wanted to be a hero. When the shooting stopped and the smoke cleared, the people who'd run behind walls or buried their faces in the dirt suddenly became witnesses to the greatest shootout in the history of the West. It was all anybody talked about. He was the boy who went head to head against a madman with a Gatling gun. Nobody looked at the girl or the gawky stringbean with the smoking pistols, and those two, in turn, were too busy dealing with the dead and injured to make statements to the overwhelmed sheriff.

A few days later, an express rider brought word that Daniel was an escaped road agent known as the Bulldog Kid. This presented the town with a quandary. Do they apprehend the road agent, or do they celebrate the hero who single-handedly stopped a massacre by a man with an unimaginable killing machine?

The express rider was given a message to take back to Deadwood. The young man identified as the bandit Bulldog Kid was in fact the newly deputized assistant sheriff of Cheyenne. Sheriff Bullock would need a whole fleet of armored wagons with Gatling guns if they wanted to take him.

Being a hero took some getting used to. It brought its rewards, no doubt, among them four seats to the baseball game and the ability to insist that Lincoln join them in the otherwise whites-only section of the stands. Still, Daniel couldn't escape the feeling when people looked at him that they were just itching for the chance to see him shoot another bad man. And this being Wyoming Territory, in time, that was nigh on inevitable.

The three prodigies—four, if you counted Segal—laughed and relaxed in the sunshine as they watched hapless local players struggle for hits and the touring showmen inject ever-more-elaborate stunts into the game to keep things entertaining. Segal, a professional entertainer now that he had taken the place of the wounded Mr. Szabo, offered stern critiques of the comedic routines. "This material is so dusty, I'm gonna sneeze."

Lily poked Segal on the shoulder and laughed. "Listen to him. He's done a one-week run as a clown, and suddenly he's an entertainment maven. Did I use 'maven' right?"

"A fast learner, this one. Dogs, horses, Jews—she speaks just about everybody's language."

The manager of the touring team emerged from his team's bench with a step stool and a speaking cone to make an announcement after the sixth inning. The visitors, the Texas Road Kings, were always on the lookout for talent and would give every member of the audience the opportunity to demonstrate his aptitude for the sport of baseball. Any man who could hit a ball pitched by the mighty long-armed Horace Crockett would receive ten dollars in cash. Any man who could hit two pitches out of three would be offered a one-year professional contract with America's premier touring baseball team.

All along the bleachers, young and not-so-young men jumped to attention and ran down the steps to the field. Some were schoolboys, one had the powerful arms and chest of a blacksmith, plenty of them had the weather-beaten, lined, faces of cowboys.

Daniel thought of Segal, about to leave with the circus for a tour of Colorado. Daniel could do the same if he wished. He'd already turned down Stanislas twice, and he had a stack of telegrams from Buffalo Bill Cody in the wastebasket of his hotel room. He could earn a living as a target shooter, no doubt, but he'd had enough of weapons.

He thought of Lincoln, about to board a train with his family and Mr. McTaggart to take up a new job doing mechanical work at a giant flour mill in Minneapolis.

And he thought of the graveyard in New Jersey where his mother was buried.

The East had no hold on Daniel. Maybe traveling with the Texas Road Kings would give him what he longed for—a home. He stood and began to inch toward the stairs.

Segal reached out and grabbed Daniel by the sleeve. "You need some money, you can just ask me."

"It's not about the money."

Daniel looked at the gaps between left field and center, center and right, to his eyes vast as the prairies themselves.

40

---❖---

THE TITLE WAS a bit of a mouthful. *The Dead Eye of the Plains. The Youngest and Most Dangerous Gunman in the West. The Life and Deadly Adventures of the Bulldog Kid.* Vera had wanted something more straightforward, more newsy. After all, she was a newspaperwoman, and a newspaperwoman's stock in trade is honestly recording the events of the day without exaggeration. But as the editor explained, once you put a story between flimsy paper covers and sell it for a dime, you're a dime novelist. And then a whole different set of rules applies.

Her reservations didn't stop with the title. She'd originally focused her attention on what she had witnessed—the quick-draw displays outside the Deadwood courthouse and at the circus and the stagecoach robbery, with its uncannily accurate rifle shots from a hidden marksman.

She'd quoted the mesmerist, Segal, as to the Kid's origins but expressed no opinion as to the veracity of Segal's story. But at some point, as the story sat on the editor's desk, the text took on an entirely new sound. Vera's wording, "described by his friend as the son of a prominent Southern duelist made penniless by the War Between the States," somehow became "Raised to be a proper Southern gentleman, with the chivalric code and hair-trigger sense of honor of that archaic race, the youth who would become the Bulldog Kid knew the lash of poverty and dishonor when his clan was brought low by their devotion to the Secessionist cause."

Well, there was no doubt but that the latter version more successfully compelled the reader's interest. Now Vera found herself with a dilemma.

Desmond Pettigrew, the publisher of her dime novel, had required some convincing to order a print run of a story about a heretofore unknown bandit. The raid by the James-Younger Gang on Northfield, Minnesota, had inspired several more dime novels about the Missouri desperadoes. A regular stream of cheaply bound books featuring Buffalo Bill Cody had been flowing into newsagents' shops ever since the great scout had appeared in his first stage production a few years before that. John Wesley Hardin's bloody trail across Texas and the Indian Territory, factional wars in Kansas cattle towns, and forays into the Arizona Territory by the likes of Vittorio and Geronimo were familiar fodder for other dime novelists.

Pettigrew, who had ventured into the dime novel trade as a refuge from the cutthroat competition in the production of devotional tracts, had dropped a pile of dime novels onto the desk in front of Vera. From the pomade in his hair, to his artfully tied cravat, to the button-popping girth beneath his brocade vest, Desmond Pettigrew did not give the impression of a man who relished a knuckle-bruising struggle in a crowded marketplace.

So, perhaps Vera had promised a little more than she could deliver.

"The Youngers are dead or in prison, and the James brothers soon will be," she'd argued. "Buffalo Bill Cody is more interested in performing tricks on stage than living rough in the West. Dodge City is as safe now as Davenport, Iowa."

"What, and Geronimo just wants to settle down and collect stamps?"

"The Bulldog Kid is young, and he's just getting into his life of crime and adventure, and he's already the fastest and most accurate shootist in the country."

"Says you."

"Yes. Says me. And I can say that because I know him personally. I'm not getting my information from thirsty old men on the front porches of saloons. I've seen him in action, and I've spoken to him and to his friends."

"Okay. So, maybe you've got a good story here. But this is one story."

"Publish this one, and I promise I can get you more."

She'd regretted it as soon as she said it. How was she to get more Bulldog Kid stories when she was imprisoned at Mrs. Cramp's Finishing School for Girls in Kansas City? As it was, escaping the confines of the dormitory in order to meet Pettigrew for an evening meeting—a necessity, she told the publisher, because of her daytime work as a schoolmistress—required an advanced level of subterfuge and the dispersal of generous bribes to the porter.

But then, just before her book was published, news of the shootout in Cheyenne burned down the nation's telegraph wires. Pettigrew gambled on double the usual print run, and it sold out immediately. The Bulldog Kid made readers forget about Hickok, Wyatt Earp, and Frank and Jesse James. They'd slapped leather against outlaws or lawmen but never against a war wagon. Pettigrew offered her more and more money for a second book. If she didn't write it, somebody would, and that somebody wouldn't know the Bulldog Kid.

Living in Kansas City at Mrs. Cramp's gave Vera a base from which to gather information about Western outlaws and lawmen, so she neglected her studies and churned out additional dime novels to keep Pettigrew mollified until she would be old enough to hit the trail in search of the Bulldog Kid. A letter from her father proved the deciding factor for Vera. He was selling the newspaper in Deadwood. He'd be in Kansas City forthwith in order to take her back to Pennsylvania and a life more suitable for a young woman.

Vera took Pettigrew's advance, bought a ticket to Cheyenne and planned to light out for the territory, hoping to find clues in the Kid's last known whereabouts.

Now, as she packed for the journey to Wyoming—and wherever the trail led from there—Vera heard a knock on her door and opened it to reveal a familiar, plump woman of middle age. The woman produced a copy of Vera's Bulldog Kid novel and smiled.

"If it isn't the famous authoress," Mrs. Kleinschmidt said. "How many of your readers would guess that V. E. Bly is such a delightful young lady?"

"My publisher says it looks better if readers think a man wrote it."

"Typical." Mrs. Kleinschmidt pointed at Vera's luggage. "And where might you be going now?"

Vera noticed a predatory glimmer in the woman's eyes. Mrs. Kleinschmidt had fixed that look on the young gunman who gave the workers' representatives back their money. And she had looked at Vera with that same smiling, shark-like expression during the remainder of their stagecoach trip to Cheyenne.

"I'm thinking I might work as a schoolmistress," Vera fibbed.

"If I wrote America's favorite dime novel about America's new outlaw hero, I'd want to find him and write another."

"I don't know where he is."

"But he was in Cheyenne the last time anybody saw him."

Vera smiled and nodded and agreed that, yes, that was what she had heard too. But given how rootless these bandits were and how fickle public tastes could be, would there be any point trying to find the Bulldog Kid?

"Especially if he doesn't want to be found. That's what you're thinking, right V.E. Bly? In that case, you need something that might bring him to you. I'm thinking maybe you need information."

Mrs. Kleinschmidt gestured for Vera to join her outside and linked arms with her as if they were old acquaintances going for a stroll.

"The famous V.E. Bly was difficult to track down. I'm so glad we found you before you took up school teaching somewhere."

Two men approached, a rat-faced man in a brocade vest and a Stetson riding uncomfortably atop a toupee. He was followed by a giant, bigger by far than the young muscle man in the Bulldog Kid's gang, with a patch over one eye. The rat-faced man opened his mouth in a parody of a smile, displaying a gleaming array of false teeth.

"Writers like information, don't they?" said the man, his gaze skittering up and down Vera's body. "We'd like you to have this information, but you need to share it with the Bulldog Kid. I have fond memories of him, though he wasn't a quick-draw artist when I met him. Just a boy with fast hands and fast eyes."

Mrs. Kleinschmidt silenced the man and reached out a hand, into which he placed a small framed photograph. She held the photograph out to Vera.

The photograph was of a girl a few years younger than Daniel.

Vera looked closely at the girl and recognized the eyes. They were the same eyes she'd seen above the scarf during the robbery of the stagecoach. And the girl in the photograph had the same long delicate fingers that Daniel used to conjure pistols into existence.

But the eyes were set in a face that otherwise matched those of the cooks and laundry workers in Deadwood, and the hand poked out from underneath a delicately filigreed silk robe.

"If you find Daniel before we do, tell him to get in touch," Mrs. Kleinschmidt said. "His sister is dying to meet him."

BOB ARMSTRONG IS a novelist and freelance writer from Winnipeg. The original edition of *Prodigies* won the 2022 Margaret Laurence Prize for Fiction in the Manitoba Book Awards and his writing has appeared in literary magazines on both sides of the Medicine Line and in anthologies of comedy, speculative fiction, travel writing and drama. An avid hiker and history buff, he has wandered western trails from south of Tombstone, Arizona, to north of the Yukon Territory's Tombstone Mountains. His travel misadventures and musings can be found on Substack **@wanderingwriterbobarmstrong** and at **www.bobarmstrong.ca**.